STORM

A storm-tossed crossing on the North Sea; a catastrophic ferry accident; hundreds dead. DCI Kate Beauchamp is one of the survivors but her ferocious fight to stay alive brings with it a high cost: a burden of guilt that she should live while some of her friends died; a terror of water; a frozen inner core that never seems to melt. Hoping to exorcize her demons, Kate insists on leading the hunt for a murderer who has left a unique calling card on his victim's body: a poisonous snake. Into this emotional cauldron steps the last man on earth Kate wants to see—her estranged father, Frank, in Aberdeen to conduct the inquiry into the sinking. In a sweltering heatwave, Kate and Frank conduct their highly pressured investigations. But for both of them, danger is approaching fast—a vortex of violence which will sweep them up and endanger their very lives.

STORM

Boris Starling

CHIVERS PRESS
BATH

First published 2000
by
HarperCollins Publishers
This Large Print edition published by
Chivers Press
by arrangement with
HarperCollins Publishers Ltd
2001

ISBN 0 7540 1669 2

British Library Cataloguing in Publication Data available

Printed and bound in Great Britain by
BOOKCRAFT, Midsomer Norton, Somerset

For Belinda and Mike

ACKNOWLEDGEMENTS

The editorial team at HarperCollins has been a joy to work with. Nick Sayers, Fiona Stewart, Julia Wisdom and Anne O'Brien have all kept *Storm* heading in the right direction, and their advice on character and structure in particular has been invaluable. I am also greatly indebted to Brian Tart, Louise Burke and Carolyn Nichols at Penguin Putnam in New York. Their critical counsel has been unfailingly accurate.

David and Judy Starling, Belinda and Mike Trim, Iain Wakefield, Fiona Kirkpatrick, Claire Stewart and Samantha de Bendern have all read the manuscript, and their willingness to give me honest comments has been extremely helpful. Professor Kenneth Rawson provided me with a fascinating exposition of the mechanics of ferry sinking. Any mistakes are entirely my responsibility.

MONDAY

'I have just been informed that there is a bomb on board.'

Captain Edward Sutton quells the shocked murmuring with an upraised hand.

'It's in a white Transit van on the car deck. Near the front, that's all I know. I have no idea who planted it, what they want, when it's due to explode or how powerful it is. For all I know, it could be a firecracker. But I am not prepared to take any chances. What I *do* know is that we are 150 miles from land. By the time help has arrived, it may be too late. And I am unwilling to evacuate the ship so far from shore. There are more than eight hundred people on board, and I daresay a good number are half-cut. And the glass is falling as we head towards the bad weather. We do it now, or not at all.'

His officers' features hover in the cathodic uplighting of the radar screens. Beyond the windows, the rain-softened haloes of ship lights dance gently in the darkness.

'We're going to stop the *Amphitrite* and tip the vehicle into the ocean.'

Sutton waits for dissent. No one moves.

'Second Officer Garthowen will bring the *Amphitrite* to a halt. He will announce on the PA system that we have caught a fishing net in the propellers and are stopping to clear the blockage. If any other vessel picks us up on the radar and asks why we have halted, that is what we shall tell them too. How many craft are in the vicinity?'

Garthowen glances at the twin radar screens, set to five and thirty miles respectively. The five-mile screen is blank. A small scattering of objects

3

smears the thirty-miler: two large ships, four smaller vessels, and the electronic flare of an oil platform.

'Six, and a rig.'

'Fine. We may get away unquestioned. Even so, the knowledge of the bomb will be confined to this room. Under no circumstances do I want it disseminated—certainly not to the passengers. The less they know, the better. Is that clear?'

The bridge crew nod. Sutton continues.

'I will go down to the car deck myself. Third Officer Parker will find five—no, six—deckhands to accompany me. He will tell them to meet me at the car deck, but will not tell them why. When the *Amphitrite* is stationary, I will open the bow door, supervise the vehicle's ejection, and close the bow door. We will then resume our journey. I will not open the bow door until Second Officer Garthowen assures me that the ship has come to a complete halt, and he will not restart the *Amphitrite* until I have told him that the door is firmly shut. The engines will be running throughout the entire operation. Any questions?'

They shake their heads, staccato and urgent.

'Good. Let's get this over with.'

Sutton turns on his heel and walks towards the main door. Even before he's left the room, he can hear the clipped, urgent tones of an experienced crew swinging into action: Garthowen on the intercom to the engine room, Parker to the deckhands. Sutton listens for any signs of panic in their voices, and hears none. He wonders how long it will be before the enormity of the danger he's outlined sinks in.

It is nine levels down from the bridge to the car

4

deck. Sutton takes the stairs two at a time, nodding greetings to passengers as he sidesteps them. His movements are controlled, precise. He doesn't look like a man whose vessel may be blown sky-high at any moment. He is the very model of a ferry captain: not the tall, bronzed and slim stereotype of an airline pilot, but squat and affable. Solid, that's what Sutton is. Utterly dependable. Behind his back, the crew call him Steady Eddie, pitched midway between compliment and insult. Steady Eddie, who worked his way up through the ranks. Nothing flash about him, nothing spectacular or unpredictable. His authority is unostentatious, but no less effective for that. He's the kind of man you'd want in the trenches with you.

The kind of man you'd want when there's a bomb on board your ferry.

Down and further down bright staircases he goes. The twin odours of disinfectant and diesel oil prick at his nostrils. Sounds: the metallic bleeping of arcade games, raised voices behind a cabin door, Garthowen spinning the propeller story on the tannoy. And behind it all, the pulsing beat of the Stork Werkspoor engines, their metronomic thumping beginning to slow as Garthowen throttles them back.

Sutton leaves the crowds behind.

He opens the door to the car deck, and winces at the sudden increase in noise. It's horrifically loud down here, with every sound bouncing off metal rafters and echoing across the huge vault of the roof. Sutton can hardly hear himself think for the roar of the overhead exhaust fans and the restless clanking of chains in ringbolts. He feels as if he is deep inside a sea monster, white-painted stanchions for ribs and massive throbbing engines for a heart.

The glaring deck lights illuminate the vehicles without shadow or mercy. Squat menacing lines of steel and glass. Looking towards the bows, Sutton sees the white Transit van almost immediately. There are seven columns extending from stem to stern, and the van is third from the front in the second column from port.

The vehicle nearest him is a lorry, caked with thick layers of dust in which someone has finger-written: 'Bet you wish your wife was as dirty as this.' At another time and in another place, Sutton would laugh.

Doors are set into the wall of the car deck at ten-yard intervals. The six deckhands Parker called for appear through the next door along, sullen and apprehensive. This is the low time of the journey for them, with none of the frantic activity of departure and arrival. They're not sure why they're here, and they don't know what to expect.

Sutton walks up to them. He has to raise his voice to be heard.

'Come on, you lot. Look sharp.'

They follow him through the columns of cars, turning sideways and holding their arms clear as they squeeze through the gaps. The edges of bumpers tug at their trouser legs.

Sutton tries the Transit's door handle. Locked. He does the same on the two cars ahead, a new blue Audi saloon and an older maroon Vauxhall estate piled high with luggage. They are also locked.

'What are we doing?' asks Keith, the oldest of the deckhands. He and Sutton joined Seaspeed the same day, a fact which often causes Keith to moan into his beer about how he too could have been captain if he'd had the breaks.

'Toolbox.' Sutton holds out his hand like a surgeon demanding a scalpel.

Still waiting for an answer, Keith passes him a toolbox. Sutton puts the toolbox down on the Vauxhall's bonnet and roots around inside until he finds a long, solid wrench. He taps it lightly against the palm of his left hand.

'Stand back.'

He turns his face away and swings the wrench in a short, fast arc on to the driver's window. The glass shatters instantly, most of it dropping in thick crystals on to the seat inside. Random arrays of jagged shards. He could smash a million windows, and the glass would break in a million different ways. Snowflakes and fingerprints are similar in their infinite uniqueness.

Sutton puts his arm through the open space, careful not to catch his sleeve on any stray shards, and releases the handbrake.

He steps over to the Audi, checks for the red diode of a burglar alarm, sees none. Wrench round and down, window smashed, handbrake off. The Transit gets the same treatment. Sutton hands the toolbox and wrench back to Keith.

The intercom squawks in the corner, bang on time.

'Bridge to car deck. Ferry has stopped. You are cleared to open bow door. Over.'

Sutton walks over to the intercom and picks up the handset.

'Car deck to bridge. Commencing opening of bow door. Over.'

7

He replaces the handset and starts to punch at the buttons on the adjacent control panel.

The bow door is actually two doors: an outer one, which hinges downwards from just below the bridge and forms a visor when closed; and an inner one, which pulls upwards from the hull and acts as the vehicle ramp when open. The doors are opened in strict sequence. The inner one has to remain closed until the outer one is fully open.

The control panel has six separate manual controllers. Each controller has its own indicator light, which shows red for fully open and green for fully closed.

Visor bottom lock red. Visor side lock red.

Sutton hears the visor start to clank upwards.

Open visor parking plunger red. Visor open/close indicator red. Ramp pull-in hooks and locking bolts red.

The inner door begins to ease inexorably open, like a medieval drawbridge. The world outside unpeels itself layer by layer: a night sky matt with clouds reaching down to a white-flecked sea. In the absence of a clear horizon, Sutton can hardly tell where sky ends and sea begins. A world without division.

The ramp bounces slightly at the end of its travel. Ramp open/close indicator red.

The *Amphitrite*'s mouth is gaping wide open. Sutton could step on to the ramp and straight off into the North Sea if he wanted.

The wavetops are gently frothed, and the wind darts at his face in spluttering squalls. The weather is already getting up. They're heading straight towards the gale.

Sutton turns to the deckhands.

'We've got to tip this van into the sea.'

If it were possible, some of them look even more stupid than they did before. Keith begins to ask the obvious question, and Sutton cuts him off.

'Doesn't matter why. We need to move these two cars out of the way first, and then get the Transit off. Quickly. Come on.'

His urgent authority forestalls their curiosity.

He arranges the deckhands around the Vauxhall: two at each rear corner, one on either side, and himself gripping the steering wheel through the smashed window. They roll the vehicle on to the ramp, keeping it near the port edge. The deckhands on the passenger side have less than eighteen inches between them and the sea, and they watch their own feet and the vehicle's momentum equally. There is an anxious shout of 'Watch it!' as someone gets too close to the edge for comfort.

They leave the Vauxhall halfway along the ramp and come back for the Audi. Adventurous forays of water nip at their ankles. The Audi is rolled tight up behind the Vauxhall.

Now for the Transit.

Sutton twists the steering wheel hard right the moment the van is on the ramp, so as to clear the two vehicles ahead. They take the Transit right out to the ramp's leading edge, bumping unsteadily over the transverse stiffeners underfoot. The vast canopy of the visor watches them impassively from above.

'Big push, lads,' says Sutton. 'Two, six, heave.'

The Transit lurches forward. Its front wheels slip off the ramp and into the sea. Sutton and the men on each side let go.

9

'And again.'

The four at the rear corners brace themselves and push in unison.

The Transit is in the sea now. Water tumbles over and on itself through the smashed window, filling the driver's compartment. The van tips forward and downwards, its rear end pointed skywards like a grasping hand, and surrenders itself to the sea's embrace.

The deckhands return the Audi and Vauxhall to their original positions, hurrying back and forth across the ramp.

'That's all,' says Sutton. 'Thanks very much. And not a word of this to anyone, you understand?'

They see that he's not going to explain, and set off in single file through the cars.

Sutton begins to punch the reverse sequence into the control panel, and the sea disappears with the rising ramp. Ramp pull-in hooks and locking bolts green. Ramp open/close indicator green. Open visor parking plunger green. Visor side lock green.

The visor bottom lock and open/close indicators remain resolutely red.

Sutton checks his watch. It doesn't usually take as long as this.

He strains to listen for the sounds of the visor's hydraulics above the din.

Nothing.

It *must* be shut by now.

He swears softly under his breath. It must be another recurrence of the intermittent problem with the sensors. The bottom lock sensor sometimes indicates open even when the lock is firmly shut, and this error is transmitted down the

10

line to the open/close sensor. He reported it himself three weeks ago.

There is a corresponding control panel on the bridge, but it's not as comprehensive as this one. The bridge panel only has lamps for the visor side locks and the ramp locking devices. All its lamps will be showing green. The visor's side locks are shut, and the ramp is firmly closed.

The only person who knows that the last two lamps are still red is Sutton.

He picks up the intercom handset.

'Car deck to bridge. Bow door is shut. Clearance to restart *Amphitrite*. Over.'

The ferry lurches slightly as it begins to move again.

*   *   *

The plastic banquette sticks to Kate's skin when she lies on it. She rolls up her fleece and places it under her head. It nestles warm and fluffy against her cheek.

She should be tucked up in bed, sound asleep. The journey from Bergen to Aberdeen takes twenty-four hours, and they had booked five twin cabins. When they boarded yesterday afternoon, they were told that there was more freight than expected on board, and that all lorry drivers by law must be given sleeping accommodation. So no cabin for Kate or any of the other nine members of the Aberdeen Amateurs travelling with her.

Kate's breathing gradually settles into a contented rhythm. She can feel herself in the twilight zone of half-sleep, where thoughts float in and out of her consciousness like feathers on the

11

wind, a confetti of nonsense scattering in her head.

Memories of Norway, where her amateur dramatics troupe has just been performing Alan Ayckbourn's *Way Upstream*. Ten of them in all: seven actors, plus the director, the set designer, and the sound and lighting man. She recalls cruising through the fjords on their weekend off, the air so clear and crisp that it almost hurt to breathe, the mountains towering sheer and vertiginous as they eased past isolated spits of land dotted with grass-roofed brick-red houses.

Two loud bangs reverberate through the hull and jerk Kate wide awake.

She bites on her lower lip to stop herself screaming with frustration and slowly levers herself upright. The rain hammers against the porthole above her head.

The others are looking around uncertainly.

'It could have been anything,' Kate says, more to herself than anyone else. 'Nothing to worry about.'

Then the *Amphitrite* tips suddenly and violently towards her, and she knows instantly that there's plenty to worry about.

They all go tumbling to the floor, as if a giant hand has playfully flicked them horizontal. Kate grabs hold of the banquette to steady herself, and then the ferry rolls back the other way, flipping her off the seat and smacking her hard against the floor, left hip first.

She winces at the sharp stabbing pain and fights to quell the panic rising from her gut. Maybe the ferry had to swerve to avoid a collision. Kate knows that steep rolls are possible when a large ship has to make a tight turn as another vessel cuts across her bows.

But surely the *Amphitrite* would have picked another ship up on its radar? Unless that other vessel was a small boat, but then they probably wouldn't have seen it at all, just run it over as if it wasn't there.

The ferry lists heavily again, steeper and quicker this time. Everything unsecured in the bar—glasses, plates, trays, people—is sent hurtling to starboard, towards where Kate is lying. She hauls herself back on to the banquette. Sinclair and Alex, the director and leading man respectively, slide across the floor and slam into the partition wall next to her.

Tiny bright flashes in the air, and Kate instinctively buries her face behind her arms as she realises they are shards of glass catching the light as they fly. Someone—Davenport, she thinks, the set designer—screams as a splinter catches him on the forehead. Kate can smell the cloying vapours from broken spirit bottles. She takes her hands away from her face and sees Davenport looking disbelievingly at his hands. They are stained red, and he has unwittingly smeared the blood across his face like woad.

Get out. They have to get out. Now.

They are looking at her, the police officer, to take the lead.

Kate grabs her fleece and winds it round her head, tying the sleeves together in a tight knot at the back. She knows she must think clearly. If she gets a bad knock to the head, she can kiss her chances of survival goodbye. She's not drunk. She can still think straight, make quick decisions. She must use it while she can.

The *Amphitrite* seems to have stabilised at this

13

crazy angle, at least for the time being. There is a severe tilt towards the far side of the bar, flat floor now a treacherous slope steep enough to make walking difficult. On the other side of the room is the corridor, and beyond that are the staircases towards the upper decks.

It is the only way out. They have to get across.

'We should form a chain,' says Sinclair. As usual, he looks impeccable, black polo-neck under light grey suit: an incongruous throwback to the days when people dressed up to travel. But this is the storm-lashed North Sea rather than a transatlantic cruise, and it's only in the past few seconds that the *Amphitrite*'s had anything in common with the *Titanic*.

Kate shakes her head.

'A chain will get broken when the ship starts moving again. Follow me. Do what I do.'

She grabs hold of the nearest table. The tables are all circular, with a central stem bolted to the floor, and the stools round them are the same design, though smaller and lower. They look like clumps of mushrooms. The gap between one clump and another is about three or four feet at the narrowest points: short enough for Kate to traverse if she pushes herself up on a stem with one arm and grabs the next stem with the other.

She finds it difficult to keep hold: the metal is cold and slippery against her skin, and her palms gush sweat. Kate slowly makes her way up this makeshift ladder, always with one hand in contact with a stem. Push, reach, pull. Push, reach, pull. She imagines herself in a spaceship, swinging from one fixed point to another.

Two tables from the door now and beyond that

14

the corridor, rapidly filling with people.

Her right foot slips and dangles free. Wincing, she takes the jolt of her bodyweight through her arms. Her foot scrabbles in mid-air for the reassurance of the metal cylinder, finds it, loses it, finds it again.

The *Amphitrite* begins to list back to port, and with it comes the sudden exhilarated anticipation of bodysurfing, the fear and excitement as the wave comes in and the surfers start to paddle, knowing they must time it right or risk being pounded like debris on the seabed. The *Amphitrite* is like that wave as it flattens towards equilibrium, daring Kate to fight her instincts and wait her moment.

She looks down between her legs. The others are stretched out across, the floor—the slope—like an army of ants.

'Let go!' she yells. 'Let go now!'

She swings round on herself so that her feet are ahead of her and slides the last few feet to the door, flat on her backside as when she was learning to ski. She bounces off the doorframe and into the corridor, where she collides with a steward. Absurdly, they apologise to each other, hardly able to hear each other above the screams of other passengers and the tearing of metal against metal. Kate can't remember when she last heard noise this loud, a wall of sound without tone or heart.

The steward rolls Kate away from the entrance as the others come spilling into the corridor. She counts them as they appear. They have all ended up on her side of the door apart from Sinclair and Sylvie, who have fallen the other side.

Down the far end of the corridor, a swarm of heads bobs at the foot of the staircase. Two young

15

women in grey knickers cling on to a handrail. Their dark nipples look like extra eyes. An old man stands in one of the doorways away to Kate's right, hands clamped over his ears and mouth stretched wide as in the Munch painting, and then a sudden jolt flips him back into the room behind and out of sight. A rush hour from hell, panic leaping from person to person as fast and infectious as a virus.

Without warning, the *Amphitrite* lists violently back to starboard. Kate grabs in desperation at the doorframe as her feet are swept from under her. The wood splinters beneath her grasping fingers as she is swung round on herself and back into the bar. She smacks hard into the wall, taking her entire bodyweight through her fingertips.

She daren't look down at a world bouncing beneath kicking feet.

She can't hold on. She's going to fall down the bar floor—*down*—forty or fifty feet which is usually flat and innocuous, bouncing from one obstacle to other like a tiny silver sphere in this giant heaving pinball machine before the unyielding far wall finally stops her dead. This is how it will end, an impact to break bones and crush organs, horrible sickening shuddering drowning in her own blood, agonised and paralysed, until the freezing ocean comes to finish off what the haemorrhaging has started.

Kate's fingers start to slip.

Should have been a climber and practised with those hand-squeeze grips they use.

She tries to get a tighter grip. Can't. Can't do anything through the excruciating pain oozing from fingers through wrists to forearms.

If she hits the first table, the nearest table,

16

before she's got up enough speed, she might just about be OK. If.

A hand on her right arm, and another round her waist. The weight comes off her fingers, and she feels herself being hauled back up through the door. She lets go of the doorframe and bangs her shins on the jamb. She gasps a breathless thanks to Alex and Davenport, her rescuers.

Two of the crew, their white shirts already patterned with dirt and blood, head past them and towards the staircase, attempting to restore some order to what is now a blind stampede.

White noise, all around Kate and within her.

Sinclair leaps across the open doorway and turns to help Sylvie. Kate positions herself alongside him, and they reach out to pull Sylvie across the gap. It's not far, but Sylvie is small and, more pertinently, petrified. She is standing ramrod straight, right on the edge of the gap. Kate motions at her to crouch and give herself some spring for the jump.

Sylvie yells something at them, but her voice is drowned by the noise.

She reaches for their hands.

Sylvie's back foot slips as she stretches. She plunges forward and down through the door, smacking her chin hard on the doorframe as she goes through. The impact knocks her backwards and out of control. Sylvie bounces across the bar just as Kate envisaged herself doing a few moments ago, flipped this way and that as she grabs at the tables and stools for some kind of purchase, screaming screaming screaming.

Kate can hear Sylvie now all right, can hear the awful primal fear of a human totally defenceless in absolute subjection to the laws of gravity. The body

17

is never more helpless than when falling. In its inevitable linear passage to an abrupt halt, falling is in fact the image of death itself.

Sylvie smacks into the far wall and goes suddenly and awfully silent. Her head lolls down on to her right shoulder. Her right arm dangles uselessly down to the floor, and her left arm is tucked behind her back. Her legs are splayed wide apart, a grotesque parody of sexual come-on. A halo of blood frowns on the wall behind her head.

That could have been me, that would *have been me, if Alex and Davenport hadn't grabbed me in time.*

For a moment, Kate can't tear her eyes away from the dead woman.

Sinclair's face appears at her shoulder. Kate grabs him by the shoulders and spins him around and away from the scene, pushing him bodily towards the staircase.

Alex is the last man back, making sure that everyone has gone on. Kate tries to do a quick head count of the troupe, but there are too many other people in the corridor for her to see clearly. The only thing she can be sure of is that no one's left behind her.

No one but Sylvie.

Alex motions with his head towards the staircase. Kate nods. No point in sticking around.

Alex puts one foot on the wall and the other on the floor, both of which are by now around 45 degrees from the vertical. Kate copies him, and in this way—as if they are walking on the interior sides of a ditch—they go as fast as they can towards the staircase.

They don't get very far. Within yards, the crowd

18

is impassably thick, a heaving mass of humanity pushing and jostling and making its own bottlenecks. They are squeezed so hard against each other that the air seems to vanish from the ever-decreasing gaps between bodies.

Kate looks around. She still can't see any of the Aberdeen Amateurs. The maelstrom has swallowed them. Alex's head darts from side to side. He too is looking for familiar faces.

The thought comes to Kate with razor-edged clarity.

If we stay here, we're going to die.

Simple as that. The others—everyone else in this ship—are beyond anyone's help but their own. The only person Kate can save down here is herself. Up at the top, where the lifeboats and the open spaces are, that's where Kate can do some good. If she gets there.

Alex is looking at her. She knows he is thinking exactly the same thing.

They take the decision together, without speaking. *Sauve qui peut.*

Alex puts his head down and charges. Arms ahead of him and then out and roughly round, he breast-strokes his way through the scrum, barging people out of the way like a ship's bow carving through rough water. The crowd parts, recoils, surges. Kate rides his slipstream, right up on his heels to prevent the pathway closing back in on her. She is vaguely aware of outraged shouts and blurred fists being aimed at them. A punch connects with the side of her face, but she hardly notices.

A snatch of memory from police training, instructions in the formal language of the classroom. 'Dopamine is a neurotransmitter which is released when the individual is actively pursuing a defined goal such as escape.'

The word *dopamine* starts forming and reforming in front of her eyes.

Up the staircase now and on to the next deck, even more crowded than the one below. On either side, a long line of identical doors. This is where many of the cabins are located—the cabins Kate wanted for herself—and their occupants all seem to have come out at once.

It takes Kate a moment or two to realise that this mass is not seething and fighting. Many of them are old and docile, and they are making little effort to escape. One man even steps courteously out of their way, giving them a little smile as they hurry past. People near the end of their lives, accepting that their time has come just a little earlier than they expected. In the eye of the storm, a shuffling tranquillity.

Kate and Alex are moving in a different dimension, quick quick in a slowed-down bubbleskin of time. Fast along the corridor, and then into another gridlock at the next staircase. Stop, start, stop. Everyone who can find space is clinging on to the banister, and it can't take the strain. It pops free first at one point, then at two more, until it finally unravels and comes away altogether, whipping and flexing like a snake. People topple back down and across the staircase, falling over and around each other.

Alex wastes no time. He jumps on to the human sand dune and begins to clamber up it. Someone's head is bent under his foot, another's torso touched briefly as he stumbles and recovers his balance. His

20

feet sink into the shifting surface, and he pulls them free again as if from quicksand. Kate follows. A hand grabs at her ankle, and she kicks hard at it.

The damned and the saved, survival of the fittest.

At the top of the stairs, Alex turns to her and holds up two fingers. Two decks to go. Two decks until they reach open air. She nods at him.

It would be so much easier if ferries weren't designed to keep people inside. Almost everything is geared to confining passengers within the superstructure, protecting them from the elements and keeping them safe; but the safest place to be at a time like this is out in the open and fuck the elements, fuck the wind and the rain, because you can't escape through walls of solid steel four decks down.

Kate scrambles with Alex now, and finds with bemused curiosity that she has no sensation of fear whatsoever. Fear is when she's being followed down a dark city street at two in the morning. Fear is when she's waiting for something to happen, when her imagination can run wild. Fear requires time to infect her system. And time is the one thing she hasn't got here. Just the need to act faster than she can think, and a grim determination to stay alive.

Kate feels herself looking around in slow motion. Her neck seems to be making small robotic movements, and her eyes focus like a camera lens, panning in and out—almost with a mechanical whirring—until she gets the image in focus. Half woman, half machine. She looks down, and her legs seem ridiculously long and far away.

The images she sees stay in her mind for a second before vanishing, but when she tries to get

21

them back, she can't even remember what they were. She is dimly aware that her brain is shutting down to stop itself imploding.

Her senses begin to disappear, one by one. Taste is the first to go. She wipes blood off her arm and licks her finger, and there is no coppery smarting on her tongue. Then she realises she can no longer smell the diesel in her nostrils, and now touch vanishes—she has to look down and check what she's holding on to, there's no sensation through her fingers or palms—and finally her hearing switches off as well, even at the height of all this excruciating noise, as if she's already listening to the world from under water.

The only sense Kate has left is sight, and it guides her through a silent tunnel towards the most inviting storm in the world, where driving rain and howling wind mean freedom itself.

This is it, this is now, this is all there is: the present, nothing except what is happening in this fraction of existence. No past, no future. A succession of presents, infinite and immeasurably short. Everything that has gone before counts for nothing. A life that was complex and exciting and turbulent is now pared down to its barest essence— a straight fight for survival.

The *Amphitrite* is suddenly plunged into darkness. Kate thinks she's gone blind, lost the last of her five senses. Then she sees a frenetic blue of sparks arc down past the portholes and into the water. Beats of darkness again and the emergency lighting comes on, a dirty mustard glow too dim to be of much use. It pulses twice and goes out. The last thing Kate sees is Alex's hand reaching out and closing around hers. She notices that the little

22

blond hairs on the backs of his fingers are standing upright, the way they would do if he placed his hand near a television screen.

He pulls her this way and that as he tries to navigate through the darkness. She can't feel his grip, but the motion of her body lets her know that they are connected.

And suddenly fresh air and freezing spray whip against her face, and her senses come tumbling alive again, machinery whining loud in her left ear.

They are out in the open. The *Amphitrite* is listing steeply to starboard, but seems to have stabilised again. Kate plants her legs apart as a brace against any unexpected motion and looks around her. No sign of Alex, even though he was with her just a few seconds ago. At least, she *thinks* it was seconds. Could have been hours.

A lifeboat swings extravagantly as it is lowered towards the sea. One of the occupants is bashing repeatedly at the ship's side with an axe whenever the swing takes him close enough. Sparks fly from the axehead as it clangs against the hull, and it takes Kate a few moments to realise that the man is trying to smash the portholes and release those trapped on the lower decks.

Kate half-crawls, half-slides down to the leeward side. A small crescent of people has gathered like spectators at street theatre, and they screech in the high pitches of seagulls. Kate barges her way to the front and looks over the edge. A woman is clinging on to one of the rescue ladders which leads down to the sea. She is motionless, and it is she they are shouting at. The more they scream at her to move, the tighter she holds on. No one dares to touch her. Her hands are blotched white where they grip the ladder.

Kate doesn't know whether the woman is dazed or simply petrified, and she doesn't much care. All she knows is that the woman is blocking the way for everyone else.

'You have to move,' Kate yells. 'Come up or go down, but let these people through.'

The woman doesn't even look at her.

Kate grips the top rung of the ladder, lowers her legs and kicks hard at the woman's hands. Two, three, four kicks, and the woman can't hold on any longer. She peels away from safety in stages, hands to chest to knees to feet. She tumbles backwards, hits the water spread-eagled in an aura of foaming white, and disappears under the storm waves.

Kate hauls herself back on deck. The crowd look at her, stupefied. She grabs the nearest one and propels them towards the ladder.

'Go. Move.'

Kate's own head on that woman's body as she falls.

An inflatable life-raft comes scooting across the deck, flipped end over end by the wind. Some of those waiting for the ladder set off after it. A man in shorts and singlet sprints past the rest of them and dives head-first for the raft, clinging on and trying to drag it to a halt as a rancher might try to stop a bolting horse. The others pile on top of him in a writhing orgiastic welter of limbs, and their combined weight sends the raft over the edge and down into the sea. It spills bodies as it falls.

This is why everyone is panicking, Kate realises: not simply because they're scared of dying, and not simply because this is such a dreadful way to go, but because the odds are so cruel. Enough people

24

will live to see tomorrow to make escape worth fighting for, but far more will try and fail. When an airliner plunges into the sea, everyone on board dies, and more or less instantly to boot. But here, fate plays with its victims. It gives them time to hope but not necessarily to believe. It toys with them, dares them to look inside themselves and see if they've got the skill and nerve to joust with death.

And just when you think the odds are long enough, you see that human folly and caprice makes them longer. Kate feels a tight knot of anger at the arrogant incompetence of the *Amphitrite*'s preparations. Ships this big shouldn't go down this fast, and when they do, they shouldn't have lifeboats which can't be lowered because the lashings are too rusty, like that one dangling uselessly from its davits over there, and they shouldn't have crew members handing out batches of life jackets like those piled snowfall high on the deck at her feet, bundles which can't be separated from one another because they are tied too tight together.

Suppose they thought it couldn't happen. Well, it could happen. It *is* happening.

A life jacket nudges at Kate's chest. She sees that the person offering it to her is Alex. He has one for himself too. They put the jackets on with difficulty, numbed fingers struggling clumsily with the too-fiddly toggles. The straps on Kate's jacket are too short to be fastened under her crotch. She ties them round her waist and pulls at them. The jacket slides halfway round her side. Too loose. She looks for one that fits better. Alex grabs her arm and pulls her close, cupping his free hand around her ear.

'Leave it,' he shouts. 'We have to jump now. This thing's going down.'

The hard plastic deck covering is beginning to disintegrate. They step around a section which has rucked up like a carpet, climb over the guard rail, and stand right on the edge. It is about 20 feet down to the water; soon to be less, when the *Amphitrite* goes down for good. Alex turns his face to hers again.

'When this is all over,' he yells, 'will you have dinner with me?'

When this is all over. When we come out the other side alive. When. Not if.

Kate nods, and reaches for his hand. She is able to feel it this time. She locks her fingers between his and squeezes.

They jump.

It may only be 20 feet to the sea, but it feels like 200. They fall through time and space, her stomach left somewhere near deck level and hope whipped away on the raging gale. Kate splays her limbs to make a starfish shape, and as she drops she is suddenly flooded with a long-forgotten childhood fear of diving into a swimming pool at night and finding that it had been drained. What if the sea disappears as she falls towards it?

It doesn't disappear. It swallows her whole, so cold it doesn't even hurt. The impact rips her hand from Alex's. Her life jacket flies uselessly up and away, and it takes with it the fleece wrapped around her head. Kate makes little figure-of-eight motions with her hands as she works out which way is up. She opens her eyes, but all she can see are murky patterns.

Alive alone in a hostile vastness, with the white

26

curtain of panic descending. If she lets it cover her and destroy her ability to make decisions, she's lost.

She has the sense to wait for her body to right itself. When she's sure she's upright, she kicks hard for the surface. She comes up straight into a wave and immediately has to duck back under again, no more than a snatched half breath in her lungs and a slosh of saltwater and engine oil in her mouth.

Water in her lungs too. She is drowning.

The water holds her body in suspension, but Kate is outside this. She is looking down on herself from above, and the details she sees—the patterns made by individual strands of hair plastered on her forehead—are preternaturally sharp.

She has no understanding and no knowledge, no notion of time or place. On the most basic level imaginable, she is intrigued to see what happens next—but she is simply an observer, without control or will alike. A straight fight for survival, and she is losing it.

Whatever happens to her body, her mind and soul will continue on their journey. She is simply going to the next part of the cycle. Maybe she is in the afterlife already. Perhaps this is some sort of cosmic decompression chamber made deliberately similar to the place she has just come from, so that she can acclimatise gradually to her new condition.

The sense of liberation is intense, and Kate basks in it. When the struggle is done, euphoria takes over. If they ever find her body, they'll never know how close she came to discovering true peace.

A voice in her head. Her own voice.

Leo.

Leo, the heartbreaker with floppy brown hair

and huge chocolate eyes, baggy trousers above his pigeon-toed walk. The one who launches himself at her every time she comes home from work, a four-year-old guided missile who smothers her in kisses and hugs.

Leo, her son. Fight for him, if not for herself.

Kate comes back to herself in a long fall. Her own floating body disappears from view, and in its place she sees a sea cleaved by a sinking ship and churning with blood and corpses. It looks like an epic scene from naval warfare: Mather Brown's *Destruction of L'Orient at the Battle of the Nile*, perhaps.

This view, this vision of hell, is Kate's first memory. She is going through a rebirth, where everything is new and strange. All that has gone before is now locked away in a previous dimension.

She feels her brain reboot on to the most basic of thought processes, cause and effect.

Cold body, cold water. Get out of the water, get warmer.

The connection struggles from brain through synapse to muscle. Kate breaks surface again, coughing water out of her lungs even as she hauls oxygen back into them.

There is a life-raft directly in front of her. Twenty seconds old, she strikes out for it. She reaches the side and hauls herself inboard in one movement, feeling the ocean run in rivers off her legs. It is pitch-black inside, so dark she thinks she's alone. She stands unsteadily in inches of water and looks around her. Gradually, as her night vision adjusts, the blackness resolves itself first into hazy shapes and then into faces and bodies. The raft is full.

A spluttering from the sea nearby, and half a man's head appears above the waves. Kate leans over the side, reaches under the water and grabs his collar. She tries to haul him on board, but he is too tired to raise his arm to hers. All she is managing to do is throttle him. She lets the man go, and watches in tired disgust as he slips beneath the surface and out of sight.

The *Amphitrite* is almost gone, slipping away in deathless motion like a living thing whose soul is leaving her. It goes down bow first, its stern raised high in futile defiance. Terrified faces dot blood-smeared portholes, those desperate souls trapped in the lower cabins and in the engine room, waiting in darkness for the sea to come and devour their terror.

As the water reaches the funnel, Kate hears the bridge windows breaking. The tinkling glass sounds high over the flat drone of a typhoon signal. A distress rocket arcs away from the sinking ship, illuminating the carnage in an explosion of deep red. The sea splashes over the hatches and ventilators, around the empty lifeboat davits and broken stretches of railing, greedily taking possession of the dying hulk. It comes for those still on deck a couple at a time, as if it can't take them all in one go. The lucky ones suffocate in the smoke from the funnel before the water gets them.

To Kate, it seems that the sea itself is screaming.

And, like that, the *Amphitrite* is gone. A great round mountain of water erupts through globules of foam and hangs motionless. At the summit bobs a solitary body staked out in futile sacrifice. Then the water mountain subsides with a low roar, sending dull echoes of itself to all points of the compass, and all that remains is an untidy blotch of smoke and steam over the death spot.

Kate slumps back against the side of the raft. Something sharp digs into her thigh. She rolls away and upwards, and sees that it is the catch for the canopy. It flips open easily. Kate raises the canopy. The lights in the raft come on automatically, and for the first time Kate gets a good look at her fellow refugees: twelve in all, their drenched clothes clinging to the contours of their bodies. Most sit with their arms round their shins and their knees tucked under their chins, staring down into the bilges.

Only two even look at Kate as the lights come on. One of them looks quickly away, but the other—a man dressed only in a pair of underpants—is glaring belligerently at her. She holds his gaze.

He leaps to his feet. Her hands are up and out to defend herself, but it isn't her he's going for. He punches one of the lights with his bare fist, the bulb fizzing white light as it shatters, and then at the next bulb, and then the next. His knuckles stream bright red from the cut glass. Kate reaches up and grabs him by the shoulder.

'What are you doing?'

Already flailing towards the next light, he turns and spits in her face. Another woman gets up and yells at him.

'What the fuck are you doing?'

The man makes a wide sweeping motion with his arm.

'The horror. Don't—don't want to see the horror. Don't want to see it.'

Kate wipes the phlegm from her cheek, gets to

her feet and wraps an arm roughly round his neck. She pulls him backwards and hisses in his ear.

'How are the rescuers going to find us if you smash all the lights, eh?'

He jabs his elbow sharply backwards, looking to knock the wind out of her, but she is too quick for him. She lets go of his neck and sways her torso to one side, leaving him nothing to hit but thin air, and in the same movement reaches round his front and punches down on to his groin. He gurgles and slumps forward over the edge of the raft, where a wave reaches up and slides him gently into the sea.

Kate drops to her knees, ready to haul him back on board, but he is already gone. She turns back inboard and looks around her. No one says anything. The woman who helped her shrugs her shoulders.

'Come on, you lot,' says Kate. 'Get closer together. Body heat's about all we've got left. We've got this far. Let's not piss it away now.'

She walks round the raft, pushing people together into a close circle, making sure that everyone has contact on either side. A couple of people move themselves, but most seem to be in deep shock. They let Kate push and place them as if they were dolls she was arranging, or slices of tomato round the edge of a salad plate.

They huddle together for a while, but the circle gradually breaks as people pass out or get thrown against the sides of the raft by the waves. From time to time a large swell comes over the side, and when Kate next looks she sees a face she hasn't seen before, or she can't see a face she's sure was there earlier. The sea is exchanging people as the raft drifts: some in and some out, some alive and some dead.

The woman on the rescue ladder and Kate kicking hard at her blotched white hands, the woman peeling away and tumbling backwards, into the sea and under and gone.

The others? What happened to the others?

Alex jumped with her, he's young and strong, he'll be all right.

What about Sinclair, small and neat in his grey suit, the man who has been like a father to her these past few years? Will the terror have paralysed him and sapped him of the will to survive, like the old people who ushered Kate and Alex through?

No, please no. Let Sinclair have got out.

And creepy Jason, who breathes his halitosis on to Kate through too-wet lips and touches her whenever he can? Will he have made it?

Kate has seen so many bodies in the water, and knows there must be just as many inside the *Amphitrite*. If only by the law of averages, not all the Aberdeen Amateurs will have got out. Maybe not even most of them.

Maybe it's just her.

If she was given a number—four, say, four of them will come out of this alive—which ones would she choose? Who would she most like to have survived?

Sinclair, for sure. Sinclair, and Alex. Who else?

No. This is a dangerous line of thinking. Stop it.

The storm begins to subside, and with it the waves and the wind, and Kate knows that she's not going to die, not today.

The sky is turning from black to deep blue by the time the first rescue helicopter skims in low over the waves. A diver crouches in the doorway and

32

jumps the last few feet to the sea, holding himself ramrod straight. He disappears behind a hillock of water, and when he next appears he is almost halfway to them. Another swell snatches him from view, and suddenly this angel in grey neoprene is clambering on board the raft.

The helicopter is hovering directly overhead, and the draught from its rotors beats the water flat. The diver reaches up over Kate's head, guides the helicopter's rescue harness down, and clips her securely into it. Up and away from this hell, a lump of meat swaying on the end of the winch.

Strong hands haul Kate the last few feet, and she slumps on to the floor of the helicopter with a small wet plop. Someone puts an aluminium survival blanket around her shoulders, and a man in a flying suit is crouching next to her. He has a clipboard in his hands.

'What's your name, love?'

He has a thick Scottish accent, and his chin sprouts light brown bristles. One of the many who must have been hauled out of bed in the small hours without time to shave. She wants to hug him and thank him and his colleagues for saving her, but instead she clears her throat and says 'Kate Beauchamp.'

'Where are you?'

'Huh?'

'Where are you? Just tell me where you are.'

'I'm on a helicopter.'

'Good. What day is it?'

'Why are you asking me this?'

'Please just answer. I need to know if you've been hurt.'

'No. I haven't been hurt.'

33

'What day is it?'

She sighs.

'Monday, I suppose. Early on Monday.'

'And what just happened?'

'What do you mean?'

'What's happened to you in the last five minutes?'

'*Christ*. This is like early learning. I was sitting on a raft, and then you guys came and hauled me out. That's what happened.'

'Thank you.'

He ticks four columns on his clipboard, and writes 'A/O x 4' in a fifth.

'What does that mean?' she asks.

'Alert and oriented times four. It means you know who you are, where you are, what time it is and what just happened.'

'Doesn't everyone?'

'No. It goes all the way down from times four to times zero.'

'What does times zero mean?'

'That you're just about aware you exist. Nothing more.'

'If that happens to you, you're in big trouble. Right?'

He smiles.

'Right.'

'Where are we going?'

'Aberdeen.'

The harness appears by the helicopter door again. Another man hauls the next survivor inside, and the man with the clipboard asks the same questions for a second time. Kate presses herself in the corner and wishes it was all over,

Someone else is in charge now. She doesn't have

34

to be strong any more.

The helicopter takes them to an empty warehouse in Aberdeen harbour. It is huge, cavernous and cold—and just about the most welcoming environment Kate can remember. The clock on the wall says that it is ten past five, and the soft dawn light filters through the patches of pale plastic which dot the corrugated iron roof.

Kate finds her own bit of floor space and is given a bowl of green soup. She sips gently at it, letting it warm her gradually from the inside out. Her aluminium blanket crackles loudly whenever she moves.

The survivors enter in batches, like guests at a party. Kate looks up every time someone comes in, hoping to see Sinclair, Alex, any of the others. No sign.

A middle-aged woman, quick and efficient in jeans and loafers, comes to check her details.

'We're taking you to hospital, just for a check-up. Sorry it's taken so long, but we've had to prioritise, as I'm sure you appreciate, and there's others need the doctors much more than you. If you go out of the door and turn left, you'll find a minibus waiting on the corner.'

Kate steps out of the warehouse. The wind whips grit against her throat. Above her, yellow cranes stretch skywards from indigo bases, and seagulls hover in circles like airliners held in pattern. The ground is archipelagoed with guano and glistens with shards of green, tiny remnants of shattered beer bottles.

She waits for ten minutes, slumped in the back seat of the minibus, until the vehicle is full. The driver gets on board, gives the occupants a look in

35

which sympathy and embarrassment battle for space, shuts the door and starts the engine. He drives past serrated ranks of articulated trailers, dabs the brakes as a forklift truck scoots across their path, and then turns on to the main road which runs along the length of the docks. The granite buildings sparkle as the rising sun catches the chips of feldspar in the stones.

The Royal Infirmary is pandemonium. Under normal circumstances, the reception area for accident and emergency can seat maybe thirty people, at a push. Today, there are at least three times that many, and a dozen more are crammed into the small smoking annexe off the main area. The electronic sign announcing the average waiting time has been turned off, and the corridors are criss-crossed with blurs of colour as the staff run this way and that: green for the doctors, turquoise for the nurses, dark blue for the radiographers. One of the turquoises stops long enough to check Kate in.

'Is there anything you need?' she asks.

'Apart from the chance to live the last few hours differently?'

The nurse smiles uncertainly, and disappears back into the body of the hospital.

There is a single payphone in reception. A woman is wailing into the receiver, and whoever is on the other end isn't getting much of a look-in. Kate walks over and takes the phone from her.

'Your friend is fine,' she says into the mouthpiece, and ends the call.

The woman is too astonished to object.

'There's plenty of others who need to use this too,' says Kate, dialling 100.

'Operator, how can I help?'

36

'I'd like a reverse-charge call, please.'

She gives the numbers of her aunt Bronagh and of the phone she is calling from.

'Connecting you now.'

The ringing tone purrs down the line at her. Kate thinks of Bronagh fumbling in the dark for the receiver.

'4259,' Bronagh says. Her voice is thick with sleep.

'Operator service, will you accept a reverse-charge call, local rate?'

'I—oh, yes, I suppose so.'

'Go ahead, caller.'

'Bronagh, it's me. There's been—God, Bronagh, I've—'

'What, Kate? What is it? Where are you?'

'The Infirmary.'

'At this time in the morning?'

'The ferry sank.'

Kate hears her aunt's sharp intake of breath.

'Jesus Christ.'

'I'm OK. I mean—I'm here. I'm alive. How's Leo?'

'Fine, fine. I'll come and get you.'

'No. I'll be here for hours. I rang in case you saw it on the news.'

'Oh Lord, Kate. Poor you. How—how serious was it? Did you all get out?'

'It was awful. There must be hundreds lost. I don't know about the others.'

'Kate, I don't know what to say.'

'Don't say anything. Especially not to Leo. I'll be round as soon as I can.'

'But Kate . . .'

'I've got to go. There are others who need the

phone. I'll see you later.'

Kate puts the phone down and slumps to the floor, finding comfort purely through contact with terra firma again.

She looks at the clock on the wall, and then into space, and then at the other survivors again. She still can't see any of the troupe. Some of them must have got out. *Must have.*

With a start, she sees Alex, lying flat on his back by the Coke machine in the corner. He is gazing unblinkingly up at the ceiling. She gets up and hurries over to him.

The left side of his face is torn up, scratches and cuts lined with dirt. There is a livid bruise across the front of his neck, just under the point where his goatee beard is trimmed square, and an ugly pair of scrapes on the underside of his right arm.

He pushes himself up to a sitting position and wraps his arms around her. She presses herself close, careful to avoid any of the places where he's been hurt, but it is she who winces with the pressure. She must have been knocked around more than she thought.

'I thought you—you—after we jumped . . .'

She mumbles into the short hairs of his neck.

'Me too.'

'What about the others?'

'Sinclair, Lennox and Emmeline I've seen. They're OK.'

Sinclair's all right. Kate exhales with relief.

'Sinclair thinks that Jean made it too,' Alex continues.

'You saw what happened to Sylvie?'

Kate feels him nod.

'Matt and Davenport?'

38

'Don't know.'

'Who else?'

She ticks them off in her head—her and Alex, Sinclair, Lennox, Emmeline, Jean, Sylvie, Matt and Davenport—knowing she's missed one. It takes a second to come to her, and it does so with a pang of guilt attached for forgetting him.

'Jason?'

'No idea.'

'God. Please let them be OK.'

'You call this OK?'

'You know what I mean.'

He nods again.

'You still on for dinner?' he asks.

She leans back from him, so she can look him in the face.

'Try and stop me.'

*   *   *

In Seaspeed's Aberdeen headquarters, pandemonium.

The sheer kinetic energy of a hundred employees doing their best to cope with the uncopable. They have all read the contingency plans and run through the simulation exercises with specialist consultants, but deep down they never really thought it would happen—and when it does, it is all so fast and confusing and tragic that it is all they can do to keep themselves together. It is far bigger than they could ever have anticipated. The simulation exercises started with a premise and dripped through information and incidents piecemeal. They didn't throw the whole lot in at once.

39

Some of them have been here for three or four hours already, trying to remain calm and helpful against a barrage of noise: ringing phones, clipped shouts of casualty figures and passenger names, loud keening sobs as the impact of the disaster bites. Hayley on the reception desk, two weeks on the job, two weeks out of *school*, juggles three phone calls at once, trying to explain to hysterical and frustrated relatives on the end of each line that she simply doesn't know who has survived and who hasn't, and that's all she can tell them, of course she appreciates their concern but she simply doesn't *know*, and them yelling at her isn't going to change that.

It is six-thirty on Monday morning. What a way to start the week.

Sir Nicholas Lovelock strides across the open-plan floor towards his corner office. He walks stiffly, almost marching, and his face is set in lines of determination. Seaspeed's chairman and chief executive, the titles do his attachment to the company scant justice. He runs an empire now— the *Aberdeen Evening Telegraph*, department stores, golf courses, Urquhart's auction house, property development and airport car parks, all thriving in the city's oil-soaked economy—but his business-hardened heart is with Seaspeed, where he first started thirty years ago. When it comes to Seaspeed, Lovelock is a jealous lover harking back to his first passion, obsessive and possessive in equal measures.

One of the marketing assistants puts down her phone and bursts into tears as Lovelock walks past her desk. He puts his hand on her shoulder and lets her rest her head against his forearm. She chokes

40

out the words between gulping sobs.

'It's just so awful. All those people desperate to find out, and we can't tell them anything. They must be going mental.'

'You're doing great, Sarah. Hang in there.'

The staff know that this is hurting him. They know what he feels for the company—in his occasional moments of whimsy, Lovelock likes to look at Seaspeed as an extended family, with himself as the benevolent patriarch—and so they know what, by extension, he feels for them. Seaspeed looks after its employees, makes them feel valued. And when staff move on, Lovelock refuses to attend their leaving parties. He regards departure as an act of personal betrayal. He understands the need for it, of course—he wants ambitious people, driven people—but that doesn't mean he has to like it.

He squeezes Sarah's shoulder and sets off towards his office.

He'll have to make a statement to the press, of course. He knows how important PR is at times like this, how much can be won and lost merely on the image which he manages to portray, irrespective of what he actually says. And he knows he'll come across well: the successful executive humbled by catastrophe, who in adversity shows himself to be a fine man as well as a fine businessman.

He'll look serious but sensitive, shaken but still in control. Sufficiently human to appeal, sufficiently professional to reassure. A good balance, and one which is deceptively difficult to achieve. Patrician. That's how journalists describe him when they can't think of anything original to

41

say. Patrician, because he's tall and thin and slightly lupine. In fact, he's a cartoonist's dream, there's so much in his face to distort: the extravagant sweep of whitening hair, the deep trenches in his forehead and on his cheeks, the sharpness of the nose which splits his features.

Lovelock's PA, Marita Rudolph, looks up from her computer as he approaches.

'Is Cameron in there?'

'Just arrived.'

'Good. No interruptions, for *anybody*.'

He walks into his office and closes the door behind him, shutting out the hubbub.

Cameron Shillinglaw, the editor of the *Aberdeen Evening Telegraph*, is sitting at the table by the far window. The oval patches of his paunch spill between the lower buttons of his shirt, and the tips of his thumb and middle finger are stained nicotine-brown.

Lovelock is dressed in a pinstripe suit, pink shirt with white collar, and he looks as if he's just stepped off the pages of GQ. He pulls out a chair, sits down, and glances out of the window, over towards the harbour. One of the rescue helicopters is sitting on the tarmac by a warehouse. Its rotors turn languidly at idling speed. As Lovelock watches, a man in orange overalls emerges from the warehouse and runs across to the helicopter. He gets on board and it lifts off, swaying slightly as it climbs.

Shillinglaw is saying something.

'The passenger manifest, faxed from Norway.'

He points to several photocopied pages on the table. Lovelock flicks through them. A full list of those on board the *Amphitrite*. No indication as to who made it and who didn't.

Shillinglaw clears his throat.

'We've cleared the decks for this story, obviously. We're giving it the entire news section. One extra edition, maybe two. The printers will run editions up till seven-thirty. That's two and a half hours later than usual.'

'Good.' Lovelock puts the manifest back down on the table. 'What we've got to sort out is what we're going to say.'

Two years ago, when Lovelock first bought the *Aberdeen Evening Telegraph*, this kind of comment would invariably spark long and bitter argument. Shillinglaw is a journalist of the old school, a man who worked his way up the ranks from cub reporter to sub and then through the higher echelons of editorial management. He remembers the days of metal plates and union power. Although he likes to think that he has moved with the times, there are a few beliefs which he has never modified, and one of them is that owners should own and editors should edit.

But he is late in his working life, is Shillinglaw, and his fires are being slowly doused. Lovelock made it clear from the outset that when he wanted a story run, Shillinglaw would run it. Lovelock's companies and dealings would be praised. Competitors would be knocked. If Shillinglaw didn't like it, all he had to do was say so. Lovelock could easily find a new editor.

Shillinglaw didn't like it, and he still doesn't. But he has worked hard to get where he is, and his principles fall short of self-destruction. Besides, it doesn't happen that often. For the most part, Lovelock lets him alone. It's only when he has something to say that he hauls the editor in and does everything but dictate the copy to him. Like now.

The *Amphitrite* is going to be the lead story in all the nationals, and across television and radio too. Lovelock can't influence what *they* write or say, but he knows the importance of favourable local coverage. Not only will many of the big boys look to see how the locals cover it, but in days and weeks to come, when the story has died and the out-of-town reporters gone home, the *Aberdeen Evening Telegraph* will still have its own constituency to serve.

'There are four things I want covered, whatever,' says Lovelock. He hands Shillinglaw a Seaspeed compliments slip, on which he has hurriedly scrawled the headings. Shillinglaw reads it aloud.

'Safety record, hearts and minds, my own profile, and our legal position.'

'Right. Safety record first. Our safety record is exemplary. We've been operating thirty years, and this is the first accident we've had—of any sort. Airlines would kill for that kind of record. So would most of our competitors. Our maintenance team is the finest in Scotland, and the *Amphitrite*'s captain, Edward Sutton, was our second most experienced officer. He took the mandatory biennial simulator test two months ago, and passed with flying colours. And the *Amphitrite* was of course compliant with all necessary regulations. I've got them all here. SOLAS, ILLC, MARPOL, COLREG. You name it, we were registered.'

'It wasn't your fault. That's what you want me to say?'

'Exactly. Blame the weather, blame divine

44

justice, blame Bonnie Prince Charlie for all I care. Just don't blame us.'

'The manufacturers?'

Lovelock permits himself a thin smile.

'You're ahead of me. The *Amphitrite* was built by a German outfit called Kremer-Steinbach. I've got two people trawling through shipping records right now, looking for accidents involving their vessels. We'll have that to you as soon as possible.'

'And if there aren't any?'

'Then we'll have to use innuendo. You've got good lawyers. They'll tell you what you can and can't get away with.'

'I guess.'

'Good. Hearts and minds. Seaspeed will provide counselling for anyone who wants it—survivors, victims' families, rescue workers, whoever. We're having counsellors brought in from Edinburgh and Glasgow, and they'll stay here as long as we need them. Every director of the company will be visiting the survivors in hospital today. They'll also be going to selected funerals. I want snappers and scribblers at these places. Big coverage of what a caring company we are, how we're doing all we can to ease the pain.'

'We're stretched for staff as it is. My people are being run off their feet already.'

'We'll tell you where and when. Get people there, I don't care how.'

Shillinglaw nods.

'Next, my own profile. You must have that on record somewhere. In my obituary, if nowhere else. I can fill in any gaps. Rags-to-riches stuff. How I started Seaspeed with a name at Companies House and a single, clapped-out ship plying the Dover-

Calais route. Heavy borrowing, fleet of new ferries, route expansion, aggressive marketing. The gambler who took risks and won. The man who slashed prices and agreed special offers with tabloid newspapers, banking that tourists would jump at the chance of going to the Continent for a fortnight, a week, a day. The country's leading ferry company by the late eighties. Entrepreneur of the year, 1986 and 1988. They would have given it to me in 1987 too, but then Zeebrugge happened and the whole industry was in the doghouse. How I beat off three takeover bids in five years. And then all the philanthropy stuff too.'

'This might all backfire, you know.'

'Bollocks. I'm a fighter. That's what the public like to see. And I want them to know that I don't associate myself with losers.'

'You posted a profits warning two weeks ago. People are going to remember that.'

'Maybe. But you don't have to remind them.'

'It's . . .'

'I said: you're not going to mention it.'

*   *   *

Kate sits on her bedroom floor, stark naked.

Her body doesn't look bad for thirty-five, she'll give herself that. Her breasts are still fighting gravity with gusto, and there's not too much excess around and below her arse. She knows that the cellulite stays off more through nervous energy than exercise, but the ends justify the means, that's what she tells herself. The only thing she'd really change are her feet, which are a size and a half too big for her liking.

She is glistening with sweat. It is warm outside anyway, and the weather forecast is predicting a heatwave from tomorrow, but Kate has started early. The central heating is turned up as high as it will go, and two portable heaters blast scorching air on to her bare skin.

She is sweating because she wants to excrete the horror as a physical function. She wants to drive the memories of the *Amphitrite* out through her pores, feel them prickle on her arms and legs and breasts before evaporating into the heavy air. Purge herself of what happened, make herself clean and start her life again for the second time today. So she sits and lets the sweat—salty as sea water—run in rivulets down her body.

But still she feels cold. The hospital checked her quickly and cursorily, said she wasn't suffering from hypothermia, told her to keep herself warm, and sent her on her way. As she left, she saw Jason, worse for wear but very much alive. Seven of them now accounted for, and Sylvie definitely gone. No word of Matt or Davenport. She wants to grieve for Sylvie, but somehow she feels it improper until she knows for sure who else didn't make it.

Kate went straight from the Infirmary to Bronagh's, where she spent long minutes clinging on to her son and her aunt in turn, no one saying anything. That's one of the things Kate loves about Bronagh: she knows that Kate will talk when she wants to talk, and won't when she doesn't. Bronagh didn't bombard her with a million and one questions, as David would have done if he was still around. And Leo doesn't know anything about the ferry disaster. He was thrilled to have his mum back after two weeks away from her, though he did

47

tell her she smelled funny when he hugged her. That's what sloshing around for hours in the North Sea does for you.

She has left Leo with Bronagh, because she wants to be alone for this.

The only person she rang was Sinclair. She left a short, simple message for him, and then unplugged the phone in her bedroom. She can hear the other extensions ring through the flat, and her own voice as the answerphone takes a string of messages. She doesn't want to talk to anybody. All she wants to do is stay here and force the demons out, mind whirling and body motionless.

She raises her right arm to her face and licks the smooth skin on the inside of her wrist, wondering if she can taste the savagery of the fight for survival. She can smell the alcohol on her skin when she sweats off a hangover, so maybe there'll be something there now. The warm cloying of fear, or the cold tang of floating corpses.

She can't taste a thing.

This time yesterday, before the ferry left Bergen for the long run back to Aberdeen, Kate knew who she was and what she was doing with her life. She knew what she believed in and what her morals were. Her entire existence was neatly packaged in a lattice which was at once phenomenally strong and alarmingly delicate. Rather like the human body itself.

And then the North Sea smashed that lattice into a thousand tiny pieces and scattered the driftwood away on the waves *and the woman on the ladder with them.*

Kate never expected to be caught up in something like that. Disasters are things which

48

happen to other people: God knows, she's had to deal with enough of them in her time on the force. But suddenly *she* was the one fighting her way through upturned corridors with the clock ticking remorselessly down on her life span, and now she doesn't know how to deal with it. The maps inside her head have been ripped to shreds, and she has to draw new ones from scratch.

The *Amphitrite* is Kate's only fixed point. It is the only thing in her life that feels real. More real than the Bangladeshi throw on the bed and the photographs on the wall. More real than her job with Grampian Police. Right now, and it cuts her to the quick even to think it, more real than Leo.

It *is* her life. The *Amphitrite* is there wherever she turns, a huge enveloping shadow that she can feel but can't understand. And she hates not being able to understand.

Kate has lost her past and has no vision of her future. Of all the knowledge she's lost, there's one piece that remains, and it's this: she won't be able to crawl out from under the shadow and resume her life until she comes to terms with what happened on the *Amphitrite.*

*   *   *

It's only a bath. She's taken thousands of them in her life. It can't hurt.

Logic and emotion scream at each other inside her head. This pulverising fear of immersion she didn't even realise she had until she walked into the bathroom and began dry retching at the prospect.

She reaches out for the hot tap and twists it

slowly. The tap gurgles and releases a trickle of water. Her knuckles are white with the force of her grip on the tap.

A trickle. That's all. Nice and gentle. She can deal with that. If she turns the tap any further, it will start to gush, and that will make the water churning and angry.

The tap coughs, and Kate jumps back. It coughs again, and the trickle resumes. Her heart pounds hard against her sternum.

It takes ten minutes for Kate to fill the bath half-full, and another five until the surface is perfectly still. The enamel tinges the water green.

Steam wafts in lazy spirals above the surface.

Kate shivers. The cold is still with her. Inside her, even. Like a microwave in reverse, freezing her from the inside out.

She looks at herself in the mirror. Small nose, big mouth, brown eyes, quite a square face. Her jaw comes across sharply, and it dips slightly in the middle before appearing to think better of it and resume its previous course.

Her eyebrows sweep down and round in extravagant arcs on to the upper edges of her nose, and her hair falls like curtains down either side of her face, past her eyes and on to her ears. She pushes a matted clump back from her forehead to reveal a weal up near the hairline. There is another on her right cheek, and a purpling triangle of bruising on her stomach.

Kate tries to lift her foot. It feels incredibly heavy.

Naked in her own bathroom, cold in clouds of steam and rooted to the spot with fear.

She puts her hands on the side of the bath,

holding tight so she doesn't slip, and swings her leg slowly up and round. The water will rear up and bite her any moment, she's sure of it. She watches it like a hawk, untrusting.

The end of her big toe touches the water, breaking the surface tension.

She can't do this. She can't put herself underwater again. Not even the tiniest part of her.

It's a *bath*. She tells herself not to be absurd.

Thinks about something else.

Their time in Bergen. Drinking Aquavit till four in the morning in twelfth-century timbered bars, going to the leprosy museum and gawping at the gruesome pictures of dropsy sufferers, wandering through streets of houses painted fantastic combinations of mustard and indigo or ochre and salmon.

Sinclair, a whirligig of energy in rehearsals, making them stop and do scenes again, again, again until he was satisfied. Them clapping him on to stage every night, knowing that he pushed them hard because he demanded that of himself too, and that he helped some of them find places in themselves they never knew existed. Alex, for example, in his transformation from happy-go-lucky sailor to raving psycho. When they started rehearsals, he couldn't do it at all. By opening night, he'd have given Hannibal Lecter a run for his money.

Matt and Alex scrapping on stage, in the shallows which Davenport had so painstakingly built. Matt, still missing, and Alex, who at the last-night party kissed her on the mouth and she so wanted to prise his lips apart with her tongue and kiss him back properly, and everyone was there and

51

she wasn't drunk enough not to care.

Kate dunks a flannel in the water and begins to dab at herself. Under her armpits, across her breasts, between her legs, as if cleaning her most intimate parts will compensate for her refusal to immerse herself. She smears and wipes with increasing fury, trying to make herself so angry that she'll just leap into the bath. Anger against fear. Anger born from fear.

Fear wins hands down. She didn't die today, and she's not going to get into the bath today.

In a sudden disgusted movement she yanks at the plug chain just below the overflow channel. The water sloshes impassively back and forth as the bath starts to drain, and in the gathering whirlpool Kate fancies she can see tiny bodies being carried to their death.

*   *   *

The recording of the *Amphitrite*'s last radio conversation arrives at Seaspeed headquarters before lunch. Lovelock shuts his office door and listens to it alone, hearing the vortex of desperation and terror under the calm delivery of the radio officer as he tells the world that a ship is dying. The conversation has not been edited, leaving long gaps between transmissions of nothing but static.

The recording starts with a long electronic warbling, the alert signal comprising alternate transmissions on 2200 and 1300 Hz, and then the voice on 2182 kHz, the international maritime distress channel.

'Mayday Mayday Mayday, this is *Amphitrite, Amphitrite, Amphitrite*. Mayday *Amphitrite*, 58 36 degrees north, 00 54 degrees east. We have a bad list to starboard and are in sinking condition. Require immediate assistance. Will fire distress rockets at intervals. Over.'

'Mayday, *Amphitrite, Amphitrite, Amphitrite,* this is Peterhead, Peterhead, Peterhead. Received Mayday. Over.'

'Mayday, this is *Harwich Venturer.* We are proceeding full speed. Estimate passage time at thirty-four minutes. Over.'

'Mayday, this is *Amphitrite.* Engines have stopped. List to starboard worsening. Lifeboats launched. Need air and sea rescue soonest. Over.'

'Mayday *Amphitrite.* All ships. This is MRCC Peterhead, Peterhead, Peterhead. *Harwich Venturer* will assume responsibility of on-scene commander on arrival at the casualty. *Harwich Venturer* to co-ordinate evacuation if required. Helicopters scrambled, en route to casualty; two Super Puma, one Boeing Kawasaki, one Agusta Bell 412, one Sea King. Over.'

'Mayday, this is *Amphitrite.* Bad. This is really bad now. This is—'

Silence.

*   *   *

The search for survivors goes on until nightfall, hope fading with the daylight.

Every passenger ship in the vicinity alters course when it hears the *Amphitrite*'s Mayday. They arrive at full ahead and then stand on their brakes, their captains ordering emergency stops so that their propellers won't catch stray rafts or floaters and slice them up. Ships bob in clouds of smoke

53

beneath whining aircraft. Helicopters and light planes come from Scotland, Norway and northern Denmark, outsize insects criss-crossing the area, setting briefly down to pick up survivors and offloading them at the nearest safe point—the less seriously injured on the rescue ships, the more urgent cases back to Aberdeen. The pilots rely entirely on visuals and their innate skill to prevent collisions. Distress frequencies are already overloaded, air traffic radar is unable to follow helicopters at such low altitudes, and there is no supervision or tracking system over the sea. They fly deaf, and they do it brilliantly.

The rescue men crouch in the helicopter doorways, waiting for the signal telling them they're 'ten at ten'—ten feet above the waves at ten knots. They spear the water feet first with hands by their side, the neoprene layers muting cold water shock. When they come up, they clear their snorkels, settle their masks, and strike out for the life-rafts. The swell is so pronounced that the divers feel as if they are swimming up and down hills rather than across a level surface. When the wind blows the crests off the waves, they have to dive under cascades of white water. They search the life-rafts fast and urgently and then slash the canopies, to denote that the raft has been checked and save subsequent rescuers unnecessary duplication.

A vignette from the early hours. The *Harwich Venturer*, first there, lowers one of its own life-rafts with three volunteer rescuers on board, and begins to take in survivors. The life-raft is full, and still the survivors keep coming. The rescuers tell them they'll be up and down again in no time. The

54

survivors don't care. They try to climb on board, even though there's no room. The rescuers try to repel them, and signal to the deck crew—begin winching. The crew start to hoist the raft upwards. The raft's bottom strains and bulges under the combined weight of people and water, and suddenly it rips clean open, tipping five of the occupants straight back into the sea and forcing the others to grab at the sides as they fall. Twelve hanging on for dear life, suspended halfway between deck and sea.

James Hertford, the *Harwich Venturer*'s captain, takes one look and orders the raft to be lowered back to the sea. The occupants scream. He yells at them to shut up. The crew look at him, uncertain. He motions with his head and they lower the winch, returning the desperate to the water. When the raft is back on the surface, Hertford has the ferry's evacuation slide inflated, flat-packed creased yellow plastic bursting into shape and gently settling on the sea. Two of his crew go down and bring the survivors on to the slide one by one, scrambling up the air-filled plastic and to safety. When the survivors see there's room for everyone, the savage fight to be first in the queue stops.

Cold statistics mask the human cost. The numbers in the helicopters' mission logs don't tally with the numbers registered onshore. No one can remember who was rescued when, or how many they plucked from the sea. Name sheets are lost, passed to the wrong people, forgotten. Passengers are divided into three categories: alive, missing, dead. The missing category begins as the largest and is whittled away as the day goes on, more and more of its occupants ticked off as either drowned or saved.

By the time the search is called off at dusk, 529 of the 881 passengers have definitely survived. Of the 352 left, 158 are confirmed dead, but little hope is held out for the 194 still listed as missing. Most of them are entombed in the *Amphitrite*, and those that aren't have almost certainly drowned anyway. The rescue mission has been comprehensive, and the North Sea is unforgiving. This is not an earthquake, where people can survive for days before they are rescued.

Davenport Leivers and Matt Kellman are among the missing.

Back at their bases, the helicopter pilots slump in tatty chairs and look blankly into space. Those. who can muster the energy begin to cry. They are hard men and used to death, but the sheer scale of this thing makes it impossible to brush off.

In Aberdeen's Royal Infirmary, the night shift takes over, accepting the grateful thanks of exhausted staff who have been on the go since before dawn. The litany of injured who pack the wards make the place look like a wartime field hospital: broken arms and legs, head wounds and hypothermia. Streams of relatives and reporters traipse through the corridors.

Lovelock has been on his feet all day, shuttling between hospitals, newsrooms, press conferences and his own office. He is meeting the official government inspector tomorrow. Most of the staff have gone home, but a handful remain to deal with further enquiries. He goes round each of them in turn and thanks them for their help. They look at him with glazed eyes.

Out beyond Aberdeen's harbour, the North Sea

56

settles back into its timeless rhythm of ebb and flow. The weather is calm now, and murmuring waves lap gently over the spot where the *Amphitrite* went down. The sea is innocent and beguiling once more. It gives no clue that its treacherous alter ego has just claimed 352 lives.

*   *   *

Sinclair is the only person Kate wants to see.

He comes round to her house late in the afternoon, and they hold each other for long minutes. They have always been comfortable in each other's silence, and that ease serves them well now. Neither particularly wants to talk about what has happened. They just want to be with someone who shared the horror, and can understand the pain and the anguish.

Sinclair makes tea, strong and shot through with brandy. Kate watches as he busies himself in her kitchen, finding tea-bags and milk and sugar as easily as if he were in his own home. Even in such mundane domesticity, his energy is noticeable. He moves quickly and with the odd hint of flamboyance, flicking his wrists as he pours the liquor into the steaming mugs. The kitchen light shines on the top of his head, where what was once a widow's peak is now an island of greying hair, cut off from the rest by a tide of scalp.

They sit without talking. This is their companionship, contented and undemanding. In the time they have known each other—since Kate first auditioned for the troupe, just after she moved to Aberdeen five years ago—they have both essentially been singletons. Kate's relationship with

David, Leo's father, broke up while Leo was still trying to kick his way out of the womb. Sinclair has never been married. Kate lives with her son, Sinclair alone.

What they have is a state often sought and less often achieved in male–female relationships: affection without lust. For Kate, it is the simple pleasure of being friends with someone who doesn't want to fuck her; for Sinclair, the fulfilment of having someone to care for and advise. In simple terms, they are the father and daughter each other doesn't have.

* * *

Bronagh lives on the north side of the harbour, a small cottage in the old fishing community of Footdee. Kate loves this part of town. It is endearingly disordered, and on warm days old women sit outside their cottages and gossip with whoever comes past. The city centre is less than half a mile away, but it may as well be in a different galaxy.

Kate rings the bell. She normally has a set of keys, but she's given them back to Bronagh for the time being, for the builders while they do some renovations.

The intercom buzzes to let her in. Bronagh's twin Pekinese, Vodka and Tonic, snuffle round Kate's feet as she walks through her aunt's front door. Kate bends down and rubs the dogs on their noses.

'Up here!' yells Bronagh from upstairs.

Kate turns sideways to squeeze past a stepladder and some paint pots. She climbs wearily, one tread at a time. The dogs scamper behind her.

Bronagh and Leo are in the sitting-room. Leo is watching cartoons on TV, and Bronagh is dabbing at a watercolour on her easel. A can of Foster's balances precariously on a rickety table nearby— Bronagh might be Irish, but she detests Guinness with a vengeance—and two budgies waddle round a large cage at Bronagh's feet. One of the budgies is blind, and the other leads it round. There are about three hundred more in the garden shed.

The house smells as revolting as usual, a sharp mixture of birdfood, dogs, paint, menthol cigarettes and whatever Bronagh has cooked in the past couple of days. She's about as bad a cook as it's possible to be without being actively dangerous, and her kitchen window has been jammed shut for as long as Kate can remember, channelling the smells through the rest of the house.

Bronagh is wearing voluminous purple flares and a black artist's smock, an outfit which Kate knows ranks amongst the more sober in her wardrobe. Her hair, streaked with grey and henna, is swept up, back and round in full Thatcher style. A tube of silver bangles encases Bronagh's left arm virtually from elbow to wrist, and the skin on her right is blotched from years of dedication to the amber nectar.

Kate loves her aunt for all of her eccentricity, and wouldn't have her change a thing.

Leo looks up and sees Kate come in. He pushes himself off the sofa and scoots over to her. She scoops him up and presses her face against his.

'You smell nicer now,' he says. She kisses him, and he clings on to her neck as she walks over to Bronagh.

'Feel better?' Bronagh's voice is deep and rasping, and Kate can smell the beer on her breath as they kiss.

'A bit.'

'Long hot bath must have helped.'

'Hmm. I see the builders are still here.'

'Three weeks late, and counting.'

Something in Bronagh's face brings Kate up short.

'What's wrong?' she asks.

'Katie—there's something you should know.'

Still looking at her aunt, Kate leans down and sets Leo gently back on the floor.

'What?'

'This is going to be a bit of a shock to you, and God knows you've had enough, but—'

'Auntie B. Just tell me.'

Bronagh pecks at the neck of the Foster's can. It is unlike her to be coy about anything.

'It's your father. He's in charge of the investigation into the ferry.'

Kate hears the breath whistle out of her lungs. She suddenly feels very weak.

She reaches down for Leo, but he is already back on the sofa, watching the cartoons again. Kate decides to leave him there.

'He's—he's doing the investigation?'

'Uh-huh.'

'Why? *How?*'

'He's head of the outfit which handles all these things. You know, the Marine Accident place. The one down in Southampton.'

'I knew he worked there. I didn't know he was in *charge* of it.'

'For the past three years. Took over when the

60

previous chap died.'

Three years Frank's been head of the Marine Accident Investigation Branch. And Kate hasn't seen him for four. Four years since Angie, her mother—his wife—died. When father and daughter spoke at the funeral, it was only to exchange words heavy with bitterness and recrimination. Sixteen years before that when she cowered at the top of the stairs in teenage fear while her parents had the most almighty argument, and the next morning they told her that her father had met another woman and was leaving.

From that moment on, Kate acted as though her father didn't exist. She took his photos off her bedside table and ripped them up. He sent her cards and presents on her birthday and at Christmas, and she dropped them in the bin unopened. And Bronagh, even though she was Frank's sister and therefore came encumbered with a very obvious set of loyalties, was as fair and even-handed as anyone in her situation could have been. She sat with Kate and Angie for nights on end, drinking and talking with them as they went round in circles looking for reasons why.

Bronagh never pretended that her feeling of betrayal was anywhere near as deep as theirs, and she never hid anything from them when they asked—though equally she never went out of her way to tell them when she saw Frank and what he was doing. When Angie died, it was Bronagh who turned up at Kate's flat with a bag full of clinking whisky bottles and an endless capacity to listen: Bronagh to whom she turned rather than David, who had decamped to Seattle a few weeks after his son Leo was born.

'Do you think I'll have to see him?'

He. Him. Never 'Dad', never 'Frank'.

'They'll want to talk to the survivors, I'm sure.'

'He doesn't know I was on the ferry.'

'He'll find out soon enough. They'll have passenger lists.'

'I'm not seeing him. They can get someone else to interview me.'

Bronagh glances over at Leo.

'It might not be as simple as that.'

'Why not?'

'They're setting up shop in the Michaelhouse.'

Kate blinks in disbelief.

'But that's right across the road from Leo's school.'

*   *   *

This madness is the price he pays for murder. Heaven itself has made him mad.

Breakneck for the finish they come again, dead weight in their crashing footfalls as they stamp him down, their black cloaks like nets. In his ears the heavy rasp of their breathing as they race him on, their moment of yielding drained away like her blood into the earth.

He takes his time with her, of course. All the pain and anguish she has put him through must be repaid, and repaid in full. She is bound hand and foot, and her eyes plead with him. Does she think he's simply going to relent? He knows that her supplication is a cynical tactic, nothing more. If he releases her, she will simply resume the torment. But the torment now is all his, perpetrated *by* him rather than *on* him. He requires, he requests and requires that she suffers. When he takes the dirt out of her mouth to let her scream, it is a siren song to him.

The torture goes on for hours, and it only stops when he decides.

He comes fast for her now. When snakes strike, they are so quick that the human eye can barely follow them: one frame of a film, that's all. He is like that snake.

The joy of relief and release as she squirms under him, her body jerking and spurting with the knife-blows. He feels the triumph as the life goes out of her, the evil driven away, exultation as he sees her death. The last plume of breath leaves her body and is borne by the wind away to the sea. He watches as the light fades from her eyes.

At that moment, the instant when she passes, he possesses her. To the victor, the spoils. He has faced down his pursuer and engaged her in combat. Stealth and surprise on his part, and she is his. Her cohorts disappear in wingless cowardice.

She is his. The ground where he kills is sacred. Dogs may defile it and humans may be ignorant of it, but from now on it is hallowed turf, a holy area of possession that can never be deconsecrated. The sweet release of triumph.

But the blood that Mother Earth consumes clots hard. It won't seep through, it breeds revenge, and frenzy seethes like infection through the guilty.

There is a farm off the Inverurie Road, nestling against a hill above which the waxed moon holds itself still. He has been here many times: huge beef stews in the kitchen, red wine and tall stories flowing at an equal lick. Happy faces in the candlelight, friends who demand little more of life and of each other than good humour and toleration. An easy matter, the last time he was here, to take a walk through the farm, pacing out the distances between buildings and noting where everything is kept: the feed, the machinery, the fertiliser.

And the pigs.

He comes here now.

He licks his finger and holds it up away from his face. The wind gusts gently from the west as it dries the saliva. Ideal. He will be coming from downwind. He will smell them long before they smell him.

The pigs sleep, their backs ridged low in the sty like ploughed furrows.

Gently on his feet across the gravel strip. He rocks on his feet, heel first then toe to minimise the crunching. When he glances back at the house, he sees with relief that the windows are still dark, no squares of sudden light to send him running for cover.

At the edge of the sty, the wooden rails bump his shins. He climbs over and stands in the corner. Lines of restraint left and right, a boxer before the fight.

Snuffling as the animals stir, sniff, sense his presence.

The nearest one noses at his legs.

The blood of the pig, to assuage the guilt of his own blood.

He moves the knife in a wide ellipse around his shoulder joint, high and back then round and down with sudden venomous speed, *shlock* as it punctures the pig's skin, one hand holding the beast still while the other plunges and withdraws, plunges and withdraws, the pig squealing squeaking roaring, yellow dotting the farmhouse walls as the lights come on, his hands in the wounds and the blood warm and delicious on them, smeared on his face, another blow and this one hits an artery, the blood quite black in the moonlight as it spurts heavenwards, and he puts his head and body in the spray as if it were a geyser from the earth itself, a familiar voice from the farmhouse and he's back over the rails and running, away from the heaving porcine mass and the erupting house, cries from behind him as the farmer and his wife discover the carnage.

The darkness swallows him as he runs.

Down to the stream beyond the farm's edge, and at last he stops and catches his breath. His lungs heave in the warm night air, and his clothes are coated in human and pig blood, one his vengeance and the other his cleansing.

He strips naked and steps into the water at the point where it eddies around a boulder worn perfectly smooth. The water is cold, and he gasps as he lowers himself as far as his waist, his shoulders, his hair. He ducks his head under, and when he surfaces he sees the blood leaving his skin in long tailing streams.

He is purified.

Back to the car and home and bed, to a hard dreamless sleep.

When he wakes, it is because their screeching has snatched him from sanctuary. The reek of human blood is laughter to their hearts, and the madness is back.

TUESDAY

Two duvets and a blanket on top of her, but still Kate is freezing when she wakes up. She leaps out of bed and runs to the wardrobe on the far side of the room, where she grabs anything warm she can find: thick socks, tracksuit bottoms, two sweatshirts. Her bulging reflection in the full-length mirror on the inside of the wardrobe door stares pudgily back at her.

Leo is still asleep. Too hot in the night, he has kicked the bedclothes away, and now the sheets are rumpled over the lower half of his body.

Kate looks at the alarm clock. Ten past six. He can sleep a while yet.

She walks out of the bedroom and across the hall. She opens the front door, picks up the *Scotsman* lying on the mat, and goes into the kitchen, where she fills the kettle—putting the spout right under the tap so she doesn't have to see the running water.

While the kettle boils, she flicks through the paper. *Amphitrite, Amphitrite,* more *Amphitrite.* Photos of survivors, diagrams of the ferry, tables of similar accidents. At the bottom right-hand corner of the front page is a small column entitled 'Other news'. 'Other news', indeed. What 'other news' can there be?

She flips to the weather forecast, which tells her that today's going to be the warmest day of the year, 28 degrees come mid-afternoon. Hot and humid, with the heatwave scheduled to last into the weekend.

Sod it. She's cold, and that's all there is to it.

She makes herself a cup of coffee and drinks it

as hot as she can stand, hoping that the liquid will thaw her from within, for this coldness is right at the heart of her.

Out of the corner of her eye, she sees the red pulsing of the answerphone light. All the messages she received yesterday. She counts the flashes. Eighteen. With a sigh, she pulls the telephone pad towards her and presses 'play'.

Endless voices suffused with concern, all asking what they can do. Her friend Mary. Chester Renfrew, Grampian Police's Chief Constable, telling her not to come into work until she's ready. Bronagh, twice—before Kate went round to see her. Someone called Jane Bavin, who says she's a counsellor. Peter Ferguson, her deputy. A couple more of her colleagues, some of her friends. When the machine's disembodied voice announces: 'That was your last message', Kate notices that she's been transcribing for about fifteen minutes.

She looks at the pad. She has written Renfrew's message in larger letters than the rest.

'Don't come into work till you're ready.' His words, verbatim.

Kate thinks about having a bath, and knows instantly she won't be able to. But equally she knows she has to start somewhere. Her fear of water is like an injury: she'll have to recover one step at a time.

She goes into the bathroom and peels off her clothes. Stands in the bath, pulls the shower curtain shut, and reaches up for the shower head. It feels like a snake in her hands. She turns the tap, and the shower head spits water. Kate holds it away from her body until it's warmed up.

Now.

70

Needles of water jab against Kate's skin. She turns the shower head away and then instantly back again, knowing that she has to force herself through the fear. The water plays on her stomach, up and down her legs, across her breasts. Kate's skin is red where the jets strike, but the sharp pain has subsided to a dull ache. It's not as bad as she thought it would be.

When she tries to move the shower head up to her throat, it seems to lock itself still. Not the face, not the head. Not yet. One step at a time.

She turns the shower off and wraps herself in the largest towel she can find. Then she goes into the bedroom and wakes Leo up. She helps him get dressed and makes him his breakfast. Renfrew's words stare at her from the pad.

'Don't come into work till you're ready.'

If she wants to come to terms with what happened on the *Amphitrite*, the best way is surely to behave as normally as possible. She mustn't let it dominate her life. Not pretend it didn't happen, of course, but not let it swamp everything either.

She's ready. She's going to work. Better than moping round the house all day.

While Leo eats, Kate roots out some work clothes—skirt, blouse, a thick pullover—and puts them on.

The replay starts in her head the moment she walks back into the kitchen. First behind her eyes and then in front of them and in her ears and nostrils and on her fingertips and all around her. The *Amphitrite* happening all over again, in broad daylight in her flat in Aberdeen, for God's sake, and yet it feels as real as it did the first time.

Kate feels the floor tipping from side to side in

big violent swings. She takes two quick strides to the table and sits down heavily in one of the chairs, gripping the sides of the seat to prevent herself from being flung across the room and slammed against a wall.

Leo gives her a quick, incurious glance and munches happily on, oblivious to what's happening to his mother.

It is sunny and warm outside, but inside it feels cold and wet, spray on her skin and water in her face. Mechanical crashings and human screams, angry terror on the faces that float past her vision.

And yet Kate isn't scared. Far from it. The replay makes her feel secure. It is something she knows, something she can relate to, because she got out of it alive and, no matter how horrible it was, she knows the ending won't change. In her little video of the sinking ferry, she's the one who's in control.

Half-crawling half-sliding down to the leeward side, the people round the woman on the ladder like spectators at street theatre.

The tape stops just as she and Alex are about to jump. The deck covering cutting up under her feet, and then nothing. Kate sits stock still, just to make sure. The room comes back into focus, warm and bright and dry, Leo lifting his glass of milk with both hands, the digital clock on the microwave.

Motion in front of her, and she starts.

The wall. That one over there, right opposite her. It moved.

Don't be absurd. Walls don't move.

She looks again. It seems to have got a little closer. Quick look around the room. No breaks at the corners. If that wall is getting closer, the other three must be as well.

The walls. Closing in on her. Crushing her in this room.

Get out. Had to get out of the ferry. Has to get out of the house.

She leans across the table and takes Leo's glass from him.

'Leo. Come on. Time for school.'

She puts the glass down on the table.

'But Mum . . .'

'*Now.* Don't argue. Let's go.'

Kate runs out of the kitchen and across the hall, snatching the keys from the hall table on her way out. Leo follows her, his satchel bouncing against his legs and his face twisted in puzzlement.

She flings open the front door, and stops.

A bizarre thought pops into her head. Is the iron turned off?

She runs back into the kitchen to check, quickly so the walls don't know she's coming. The ironing board is stacked up against a wall and the iron is on the window shelf behind it, standing on one end with the flex wrapped firmly round the base. She hasn't used it since getting back.

What about the taps? Taps in the kitchen. The bathroom too. She's used *those.*

She runs over to the kitchen sink and checks that the taps are off, and into the bathroom to check bath and basin, valves all shut tight, and then she has to check that the television and the hi-fi are off and that the remote controls for the television and the video are resting face up, because fires can start if they're left face down, sounds stupid but it's true, the constant friction of a button being pressed against a surface can set off sparks, she saw it up in

73

Rosemount last year, and check that all the windows are shut in the sitting-room and the bathroom and the bedroom and the kitchen and the telephone's on the hook and the fridge door is shut—and then, only then, can Kate get out of the house and slam the door behind her.

From Jane Bavin's notes, copied to Sir Nicholas Lovelock at Seaspeed.

Post-traumatic stress disorder, or PTSD, is a natural human reaction: people have suffered from it since time began. If it seems relatively new, it's because we have a more scientific explanation for it than our ancestors did. There's a good account of PTSD in Samuel Pepys' diaries, when he describes how Londoners wandered around like zombies after the Great Fire.

Basically, there are two main types of trauma: type one, brief exposure to an isolated incident; and type two, prolonged or repeated exposure to traumatic events. Type one covers incidents as diverse as earthquakes, kidnaps, rapes, industrial accidents, fires and so on. Type two includes chronic sexual abuse, the after-effects of a toxic spill or nuclear explosion, and of course experiences in wartime. The good news for those who were on board the *Amphitrite* is that people are far more likely to make a rapid and substantial recovery from type one trauma than from type two. The longer the exposure, the longer the recovery. So the survivors of the *Amphitrite* disaster will mend far quicker than,

74

for example, an American GI would recover from his tours of duty in Vietnam.

Individuals suffering from PTSD traditionally exhibit three main strands of behaviour: intrusion, avoidance and hyperarousal.

Intrusion. This involves persistent and distressing recollection of events. These recollections can often seem all too real, as if the traumatic incident itself were literally taking place all over again. Replays may not be exclusively visual, but may involve recall of sounds and smells as well. And because recall is multisensory, intense psychological distress can be caused by exposure to a variety of triggers. These triggers can be perceived by any of the five senses: they can be sights, sounds, smells, tastes or touches.

Avoidance. Because recollection can be so distressing, individuals often go out of their way to avoid any stimuli which they may associate with the trauma. Avoidance manifests itself in various ways. Sufferers may try to avoid thoughts, feelings or conversations connected with the trauma, and throw themselves into work or hobbies with all-consuming zeal. Maybe they steer clear of activities, places or people which arouse recollections of the trauma. Or perhaps they find that they can't remember large chunks of what happened that night.

Hyperarousal. Victims of post-traumatic stress disorder may have difficulty sleeping or concentrating for long periods of time. Perhaps they're more irritable than usual, or feel on edge the whole time. While their brain continues to replay the traumatic event, it fools the body into thinking that the emergency is happening again. This in turn prompts the body to release what are called catecholamine neurotransmitters— basically adrenaline, the chemicals needed to prepare one for fight or flight. This in turn ensures that the nervous system is on permanent or semi-permanent alert.

Many people point to an apparent paradox between avoidance and hyperarousal—in that it seems impossible to be simultaneously avoiding an event and over-reacting to it. However, the concurrence of such reactions makes perfect sense once it is accepted that time is needed for a victim to assimilate and integrate the traumatic experience into the larger framework of their life. Until this is done, their body and mind are demanding vigilance and rest so intensely that they cannot make normal compromises between these competing demands. So they either react excessively or not at all.

Kate hugs Leo goodbye and watches him trot off towards the school buildings. He falls in step with one of his friends and they walk the last few strides to the door together, their little legs keeping perfect time. Leo waves to Kate from the door and then disappears inside, swallowed up by Woolmanhill Primary for another day.

Across the road, liveried doormen stand under the massive granite canopy of the Michaelhouse. The MAIB obviously doesn't expect its inspectors to slum it. Kate watches the entrance nervously, as if her father is going to appear at any moment. Three men come out and set off down the street without looking at her. They are in shirtsleeves, and their jackets are slung over their shoulders. It must be warm already, though Kate can't feel it.

She walks quickly back to her car, takes out her official police-issue mobile—her own personal one is at the bottom of the North Sea—and dials Renfrew's private line before she can change her mind.

'Chief Constable's office.'

'Tina, it's Kate Beauchamp.'

Kate was hoping to get Renfrew himself. Tina can be somewhat overbearing, and right now she'd much rather have Renfrew's brisk no-nonsense approach to life.

'Kate, how *are* you? My God, what an awful thing to happen. You must be . . .'

'I'm OK, I'm OK. Is he there?'

'He's just on a call, but I know he wants to talk to you. Hold on a sec while I get his attention. You take care now, you hear?'

Kate drums her fingers on the steering wheel while she waits in electronic limbo.

'Kate.' Renfrew's strident voice. 'How are you?'

'I'm coming in.'

'What, today?'

'Now.'

'Kate, there's no need. Take your time. You've had a dreadful shock.'

'No. I want to. I've lots to do.'

'Such as what?'

'The three-year plan, for a start.'

Three-year plan. On any other day, she'd run a mile. Divisional restructuring, devolved control of

CID, tighter financial management. Paper pushing, basically.

'You want to do the three-year plan?' Renfrew chuckles. 'What happened? You get a bang on the head?'

'I'm fine. Really.'

'Anything to keep you occupied, eh?'

'Yes.'

'And you're just going to throw yourself straight back in?'

He could have picked a better choice of words, but she knows what he means.

'Exactly. Back with a vengeance.'

'Well, if you want occupied, I've got just the thing.'

'What is it?' Eager, almost grasping.

'But I'm not sure . . .'

'Tell me. What is it?'

She hears Renfrew exhale as he weighs up his options. 'Ferguson's there at the moment, but you can pull rank on him.'

'Ferguson's where?'

'Woodend Hospital, in the grounds. Out towards Hazlehead.'

'What's happened?'

'I think you'd better go look for yourself. Then you can tell me whether you want it.'

*   *   *

Woodend Hospital is aptly named. It is located in glorious woodland to the west of the city centre, and the trees are luxuriant at this time of year.

The blue-and-white police tapes strung between trees direct Kate towards the scene. She parks her

78

car next to the bridge which leads over the river Denburn to the hospital, flips her badge at a uniform who comes across to intercept her, and strides across a patch of grass towards the cluster of forensics and photographers. Away to her right, the morning sun blazes from behind the hospital's Gothic clocktower.

Ferguson, Kate's deputy, is squatting on his haunches by a peeling wooden bench. He looks vaguely in her direction, and then pushes himself upright in surprise when he sees who it is. His forehead shimmers with sweat, and his glasses reflect the world in green tint.

'I didn't expect you . . .'

'What's happened?'

'It's not pretty.'

'That's not what I asked.'

Ferguson's fingers scrabble nervously in his hair, pushing the dark of his fringe off his forehead. He is only a couple of years younger than Kate, but right now, squinting into the sun, he looks barely old enough to be shaving.

'Boss, I've got this under control, and don't you think that maybe . . . ?'

'Jesus Christ, Peter. I wish everyone would stop treating me like a fucking invalid. The ferry sank. I survived. I'm here. End of story.'

'I'm sorry, I'm sorry.'

She knows why he's trying to protect her. Ferguson's feelings for Kate go beyond the professional. She's known this since last Christmas, when he got stupendously drunk at the department party and told her in great detail how much he loved her and how she was everything he'd ever looked for in a woman. She told him that she was

79

flattered, but that the feeling wasn't mutual and wasn't ever likely to be. The issue has never been mentioned since. But she knows it's there, and she sees how it colours his behaviour at times. Like now.

'What happened?'

'She's through there.' He gestures towards the melee.

Kate elbows her way through. Her body moves uncomfortably inside her multiple layers. She is aware of Ferguson at her shoulder.

'Excuse me,' she says. 'Let me through. I'm the senior officer here.'

The last photographer steps aside, and Kate stops dead.

Ferguson was right. It isn't pretty.

A pair of legs stick out from under a tree. Female legs, slender and young.

With bloody stumps instead of feet.

Kate clamps her teeth together and swallows in the back of her throat.

Ferguson starts forward as if to tell her something, but she holds up her hand to stay him.

There is a dreadful pathos about outdoor homicide victims. Whatever violations have been inflicted on them, they also suffer the indignity of being exposed not only to the elements but also to the casual eyes of passersby. Even the most mutilated of indoor victims is afforded some measure of privacy.

'Who found her?'

'An early-morning runner,' says Ferguson. 'He's being interviewed now.'

Kate squats down to get a closer look.

The soil beneath the victim blends gently with

the brownish red of the blood which is drying in patches on her body. Her tattered shirt gapes with the smiling mouths of knife wounds. She has been stabbed repeatedly and violently.

One arm is folded across her chest, and the other lies on the ground by her side.

Her hands have been removed as well.

Kate forces her gaze upwards, towards the woman's face, knowing that it may well have been beaten unrecognisable. This attack is as savage as any she's seen.

She never gets to the face.

A rope has been tied round the victim's neck, under her armpits and round her upper arms. Off this rope hang the missing extremities: one hand and one foot on each side of the body. The feet rest on the collarbones, and the hands are splayed across thin biceps.

Bishops and knights, chess pieces lined up before a game.

And right in the middle, pinned behind its head at the dip of the woman's throat and darting malevolently at anyone who comes too close, is an adder with skin of unbroken black.

*   *   *

Before the MAIB was established in 1989, investigation into marine accidents was carried out by surveyors in the Department of Transport's Marine Directorate. Now, the MAIB is a distinct and separate branch within the department (which has itself been expanded to incorporate the environmental and regional portfolios), and the chief inspector reports directly to the secretary of state. Its independence is reinforced by its location in Southampton, far from the incestuous Whitehall corridors.

The MAIB deals with around 2,000 accidents each year. Of these, about 600 require investigation, though most of them can be dealt with by correspondence or telephone. Only around 70 necessitate an on-site visit. And virtually none require the kind of commitment which the *Amphitrite* investigation does. In terms of lives lost, it is the biggest disaster involving a British vessel since the *Herald of Free Enterprise* in 1987. Frank has brought seven inspectors and sixteen assistants with him to Aberdeen. All the stops have been pulled out.

Christian Parker, the *Amphitrite*'s third officer and only surviving member of the bridge crew, has been moved from accident and emergency to the main body of the Royal Infirmary, a couple of hundred yards up the hill. The entrance is crowded with journalists, trampling over the increasingly haphazard arrangement of flowers and small trees in the earthed roundabout outside the door.

Frank walks fast through them and inside, before they recognise him and the shouted questions begin. He shows the receptionist his ID, a small laminated card with the MAIB crest in the top left-hand corner, and she gives him Parker's room number. He goes down the stairs and back on himself, through half-lit corridors which smell of under-cooked food and the leather from new cars.

A doctor stands in a doorway, scribbling on a clipboard. Frank's mobile trills at his waist. The doctor looks up sharply.

'Could you turn that off, please?' he says. 'They

interfere with hospital equipment. There are signs.'

Frank reaches down and locates the phone's 'off' button with his fingers.

He finds Parker's room at the second attempt, after an abortive sortie which ends with him striding confidently into a cleaning cupboard. There is a policeman outside Parker's room. Again Frank flashes his ID, and the policeman opens the door and lets him through.

Parker turns his head towards Frank as he enters. His face is virtually untouched: a small slice of bruising above his right eye, purple fading to yellow, and a slight cut near the bottom of his left cheek. Those apart, nothing.

The damage that Frank can't see, of course, is inside Parker's head: the nightmares and flashbacks which beat against the walls of his skull.

The room's walls are painted pale blue, the window looks on to the looming circular backsides of the hospital ventilators, and the bed is jacked up high. There are two chairs. Frank sits down on one of them. Parker watches him all the way.

Frank knows that, at first glance, he doesn't look the most accommodating of people. He is short and squat, with a small sphere of belly teetering above his belt. His white hair is razored to a cricket pitch stubble, and its shortness accentuates his ears. He has a boxer's nose, big and flat and barely narrower than his mouth. He tries now to put Parker at his ease.

'I'm Frank Beauchamp, head of the inquiry into the *Amphitrite*'s sinking.'

Parker nods almost imperceptibly.

'How are you feeling?'

'Hungry. And hot. Do us a favour and open the

window.'

Frank gets up and goes over to the window.

'Didn't they give you breakfast?' he asks, fiddling with the latch.

'Didn't feel like it. And now I'm hungry. Got to wait till lunch, though.'

Parker's voice is heavy, his words slow.

The latch squeaks irritably and yields. Frank pushes the window open as far as it will go and comes back to the bedside. He takes off his jacket and hangs it on the back of the chair. His forearms, forged through decades of hauling winches and holding sheets, are massive.

'Christian, I'm here to ask you about what happened on board the *Amphitrite*. I know this might be painful for you, but I need you to tell me as much as you can remember about that night. I'm going to tape this conversation, just for the record. Is that OK?'

Parker shrugs. Frank pulls a microcassette recorder from his pocket, places it on the bedside table and switches it on. The 'record' light glows red.

'What do you remember, Christian? About that night?'

'I remember hitting the water. It was cold. Aye, it was cold.'

'And after that?'

'Nothing.'

'What about before that?'

Parker is silent. Frank prompts him.

'Before that? You remember anything before that?'

Parker nods.

'Just give me a couple of seconds, yeah?'

84

'Sure.'

From the corridor outside, the squeak of rubber-soled shoes and a trolley's muted clanking.

Parker clears his throat.

'There was a bomb.'

'A *bomb*? You're sure?'

'Positive.'

A bomb. Forty years in the maritime business, in one form or another, and Frank has never heard of a ferry being bombed. His first instinct is to think Parker is delirious or otherwise confused, but he is palpably lucid. Parker's words may be coming out slowly, but there is nothing wrong with his memory.

'What happened? Start from the beginning.'

Parker runs Frank through events on the bridge in the minutes after midnight, when he had just come on watch for the four-hour graveyard shift. Captain Sutton—Steady Eddie—calling them together and telling them there was a bomb on board. Second Officer Garthowen throttling back the engines while he, Third Officer Parker, puts out a call for the deckhands. The cover story for the passengers about catching fishing lines on the propellers. Watching the activity on the car deck through the four cameras there—one for'ard, one aft, and two amidships, port and starboard—feeding into monitors on the bridge. The door lights going from green to red and back to green again. Position indicators for the visor side locks and the ramp locking devices.

'And when Captain Sutton had finished, he came back up to the bridge?'

'Aye.'

'How did he look?'

'Shaken.'

'That's hardly surprising. If that bomb had gone off when he'd been moving the van, he and the deckhands would have been blown to pieces.'

'Aye. When it was all done and he'd had a chance to think about it, that's when it really freaked him out.'

'How did he know about the bomb in the first place?'

'Dunno. Must have got a tip-off.'

'On the radio?'

'I would have thought so.'

'But the radio operator didn't mention it?'

'Sparks? Not that I heard.'

Frank scratches his ankle. The tape loops relentlessly forward.

'There's something bothering me. You said there was a bomb.'

'Aye.'

'But Captain Sutton and the deckhands tipped the vehicle with the bomb into the sea.'

'Aye.'

'So there was no longer a bomb on board.'

'That's what I thought. At first.'

'What do you mean, "at first"?'

'Like everyone else, I thought the danger was past. Then suddenly there were two massive bangs. That's what started us going down.'

'Bangs? Like bomb blasts?'

'Aye. Explosions. They shook the hull. You could feel the reverbs from the bridge.'

'But the first Mayday was put out at 1.12 a.m. BST. You said the van was tipped out shortly after midnight.'

'Aye. That's why we thought the danger was past. We got the engines back up to cruising speed and thought no more of it. Then we had to cut the speed a bit, when the storm started to come up.'

'The weather report said it was—what? Beaufort seven, eight?'

Seven is a moderate gale, 28–33 knots with large waves. Eight is a fresh gale, 34–40 knots, moderately high sea with blowing foam.

'About that. I've been in worse. Up to eleven one time, a real fucker off Fraserburgh. But it would have been bad enough for the passengers.'

'How much did you cut the speed by?'

'Two or three knots. From 17 to 15, I think.'

'So you must have been losing time, what with having had to stop as well?'

'Aye. The skipper was calculating how far behind schedule we'd be arriving.'

'What did he reckon?'

'An hour, he said. But that was miles wrong. We were half an hour up to start with.'

Parker looks at Frank. There's something in his voice, his manner, which makes Frank think he's trying to tell him something.

'It can't have been a very difficult calculation.'

'It wasn't.'

'But he messed it up.'

'Aye.'

Shaken enough to mess up a calculation. Shaken enough to do—or not do—what else?

'That wasn't the only mistake he made?'

'You won't hear that from me.'

But of course Frank will. Parker wants to tell him, but also to be able to say that Frank wheedled it out of him, that he didn't just offer it up on a plate.

'He's dead. You've got nothing to gain by

protecting his reputation.'

Parker says nothing.

'I need to know what happened.'

Parker fingers the bruise on his face, decides that honour is satisfied, and relents.

'OK. He panicked. He lost the plot. Totally.'

'In what way?'

'He was gibbering. Muttering away to himself like a loon. He could have done that calculation in ten seconds flat. But he kept punching at the calculator, over and over. Scribbling numbers on pieces of paper and ripping them up. And that was only the start of it. When the *Amphitrite* began to sink, he grabbed the intercom and started yelling instructions. But they were rubbish. Not to start the cars up until the doors were opened. People to disembark according to which deck they were on. And then a whole heap of nothing. I don't even know if it was English. The fucking ship was sinking, and he's telling things as if we've docked safe and sound in Aberdeen.'

'Had you ever seen him like this before?'

'Never.'

'What did you do?'

'I knocked the intercom out of his hand and yelled at him. "You didn't get the right vehicle, did you?" That's what I said.'

'And what did he say?'

'I thought he was about to bite me. He looked like he'd lost his mind. He grabbed my shoulders and said: "You could say that, Christian. You could say that."'

'"You could say that." They were his exact words?'

'Aye.'

A white Transit van. By the law of averages, there would have been more than one on board. An easy mistake to make. Easy, and fatal.

'And after that?'

'He grabbed the wheel and turned the ship hard a-starboard.'

A ship travelling west-south-west. Westerly winds, and a storm crabbing its way down from the north. Frank knows instantly what Parker is saying.

'Sutton turned *into* the storm.'

Parker nods. Frank goes on, half to himself.

'He should have turned to port and tried to run with it.'

He looks at Parker.

'Didn't you try to stop him?'

'Of course. Me and Ken—Second Officer Garthowen—we went to take the wheel off him, both of us together. But before we could get there, the ship tipped suddenly and sent us all flying.'

'Had he turned to port, do you think the ship would still have sunk?'

'With bomb damage? Oh, aye. But not so fast. We'd have had fifteen, twenty minutes extra. Could have saved hundreds more in that time.'

'How did you escape?'

'I got lucky. When I was going for the wheel and the ship threw me down, I was hurled back into the chartroom, so I had some shelter when the water broke the bridge windows and came piling in. Most of those poor buggers by the windows would have been killed instantly. And when the *Amphitrite* tipped back the other way, the water drained out of the bridge, and I went with it. Right past all the bodies. Sutton, Ken too. Sparks, still with his headphones on. Jesus Christ, it was awful.

89

Terrible.'

He looks Frank right in the eye.

'You can talk to everyone who survived, ask them as many questions as you like, but you still— it still won't tell you what it was like. More awful than you could imagine.'

Frank shakes his head.

'It was a preview of hell,' says Parker.

*　　　*　　　*

The autopsy room is bright, clean and cool. To Kate, it feels like the inside of a fridge.

Autopsies are never pretty, but some are more savoury than others. The one Kate is attending now is about as unpalatable as she ever hopes to experience.

She rang Renfrew from the crime scene and told him she wanted the case. She'd have been given it as a matter of course were it not for the *Amphitrite*, she said, and she has no substantial physical injuries which might in any way incapacitate her. He didn't ask about the mental damage, and she didn't tell him.

Renfrew is a former head of Edinburgh CID, and also did a stint as head of policing at Ibrox, where at least twice a season Rangers and Celtic do sectarian battle thinly disguised as football matches. He knows which arguments he can win and which aren't worth fighting. He told Kate the case was hers.

Kate also rang Bronagh and told her she'd be working late. They have a well-established arrangement. Bronagh will pick Leo up from school, take him home and give him his tea. If Kate isn't back by seven, Bronagh will cook Leo dinner as well. She dotes on Leo, and it is the easiest thing in the world for her to help Kate out in this way. She paints and she plays bridge, and the former at least is infinitely flexible.

Kate turns her attention back to the body on the slab.

The victim has been identified as Petra Gallacher, eighteen years old and a trainee reporter on the *Aberdeen Evening Telegraph*. Her handbag was left near the body and a name tag was sewn into the waistband of her skirt, a legacy of schooldays barely left behind.

The adder has been removed, tranquillised by the university's professor of herpetology. Petra's hands and feet have been untied from the rope, and are lying neatly on the autopsy table next to her body. The rope has been taken away for forensic analysis.

Dr Thomas Hemmings, the pathologist, busies himself with his instruments. He has completed the external examination of Petra's body, and is going to show Kate what he's found before he has to cut Petra up for the internal examination. His bald pate shines under the lights, and the ring of white hair around the sides and back of his head reminds Kate of winter crocuses at the foot of a hill.

'Ready?'

'Yes.'

Hemmings walks over to the slab, murmuring under his breath. It takes Kate a moment to catch his words. 'This is the place, where death rejoices to teach those who live.'

He clears his throat.

'Body temperature and extent of rigor mortis

indicate that the deceased was killed between midnight and two o'clock this morning. Her cause of death was multiple sharp force injuries. There are more than twenty discriminable wounds on her face, neck and torso. In addition, there are cutting wounds and blunt force injuries compatible with defensive wounds on both hands, and some of the stab wounds on her torso don't line up with the rips in her shirt.'

'All of which suggest that she struggled.'

'Exactly. I'll give you a full report later, but right now I'll just point out the major things to you. Any one of four wounds could have killed her.' He points at Petra's body. 'There, there, there and there.'

It's hard to see which wounds he's indicated, there are so many.

'The first one is here.' He touches her neck. 'Sharp force injury to neck, left side, transecting the left internal jugular vein. About 3 inches long, beginning over the left sternocleidomastoid muscle and going up and backwards. It is a complex wound, and appears to be a combination of cutting and stabbing.'

His hand moves down to below her right breast.

'Wounds two and three. Both stab wounds, both perforated the right lung to 2 or 3 inches, both helped cause a haemothorax.'

He goes to the higher one first.

'Number two, 5 inches from the back, incised the seventh rib at the approximately mid-axillary line. It is a 5/8-inch wound with a 4-inch wound path, going from right to left and from back to front. The wound path terminates at the right fourth rib on the anterior cage at the approximate mid-clavicular line.

'Number three, 2 inches from the back, penetrated the eighth intercostal space without rib damage. The pathway is similar to number two. It is a 1-inch wound on a 3-inch wound path.'

He moves his hand across her body and down.

'Number four. Transversely orientated ³⁄₄-inch wound on a 5-inch wound path to the left side of the abdomen. The path runs from left to right and slightly back to front. The wound perforated the abdominal aorta and caused severe retroperitoneal and intra-abdominal haemorrhaging.'

The stark medical language in no way mitigates the horror of what Kate is seeing.

She knows that Hemmings is a kind man, and eminently sensitive to the emotions of those involved on such occasions. Nonetheless, Kate wonders whether he—whether all pathologists—look at living people purely as walking bundles of ligaments and bone and organs, knowing that everyone ends up that way in the end.

'Can you tell what kind of knife he used?' she asks.

'Almost certainly a single-edged one. Many of the wounds—particularly the more superficial wounds—have one end squared off and the other V-shaped.'

'Not all of them, though?'

'No. But that's to be expected. As you know, the depth, width and length of individual sharp force wounds is not a predictor of knife type. Each stab or cut is a hypervariable incident of its own nature, and is dependent on a multitude of factors—force applied, direction, angle, obstructions of tissue and bone. For example, the fatal wounds I just showed

93

you all have irregular configurations and varied shapes. But when you consider Langer's lines, or the . . .'

'What are Langer's lines?'

'Sorry. The grain of the skin. When you consider those, and the likelihood that the killer was twisting the knife and the victim moving as the blade was withdrawn, then you see that variety is not only possible but probable.'

'Smooth or serrated?'

'Smooth. There are hardly any serrations in the wounds. The ones that *are* there can be explained by the factors I've just mentioned.'

'How long would she have lived, once he started stabbing her?'

'A minute, maybe ninety seconds. No more.'

'And'—Kate can hardly bring herself to ask this—'the extremities. Her hands and feet. Did he . . .?'

'Afterwards. The blood patterns around the stumps are limited, and the cuts are reasonably clean. He didn't dismember her until she was dead.'

Kate breathes a sigh of relief, and is instantly struck by the absurdity of her reaction.

'However, there *are* serrations on the skin at the points of amputation,' continues Hemmings. 'Small serrations, close together. A surgical saw, no doubt. And he knew what he was doing.'

'In what way?'

'For a start, surgical saws cut much quicker than knives. And secondly, he's severed at the weakest points. He's avoided the bones as far as possible, and instead gone through the ligaments. Look here.'

He takes hold of Petra's left wrist. No hand attached to it.

'See where he's cut. About an inch and a half above the heel of the hand. If he goes too close to the hand, he has to cut through three bones—the scaphoid, lunate and triquetral—which between them span the entire width of the joint. But where he's chosen, he only has two bones to cut, the radius and the ulna. And they don't span the width of the wrist, not nearly. There's a substantial amount of collateral and radiocarpal ligament between them.'

He lays Petra's wrist carefully back down on the table and takes a couple of strides down towards her feet. No. Not her feet. Where her feet were.

'Similarly with the ankle. Again, he can't avoid bones altogether—he has the medial and lateral malleoli here—but he's also got as much tibiofibular ligament as he can. And that's no easy matter. The ankle joint is complex: the bones and ligaments are recessed into each other more than in the wrist. Whoever did this must have a working knowledge of anatomy.'

'Medical training?'

'Not necessarily. He could have spent an hour in the library with Gray's Anatomy, if he took good notes. But he'd have had to have done some research, yes.'

'Did he rape her?'

'There's semen inside her vagina, though vaginal tearing is minimal.'

'It may have been consensual sex, then?'

'Maybe. Or with someone other than the killer. I've sent a sample off for DNA analysis, of course.'

Kate nods to herself, and looks at her watch.

95

'I've got to go. We've got a case meeting in fifteen minutes. Thank you, Doctor.'

'Not at all. You'll have the full report by mid-afternoon.'

He pauses.

'There is one more thing.'

He reaches over Petra's body and picks up one of her feet.

'The histamine levels and petechial haemorrhaging will confirm this, I'm sure, but you should know now.'

He holds up the foot so Kate can see the sole. It is criss-crossed with welts.

'Blunt force injuries,' says Hemmings. 'In this case, bastinado, beating the soles of the feet. He tortured her before he killed her.'

*   *   *

The Queen Street police headquarters is an ugly, functionalist building. Its roof bristles with antennae, and the lines of windows seem somehow uneven. It is shamed by the surging, soaring lines of the nearby Marischal College, Aberdeen's most imposing edifice and the second-largest granite building in the world behind the Escorial in Madrid. Kate knows this in the same way that she knows most things about the buildings of her adopted city—via Ferguson, who fancies himself as something of an expert on local history and architecture.

The Marischal's tall, steely grey pinnacles gaze imperviously down on Kate's car as she drives into the underground car park beneath police headquarters. Her mind races as she brings the

96

vehicle to a halt.

The darkest year of my life, chasing the maniac we knew almost until the end merely as Silver Tongue, one of the bloodiest butchers in London's history, the man who ripped his victims' tongues out as he hanged and bludgeoned and beheaded and flayed them and worse. And worse, like sawing one of them—an MP—in half. Red Metcalfe and me in a Victorian living-room in Westminster, looking at a body cut in two, a sandwich in cross-relief, the skin as bread round the outside and the organs the filling within, glistening livid shades of red and turquoise and purple and yellow and black. And me knowing that all that stuff, all that mess, is in me too.

Sawn in half. Petra Gallacher on the slab with her hands and feet sawn off.

She takes the lift up to the fourth floor and goes straight to the incident room. There must be fifty people in there: not just uniformed officers but civilians too, typists and copytakers and secretaries. Kate calls for quiet, and the room gradually settles.

She perches on the edge of a table and looks around her. They are a tough lot to impress, the Grampian Police Force. She's had to earn her respect from them the hard way since she moved here from London, by taking on the most difficult cases and running herself into the ground to solve them. Like their city itself, Kate's colleagues are conservative and disinclined to rapid change. But they give credit where it's due, and there's not a man in the room who doesn't think she's worth her position.

They know about the *Amphitrite*, of course. But if things go wrong, she won't use it as an excuse and they won't let her. It's her choice to come back to work, her choice to take this case. They won't cut her any slack because of what's happened to her, and nor would she want it.

She blinks twice to banish the images of Petra Gallacher on the slab.

'I've just been speaking to Dr Hemmings, the pathologist. He's going to have a full report by mid-afternoon, but in the meantime he has confirmed a few things. There was semen inside Petra, though vaginal tearing was minimal. Petra was tortured before she was killed, though she was dismembered only after she was dead. He used a single-edged knife on her, more than twenty times. Four of her wounds were fatal. Both of those are high numbers. This is a crime of power and rage.'

And Kate doesn't know any cure for those, not in such extreme forms.

'From all this, I would guess that she knew her killer. Most victims do anyway. And it would be hard for the killer to have summoned up that amount of anger and hatred for someone he didn't know. Consider that Petra may also have had sex with him voluntarily—either in a desperate attempt to stop him killing her, or because she had no idea he was going to turn on her. So I want her life turned upside down. Boyfriends, past and present. Had she split up with anyone recently? Had she given someone the brush-off? She was a reporter. Maybe she was doing a story and met some weirdo who developed a fixation with her. Internet chat rooms, even. Anything which would have brought perp and victim into contact.

'Right. I'm going to divide you up into various groups, each with a leader.' She ticks them off on her fingers as she goes. 'Wilcox, incoming calls from the public and following up on any leads generated there. Also claims of responsibility. The details about the extremities and the snake are being withheld from the public: use them as controls to weed out the cranks. Atkins, search HOLMES and other databases for known sex offenders. This killing is absolutely brutal. I can't believe it's his first offence. He simply couldn't graduate from being a law-abiding citizen one moment to leaving Petra like that the next. He may not have killed before, but he might well have a record for rape, assault, battery, indecent exposure, bodily harm, things like that. Sherwood, house-to-house among Petra's neighbours. Four hundred yards in every direction. Ripley, vehicle and pedestrian checks in the city centre and out at the murder site, asking people if they saw anything untoward. Peter, you and I will go down to the paper where she worked. And I'll also go and see the guy at the university who took the snake away. Everyone clear?'

The detectives she's singled out nod their heads.

'Most of it's going to be thankless and useless.' Kate indicates the Scottish police crest on the far wall. 'Remember what it says there: "semper vigilo". Cross-refer, cross-refer. We keep at it, and one name will start coming up again and again on people's lists. It might be the smallest thing which helps us crack it. Part of a numberplate, a sketchy description, a blood type. That's why I don't want anyone stinting on this.' Kate glances at her watch. 'You all know the 24–24 rule. The twenty-four hours before the killing and the twenty-four hours after it are the most crucial to solving the case. It's now ten-thirty. We reconvene here at four-thirty.

By then, I want to know what Petra Gallacher was doing for every minute of the last twenty-four hours of her life. And I want sightings, suspects. I want someone in custody by midnight tonight. I want this thing over with, and I want it over with fast.'

'What are we going to call him?' asks Sherwood. 'We need a name for him.'

'How about Blackadder?' says Atkins.

The room laughs.

Kate would rather they chose something else, because of the adder's existence being kept secret, but a quick look around the room convinces her that the point's not worth fighting. They seem taken with Atkins' suggestion.

Blackadder. Under different circumstances, the name would make her chuckle. Like hurricanes, killers are often given the most inappropriate names: flippant, comic even, entirely at odds with the havoc and destruction they cause. Kate recognises the instinct, to humanise the inhuman and thereby better deal with it.

'All right,' says Kate. 'Blackadder it is. But that name doesn't go outside this room. It's not used in public, or on any written memoranda. And the sooner we can replace it with his real name the better.'

*   *   *

'I have Christian Parker's statement on tape here, and I will have a transcript made the moment I get back to the hotel. But what he said was very clear. There was a bomb on board. Captain Sutton received a warning, and supervised the ejection of what he thought was a suspect vehicle. It appears that he picked the wrong one. There must have been more than one white Transit van on board. He was so shocked by the mistake that he turned the *Amphitrite* the wrong way, into the storm rather than away from it.'

Lovelock doesn't miss a beat. He's so controlled, so much the consummate executive, that he shows no emotion. No surprise, shock, concern. Nothing.

Renfrew is here too. Frank asked him to come along in his capacity not only as Grampian's Chief Constable, but also as liaison with the anti-terrorist squad.

The air conditioning hums gently from the ceiling vents. Renfrew in particular is grateful for the cool air. He is not in the best of health: he had a heart bypass last year, and his doctors warn him that another may yet be necessary. His skin is florid under his curly brown hair, and his face sags like melted cheese.

Frank waits for the import of what he has said to sink in, and then continues.

'I'm going down tomorrow in a submersible to inspect the wreck. I fully expect there to be visible and substantial damage to the hull. A large bomb on the car deck will have holed the *Amphitrite* virtually flush at the waterline.'

'This is very unusual,' says Renfrew. 'I've never heard of terrorists attacking ferries before. Airlines, of course. Trains, even. But not ferries. There was an Irish Republican car bomb found on a ferry to Holyhead in April 1998, but it was en route for the Grand National. The ferry was simply the chosen method of transport.' He looks sharply at Lovelock. 'The *Amphitrite* wasn't carrying

101

anything dangerous or controversial, was it? Chemicals? Animals? Weapons?'

'Not that I know of,' says Lovelock. 'There's nothing on the passenger manifest to indicate that. Bergen customs checked and accounted for all the lorries before embarkation. Just the usual. Foodstuffs, beer, furniture. Nothing that needed special clearance.'

'And nothing in your empire—other business interests—which might prompt environmentalists or issue groups to target it? You're not involved in nuclear power or GM crops or live animal exports?'

'Not at all. Is this the line you're pursuing?'

'It seems the most obvious. Animal liberators, or the anti-genetics mob. But they rarely resort to such extremes, especially because most of them can't shut up about how much they value life.'

'What about Greenpeace? They've been campaigning against oil exploration west of Shetland for years.'

'Greenpeace wouldn't do a thing like this, not in a million years. They of all people trade on non-violence. Their publicity is predicated on being the victim, not the aggressor. And you don't have many connections with the oil industry anyway, do you?'

'Not directly. Most of my business is in the service sector. Yes, oil workers are a substantial part of the clientele, but then again they are for everything in Aberdeen. I don't own exploration companies or anything like that. What about disgruntled former employees? There are always a few of them around.'

'With the ability to sink a 20,000-ton ferry? I doubt it.'

'You mentioned the Irish earlier.'

'Always a possibility. I'll talk to Special Branch and MI5. They'll put their feelers out. We should have answers back from them within a day or so. But I wouldn't hold out much hope. If any of the known groups had been planning something like this, I'm sure we'd have got a sniff of it before now.'

Frank can't help but admire the adroitness with which Lovelock has flipped the conversation on its head, so he's the one asking the questions of Renfrew rather than vice versa.

Renfrew turns to Frank.

'How did Captain Sutton know about the bomb in the first place?'

'Parker presumes a radio call. We're checking all radio communications as a matter of course. If something did come through to the *Amphitrite*, we'll know.'

Renfrew purses his lips.

'Or maybe one of the crew saw or heard something suspicious and told him.'

'Or maybe the driver of the van itself tipped him off, for reasons unknown.'

'I doubt it. Certainly not if he knew what he was carrying.'

'What about the rest of the investigation?' asks Lovelock.

'My forensic team are currently conducting scale-model weather and wave simulations in our Southampton laboratory. They are using as their benchmark the original tests which you carried out with Kremer-Steinbach when the *Amphitrite* was first built, and hope to have some preliminary results later in the week. We are interviewing

103

survivors as fast but as thoroughly as possible. Many of them don't want to talk about it, understandably. Others, you can hardly shut them up. It's very trying for all concerned, and we have to act with great sensitivity, as you can imagine. Two of my inspectors are seconded to your shipyard, where they are conducting an audit of maintenance records and talking to the employees who worked on the *Amphitrite*. We are in constant touch with the DETR, and they will be formally asking in the next day or so that we all consider ways in which safety could be improved in the light of the tragedy. We have a representative in Germany talking to Kremer-Steinbach, who like Seaspeed seem to have had a hitherto spotless safety record. And that's just about it. I'll be back here first thing on Thursday morning to present the findings of the submersible survey.'

Renfrew stands up.

'This is all very interesting, but I must be on my way.'

'The murder out at Woodend?' says Lovelock. 'I heard it on the radio.'

'That's it. Nasty bit of work.'

'A girl, they said. Who was she? A prostitute?'

'No.'

'I'll come with you,' says Frank.

Lovelock's PA Marita walks in silence with Renfrew and Frank to the lifts. The atmosphere in the Seaspeed offices has simmered from churning chaos to usual high pressure.

The lift doors have barely shut before Renfrew is punching numbers into his mobile.

'DCI Beauchamp, please.'

Frank looks at him in surprise. Renfrew doesn't

notice.

'Kate, Renfrew here. What progress?'

Her voice comes to Frank tinny through Renfrew's earpiece. He kids himself that he would have recognised it even if he hadn't heard Renfrew ask for her by name.

'Good, good.' Renfrew nods to himself. 'Four-thirty, you say? I'll sit in on that, if you don't mind. See you then.'

He ends the call.

'That was Kate Beauchamp?' Frank says.

'Aye. You know her?' Renfrew's brows knit briefly. He fishes Frank's business card out of his jacket pocket, and looks at it. 'Any relation?'

'She's my daughter.'

'Well, well. Small world.' Renfrew pauses. 'Remarkable woman, coming in so soon. Absolutely remarkable.'

'So soon after what?'

Renfrew looks at him in surprise.

'The *Amphitrite*, of course.'

*   *   *

'Where was Petra yesterday? That's easy. Running around on the *Amphitrite* story, like the rest of us.'

Ferguson, wearing his usual expression of brooding resentment at all the slights the world sees fit to inflict upon him, is jotting Shillinglaw's answers down on a pad in shorthand. This is the way he and Kate work: her talking, him writing. They've found over the years that this works well, not only because it frees Kate to keep thinking, but also because Ferguson's silent scribbling tends to unnerve people who have something to hide.

105

Shillinglaw leans back in his chair and clasps his hands behind his head. Kate notes with distaste that the neck and armpits of his shirt are patched darker in the heat. He nods towards her.

'Are you not hot in all that gear? I can't remember weather like this. You'd have thought we were on the equator, not halfway to the Arctic.'

'I'm fine. Thank you. What time did Petra come to work yesterday?'

'I got in at half two, and she wasn't long after me. Quarter to three, three maybe. No later.'

'Three in the morning?'

'Aye. The ferry went down just after one o'clock.'

'I know. I was on board.'

Shillinglaw cocks his head slightly and looks at Kate askance, as if she might be taking the piss. She gives him a level stare in return.

'And no, I'm not going to give you an eyewitness account.'

If she's read his mind, he gives no sign.

'I can't believe that about Petra,' he says. 'Who would do a thing like that? I mean, you see it often enough in this line of work . . .'

'In ours too,' interjects Kate, drily.

'. . . maimings and killings and that, but they always happen to other people, you know what I mean?'

'And those other people always have friends and families and colleagues, who in turn have sensitivities. Murder affects people, Mr Shillinglaw. That's something your profession seems to forget sometimes. It's not just a juicy story for a day or two. It changes people's lives.'

'Detective, I'm as shocked as you are by this. I've just had my crime correspondent on the phone barely able to speak, it's choked him up so much. If it wasn't for this whole ferry thing, it would have knocked us all a lot more. But spare me the lecture.'

Kate flicks at the top of her biro.

'Can you give me a detailed breakdown of Petra's movements yesterday?'

'Off the top of my head—she was here in the office until the news conference at eight.'

'What was she doing?'

'Mainly taking calls from other reporters out at the docks, and transcribing them on to the system.'

'Because she was a junior?'

'Someone had to do it.'

'What then?'

'After the news conference, with the subs in, I could free up some more reporters. I sent Petra up to the Infirmary to see what was going on there, talk to some of the survivors.'

Kate was there for hours, waiting to be seen. She wonders vaguely whether she saw Petra in the hospital: Kate having just stared death in the face, Petra not knowing that she was hours away from doing so. Petra's face, pretty and blonde in the crowd of rushing doctors and zombied survivors? She can't be sure.

'Which she did?'

'She got some quotes.'

'That was it? Just some quotes?'

Shillinglaw twists his mouth.

'Yes. Ones that I could have sat here and made up off the top of my head.'

'You weren't impressed?'

'You could say that.'

At least Shillinglaw's being honest. Most people

107

are anything but, after a death: they think it rude or tasteless to speak ill of the deceased. But courtesy and tact don't solve murder cases, and Kate appreciates Shillinglaw's candour.

'What time did she come back?'

'Lunchtime, I think.'

'Did you bawl her out?'

'Yes. I was livid. I set her to work doing background stuff. Biggest ferry accidents in recent years, design and safety, rescue procedures, that kind of thing.'

'All afternoon?'

'Yes.'

'What time did she leave?'

'Not sure. Six or seven, probably.'

'Did you see her go?'

'No. But I left at quarter to eight, and she was gone by then.'

'You don't know where she went?'

'Home, I would think.'

'Not to the pub?'

'No one really felt like drinking. You know what I'm saying?'

Kate nods.

'Who's her immediate boss?'

'Irvine Scoular. News editor.'

Kate looks through the glass wall across the newsroom. Today's first edition can't be very far away. Half the staff are tapping furiously at keyboards, and the other half have phones crooked into their necks. Some are doing both at once.

'Which one is he?'

'He's not here today. Got mugged last night.'

'That's unfortunate.'

'And they say bad luck runs in threes. In the

chain of command, I'm next.'

The door to Shillinglaw's office opens, and a man enters. He is carrying a galley proof of the front page. Shillinglaw gestures towards a small table by the window.

'Just leave it there, Bruce. I'll look at it in a sec.'

Bruce glances at his watch.

'It has to go in . . .'

'I know.'

Bruce puts the proof on the table and smooths it flat. He looks curiously at Kate and Ferguson on his way out. Kate waits until the door clicks shut behind him.

'You said Petra didn't do very well up at the hospital. Was that usual?'

Shillinglaw leans forward in his chair and rests his elbows on the desk.

'She was a trainee on six months' probation. Her contract ended a month from now. I was going to let her go.'

'Did she know this?'

'No.'

'What was wrong with her?'

'She just didn't have it. Oh, she was a nice kid— young, sure, and immature, but a nice kid nonetheless. People liked her. She held her own with the banter, and that's no mean feat in a place like this, as you can imagine. And it wasn't that she lacked ambition or drive either. She was always talking about how she wanted to go to Kosovo or Indonesia and duck bullets with the foreign correspondents—even though she had no idea what those kind of places are really like. But like I said, she just didn't have it. When she went on a story, more often than not she didn't know the right questions to ask. Didn't go one step beyond the obvious. It's not rocket science, Detective, it's really not. Yesterday, at the hospital, with all those people wandering round, shocked and tired . . .'

He stops short, remembering that Kate was one of them. She nods at him to continue.

'. . . she should have been able to write a cracking article. A really good colour piece. The reality of a disaster, how the hospital was coping, the sheer scale of the whole thing, but with individual touches too. And what did she come back with? Like I said, some quotes that I could have made up myself. I don't want to sound cynical, but what happened yesterday doesn't come along very often, not in terms of news values. It was a perfect opportunity for her, and she messed it up.'

'In general, did you send her out a lot?'

'Oh, aye. There were any amount of stories that even she could do.'

'What kind of stuff?'

'Little things. Gardening shows. Roadwatch. The odd bit of local government.'

'Nothing controversial?'

'Not that I can remember. We've got an archive, if you want to see the articles she wrote.'

'She wrote nothing that would have offended someone to the point of revenge?'

'God no. This is Aberdeen, not Sicily.'

'Did she meet anyone weird or unusual? Anyone who tried to contact her after a story?'

'Not that I know of.'

Kate gets up.

'Peter, you come back this afternoon and check the archive, talk to Petra's colleagues.'

'They're very busy, Detective, as you can see. I

110

would appreciate it if you could come after five o'clock, if possible. This is big news, you know, this ferry thing.'

'And this is murder,' says Kate. 'Thank you for your time, Mr Shillinglaw.'

Kate strides through the newsroom. Her gaze sweeps over the rows of desks like the arm on a radar screen. She has a sudden and intense flush of anger at Petra's death. Even though it's academic now, she finds herself rooting for Petra. Fight, girl, fight. Get away while you can, fight like hell, because if you bide your time then there won't be time.

Young and ambitious and full of big dreams, a life ahead of her, struggling to make it in a man's world, wondering whether she was up to scratch, in turn doubting and praying that she was. Kate knows what Petra felt, because she felt it herself when she first joined the police. She grieves for Petra because in the dead girl she sees what used to be herself.

*   *   *

Petra Gallacher lived alone. Kate walks through her one-bedroom flat on the third floor of a tower block in Mastrick, a housing estate north-west of the city centre, and thinks of the old adage about cats and swinging. A tiny living-room with a kitchenette off one side, an impossibly small bathroom—one could sit on the toilet and turn both the bath and basin on without moving—and a bedroom which barely exists beyond the double bed wedged in there. There is so little space between bedframe and walls that Kate wonders how Petra ever managed to tuck the sheets in. The windows look out on to a grimy courtyard: the interior wall backs on to the flat next door.

Eighteen years old and just out of school. Petra must have thought it was paradise.

Kate glances through Petra's mail, which she picked up from the main hall downstairs. Two envelopes from the credit-card company, postmarked yesterday. 'You may already have won . . .' also postmarked yesterday. A dark blue envelope with writing in silver pen and a nondescript brown one with name and address on a typed sticker, both postmarked Saturday. All first-class mail.

Saturday postmarks would have arrived yesterday. If Petra came back from work last night, she didn't pick up her post. But the dark blue envelope looks like personal correspondence. No teenage girl would put that aside for later. She might not open the boring business mail for weeks, but she'd open something from a friend—a boyfriend?—immediately.

Likelihood is therefore that Petra didn't come back from work at all yesterday. Sixteen hours chasing the ferry story, and then she went straight out. To meet her killer? Or somewhere where he saw her, followed her to? Tired and emotional after her day, probably knowing deep down her job was on the line, she'd have been vulnerable. Easy pickings.

But wherever she and he made contact, it wasn't here. There are no signs of a struggle. In fact, the place is much neater and tidier than Kate would have expected of a teenage girl.

Too neat? Could Blackadder have come here,

killed her, and then cleaned the place up?

Images of Petra's mutilated body rise unbidden in Kate's brain. Feet and hands, chopped off as cleanly as if he'd used a guillotine.

Contrast. Frenzy of the attack, twenty discriminable stab wounds. And here, order and geometry, everything in its place. He couldn't have tidied this place up, couldn't have been hyped up for the attack and then come down that far again.

And besides, the earth where they found her was soggy with her blood.

Maybe Petra was just a neat person. The first time she had lived away from home, thinking she was all grown-up. Her little rented flat in a tower block, in amongst the welfare scroungers and the junkies—70 per cent of Aberdeen's crime is drug-related in some way—and those with low-paying jobs, like hers. She would have been as proud of this flat as of a country cottage all her own. Petra Gallacher, trying so hard at playing the young professional.

Kate looks round the flat with Ferguson half a pace behind, like a prospective buyer and the estate agent. She tries to sense the minutiae of this young woman's life. The books on her shelves. A couple of early Jilly Coopers, the ones with girls' names as titles. *The Beach, Rancid Aluminium,* the screenplays of *Pulp Fiction* and *Reservoir Dogs* side by side, *Paddy Clarke Ha Ha Ha.* CDs stacked on a shelf above the small hi-fi. Kate turns her head sideways to read the spines. Blur, the Propellerheads, Travis. A dance compilation which shrieks a lurid-coloured 'Ibiza!' The *Chicago* soundtrack. *Soul Mining* by The The. Kate wonders where Petra found *that.* The The was Kate's generation. She is surprised that Petra's taste goes back that far.

Next to the CDs, a photograph album. Petra with her friends, her parents. Christmas, a birthday, somewhere in the sun. Petra smiling, pouting, diving into a pool.

The small bathroom cabinet is packed with make-up bottles and a half-empty box of Tampax. Kate glances at the bin beneath the basin. A couple of tissues and a plastic bag, but no Tampax wrappers. Petra wasn't on.

Her clothes in the wardrobe. Jeans, a couple of skirts, some blouses, a bright red jacket. Not much, but enough for her to mix and match without it being obvious how often she was recycling clothes.

Ferguson is writing, but he's male and this space they're in is female. Kate knows he won't have seen half of what she has.

She recognises it all. She wants to cry for the woman who never was.

On the floor by the bed—there's no room for a bedside table—an alarm clock with a fold-out cover showing a stylised map of the world with time zones, and a photograph in a small silver frame. Petra and a man, an older man. Late thirties, early forties. It could be her father, except he's not holding her in a very fatherly way. He is standing behind her with his hands on her chest, just under her breasts, and she is bending back to kiss his neck.

Kate recognises him with a cold start.

Drew Blaikie.

*   *   *

They pull Blaikie in for questioning just before midday. He comes with bad grace, swearing at the officers and grumbling at how unnecessary it was for them to humiliate him by coming to his office in person. A respected architect, he says. Standing in the professional community. Clients, colleagues, friends. He would have come if they'd simply rung and asked him down. But now—well, he'd better not have lost any business, that's all. And what's this whole thing about, anyway?

Nothing he says or does indicates that he knows about Petra's death. He doesn't mention her, and Kate finds it hard to believe that even Blaikie would be at work hours after her body was found, humiliatingly exposed for inspection by anyone who happened to walk—or run—past. But he could be lying, of course. And if he is guilty, what else could he do other than go to work and wait for the police to come and tell him that his girlfriend's dead?

He sits alone in the interview room. His right cheek is scratched and he has a swelling over his right eye, a small purple egg which he presses gently from time to time. Kate watches him through the one-way glass for a few minutes, looking at the scratches on his face, looking at his clothes, fresh and clean. As always, he is dressed like a film director, or at least how he imagines film directors would dress—linen jacket, white T-shirt, khaki slacks, docksiders. Clothes more suited to Florida than north-east Scotland, even if Aberdeen is (as Ferguson told her on the way back from Mastrick) hotter than Miami today. They look faintly absurd on him. He's at least five years too old to carry them off successfully.

115

Drew Blaikie, *Miami Vice* wannabe and proud recipient in the past of two charges relating to domestic violence. Both charges were ultimately withdrawn by the victims, Margerita Mason and Therese Hewson, as Blaikie will no doubt remind Kate when she mentions them. Withdrawn after he kissed and made up and promised it would never happen again. In their revised versions, Margerita and Therese said that they fell down the stairs. Both of them, three years apart.

But Kate saw them, saw what he had done to them in fits of rage. Too smart to hit them on the face, he beat a fearsome tattoo on their bodies. Red weals up their flanks, patterns of bruises overlaid and interconnected. But more than that was what he'd done to their minds. The shaking and cowering, the instinctive flinching at other people's most innocuous gestures. Reaching for a telephone, putting a hat on—flinch. They didn't get that from falling down the stairs, did they, Mr Blaikie?

Common or garden thuggery, Kate can just about deal with. The poor, the dispossessed, those with reasons to be angry and energy to burn. Even if she can't excuse it, she can understand it. But for a man like Blaikie, with everything going for him— he's a genuinely good architect, they say, and he's undeniably good-looking, something which everyone can see, especially himself—for such a man, she feels real contempt. He does it because he *can*.

All criminals are liars. They have an inflated self-image in which they regard themselves as special and superior, and assume that people will do their bidding. They view the responsible world as a barren wasteland. Drew Blaikie may not technically be a criminal, but his mindset is spot on.

Petra would have had no idea what she was getting into. He would have charmed her and made her feel the most special person on earth, would have used twenty-five years of sexual experience to drive her and her youthful hormones wild in bed—and then he would have turned on her, just like that. She'd have seen what he was really like, and it would have been too late. Callow Petra Gallacher, callous Drew Blaikie.

Kate so wants Blaikie to be Blackadder. She said the killer would have offended before, and Blaikie has, even if there are no convictions to show for it. She said Petra knew her killer, and she certainly knew Blaikie. And she said she wanted a suspect in by midnight. She's twelve hours ahead of schedule.

But what she saw in the woods this morning—could even Blaikie have gone that far?

Kate walks out of the viewing room. She thinks of Occam's Razor, the philosophical maxim by which William of Occam, the fourteenth-century Franciscan, is best known. 'Entities are not to be multiplied without necessity.' In other words, the most obvious solution is usually the right one. Even more basically, KISS: keep it simple, stupid.

Into the interview room. He looks up from his fingernails.

'Would you mind telling me what this is all about?'

'Nice to see you too, Mr Blaikie.'

'Detective Inspector, I'm a . . .'

'Detective *Chief* Inspector.'

'. . . busy man, and I haven't got time for this. Why have I been brought here?'

'You're entitled to a lawyer.'

'Criminal Procedure Act 1995, section 17. I know my law.'

'I can see. Do you want one?'

'Well, mine is next to useless. I should have fired him a long time ago.'

'We can provide one for you free of charge.'

'Yeah. Some spotty trainee who's done a conversion course and thinks he's George Carman. I haven't done anything wrong. I'll take my chances.'

'You always do, Mr Blaikie.'

She prefers him indignant to smarmy, but it's a close call. Kate sits down, not daring to look at her hands for fear that she'll see her skin actually crawling, and presses the record button on the tape recorder.

'Interview with Drew Blaikie.' She looks at her watch, gives the time and date. 'Mr Blaikie, what is your relationship with Petra Gallacher?'

'My relationship with her?'

'You don't have to repeat everything I say.'

A flash of *'don't-fuck-with-me'* momentarily wipes the studied innocence from his face, like a cloud passing across the face of the sun.

'She's—a friend.'

'Is your relationship a sexual one?'

'What's this got to do with anything?'

'Just answer the question.'

'Yes. Our relationship is a sexual one.'

Is. And still he hasn't asked whether anything's happened to her. He doesn't know she's dead. Or else he's a very good actor.

'We have sex,' he adds, unnecessarily.

'Rough, by the look of it.' She gestures towards

118

his face.

'That's not how I got these.'

'How *did* you get those?'

'Went ten rounds with an Asian tiger.'

She rolls her eyes heavenwards.

'How did you get the scratch and the black eye, Mr Blaikie?'

'Can't remember.'

His look challenges her to keep asking.

'Is Petra the only person you have sex with?'

'I'm not answering that.'

'Are you the only person she has sex with?'

'No idea.'

'But do you know of any others?'

'If there are any, they're not as good as me.'

The kind of remark Kate would have expected to hear in a school playground. Even from Blaikie, she would have predicted more.

'When did you last see her?'

'What *is* this? What's happened?'

At last. A spark of interest in Petra herself. Not before time.

'We're going to get through this a lot quicker if we stick to the simple question-answer format. I've got as long as I need. You, on the other hand, were just telling me what a busy man you are.'

Blaikie sighs the sigh of the deeply misunderstood, those who feel that they have to humour lesser mortals.

'I last saw her on Sunday night.'

'Did you stay with her?'

'She stayed with me.'

'What time did she leave the next morning?'

'Middle of the night. She got called in to do the ferry story. I don't know. Two, three?'

119

'If she was at your place, how did they get hold of her?'

'Ever heard of mobiles?'

'And you haven't seen her since then?'

'I told you. I last saw her on Sunday night.'

'Or heard from her?'

'No.'

'Not a phone call, fax, e-mail?'

'No means no, Detective. I thought all women knew that.'

Kate clamps her teeth together and inhales hard through her nose.

Don't let him get to you.

She drops the bombshell.

'So you don't know that her body was found this morning?'

She doesn't take her eyes off him for a moment. It is an action of hers honed so well over long years trying to tease confessions out of suspects that it's now instinctive: spotting how people react in the split second of unguardedness which follows a revelation. Whatever he does, it'll be imprinted in her mind like a photograph, every nuance and hint recorded in stark detail.

He gets it all right. His head comes down and forward, eyes and mouth widening together. The timing is right: not too early, as can be the case when someone's anticipating a statement, and not too late, as they try to figure out how they *should* react in order to make it look genuine. Anybody else, she'd have said the reaction was genuine. But with Blaikie—he could still be faking it. He knew she was dead, because he killed her. Or he didn't know, because he didn't kill her. Kate is angry that she can't tell the difference.

120

'Her *body*? She's dead?'

'Murdered.'

'Where? When? Who?' The words flood like a spring torrent.

'Her body was found this morning in the grounds of Woodend Hospital.'

She sits back and watches him as a mongoose would a snake.

'You think I did this? That's why you called me in here? You think I did this?'

'I didn't say anything of the sort.'

'But that's what you think?'

'You have a history.'

'Of what?'

'Violence against women.'

'Those charges were withdrawn. You know that perfectly well.'

'Where were you last night?'

'Home.'

'Alone?'

'Yes.'

'All night?'

'Yes.'

'From what time?'

'From when I left work. Six, six-thirty. I took work home with me. I had— *have*—lots to do.'

'Anyone who can verify that you were alone?'

'No. Because I didn't know that anyone would have to. If I'd killed her, I'd have been careful to give myself an alibi, wouldn't I?'

'You didn't phone anybody?'

'No.'

'Friends? If you have any. Takeaway pizza? Porn lines?'

'I told you. I was working.'

121

'Then how did you get that fucking scratch?'

She knows even as she snaps at him that she shouldn't, that in doing so she's handed the initiative back.

He cocks his head and looks at her appraisingly. She might be imagining it, but she thinks he's trying not to smile.

'I didn't kill her. Anything else I do is my business.'

'You haven't asked how she was killed.'

'Maybe I don't want to know.'

'Maybe you already do know.'

'Maybe you have absolutely no evidence, and you know it.'

'But we know you have history. Try this for size. Petra's out all day, working on the ferry story. It's the hardest she's ever had to work. Fourteen, sixteen hours straight, and emotionally searing to boot. A harder day than any you've ever worked, I'd imagine. When she clocks off, she comes round to your house. She's tired, she's emotional, she just wants you to cuddle her. But that's not what you want her for. She's young and nubile and got a great body and she fucks like a train, which is why you sleep with her—but you don't see her as any kind of friend, she's just a fucktoy for you. You have nothing in common with her, you don't hang out with her friends. You want sex.

'This time, she's having none of it. You keep pushing. She relents. And afterwards she wants a shoulder to cry on. It's not much, what she's demanding, but still it's too much for you. You have an argument. And you know where we're heading with this, don't you, Drew? The same place we went with Margerita Mason and Therese

122

Hewson. You snap. You start to smack her. She fights back. And now you go mental. No one fucks with you, especially not someone less than half your age. She's terrified, she's never seen you like this before. But this time it goes too far. You beat her half to death.

'When you've calmed down, you realise what's happened. You're going to be in big trouble, unless you wrap it up as something else. So you take her out to the back of beyond. You torture her, to punish her again for standing up to you. Then you kill her, and make it look like she just happened to run into a psycho.'

There. She's told him.

Kate is breathing hard, and her skin prickles.

'I can say this till the cows come home. I didn't kill her.'

'You don't have an alibi. You won't tell me why your face is scratched and bruised. You have a history of violence against women—against girlfriends, in fact. Half the countries in the world would have banged you up and thrown away the key by now.'

'I didn't do it. I'll say it again and again, for now and the next few times you don't get the message. I didn't do it. I didn't do it. I didn't do it.'

Kate gets up.

'Ring your company and tell them you're not coming back today.'

'You can't do this.'

'I can hold you without charge for forty-eight hours before you have to be brought before the sheriff for examination.' She looks at her watch. 'Take away the forty-five minutes or so we've just used up, and you've still got the best part of two

123

days. And believe me, Drew, I intend to use every minute of that.'

Kate walks out of the room and into the corridor, where Ferguson is waiting. She jerks her head back towards the door.

'Read him his rights.'

*   *   *

Hemmings' autopsy report is with Kate by mid-afternoon, as promised. She scrawls wavy lines in orange highlighter pen across the points which catch her eye.

Petra's histamine and serotonin levels are extraordinarily high. Petechial haemorrhaging is found inside her eyelids, and on her eyes and shoulders. All these factors confirm that she was extensively tortured before being killed.

Traces of water are found in the left pleural cavity. Hemmings understands that the victim was found near the river Denburn. It is impossible to tell whether there is also water in the right pleural cavity, which holds 200ml of blood as a result of the haemothorax caused by fatal wounds two and three.

The lower abdomen is covered in small teethmarks, presumably from woodland rodents attracted to the cadaver post mortem.

Traces of wood are found on the back of Petra's head, presumably from impact against a tree. The wood is identified as *quercus pedunculata*, the common oak indigenous to the UK.

Petra's stomach is empty, indicating that she didn't eat for several hours before her death.

Dried blood is found under the fingernails of the

left hand. This blood is typed AB, a group common to approximately 3 per cent of the Scottish population. It has been sent to the laboratory for DNA analysis.

There are no traces of sedative in her body.

Rope marks on Petra's wrists and ankles, just above the points where her extremities were severed, indicate that she was tied up prior to being killed.

There are no fingerprints, hairs or saliva on the body.

The snake attached to Petra's body is an adder or northern viper, *vipera berus*. It was tranquillised and removed from the scene by Miles Matheson, professor of herpetology at the University of Aberdeen.

The incident room is close and smoky, and in it hangs the arch smell of sweat and a lingering tang of cooking grease. Kate decides to get some fresh air before the four-thirty meeting.

Going down in the lift, she turns over Hemmings' points in her mind.

Type AB. Blaikie is also type AB, she checked earlier. A full DNA match will take a week to come through, but 3 per cent of the population narrows the odds somewhat. It's much more likely to be his blood than not.

Empty stomach. If Petra did go somewhere with her killer last night, it wasn't for dinner.

Water traces in her left lung. Maybe she slipped into the river, maybe he tried to subdue her by holding her head underwater.

Her face immersed and inhaling water, please no.

The lift doors open. Kate steps out and starts to walk across the lobby. Annette, one of the

125

receptionists, glances up and calls across to her.

'DCI Beauchamp?'

Kate turns.

'Yes?'

'I've been trying to get hold of you. This gentleman's here to see you.'

Annette indicates a man on one of the fake leather sofas by the windows. He has a newspaper folded across his lap, and he is looking intently at Kate.

Her father.

Kate beats down a sudden swell of nausea. A wad of saliva materialises in the back of her mouth. She swallows it, and takes a deep breath to steady herself. Her instinct is to head back inside the station, beyond the security barriers where he can't get her, but she doesn't want to be seen as running away, and nor does she want to make a scene.

Frank gets up from the sofa and tucks the newspaper under his arm. Kate gestures with her head towards the front doors.

They walk into the sunshine. He puts his dark glasses on, she squints into the glare. She rounds on him.

'What the fuck are you doing here?'

'Well, that's friendly.'

'What do you expect?'

'You know why I'm here. I'm investigating the *Amphitrite*.'

'No. What are you doing *here*? Right here?'

'I was coming back from the Seaspeed offices. They're just down the road. I thought I'd come and see that you're all right. Your Chief Constable told me that you were on board. And that you're back at work already.'

126

'Don't I look all right?'

'You look as if you're about to expire in that big jumper.'

'I'm fine. I'm also very busy, so if you'll excuse me . . .'

'Kate!'

His voice is unexpectedly sharp. A uniformed constable walking out through the doors glances across at them.

'Talk to me, Kate,' says Frank. 'Tell me what it was like.'

'Get someone else to take my statement. I'm not giving it to you.'

'Take your statement? Kate, I'm not asking you as part of the inquiry. I'm asking you as your father.'

'Just like when . . . ?'

'Whatever you think of me, I'm still that. Now please, tell me what it was like.'

She tries to summon up the resentment she felt when she last saw him, at her mother's funeral. It takes a moment to come, and when it does, it's not as powerful as she remembers. It's as if her well of anger is half-empty. Maybe she's used too much up on Drew Blaikie already today.

She decides to make the effort, however half-heartedly. At least she'll be able to say that she's tried.

'What it was *like*? God, it was like—you can't imagine. I wouldn't have wished it on my worst enemy. I can't describe it. I don't have the words.'

What was it like? Fine, if you enjoy fairly acute hydrophobia and think the kitchen walls are closing in on you. Fine, if you can live with kicking a woman's hands until she falls off a ladder to her

127

death.

'I understand. I know what you're feeling.'

Why should she bother, if all he's going to do is come out with some jerk-off platitude?

'You're such a berk. How can you understand? You can't possibly.'

'I've talked to hundreds of people who've survived accidents. I have a pretty good idea of what they think.'

'I don't care how many people you've spoken to. You weren't there. Did you kick a woman into the sea'—*the crowd around her screeching like seagulls*—'so other people could escape? No. Did you see faces pressed against portholes as the ship went down? No. Did you sit in a life-raft for hours asking why, over and over again? No. You didn't. So keep out of it.'

'Kate, you need help.'

'I don't.'

'You do. Everyone in your situation does. You'd have to be an android not to. If you won't talk to me, talk to someone professional. Seaspeed are providing counsellors.'

'I know. One of them rang me yesterday. Jane someone. Jane Bavin.'

'Talk to her.'

'No. I've got a murder case to run and a son to look after. I'm not an invalid. I don't want to talk to you, and I don't want to talk to Jane fucking Bavin either.'

She looks down and away. Then back again, to the headline she can see on his newspaper.

FERRY BOMBED?

'Let's have a look.'

He hands her the paper. She shakes it open.

128

Aberdeen Evening Telegraph exclusive, trumpeted in a red text box.

The *Amphitrite* ferry sank because it was bombed, the *Evening Telegraph* can reveal. Captain Edward Sutton received warning that a massive vehicle bomb was on board about an hour before the ship went down. Third Officer Christian Parker, the only member of the bridge crew to survive the disaster, told investigators this morning that Sutton stopped the ferry and personally supervised the ejection of the suspect van.
But he got the wrong vehicle.
An hour later, the real car bomb exploded.

Kate looks up.
'This isn't true?'
'It's what Parker told me. It shouldn't have gone in the paper.'
He pauses.
'Did you hear the explosion?'
'I heard bangs. Two loud bangs. But I didn't think they were explosions. Well, not until . . .' She gestures at the paper, catches herself. 'No. I'm not sure. I've heard bombs go off. I was at Paddington Green when the IRA attacked it once. You *feel* bombs as much as hear them, sometimes.'
'But not always?'
'No, not always.'
Kate looks down the front page.
On the bottom right-hand side, a small headline: **Reporter Murdered**. A few paragraphs. Full story, page 5.
She turns the pages, skims the text. No mention

of the extremities or the snake. Good.

In a column down the right-hand side of the page, an editorial comment. 'Today was a black day for the press,' it begins.

And suddenly Kate sees it all. Petra was one of their own, and so the paper is going mental about it. Navel-gazing and pieces on 'Are our reporters safe?' Ignoring or moulding the truth, because it's a death in the family. She wasn't a good reporter, and her career had less than a month left to run— and yet they've made her out to have been a budding Kate Adie, giving it the full 'bright future cut short' routine.

The irony is laughable. In death, Petra has finally got the recognition she craved in life.

If that body out in the woods this morning—*this morning*, it already feels a lifetime—was a common prostitute, face smeared with mascara and dark roots jagging under her peroxide thatch, Kate knows that they, police and reporters alike, they'd have said she deserved it, more or less. They'd have given the case a cursory investigation and a couple of paragraphs respectively, and let it die a quick and painless death: much quicker and more painless than the one Petra suffered. The hypocrisy makes her choke.

Kate snaps the paper shut and thrusts it back at Frank.

'I've got a case review,' she says. 'I can't pretend this has been a pleasure.'

'Well, I hope we get off on a better footing next time,' says Frank.

'I hope there won't *be* a next time.'

'Why are you so hostile, Kate?'

She turns away and walks back into the station,

130

away from her father and everything he represents to her—his betrayal of her mother and herself, the panic and the cold of the *Amphitrite,* shadows across her life.

In the lift, alone and enclosed by metal around and above and below, the thought which she's too intelligent to suppress tugs at her.

If she wants to forget it so badly, why did she grab the paper when she saw the headline?

*   *   *

'Come on. We haven't got all day.'

Kate snaps her fingers. The room quietens and comes slowly to rest. Officers settle in their seats, checking they have the relevant information to hand. Kate is impatient, she wants to get on with it.

Renfrew perches on the edge of the table next to her. He doesn't come to progress meetings on any but the big murder cases, and his presence is a sign of the importance he's attaching to this inquiry.

Kate clears her throat.

'Blackadder case review, day one. Progress so far. As you know, because you've all been given his photograph to show people, the victim's boyfriend Drew Blaikie has been detained in custody pending further investigation. Blaikie's blood type, AB, matches that found under Petra Gallacher's fingernails. DNA tests are under way. Results are expected back within a week. Blaikie has a history of violence against women. He also has visible and recent facial scarring, which he refuses to explain.

'It's a lot to go on. But, at this stage, it's all circumstantial. Personally, I would like nothing more than to find that Blaikie and Blackadder are

131

one and the same. But we need more evidence before we can be sure. And in the meantime, we have to assume it's *not* him. So. Round the room. House-to-house. Sherwood?'

'The last sighting of Petra we've got was on Sunday afternoon, walking down Greenfern Place and talking into a mobile.'

'Who saw her?'

'An old biddy. Vanessa Ewart. She remembers it well, because she thought at first that Petra was talking to herself. It was only when she passed her that she saw that Petra was using one of those ear and mouthpiece things.'

'I thought teenagers refused to use them because they're so uncool.'

'Maybe Petra thought she'd get brain cancer.'

'Maybe.' *Brain cancer, killing her slowly. Like it matters now.* 'No sign of Blaikie?'

'No. A couple of people in Mastrick have seen him around over the past couple of weeks, but none in the last forty-eight hours.'

'Vehicle and pedestrian checks. Ripley?'

'A couple of sightings of Petra yesterday morning. One up at the hospital, the other by the newspaper offices. They only confirm what we know about her movements. Nothing after the time she left work yesterday. No sightings of Blaikie.'

'Keep those checks running. People come into town on different days. Atkins. Sex offenders?'

'We've identified thirty-two known sex offenders on parole within fifty miles of here, and we're interviewing them right now. It'll take a couple of days to work through them all.'

'Good. Do it as quickly as possible, but don't cut corners. I want them all accounted for, one way or the other. Who's handling the incoming calls?' A hand goes up. 'Wilcox. What have you got?'

'The usual. Twenty-seven claims of responsibility so far, none of them remotely feasible.'

'You tried them with the controls?'

'Yup. None of them mentioned the extremities or the snake.'

'Other leads?'

'A few busybodies ringing in to finger their neighbours. We've followed them all up. Personal grudges, mainly. Nothing doing.'

'Threaten them with wasting police time. That should shut them up. Peter. Anything from Petra's cuttings?'

'No. Shillinglaw was right. Everything she wrote was totally harmless.'

Please let it be Blaikie. Because if it isn't, we've got bugger all else to go on.

'Keep at it. The ones who were doing house-to-house, you join in with vehicle and pedestrian checks. Atkins, keep me posted on how you're doing with the sex offenders. Time's slipping away, guys. More than half our twenty-four hours are gone. The longer it goes on, the longer our odds become. Peckers up.'

They get back to work. Renfrew nods at her and leaves the room. Kate turns to Ferguson.

'Hold the fort, Peter. I'm off to see a man about a snake.'

*   *   *

Whatever Kate was expecting Miles Matheson to be like, this wasn't it. He stands six three or four in sandals, chinos and khaki shirt, broad and with a belly to match. His dirty blond hair rises from his skull in dense tufts, and the booming 'G-day, officer' with which he welcomes her is pure Queensland.

He gestures at her jumper.

'Jeez. I thought I felt the cold, but you leave me standing. Even I can't complain today. Reminds me of Brisbane. God knows what most of your lot make of it. Everyone's down to shirtsleeves the moment the temperature gets above freezing. They must be dropping like flies.'

Kate notes with mild alarm that Matheson is holding a small snake flecked in dark and light blue. His right hand grips the back of the snake's neck just behind its head, and his left hand holds the top of the tail, leaving several inches free at the end. The reptile squirms half-heartedly, looking as slender as a piece of string in Matheson's outsize hands.

'Is that . . . ?'

'Little grass snake. Cute as you like. Aren't you, my darling?'

The snake's tongue shoots out, flutters in the warm air, and disappears back inside its mouth again. Matheson holds it out towards Kate.

'You want to hold him?'

Kate raises her palms.

'No. Thank you.'

'Suit yourself. He's real friendly. Ain't that right, Natrix?'

'Matrix?'

'Natrix. "N" for November.'

'Why do you call him that?'

'*Natrix natrix*. Proper classification name for the grass snake. This is a baby one.' He turns and walks

134

over to a glass-fronted cage in the corner, talking as he does so. 'Little bit of an experiment, this. Folks don't often try and breed *natrix natrix* in captivity, though Lord alone knows there's enough of the beauties about. Go down any flooded quarry or abandoned gravel pit, and you can hardly move for them.'

He lifts the snake over the top of the cage and places it inside. *Natrix natrix* slithers over a low rock, between two plants, and curls itself next to a small pool of water. Matheson slides the roof back on the cage, checks the ventilation holes are open, and wipes his hands together.

'The snake found at the murder scene today?' says Kate.

'Ah, yeah. She's still down the vet's.' Matheson starts to head towards a pair of swing doors on the other side of the room. 'Probably got a bit of a headache from the tranquilliser I gave her,' he says over his shoulder, checking that Kate's following him. 'I can sympathise. Jeez, what a dreadful sight.'

'The body?'

'Yeah. Suppose you're used to it, eh?'

Kate shakes her head. 'You never get used to something like that.'

'That was worse than most, yeah?'

'By far.'

'Oh.' He rubs his forehead. 'Right.'

'Where are we going?'

'To the tropical room. You've caught me at feeding time, though it's nothing I can't do without talking to you.'

Matheson pushes open the swing doors. It is dark, but appreciably warmer and more humid even than outside. The damp heat wraps itself across Kate's face like the steaming towels provided in curry houses.

'This is what it's like in the rainforests of northern Queensland, year round. You ever been there?'

'No.'

'You should do. It's fantastic. Two seasons: hot and dry, and hot and wet.'

Matheson walks along the nearside wall, all the way to the end. The only light is from the cages themselves. In the last cage is a long green snake striped with thin red and white crossbars. Its environment is much more elaborate than that of *natrix natrix*: a canopy of leaves, creeping trellises, water, damp soil. The snake hangs between two miniature trees, its lowslung midsection almost touching the ground. It watches Kate through vertical pupils.

'Now this one isn't too keen on its grub, even though it only gets fed about once a fortnight. We had school food at Toowoomba like that. So we have to get him a bit angry.'

'What is it?'

'*Tropidolaemus wagleri.* Malaysian temple viper. Comes from a place in Penang called the Temple of the Azure Cloud. There are hundreds of them there. They defang some of them and let the tourists pose for pictures. Imbeciles.'

'But this is nothing to do with the adder found today?'

'They're cousins. The one at Woodend is *vipera berus*'—the way he says it, stressing the second and first syllables and rhyming them with 'air', invests the name with a curiously singsong quality—'the northern viper. It's the UK's only indigenous

136

snake, though you can also find it all the way through Scandinavia and central Europe, into northern Asia and as far east as Sakhalin island, between Russian and Japan. It's even been found way inside the Arctic Circle. The ones this far north are often black, because the darker skin helps them absorb as much light and heat as possible. Most *vipera berus* have got paler zigzag markings.'

'And it's poisonous?'

'Venomous, yeah. It's got a pair of long, hollow fangs in the front of the upper jaw, which fold back against the roof of the mouth when they're not in use. When it's about to attack its prey, *vipera berus* raises its head and strikes its victim. Its fangs make two small punctures, and the poison is injected down these—they're hollow, remember—and into the victim.'

'So the one pinned to Petra's body today could have bitten someone?'

'The state you found it in, perhaps. It was restrained, surrounded, angry. That's why it was trying to lash out. But that's unusual for *vipera berus*. You've really got to piss it off to get it like that.'

'But when the killer left it there, it might have been calm?'

'Sure. Certainly if he was a halfway decent snake handler.'

'He could have drugged it before he secured it?'

'Maybe. But we couldn't tell that now. Any tranquilliser he used will be masked by the shot I gave it. I could run a test for you, but I'd be wasting everyone's time. My shot will be stronger and more recent, that's what'll show up.'

Matheson takes what looks like an outsize pair of tweezers from a tray. Kate sees that there is a small greyish object between the ends. She looks closer.

A mouse. Dead.

He turns to her.

'I'll tell you what would have worked in his favour. *Vipera berus* had eaten very recently. We found an adult mouse, partially digested. Catch snakes when they've just finished a meal, they're pretty docile. Catch them when they're eating, though, and all hell can break loose.'

'How would you go about getting hold of *vipera berus*?'

'Piece of piss, excuse my French. Commercial breeders, probably. There are plenty around: some legit, some not so. Or just go out and find them. They're all over. Woods, heaths, rocks, cliffs, mountainsides, meadows, bogs, lakes and rivers. Once they've got somewhere, they stick to it. They move sixty, maybe a hundred metres round their habitat, tops. They hibernate in the same place, year after year. Go after them at night, especially on warm nights like now, in the few hours after sundown. That's when they go hunting. They're nocturnal.'

Matheson reaches into the cage with the tweezers. *Tropidolaemus wagleri,* head turned, watches him through one unblinking eye.

'What would you use to pick them up? A net?'

'No. Some kind of forked stick, probably.'

'Would they be found in the woods, where the girl was?'

'No. Too built-up. They don't like human contact.'

'So the killer would probably have had that one in captivity to start with?'

'I would suppose so.'

'Are they hard to keep?'

Matheson taps the mouse on the snake's tail, quite hard. It doesn't react.

He taps again, harder. Still no movement.

'What did you say?' he asks, without taking his eyes off *tropidolaemus wagleri*.

'Is *vipera berus* hard to keep?'

'Nah. You don't need a big cage: *vipera berus* spends most of the time coiled in small cavities anyway. Shove a heater at one end, to provide a temperature gradient. Then all you have to do is keep it fed. Mice, frogs, lizards. We're not talking gourmet eating here. You can buy frozen rodents in bulk. Then you just slam them in the freezer and thaw them as required. Hold on a sec.'

Matheson moves his arm along the top of the cage, towards *tropidolaemus wagleri*'s head. He does not shake. His arm is held dead steady, as though it were moving on rails.

Above the snake's snout and the mouse hovering, pinched between the tweezer ends like a bomb clinging to the belly of a fighter plane.

Tropidolaemus wagleri looks at the mouse.

Matheson brings the mouse down hard on the snake's snout. Movement sudden and flurrying; *tropidolaemus wagleri*'s head darting forwards and upwards in a flash of green as it strikes hard for the prey; Matheson yanking his arm up and out of the cage; the tweezers opening; the mouse bouncing off the snake and down on to the cage floor.

'Come this way.' Matheson takes Kate's arm and pulls her a few paces to the side. 'If we don't distract him, there's a good chance he'll eat.' He wipes the tweezers on his trouser leg. 'Now. Where were we?'

'Restrictions. There must be restrictions on keeping them?'

'For sure.' He laughs. 'Never thought I'd be telling a police officer the law, but here goes. Under the Wildlife and Countryside Act of 1981, you can't kill, injure or trade *vipera berus.* You can keep them all you like, but under the Dangerous Wild Animals Act 1976, you have to be licensed to do so by the local authority.'

'So there's a register?'

'Yeah. You'll have a copy down the station, I'm sure.'

'What about magazines? Trade publications?'

'A couple. Small ones, low circulation and pretty amateur, truth be told. Most contact in the herp community is now done via the Internet. I can give you some website addresses.'

In the dim glow of the cage lights, Kate sees the expression on Matheson's face: utter contentment, a man at peace with his world.

'You really love this, don't you?'

He smiles.

'All my life. My great-great-grandfather was Gerard Krefft, Australia's first really serious herpetologist. He wrote a book called *Snakes of Australia* in 1869. It's still being reprinted now. It's something of a classic.'

Her turn to smile.

'And you can't see it,' he adds, though without rancour. 'You see only the scales and the venom and the danger. You don't see the glorious array of colours on their skin. You don't see the beauty with

140

which they move. It's art, it's dance.'

'I guess not.'

'They're everything, snakes. Marvellously designed, incredibly diverse and amazingly beautiful. And they're the purest of all animals. No limbs, no ears, no eyelids. Evolution pared down as far as it will go.'

Pared down. Occam and his bloody razor again.

'They spend less time hunting and killing than any other predator in nature. More people are killed in the UK by bee stings every year than by snakebites. Yet you give me an animal which gets half as much bad press as snakes do. They're shorthand for evil, they're seen as dangerous and repulsive. "Speaking with a forked tongue" and all that. For a start, the snake's tongue is used for smelling. Not to mention the Garden of Eden—a place which, as any halfway competent scientist will tell you, could never have existed. Let me ask you something, Inspector. You have children?'

'I have a son, yes.'

'How old is he?'

'Four years old.'

'And has he ever seen a snake?'

'Not to my knowledge.'

'You haven't taken him to the zoo?'

'Not yet.'

'You take him along there one day and show him a snake. I guarantee you he'll want to pick it up, play with it.'

'He wants to pick up the household bleach and play with that too.'

'Maybe. But my point is this. Young children are not instinctively afraid of snakes. They're perfectly happy to handle them. Not because they don't

141

know better, but because they don't know worse. It's only as they get older that they start to dislike and mistrust snakes, and you know why? Because they're encouraged to. By adults. When those children become adults, they pass it on to *their* children. And so it goes on.'

*   *   *

Leo is asleep by the time Kate gets to Bronagh's home. Bronagh is at her easel, frowning as she mixes colours in a palette.

'Bad day?' she asks.

'About as bad as I'd ever want it to be.'

'Whisky's on the side.'

Kate pours herself a thumbsworth and sits down on the sofa, checking as always for wandering budgies before she does so.

'Don't overdo it now, Katie. I'm not going to lecture you, but you've had a big shock, and you must take it easy.'

'I will. You know I will.'

'I know you *won't*. That's why I'm telling you. To try and get some sense into that thick skull of yours.'

In the car home, Leo asleep in the child seat, Kate thinks of how right her aunt is. Of course she'll overdo it, that's the whole point of her taking it on in the first place. To fight someone else's battles rather than her own.

It is only when she's inside the front door, the world held temporarily at bay, that Kate remembers something. She didn't tell Bronagh that she'd seen Frank today, and nor did Bronagh mention it. But Frank and Bronagh are very close.

142

He's bound to have rung and told her.

Kate smiles at the old woman's canniness. Bronagh knows when she can push Kate and when she can't, and she knows the best way to push Kate is not to push her, if that makes sense.

Kate glances at her watch. Quarter past eight.

On an impulse, fast so she does it before she loses her nerve, she picks up the phone and dials Alex's number.

'Alex Melville.'

'Alex, it's—hi, it's Kate.'

'Hi. Can I phone you back later? I'm just on my way out to play football.'

'Sure.'

'I'll be through at half nine. I'll call you then.'

'If you haven't eaten—which I suppose you won't have, because you're playing football, and you'—*for God's sake, Kate, get a grip, you're talking gibberish*—'then you could always come round . . .'

She hears him push out a short, friendly laugh.

'Is this our dinner date?'

'Yes. If you want it to be.'

'OK. I'll see you later.'

'Where do you play football?'

'The rec centre. Round the back of the Marischal. Gotta go, or I'll be late.'

*   *   *

An hour later, having pottered around the house and achieved precisely nothing, Kate checks that Leo is sleeping soundly and leaps into the car. She's going to be ten minutes, twenty at the outside. Leo won't even know she's gone.

Kate stands by the railings and watches him. He

143

is long and fluid, twisting like liquid mercury as he looks for gaps in the defence. When he runs, he kicks his legs up so high behind him that his heels touch his bottom.

And he is throwing himself into tackles like a man possessed. The laid-back Alex whom Kate knows has disappeared as completely as he did on stage in Bergen, when he had to spend the last half-hour of every night in psycho mode. Kate can see the rows of moulded rubber grips on Alex's soles as he slides across the sanded Astroturf surface and clatters into opponent and ball alike. He does it two or three times in as many minutes, and none of his team-mates say a thing. They know what happened on the ferry.

At half past nine on the dot, another team walks on to the pitch, and Alex's lot troop off to the sidelines. Kate listens to their banter as they peel off their shirts and delve into their bags.

'You should have seen the bird Steve pulled last Friday. She was rank.'

'Leave it out. She had a body from *Baywatch.*'

'Yeah. And a face from *Crimewatch.*'

They laugh in unison, hearty and male.

Alex slings his bag over his shoulder and catches sight of Kate. He winks at her.

'See you next week, lads,' she hears him say.

'You all right, Al?'

'Yeah, yeah, I'm fine.'

His voice is perfectly normal. Three minutes ago, he'd been coming in on people like a Mack truck.

Alex walks through the gate and kisses her on the cheek. A couple of his team-mates start whooping. He raises his middle finger above his

144

shoulder without looking back.

'I didn't know you were going to come and pick me up.'

'Nor did I.'

Back at her house, Kate chops up some salad while he showers. She feels a brief, absurd pang of envy at the ease with which he can stand there while the water splashes around him.

He comes back into the kitchen in a white ribbed T-shirt and combat shorts.

'Your shower's too low. I was almost sitting down in there.'

'That'll teach you to be absurdly tall.'

'Six three is hardly absurdly tall.'

'It is in this house. Now shut up and eat.'

They talk easily over dinner, about anything and everything bar the ferry disaster. She tells him about Petra Gallacher's death—broad outline only, no operational details, of course. He tells her about the latest gossip at Urquhart's, Lovelock's auction house, where he is a junior in the popular arts department. Sinclair and Jason work there too: Sinclair is head of fine arts, with a special interest in Old Masters and Impressionists; and Jason is deputy head of the antiquities section, which comprises ancient art and archaeology spanning an area from Western Europe to the Caspian Sea.

In fact, it was through the three of them that Lovelock first became involved with the Aberdeen Amateurs. Lovelock is now the society's patron, and it was his funding which helped them go to Norway in the first place: he simply wrote a cheque for the difference between the amount they'd raised and the amount they still needed. At one stage, he was even going to fly over and see a performance or two, but business pressures forced him to cancel at the last moment.

'You've been at Urquhart's how long?' Kate asks.

'Five years, more or less.'

'Don't you ever think about moving on?'

'Sometimes. Setting up a business, going travelling, whatever. I've got friends who want to do one or the other, and have asked me if I want to join them. And I know I should do all that kind of stuff while I can. I'm still single, I'm not going to get married any time soon. But—it's a good job, and the people are nice.'

'You mean you can't be arsed to make the effort.'

He laughs.

'Yes. Basically.'

'Just at work, or life in general?'

It comes out harsher than Kate meant it to be. But the subtext is unmistakable, and she meant that too.

She doesn't even give him the chance to answer. She leans across the table and kisses him. Lightly at first and then longer and harder, hot breath from opening mouths as his tongue slips between her teeth and licks against hers. Eyes shut, of course, because kissing is all about taste and touch, and the view—one outsize eye and a surround of pink skin—isn't great.

Now they are up from the table, and she's pulling him backwards into the sitting-room. They half-fall on to the floor and begin to slowly remove each other's clothes, two items of hers for every one of his because she's wearing so much. Her cold skin rises to his touch in angry goosebumps.

146

Kate is on top of him as she wriggles out of her knickers. She watches as he does the same with his boxer shorts, driving them down past his knees. They tangle in his ankles, and the long muscles in the front of his thighs flex as he kicks them clear.

She reaches down and guides him inside her, letting him open her up until he is up to the hilt. He lies perfectly still. His eyes are closed, and his fingertips rest on her hips.

'Are you all right?' she asks.

He opens his eyes, and she could swear that they are damp with tears.

'I'm fine.' He grips her tighter and lifts her slightly off him.

'You're sure about this?'

He nods a yes, and moves himself up to meet her.

They begin to undulate, separately and clumsily at first, and then suddenly Kate feels him relax. They slip into a seamless rhythm, rocking against each other in long slow lazy movements. Her hair falls across her face, and it's him who reaches up to push it away so that he can look at her, him who starts to thrust faster and faster, him who finishes first, him who keeps pushing up and back even after he's spent so that she can get there too, and him who notices that she's shivering as she collapses on to his chest and gasps in his ear.

*   *   *

The *Aberdeen Evening Telegraph* has all but gone to bed. Only three people are left to prowl the offices: the night editor, Iain Lavelle, and two assistants. They check the wire services, drink coffee, watch

147

TV. Even with a story as massive as the *Amphitrite*, there's only a limited amount which can be done in the small hours—the first frantic night apart, of course.

The phone rings. Lavelle picks it up.

'Night desk.'

'This is Earth First environmental group.' Female voice, educated. 'We are not responsible for the *Amphitrite* sinking, and nor are any of our fellow organisations dedicated to preserving the planet's future. Our campaign tactics do not, have not and never will involve the taking of innocent lives.'

The line goes dead. Lavelle finishes transcribing the message in shorthand, and then picks up the phone to call the Press Association in London.

*   *   *

Where does this all begin? At the beginning, of course. Just down the coast from here, in a little village outside the town of Stonehaven. He calls it a village, but the word carries overtones of tranquillity and cosiness, and neither is appropriate. Come here, on any day other than during the fleeting period of summer balm, and you'll see what he means. The houses are clustered on the clifftops and shy away from the drop even as they peer over it. The windows and doors all face inwards, to protect not only against storms but also against the devil sneaking up the cliffs and in through the back door. The wind is never still: it twists this way and that and back on itself, moaning as it hunts the fisherman hurrying across the harbour, screeching as it rattles windows and slams

148

gates open and shut.

On the shore is an archipelago of rocks scarred brown and black. He looks at these rocks for hours on end, fancying that he can see in them the shapes of living things. Two large ones squat side by side like crocodiles feeding in the shallows, and another appears to him as the head of an old man looking out to sea, grass as sparse hair on the back of his skull.

Beyond the houses and the harbour and the rocks is the wind's twin, the sea. The sea here is alive, it's angry. It kills. Its rage is never spent, never assuaged. It batters against the rocks with unrelenting purpose, gathering itself with unrelenting energy and exploding in spraybursts of pure white. When he dares to peek out over the clifftops at night, all he can see are the haloes of the wave crests and the million shattered pieces of the moon's reflection on the water.

His first conscious memory is of the sea. He waddles on the shore, the rocks tilting underfoot. Their surfaces are slippery with a smooth treacherous green skin of seaweed, and he is too small to step from rock to rock with ease. The bladderwrack pops beneath his soles, short sharp death screams which make him wince. The sea is sharp cold against his ankles, his shins, his knees, crawling up his body and tempting him all the way in.

A voice snaps his name, sharp and close behind him. Stringy forearms lasso him and lift him clear of the water, and then stinging pain as she bats him across the head.

'Stupid child! You go ahead and drown yourself, do us all a favour. Should have done it myself, the

149

moment you popped out. You're lucky your da saw you this time. You sneak off when he's not around, and see who comes to get you then.'

He starts to cry. Another smack.

'You snivelling bastard.'

She puts him roughly back down. They walk back across the rocks and on to the road which winds up from the harbour. Her face is set in its familiar twisted rictus of resentment. The squalls fluff her thin brown hair into proud strands, and her arms are alabaster white against the red of her apron.

The family cottage is grey pebbledashed, and twice as gloomy inside. There is a small living-room where they cluster around the fire, Ivan in his sunken brown armchair on one side, Ailish upright and straight in a highbacked chair on the other, and between them a small sofa where he sits with Kathryn and Connie. Hero the lurcher lies on the floor, its head on its front paws or stretched out with its flanks rising and falling like bellows.

They eat in the kitchen, on an old pine table whose soft wood is pitted and scored with the marks of plates and cutlery.

In all the time when Ivan was there, the boy cannot remember a single conversation worth the name. When Ailish and Ivan speak to each other, it is clipped and staccato. Ivan speaks and Ailish looks quickly away, maybe answering him briefly, maybe not. Ivan tells Ailish or one of the children to do something. Sometimes Ailish asks Connie or Kathryn what they've done at school that day. She never asks the boy.

In between times, Ivan looks at the boy and smiles, except Ivan smiles so rarely that he doesn't

150

really know how to do it. His mouth twists over on itself and a couple of teeth poke out, and his eyes crinkle. He holds his face like that for a moment or two and lets it go back to what it was before, his mouth unwinding like a rubber band and the lines round his eyes smoothing themselves out. Then he says, 'You'll be right, boy', and looks out of the window.

The children all share a bedroom. Connie, as the eldest, has her own bed. The boy and Kathryn share the other. The nights are cramped and lonely. Connie fidgets in her sleep, and often he can hear Ivan grunting from next door. And all the time he listens for the monster outside, climbing the cliffs with great wet hands to sweep them away.

When the children have gone to bed, Ailish and Ivan get drunk, and then they fight. He remembers the phrases they use, and he remembers them even though they make no sense at the time, as if he knows that one day he will put them all together and understand. Snippets of words like the splashes of colour on jigsaw pieces which turn out to be the gables on a rooftop or the ear of a doll when the whole puzzle is done.

His mother:

'It's quick, with you. That's the one good thing.'

'Course he looks like you. That's why I hate him.'

'Don't be stupid. You think any other fucker would touch me now you've been there?'

His father:

'You think I'd fuck you when I was sober?'

'Aye, and I'd have kept on until we'd got one.'

'They'll grow up like fucking sluts, just like their fucking mother.'

151

Village dance, whisky and beer all around, and they go round the back and do it up against the wall. That's how Ivan and Ailish get together. He's twenty-one, she nineteen. They're married five months later, and four months after that comes Connie. No chance of Ailish having it vacuumed or Ivan buggering off and leaving her to look after it on her own. Their parents are adamant, and that's it. So they're shoved into a marriage they don't want with a baby they didn't plan. Ivan and Ailish, a few months hitched and already hating each other.

A daughter is all well and good, but what Ivan wants is a son—someone who'll grow up and work the fishing boats like he does. He won't rest easy until he has one, and he forces himself on Ailish more and more until she's expecting again. He prays and prays for a boy, and when Kathryn comes out he goes berserk, saying it's not his, accusing the hospital of switching the babies, anything and everything to excuse the fact he hasn't got a son.

He goes away for five days after Kathryn is born. When he comes back, he doesn't say where he's been, and Ailish doesn't ask. It's never mentioned again.

The more Ivan and Ailish hate each other, and the more he resents Kathryn and Connie for not being boys, the closer Ailish becomes to them. It is like their own little female conspiracy. And Ivan's wasting no time trying again. He gets drunk and smashes Ailish around, slamming her up against the walls, and then he sticks it to her half-conscious. For nine months Ailish carries the boy inside her, wanting him to be a girl and yet fearful of what will happen if he is: and then out he comes, the spitting image of Ivan, and she hates the boy with a passion. Like father, like son.

*   *   *

He is seven years old, and he is on the beach with Connie. Above their heads, the seagulls whirl on warm helixes and squawk their constant soundtrack. Kathryn is up in the house, with Ailish. Ivan is keeping an eye on them, but he's not really paying attention. He stands by the orange-roped anchor on the harbour wall, between piles of crates and net-hauling winches. The trawlers bob gently in the calm of the harbour swell, radar equipment clinging like squirrels to their masts. Their names flicker across his consciousness—Ivan's boat *Orca, Harvest Reaper, Sunbeam I.*

The children play in the shallows. Connie finds a smooth pebble and skims it across the water. It skips twice, three times, rearing up out of the ocean in small puffs of white, and then an incoming wave catches it and swallows it whole. He pokes around the stagnant pools for small creatures, and finds none. Connie walks out further into the water. She sits down heavily and moves her hands in huge scooping motions, trying to splash him with water. He ducks under the spray and dives in the sea towards her, using his own arms like windmills to churn up long looping arcs of water. They soak each other and cough spluttering giggles.

When he looks back in years to come, he cannot remember being happier than he was at that moment.

The sea comes for them so fast that they are underwater and being spun in every direction at

153

once almost before they know what's happened. It is as if the ocean literally rears up and snatches them. He is standing up to his chest when the undertow takes his feet away. It smacks him hard on the rocks and yanks him down and out to sea. Connie screams, short and sharp and cut off in a hurried panicky gulp. When he opens his eyes underwater, he can see her legs kicking open and shut like a pair of scissors.

Water around him rather than over him as he breaks surface. He shouts as loud as he can, saltwater spilling out of his mouth with the scream, and he sees a flash of pink by the harbour wall as Ivan's head turns towards him. Then he goes under again.

Connie hazy now through the green water. She is turning over and over on herself, half in and half out of the sea, but she is no longer struggling. The boy starts to swim towards her. Another wave spins him over and flings him first down and then skywards. He sees Ivan in the sea now, his big fisherman's arms cleaving the water as he comes towards the children. The boy is here and Connie is there, and Ivan is an equal distance from both of them. The boy yells once more before he is dragged under again, his lungs bubbling, and as he goes he sees with blinding clarity that the riptide is too strong for Ivan to reach both Connie and him. By the time he has got to one, the other will have been carried out of reach.

He begins to drop towards the depths, passing through the lighter shallows to ever-densening rounds of blackness. Under the silent weight of the water, he hears a droning slowed-down voice, a mixture of every voice he has ever heard. On his skin he feels the warmth of the sun, and in his eyes there are visions of breaks in the dark wild sky, heavenly shafts of light searching the grumbling sea.

Ivan's face appears, massive in his vision. There is a huge pressure on his chest. He raises his head a fraction to look down, and sees rather than feels Ivan smacking him with the heels of his hands. He tries to gulp in air even as the water comes out, and his chest hurts and he can't breathe, quick frightened panting. Then the last dribble of water runs down his cheek and the air floods in. His lungs heave in and out like Hero's when it lies by the fire in the evening.

That night, when the other villagers and the police have gone and it is just the four of them, the house is petrified in shock. Kathryn and the boy go to bed. The moment they're out of the way, the spell is broken. Ailish and Ivan have their biggest fight ever. The children huddle together—Kathryn refuses to take Connie's bed, not before she's been buried—and listen to an insane symphony rising from the kitchen. The clanging of pots and pans reverberates around the house. Their voices get louder and more agitated, never quietening, neither prepared to back down or cede an opening.

'You said you'd watch them.'

'I *did* watch them. It came so fast.'

'You let her die. You let my Connie die.'

'The lad was nearer. By the time I'd got to him, she'd gone.'

'You could have saved her.'

'I could not!'

'You'd have gone for the little bastard if he was halfway to Norway.'

155

'You weren't there.'

'How could I have trusted you? Fucking idiot I was. You fucking useless—'

He hits her now. The sharp smack of skin on skin, and then the duller thumping of a man using his fists. Kathryn turns to the boy and hugs him so tight he thinks she's trying to smother him.

WEDNESDAY

Dawn, and a pale sun peers over the rooftops of Belfast's troubled city.

On the mean streets of the Falls and Andersonstown, the police patrol in packs of four. They face outwards to cover all angles, and their ears are black with the radio pieces which keep them in touch with base. The house-high murals of fallen Republican heroes loom above them as they prowl.

A city centre coming to life. A man in overalls squeegees the plate-glass windows of the Europa, for long decades Europe's most-bombed hotel until 'overtaken' by the Holiday Inn in Sarajevo. In the shopping streets which radiate from City Hall, the dustmen clear the bins and the sweepers clean the gutters. On the eastern skyline stand the twin cranes of the Harland and Wolff shipyard, where the *Titanic* was built.

And, in the university gardens south of the city centre, the early-morning runners are out in force. The gardens are lovely at this time of year, the flowers in bloom and the grass a rich green. Those who have made the effort to be up so early could be forgiven for thinking that little is wrong with the world.

A short, stocky man pounds the paths, heavy on his feet. Without warning he pulls up, clutching the back of his left leg. He hobbles the few yards to the nearest bench and sits abruptly down on it. He straightens his leg and curls his foot upwards. Cramp, evidently, rather than a hamstring problem.

One of the runners coming the other way stops next to him.

'All right, mate?'

'Cramps. I'll run it off.'

A quick look around, to check no one can overhear.

'Nothing from the INLA, nor the Continuity. Any other jokers wouldn't have had the wherewithal to pull a stunt like that.'

'Thanks.'

The second man moves on. After a few seconds the first man gets off the bench and starts running again, gingerly at first in case anyone is watching.

Northern Irish intelligence has just learned that, whoever bombed the *Amphitrite*, it wasn't the Irish Republican movement.

* * *

Kate works the shower up her body, a little at a time. It's easier today than it was yesterday, now she knows she can do it. But since it's easier, she has to compensate by going a little bit further. When she ran at university, her coach would tell her that the only way to improve was to run faster or further each time she trained. And since speed means nothing here, she has to go further.

Put the shower on her face. That's all she has to do.

She shuts her eyes and closes her mouth. If she could seal up her nostrils and her ears, she'd do that too.

The water moves up her neck as if of its own accord.

A splash on her chin.

The woman motionless on the rescue ladder, hands blotched white where she grips tight.

160

Kate goes for it before she loses her nerve. The water on her lips against her nose battering her eyelids her head shaking in the spray like a dog's, but she keeps the shower there, breath held to stop her from drowning, water on her forehead and her hair now and streams running into her ears, and only when she can physically no longer keep the air in her lungs does she take the shower away and gasp a grateful exhalation.

*　　　*　　　*

Frank walks into the Michaelhouse conference room which the MAIB has commandeered for the duration of the inquiry. A cup of coffee from the hotel restaurant is cupped between his palms. Careful not to spill any, he heads for the far corner of the room, where he and his secretary Kirstie have established a makeshift enclave behind a partition. It's not a power executive corner office like Lovelock's—Frank's view is of the street outside, rather than a sweeping panorama of the harbour—but it'll do. It has to.

'Morning, Kirstie.'

'Morning, Frank. Here you go.'

She slides the post towards him. A pile of papers from the ones she's opened, plus two brown envelopes marked 'Personal' which she hasn't. He picks them up and taps them.

'You *can* open these, you know. I should be so lucky to get something personal.'

'Have I never told you why I don't?'

'No.'

'It was when I was working in London for that awful law firm, just before I came to you. My boss

161

said the same thing as you do—open everything. So I did. And one day, there's me just casually riffling through his mail, and what do I find? One of those penis enlargement brochures. No wonder they marked it "Personal".'

Frank laughs.

'Whatever's in there, I can assure you it won't be *that*.'

'Lucky you offered me the job when you did. I couldn't look him in the eye after that. So, what says "Personal" stays personal. Whether you tell me to or not.'

'All right. Have it your way.'

He sits down behind his desk and opens them. One is a letter from a woman in Maidenhead, saying she saw him on the telly the other night and she thinks he's very handsome.

The other is typed. Bold, serif. No heading, no signature.

We blew up the ship. If you don't lay off the investigation, we'll send you a small present (bomb) in the post. Let the dead rest.

Frank's throat suddenly feels very dry.

He reads it again, slower, and finds he read it right the first time. There is a dry crawling in his belly.

Must be a crank.

He looks up. 'Kirstie, has there been any news about responsibility claims?'

'It's all there.' She reaches across, picks up the pile of papers, and unearths a memo from the middle. 'The *Aberdeen Evening Telegraph* got a call late last night denying any environmental

162

involvement, and Renfrew left a message about fifteen minutes ago saying the Irish Republicans were nothing to do with it either.'

'Right. Thanks.'

He sounds distracted, and she picks up on it. Kirstie, Sheffield blunt and tintack sharp.

'Why?'

He slides the letter across to her. 'That's what Mr Personal wants.'

She reads it fast, her eyes widening over the top of the sheet. 'Sounds like a nutter.'

'That's what I reckon.'

'But . . . you never can tell.'

'That's also what I reckon.'

'We should call the police.'

'I think so.'

The police. Kate. What would *she* say if he showed her this letter?

Frank looks out of the window. Mothers and children arriving at the school opposite, the road half-blocked by cars. A frantic, edgy noise of engines and high voices. He tries to blot them out and think, deal with something totally new and unexpected—and all of a sudden she's right there, his thoughts made flesh. Kate, his daughter, still wrapped up like Scott of the Antarctic. Her hands poke out from thick woollen sleeves, even though today is just as hot as yesterday was. She must have the flu or something.

She is holding a small boy by the hand. Leo, no doubt. Bronagh has told Frank more than once what an adorable grandchild he's got.

He feels a catch in the back of his throat. He looks at his daughter, and what he sees is a mother—Kate with her own child now, and that

163

child as dependent on her for love and life itself as Kate used to be on Frank. If ever he wanted proof that her life has moved on in his absence, this is it. Not in the cases he reads about in the papers or in the news of her promotions which Bronagh relays, but now, a mother with her child. Kate, who deals so much with death, part of the life cycle.

The blue cold of infinite sadness brushes Frank, and he wonders whether she feels it too. Maybe that's why she's wearing her big jumper. But for a decision he took years ago, they would never have come to this. His daughter would still love him. He would have seen his grandchild learn to walk, learn to talk, smile and laugh and cry and sleep. A decision he took because he genuinely thought it was for the best, and which has haunted him every day since.

Frank bounces the threatening letter lightly against the palm of his hand, trying to affect nonchalance.

Kate is still there, right outside the window, chatting to another mother. If she turned her head now she'd see him, her father, separated by a pane of glass and years of hurt.

Kate holds her head straight as she talks. Unnaturally straight, Frank thinks, the way one does when determined not to look at something.

Or someone.

She knows he's here, in Aberdeen. And Bronagh must have told her where he's staying, especially since the hotel is right opposite Leo's school. She wouldn't have wanted Kate to run into her father unannounced, not after so long.

Which means that Kate knows he's here, in the Michaelhouse.

Frank on his feet and quickly across the conference room, through the lobby and out into the street. The light morning breeze catches the letter and flaps it in his hand.

Kate is squatting in front of Leo, adjusting his uniform. The woman she was talking to has gone.

'Kate. I was just thinking about you.'

She looks up and at him, and her eyes flash pure anger. She turns back to Leo.

'Go on, Leo. Go inside to school. Mama or Auntie B will come and pick you up later.'

Leo looks at Frank, as if he recognises him but can't place him. Instinctively, Frank reaches down to him. Kate grabs Leo by the shoulders and spins him away, propelling him towards the school gates. He cranes his neck to look at Frank.

'Who's that man, Mama?'

'Never you mind. Have a good day, darling.'

She kisses the back of his head. Leo gives Frank another bemused look and walks through the gates. He is barely out of earshot when Kate jabs Frank in the chest.

'How *dare* you?'

'I wanted to show you this.' He gestures with the letter.

'That is my son, this is my life. No one asked you back.'

'Kate, *please.* Just read this.'

He holds the letter out to her. She pauses, and then snatches it and begins to read. Her hands move fast to the edges when she realises what it is.

'When did this come?'

'This morning.'

'Who's handled it?'

'Me. Kirstie, my secretary. You.'

165

'Either of you use gloves?'

'No.'

'And you didn't think of telling me what it was before I put my fingerprints all over it? For God's sake.'

'Jesus Christ, Kate. I'm a marine inspector, not a member of the Flying Squad. This has never happened to me before. Forgive me if I didn't get the procedure right.'

His hands are trembling.

Halfway through her fourth decade, Kate has never seen her father scared before. His face simply isn't given to fear: it is hard, uncompromising, the face of a cliff. And, because she has never known him as an adult, he has always been more of an icon to her than anything else. At first he was infallible, in the way parents often are to their children, and then overnight he was terminally fallible. No in-between. It has never occurred to Kate that he might be afraid—or hold any other emotion, for that matter.

This is the first time she has ever seen her father as a person.

The fear that Frank might be hurt curls up from inside her stomach, and she recognises it in the same moment that she tries to will it away. It is as if her body is betraying her. For two decades now she has blocked him from her life. Then he waltzes back into it, unannounced and unwelcome, and, simply by virtue of who he is, closes his hand around her heart.

Kate hands the letter back to him quickly, so she can clench her fists and stop her own hands from shaking. Too flustered to apologise, because she can't be sure of how the words will come out, she

166

mumbles something about going inside and hurries through the hotel door.

They sit in reception on sofas with backs that are too low and dig in under her shoulderblades. She watches two fish circle lazily in a tube as she tries to compose herself, and it takes her a long moment to realise that the fish are artificial and kept from sinking only by the constant stream of bubbles beneath them.

'Let's see that again.'

He hands her the letter.

We blew up the ship. If you don't lay off the investigation, we'll send you a small present (bomb) in the post. Let the dead rest.

She holds the sheet up to the light.

'Mass-produced paper. No watermarks.' She brings it in close to her face. 'Looks like bog standard laser printer typeface.' She puts it in her lap. 'Either very clever or totally harmless. Probably the latter. We get hundreds of these on every major case we work.'

'If they blew up the ferry, I can't imagine that making a letter bomb's going to cause them too many problems.'

'*If.* Much more likely to be a crank.'

'More likely? Is that the most reassurance you can give me, Kate?'

'We work on likelihoods the whole time, otherwise we'd never get anything done. You know about Occam's Razor? The most likely explanation is usually the correct one. The shortest distance between two points is a straight line. What do the Americans say? If it looks like a carrot, smells like a carrot and tastes like a carrot, it's probably . . .'

'Genetically modified.'

She laughs, a genuine and spontaneous sound, the way she used to laugh as a child when he spun her upside down and tickled her. When she hears it, she cuts it dead in her throat.

Occam's Razor. On whose edge Drew Blaikie would have killed Petra Gallacher.

'You must be going down to see the wreck, yes?' Professional again.

'This morning.'

'Let me know what you find. If there's bomb evidence, I'll have this analysed and get the forensics on to it. If there's no bomb evidence, we can assume that this is the work of a nutter. OK?'

'That makes sense. OK.'

'Right.' She looks at her watch. 'I've got to go. The traffic wardens are savage round here. Let me take this, and the envelope it came in too. I'll put it in a plastic sack so no one else can touch it. Just in case.'

He goes to the conference room to get the envelope, and returns with it dangling from his fingertips.

'Bye, Kate.'

'Bye.'

As she gets into her car, Kate thinks how close she came to calling him 'Dad' just then.

'Blaikie wants to see you,' says Ferguson, the moment Kate walks into the incident room.

'What does he want?'

'Wouldn't say. Wants to talk to you and you alone.'

Maybe a night in custody has softened Blaikie up, as Kate hoped. She gets a cup of coffee from

168

the machine outside the incident room and goes down to Blaikie's cell.

'Type of blood found under Petra's fingernails: AB. Your blood type, as listed in previous reports: AB. Percentage of population with AB blood: three. So let me guess. You've decided to confess all.'

'No. I've decided to tell you where I was on Monday night.'

'And the two are not the same thing?'

'I discovered that Petra was having an affair.'

'When did you discover this?'

'Monday evening.'

'So you beat the crap out of her.'

'No. I beat the crap out of *him*.'

Kate looks at Blaikie appraisingly. No wonder he told her he was at home that night. He's just copped himself an actual bodily harm charge. Obstruction of justice and wasting police time too, if she decides to. He lied about where he was, and he lied about not knowing whether Petra was sleeping around. Three separate offences. But even put together, they're still better for him than a murder charge, and Blaikie knows that as well as she does. That's why he's decided to come clean. He's caught in a cleft stick: he has to incriminate himself to clear himself.

Kate wonders when exactly he weighed up the options and decided to run with the lesser of two evils. The moment Ferguson read him his rights, probably. Kate wonders how far behind him she is on whatever else he's hiding.

'Who is he?'

'Irvine Scoular.'

The name sounds familiar, though Kate can't

immediately place it.

'Her boss,' Blaikie adds, as if reading her mind.

Irvine Scoular. The news editor at the *Aberdeen Evening Telegraph*. The one who called in sick yesterday morning because he'd been mugged. *Said* he'd been mugged.

'How did you find out?'

'Oh, I'd had my doubts for a while. She started staying out late, saying she was working on stories. She'd never done that before. All the time she'd worked there, she'd be home by five or six.'

An evening paper. That would figure.

Drew Blaikie, controlling. Drew Blaikie, paranoid and jealous, trigger quick to notice any shift in her routine, anything that might threaten his hold over her. Even the suspicion of an affair would have been enough, let alone the reality.

'She was on a six-month contract. She was trying to get a full-time position. No wonder she was working hard.'

'None of these stories'—his fingers describe quotation marks in the air—'ever appeared in the paper. Not one.'

'Maybe they were investigative pieces, that took weeks to research and write.'

'The only pieces of hers I saw were little itty things she knocked up in half an hour.'

'You're a regular reader of the *Evening Telegraph*, then?'

'Of late, I have been.'

'Anything else?'

'She talked about him. Too much.'

'So? I talk about DI Ferguson to my friends. It doesn't mean we're having an affair.'

'Bet he's gutted.'

170

Kate ignores the jibe. 'How did you find out for sure?'

'I went to wait for her on Monday evening.'

'Where?'

'Round the back of the newspaper offices, where the reporters park their cars.'

'She didn't know you were coming?'

'No.'

'What happened?'

'I was sitting in the car, and out she came with this geezer. He had his arm around her, and she was leaning against his shoulder. Believe you me, he wasn't exactly Robert Redford.'

'They'd been working on the most traumatic story imaginable. Maybe he was just comforting her.'

'With his tongue in her mouth?'

Kate says nothing. Blaikie continues. 'Saw it with my own eyes. She got in her car, and he leaned in through the window and kissed her.'

'And then?'

'She drove off. Right past me, this big smile on her face. And he sauntered back towards the office like he was Cock of the Fucking North.'

'Then what?'

'What do you think? I got out of the car and ran over to him. I said: "Irvine Scoular?" And he said: "Yes?" And I said: "I think you're screwing my girlfriend."'

'And that's when you hit him?'

'Yes.'

'How many times?'

'Two to the face. One to the stomach, hard. When he doubled over, I kneed him in the face, then flat-handed his neck as he went down.'

171

Typical Blaikie, able to spell out in detail the damage he's done to someone.

'Anything else?'

'A couple of kicks to the ribs.'

'That's all?'

'Yes.'

'So if he tells me anything else . . .'

'He's lying. That's what I did to him. Chapter and verse. That's more than enough for an ABH charge, I know. You think I'd admit it if it wasn't true?'

'Did he fight back?'

'Right at the start. Hit me in the face. Stopped when I did him in the stomach.'

'And that's where the black eye and the scratches on your face came from?'

'Yes.'

'And then you left?'

'Yes.'

'Did anyone witness any of this?'

'Not that I know of. It was all over in thirty seconds.'

'You talk to Petra after that?'

'No.'

Kate steeples her fingers under her chin. It seems plausible enough, regrettably. All she has to do to confirm it is to ask Irvine Scoular what happened. Would Blaikie have spun her a bunch of shit when he knows she could knock it apart in a second?

Maybe, if he fancied jerking her around.

Would Blaikie have admitted that Petra was cheating on him if she wasn't?

No. Men like Blaikie never admit that their women cheat on them. For that if nothing else,

172

she's inclined to believe him.

'How unlucky can you get?' he asks.

'Huh?'

'If Petra hadn't been killed, none of this would ever have come out. Scoular would have kept shtoom because he knew he'd be in trouble with his wife. Petra would have kept shtoom because she didn't want people to think she was screwing her way into a job'—*her job was gone long before that, sunshine*—'and I'd have kept quiet because I didn't want an ABH charge.'

'My heart bleeds.'

'Now we've got all that straight, I can go. Right?'

Kate presses her face as close to his as she can stand.

'You're not going anywhere.'

He kisses her. His lips are smoky and pungent where his cigarettes have been, and they have barely touched hers before she jerks her head back and slaps him across the cheek in one movement, her whole body swivelling to get as much force behind the blow as possible. Four perfect red fingermarks appear on his left cheek, companions to the scratch on his right, and he smirks at her retreating back as she walks out.

*　　　*　　　*

Kate goes to interview Scoular at home, unannounced. He lives in Ferryhill, tucked away behind the harbour. She finds it first time: a wide road with granite houses on both sides. Scoular lives on the corner, and his is the only house in the street without bay windows.

Blaikie was right. Irvine Scoular isn't Robert

173

Redford, not by a long chalk. His paunch presses against a brown shirt, and flecks of dandruff line the strip of scalp at his parting. He has a mouthful of food when he opens the door, and he is chewing it tentatively. Kate can see why. The left side of his jaw has come up brooding crimson, and has evidently been too painful to shave over.

Kate flashes her badge. 'I'm DCI Beauchamp.'

Scoular's wife appears beside him. He turns his head to look at her, and Kate sees the welt on his neck where Blaikie flat-handed him.

'I'll put your breakfast back in the oven, dear,' she says.

'Thank you, Sheila.'

She turns to Kate. 'And about time too. He was attacked two days ago, and only now do you send someone round. That's more than thirty-six hours. We've been waiting here night and day. I've a good mind to complain.'

Without further ado, Kate steps through the front door and into the sitting-room. A gas fire, off in the heatwave. On the mantelpiece, pictures of children in school uniform, framed in cheap blue cardboard. A bowl of pot-pourri on top of the TV set.

'Mr Scoular, could you tell me how you came by your injuries?'

'He was mugged,' says Sheila. 'Set upon by three youths, round the back of the newspaper offices. Terrible, it was. And your lot haven't done anything about it.'

'Mr Scoular?'

'Like my wife said. I was mugged.'

'Mrs Scoular, why don't you go and put your husband's breakfast back in the oven, like you said

174

you were going to?' Kate gives her a look which brooks no protest. 'This'll be easier if it's just him and me.'

'Go on, love,' says Scoular.

Sheila gets up, smoothing her dress down over her knees, and leaves the room. Kate looks back at Scoular.

'Now, Mr Scoular, do you want to tell me what really happened?'

'It was just like . . .'

'Before you do, you might like to remember that the penalties for lying to police officers are severe. You might also consider how I know that you were mugged in the first place, given that you haven't reported it. And I'm sure you know that it's hardly usual for a DCI to make apparently routine calls.'

He says nothing. She continues.

'Either you tell me what happened, or I'll call your wife back in here and tell her that her husband was screwing the office junior.'

Scoular's reaction tells Kate everything she needs to know. A globule of saliva forms at the corner of his furiously working mouth. He blinks rapidly and glances nervously towards the kitchen, terrified that Sheila might have heard.

Kate shouldn't have doubted Blaikie. For once, he really was telling the truth.

'He killed her,' says Scoular. 'When I saw it on the news yesterday, I knew it was him. You should have seen his face. Murderous. Quite literally. It was him, I'm telling you.'

'Then why didn't you ring us and say so?'

He spreads his hands wide and shrugs.

'Tell me what happened,' says Kate. 'Right from the start.'

175

'He came from nowhere.'

'Who's he?'

'Him. Her boyfriend. Drew someone.'

'Where were you?'

'Outside the office.'

'Front or back?'

'Back.'

'Go on.'

'Asked my name, told me I was screwing his girlfriend. Then he started smacking me.'

'Where did he hit you?'

'Everywhere. In the face, in the stomach, kicked me too.'

'Did you fight back?'

'I tried. Got one punch in. But he's bigger than me, and stronger.'

'Where did you hit him?'

'In the eye.'

'Scratch him?'

'No.'

'No?'

'No. *Women* scratch.'

He shows her his fingernails. They're blunt and dirty, but they're not torn.

Blaikie said that Scoular scratched him. He lied.

If Scoular didn't scratch Blaikie, then logic would suggest that Petra did.

What if Blaikie went after Petra after taking care of Scoular? What if he plumped for the ABH charge because he's *guilty*? Not to incriminate himself, but to protect himself?

Kate turns her attention back to Scoular.

'How long did he hit you for?'

'Seconds. He scarpered pretty quick, before anyone could see him.'

'And after that?'

'I came home.'

'Drove?'

'Yes. Hurt like buggery to drive the car, and I felt a bit groggy, but I made it.'

'And then what?'

'I've been here. Waiting for the police to come.' He makes the same movement to describe quotation marks as Blaikie did.

'But you never reported it.'

'Of course not. Whenever Sheila got on my back about it, I'd ring the speaking clock and tell it that I'd been mugged, and could it send someone to take a statement?'

Kate almost laughs. Scoular continues. 'It was the only way I could shut her up. That, and making sure she didn't call them herself.'

'You've been here ever since you came home on Monday evening?'

'Yes.'

That includes all of Monday night. Petra was killed between midnight and two o'clock. Scoular can't be Blackadder.

'How long had you and Petra been sleeping together?'

'A few weeks.'

'Even though you knew she wasn't going to have her contract extended?'

He looks offended. 'You think that's why I was sleeping with her?'

'I think that's why she was sleeping with you.'

'Rubbish.'

'Why, then?'

'Her boyfriend's a git. I listened to her, which he never did. I made her feel wanted.'

'I'll bet you did. And did she ever mention her job situation?'

'No.'

'No? You were her boss, you were having an affair with her, and you never talked about it? Come on.'

'Well . . . maybe once or twice.'

'Did she ask you if you knew whether she was going to be kept on?'

He looks away, out of the window. 'Yes.'

'What did you say?'

He looks at Kate again. 'That I didn't know.'

'But you did know. You knew that she wasn't going to be kept on.'

'What else could I do?'

'Not have been screwing her, for a start. Except you knew which side your bread was buttered, didn't you? You kept her hanging on, even though the die had already been cast. The moment she knew she was going to be let go, she'd have dropped you like a hot brick.' Kate finds herself rooting for Petra again, and just as futilely as before. *So you had atrocious taste in men? You go, girl.* 'She didn't deserve Drew Blaikie, she didn't deserve you, and she sure as hell didn't deserve what happened to her last night.'

Kate gets up abruptly. She looks round the room with contempt, not for the cheap furnishings but for the cheap life upon which they look. Irvine Scoular and his petty manipulations, his weaselling and his lying, deceiving his wife and his colleagues, using and being used.

'It was him,' Scoular says again. 'You want to clap him in irons.'

'Drew Blaikie is a nasty piece of work, and it's a

178

bit of a novelty to find myself sympathising with him,' Kate says. 'But on this occasion, I have to admit he has a point.'

*   *   *

Wayfarer, the command boat which the MAIB has hired for the duration of the investigation, rocks gently in the swell above the wreck of the *Amphitrite*. The wind is muted and the sea compact, rolling undemandingly against the *Wayfarer*'s hull as it uses its cycloidal propulsion system to sit dead stationary. Two cycloids shaped like giant egg beaters, one under the bow and the other under the stern, allow the *Wayfarer* to go ahead or astern, turn on a sixpence, or hold still as it is doing now.

Down below deck, Frank looks at a computer simulation of the wreck. The technicians have already worked out the *Amphitrite*'s location and orientation by a technique known as 'mowing the lawn', which involves running high-frequency sonar waves over a sunken object in alternate perpendicular directions. The *Amphitrite* has sunk in 88 metres of water, is facing west-north-west, and has a list of about 120 degrees to starboard. A line of debris, which shows up on the sonar as a straggly broken trail, stretches about a quarter of a mile south-east of the wreck.

Charlie Fox, the pilot of the submersible which will go down to the wreck, enters the cabin. 'Ready when you are, Frank.'

They walk up a clanging metal staircase and out on deck. Down near the *Wayfarer*'s stern, the submersible *Starsky* crouches like a giant yellow

179

beetle. Its remotely operated vehicle *Hutch*— basically a satellite submersible—is clamped to the starboard flank. *Hutch* has a 75-metre flexible tether, image-intensifying imaging cameras and lights, and its own propulsion plant. And the tether has a cable cutter at source in case *Hutch* gets snagged on the wreckage, thereby preventing *Starsky* from surfacing.

Fox and Frank bend down and take their shoes off. No footwear allowed on board *Starsky*.

Fox climbs the small ladder leading up to *Starsky*'s turret, opens the entrance hatch, and lowers himself delicately through the hole. Frank follows him, making sure he doesn't brush against the sides of the hatch on the way in. The hatch seal is covered in grease, and Frank has learned the hard way that the grease is an absolute bastard to get out of one's clothes.

Their seats are arranged vertically, like bunk beds: pilot below, observer above. Fox straps himself into the pilot's seat, Frank the observer's. Frank pulls the hatch closed and locks it. *Starsky*'s large observation window forms a giant transparent helmet around his head, and a soft mechanical whirring begins near his left ear: the lithium hydroxide blower, which recycles cabin air and removes carbon dioxide.

Fox waves a sketchy cross in the air in front of him. He's been wreck-diving for fifteen years, and never once can he remember feeling even the slightest bit complacent. Every journey in *Starsky* throws up a mix of emotions for him. Apprehension and anticipation, the lurking prospect of a thrilling discovery—and always the fear that something will go wrong, and if it does it won't be just slightly wrong but shatteringly and irrevocably wrong, condemning him and his companion to one of two deaths: a slow, suffocating asphyxiation as their air supply gradually drains away, or the quick, pulverising influx of flooding water.

Fox puts on his headset and starts his pre-dive checks. 'Battery. Check. Life-support system. Check. Acoustic telephone. Check. Sonar. Check. Back-up battery. Check.' He exhales. 'OK. Take us down.'

Starsky lurches slightly to one side as the davit pulleys take the strain and lift it clear of the deck. It sways more as the machinery swings it out over the *Wayfarer*'s side. This situation—when the vessel is half over the deck and half over the water—is just about the most dangerous phase of the entire operation. If for any reason *Starsky* was dropped now, they could be in big trouble: damaged submersible, injured occupants.

A loud splash as they land in the water. *Starsky* bobs gently on the waves. Fox speaks into his headset again. 'Rechecking all systems now sub is wet. Stand by.' He goes through the same checklist as before: battery, life-support system, acoustic telephone, sonar, back-up battery. 'OK. Divers to release us. Let's go.'

Through the observation window, Frank sees an inflatable dinghy come alongside. Two figures in grey wetsuits topple backwards over the bow and disappear from sight. He hears them scrabbling on *Starsky*'s hull.

After a few moments, Fox speaks again. 'Flooding ballast tanks. Going down.'

Starsky slips beneath the surface of the North

181

Sea.

Fox always feels an affinity with the dead once he's underwater. He grips the control lever so hard that it appears to be oozing between his fingers.

Frank thinks of his trips down deep, beneath the vast expanses of the Pacific. Total darkness at about 400 metres. At 800, a deep scattering blur which plays havoc with the sonar. The blur comprises thousands of tiny creatures, rather like a marine asteroid belt. These creatures are bioluminescent, and their bodies brighten when they're frightened. The pressure wake which the sub creates sets them exploding in little strings of light, starting at one end and going all the way along, like tiny passenger trains running past the window in pitch-black. No chance of such beauty on today's trip.

It doesn't take them long to reach the *Amphitrite*: 88 metres, though plenty deep enough, is small fry compared to the two or three miles of water in which some mid-Atlantic wrecks are found. The great hulk of ferry comes looming at them from the semi-darkness, and Fox slows their descent until *Starsky* comes to a hovering halt about five metres above the *Amphitrite*'s bridge. He turns both searchlights up to maximum brightness.

The *Amphitrite*'s bridge has been squashed flat, like a crumpled Coke can. Both Frank and Fox know why. A heavy object accelerating in water creates a sizeable slipstream. When this object hits an immovable barrier such as the seabed and stops dead, the slipstream comes crashing through in a massive downblast.

Frank adjusts his headset microphone. 'Let's start from the stern and work forward,' he says.

182

'The van they pushed out was near the front, but the one with the bomb in it could have been anywhere—most likely as far from the decoy as possible. We'll go along the starboard side, sending *Hutch* in under the overhang.'

Fox nods, knowing this makes sense on two levels. The *Amphitrite*'s serious list to starboard suggests that the bomb exploded on that side: the ship would ultimately have listed towards the area which was holed rather than away from it. And the decision to use *Hutch* confirms the first safety rule of wreck-diving: manned craft never go in under man-made overhangs. If for whatever reason the *Amphitrite* slips further and crushes *Hutch*, all Frank would have to do is cut the tether.

Fox pilots *Starsky* back towards the stern. The searchlights play over vast flats of twisted metal. They reach the stern. The *Amphitrite*'s rear end squats solidly in their vision.

'Propellers almost zero pitch position, and rudders hard starboard. Obviously still trying to turn when she sank.'

While Fox controls *Starsky*, Frank is in charge of *Hutch*. He has a control box which can move it forwards, backwards and laterally. A screen relaying the camera images is set into the moulding in front of his seat, and these images can be recorded on standard VHS video if need be. Frank presses a button to detach *Hutch*, which snakes towards the *Amphitrite*'s aft starboard corner, its flexible tether whipping out behind it. *Hutch* in the glare of *Starsky*'s powerful arc lights. Frank pushes *Hutch* as far between hull and seabed as he can get it, and starts to work along the length of the ferry.

Fox keeps *Starsky* a good twenty metres off the

Amphitrite, just in case anything should be accidentally dislodged. It is painfully slow progress, a small section at a time, not moving on until Frank has spun *Hutch*'s camera in all directions to ensure that they've missed nothing. Frank talks sporadically, more as if he is addressing a lecture on naval architecture than crawling along the side of a sunken ferry.

'We're looking for a large hole at or near the waterline, with the steel plating around it bent outwards rather than inwards. Ships' hulls are built to withstand pressures from outside only. The steel plates which make up a hull are fixed to the outboard faces of the network frames, which in turn are fashioned to resist water compression rather than internal expansion. A powerful internal explosion would therefore have blown the steel plates outwards.'

It takes them almost an hour to traverse the length of the starboard side. They find nothing. No holes, no bending.

'I don't believe this,' says Frank.

'Do you want to try the port side?'

'Might as well. At least we'll be able to see all that without needing our little friend here.' He presses the button to wind *Hutch* back in.

Fox steers *Starsky* round the *Amphitrite*'s bow, and both men gasp.

The *Amphitrite*'s bow door has been ripped clean off.

When they look closer, they see that it is in fact only the outer door—the visor—which has gone. The inner door, which doubles as the loading ramp, is still more or less intact, its ribbed underside like a massive dental dam in the

184

Amphitrite's gaping mouth. At the top, where the leading edge meets the hull, there is a gap of a few feet, too small to send *Hutch* through.

'OK,' says Frank. 'We'll have to get as close as we can. I'll run through what's left of the visor fittings first, and then move on to the inner door.'

Fox glides *Starsky* up close to the cavern. Frank begins to speak, adjusting the searchlights as he does so to illuminate the areas in question.

'Visor bottom lock. All three attachment lugs for bottom lock installation have failed in their thinnest sections, generally in upwards or forwards direction. Visor side locks. Locking lugs remain in front bulkhead recesses. Rotation within recesses indicate general upward movement of attachment. Visor hinge arrangements. Deck hinge fittings intact except for pounding marks above hinge centres on side plates. That's about all there is for the visor. Moving on to the ramp now. Ramp attachment and locking devices. Two port-side hinges have failed, probably because of tension fracture of ramp-mounted lugs. Mounting of pins for upper locking hooks heavily twisted.'

Frank flicks his microphone up, opens a small plastic bottle of Evian, takes a long swig, and flips his microphone back into place. He rubs his eyes with the heels of his hands.

'Charlie?'

'Yeah?'

'If a bomb exploded on here, I'm a Dutchman.'

'That's just what I was thinking.'

'Let's assume there's no bomb damage on the port side—a reasonable assumption, given the way the ship has fallen. There's nothing at the stern, we saw that before we started. Therefore the only

185

other place a bomb could have gone off is here, at the bows. But if there'd been a bomb, there'd be pieces of the door hanging on to the sides. And a blast large enough to sink a ship would have caused more collateral damage to the bulkhead. No. This visor has been *ripped* off, not blown off. You can see that in the twisting of the side locks and the piston rods. This has come off at its weakest points.'

'There's absolutely no way this could have been a bomb?'

'Only if someone placed small explosives at the contact points where the visor met the hull, and blew it off that way. That would be almost impossible to do without someone noticing. And Christian Parker was adamant that the bomb warning specified a *vehicle*.' He pauses, thinks, goes on. 'In any case, how could you have a blast which ripped the visor clean off and hardly touched the ramp? It's simply not feasible. Even if you placed explosives between the inner and outer doors to blow the visor outwards, you'd still blow the ramp inwards, wouldn't you?'

Frank lapses into silence. Fox waits him out. He knows what's coming.

When they check the port side, almost all of which will be visible because it is the exposed flank, they will also have to check the ferry's interior— visually through the portholes, and maybe using *Hutch* too. Checking the interior will involve seeing the bodies of those who didn't make it, piled on top of each other as they tried to scramble to safety, or bloated with gas and bobbing like helium balloons against cabin roofs. Fox has seen it once before, on a trawler which went down off the Finnish coast,

186

and what he saw was what he imagined happened in the gas chambers during the Holocaust: everyone rushing to get out as the showers spurted Zyklon B, and dying as they clawed at each other in the crush.

That's why Fox lets Frank take his time. On this trip, Fox is the pilot: he doesn't have to look too closely. Frank is the observer, and he does.

A sharp *slapslap* as Frank smacks his palms against his cheeks.

'OK. Let's do it.'

Frank has a list of the *Amphitrite*'s decks and their functions in a transparent map pocket strapped to his thigh, and a sick bag swiped from British Midland clutched in his right hand.

'How do you want to do this?' Fox says.

'Start at the bridge and work down, I think. We'll go stem to stern, down a level, stern to stem, down a level, and so on. If I want you to stop, I'll tell you.'

'OK. We'll have to go right up close to the windows, or we won't be able to see beyond the reflection of our own lights.'

Fox takes *Starsky* up past the bow doors to the bridge, concentrating on nothing other than piloting the submersible. He eases *Starsky* round to the bow's port corner, and from now on he doesn't look at anything he doesn't have to. He lets Frank be his eyes, and even then it's bad enough, listening and imagining.

Frank gets the first shock almost before he's begun.

'Deck nine. Bridge. Oh God—I can see two bodies. Jesus *Christ*.'

Fox hears Frank's breathing turn short and

ragged as he struggles to compose himself. He's thinking of Kate. Had she been slower, drunker, unluckier, one of these bodies could have been hers—and she'd have gone to her death still hating him.

Beats of silence, and Frank's voice comes back, firmer and more controlled.

'Two bodies. One near the door to the open deck, one down to starboard. Both in uniform. Hold it there.' Pause. 'On main manoeuvre console, port engine control lever is around 50 per cent astern position, starboard lever 95 per cent astern position. Both pitch indicators indicating around 50 per cent forward pitch. EPIRB beacon cages both open and empty. Move on.

Fox takes *Starsky* down a level, and begins to inch slowly aft along the great hulk of the *Amphitrite*. Frank keeps up the commentary, reading the deck description off his list and then telling Fox what he can see.

'Deck eight. Accommodation for senior officers for'ard, ventilation equipment amidships, additional crew accommodation spaces aft. Can't see much. Visibility poor. Most of the cabins and partitions have collapsed. Nothing doing here. Go down.

'Deck seven. Main crew accommodation. Floating debris again making visibility difficult, but I can still see bodies in cabins'—the sticking moment is past, Frank hardly misses a beat when he says this—'five in this one, now two, now three, two more here. Most bodies are piled up against the doors and walls. Can see through to main staircase area. One victim visible here. Probably many more, but debris is in the way. Down.

188

'Decks six and five. We can probably do both at once, they're stacked closer together than the other decks. Passenger cabins covering forward third, remaining area used for tax-free shop, information desk, restaurants, bar, entertainment areas. Both decks have two double-door public exits to open-air aft decks. Four aft cabins inspected. No victims. Five victims found in aft staircase, three in adjacent lounge.'

His voice is low and flat. Fox knows what Frank is doing. Taking the emotion out, making it easier to deal with. And the more bodies there are, the less they become individuals, the more their struggle is depersonalised.

'Two victims in dance saloon near stage. Three victims in shopping area amidships, maybe more hidden by floating merchandise and debris. Nine more in bar. Five—no, six victims in port-side corridors, for'ard and transverse. Eight victims in corridors outside cabins. For'ardmost port stairwell contains many bodies, corresponding staircase on starboard side empty. Down.

'Deck four. Lowest accommodation deck. Passenger cabins, cafeteria. Conference rooms aft. Three victims in cabins. One in nightclub. Main staircase.' Pause. 'There must be twenty or thirty of them, piled up on each other. That's it. There are no portholes on the decks beneath this one. Take her up.'

'What about the debris trails? And the visor?'

'We'll do the debris trails now. Not the visor. We don't know where it is. We'll have to look for it from the surface.'

Fox takes *Starsky* back round the *Amphitrite* and over the wonky lines of debris which trail away from the stricken hulk. A giant underwater rubbish dump: two cars nestling together, their bonnets touching in a light kiss; patches of floor covering; torn metal sheets; suitcases spilling their contents like mushy food from a baby's mouth.

No more bodies. All those still down here have at least been afforded the most basic dignity of being buried inside the ferry, even though the fish will get them all the same, tear the skin from their faces and their eyes from their sockets.

Fox empties *Starsky*'s ballast tanks. They return in silence to the surface, where they bob for a few minutes while the mechanics lower the winch over the *Wayfarer*'s side. A brief dangling in mid-air as *Starsky* is plucked from the sea and placed on deck. The mechanics swarm over the submersible, worker bees busy round their queen. Frank and Fox haul themselves out of the main hatch and walk back to the *Wayfarer*'s cockpit.

Frank is still clutching the sick bag. Fox gestures towards it. 'Least you didn't need that.'

'Wasn't far off, I can tell you.'

*   *   *

It is only when Kate stops to fill up on the way back from seeing Scoular that she notices how dirty the car is. It offends her. She's seen too much filth these past days to take on any more than she has to. She buys a car-wash token when she goes in to pay for the petrol.

'If it doesn't go in first time, give it a smack,' says the attendant. 'That usually does the trick.'

He's right on both counts. The token doesn't go in first time, and the smack does do the trick.

Percussive maintenance, the oldest and still the most effective way to deal with recalcitrant machinery. Kate inches the car forward until the electronic sign switches from green to red, checks all the windows are wound up, turns the engine off, and waits for the furry blue rollers to start spinning.

The moment they do, she knows she's made a dreadful mistake. The rollers erupt in a shapeless blur, sending sheets of water hammering against the windscreen. They pause as if to tease her and then advance towards the car, outriders of a malevolent presence.

In an instant, the whole terror of the *Amphitrite* comes flooding back to her. Kate's car is the ferry, and the car wash is the storm and the sea. The car begins to rock as the rollers crawl snarling over the radiator grille, and Kate knows that the rocking will become more and more pronounced as the rollers try to capsize her. She puts her hands on the dashboard to steady herself. The blue whirl has her mesmerised, waiting only for the glass to shatter and the water to come pouring in and choke the life from her. In her ears a screaming roar, as if all the storm fronts in the world have gathered at this spot. She can hardly hear herself think. The panic comes on her in debilitating swathes of white.

Kate fumbles at the key, trying to turn the ignition and start the car. A brief mechanical grinding swept away by the din, and her fingers slip and fall before the engine can catch.

She sees her eyes reflected in the rear-view mirror, so wide that the pupils are entirely encircled by white.

The rollers touch the windscreen.

Her car is the ferry, a metal cage designed solely

191

to keep her inside. *Trap her.*

Kate jerks the car door open and stumbles out. Detergent in her eyes and mouth, and the rollers reaching out to draw her into their vortex. She throws up an arm to ward them off and kicks the car door shut behind her, slipping on the wet ground, sprinting back down the car rails and out on to the garage forecourt. The drivers who hold the petrol pumps to their vehicles' flanks like saline drips stare at her in astonishment.

Kate looks down at herself. Her clothes are plastered against the contours of her body, and she is covered from head to foot in foam.

*   *   *

The cashier takes Kate into a back room. He gives her a towel to dry herself and a cup of tea to calm her nerves. She nods mute thanks and tries to quell her shaking.

Stupid girl. She's just about been able to run a shower over her face, no more. Should have thought what the car wash would do to her.

One of the drivers who was filling up, a man in a dark red T-shirt and thin rimless spectacles, takes her car out of the wash area and parks it next to the air and water pumps. He comes into the back room and hands her the keys.

'There was a bit of water inside,' he says. 'I mopped it up. I know it's hot, but there must be better ways of cooling off, eh?'

She smiles weakly at him.

When her shaking has subsided to a manageable tremens—no worse than a hangover—Kate gets back in the car and drives jerkily home. Her legs

192

feel weak, and she finds herself pumping the pedals harder than she should do.

Back home, she pulls off her clothes and shoves them in the washing machine, throws on a selection of new ones, and goes to Queen Street and straight to Blaikie's cell.

'It wasn't Scoular who scratched you. It was Petra. It was Petra, when you killed her.'

'I didn't kill her. It happened just as I said. You think I was lying about Scoular?'

'No. But you haven't told me everything.'

'I *have*.'

'Someone other than Scoular gave you that scratch. That person is most likely to have been Petra.'

Blaikie stares at her. Kate continues. 'You told me you copped an ABH plea as the lesser of two evils. That's bollocks. You were trying to head me off the scent, weren't you? Because I was right all along. You *did* kill her.'

'I didn't.'

'Then tell me everything that happened. *Everything*. And remember that posters of your ugly mug are all over this city. Someone's bound to have seen something, someone's going to come forward sooner or later. If I find that you've been holding out on me, a murder charge will be the least of your worries.'

The extra spark of defiance in Blaikie's eyes has gone. 'I didn't kill her. You have to believe that.'

'*Everything*.'

He swallows hard.

'I *did* go after her. Once I'd dealt with Scoular.'

'How did you find her?'

'I rang her mobile.'

193

Another point he lied about earlier. 'And?'

'I told her I wanted to see her.'

'Not that you'd just beaten up her boss?'

'No. She wouldn't have agreed to see me otherwise, would she?'

'You sweet-talked her into seeing you?'

'Yeah.'

'Told her she must have had a hard day?'

'Yeah.'

'Where did you meet her?'

'Back at my place.'

'Where you told her what?'

'That I'd seen her and Scoular.'

'And?'

'I lost it. Called her a slag. Said she was sleeping with him just to keep her job.'

'What did *she* say?'

'That I had no right to be spying on her. That he was sensitive. He understood, he gave her space. Everything she said I wasn't. All that shit.'

'But she never denied it?'

'No.'

'And you hit her?'

She might be imagining it, but does Blaikie duck her gaze for a second as he answers?

'Yes.'

'That's when she scratched you?'

'Yes.'

'And then?'

'She left. Told me she never wanted to see me again.' He pauses. 'And she never did.'

'She didn't say where she was going afterwards?'

He shakes his head.

Standing in the cell, Kate withdraws into herself for a moment.

Always assume it's *not* him. Doubting, always doubting.

Feet and hands chopped off. Snakes. This isn't common or garden violence.

A question to ask, whoever Blackadder is. *Why?* What does Blackadder fulfil in himself, that he has to do this?

Blackadder. The name reminds her of what she has to do next.

*   *   *

Frantic work in the incident room. Kate senses the vibe the moment she walks in: desperation tinged with determination, looking for the breakthrough. Ferguson turns to her.

'What's with the costume change? Are we all about to be transferred to onerous duties on the Milan catwalk?'

Her brittle smile just about hides the bright panicky memory of the car wash. She distils the essence of Blaikie's admissions into a few easy sentences for Ferguson, and asks him what news he has. He shakes his head.

'None to speak of. Vehicle and pedestrian checks still drawing blanks. Still bashing away with the sex offenders, as it were.'

'Who's checked the register of snake owners?'

'I was just about to do it.'

'Well, do it *now*.'

Ferguson picks up his phone and taps out the number of an internal extension. Kate looks out of the window, across the rooftops towards the long golden stretch of beach. From this distance, the sea looks like ridged plastic. Benign, impersonal. Dead.

195

In the massive blue-grey expanse of the bay, the tiny black patch of a trawler flashes sporadic white as it rides the waves and glints in the sun.

'Dangerous Wild Animals Act, 1976?' Ferguson's voice from behind her.

'That's the one.' She answers without looking round.

His voice again, talking to the archivist. 'If it's just them, you might as well give me the names over the phone.'

The whisper of his pen across the paper.

'No record of anyone named Drew Blaikie?' Pause. 'Righto. Thanks.'

A click of plastic as he replaces the receiver. Kate turns towards him.

'Four people registered in the Aberdeen area.' He taps his biro against the pad. 'Daniel Astbury, Imelda Trafford, Archie Forster, Lawson Kinsella.'

'Discount the woman. Go and check out the others.'

'You think it's one of them?'

'Not for a second. Blackadder won't be stupid enough to have registered himself. But they have to be checked. And I need a couple of people to follow up other leads. Internet reptile chat rooms. Purchases of frozen rodents, from pet shops and on-line suppliers. Wherever he gets the adders from, he has to feed them.'

'What about magazines? Is there not a *Snake Monthly* or something?'

'Matheson—the university snake man—said it's mostly done via the Internet now. But tell them to see what they can find. Any magazines, get their subscription lists.'

'Are there snake porn mags? *Playboa?*

Serpenthouse?'

Kate groans good-naturedly. 'Any more of that, you'll be directing traffic. I'll be in my office if you need me.'

*   *   *

Kate takes all the reference books she can find in the police library and signs them out. In the corridor outside the incident room, she bumps into Renfrew. He gestures at the books.

'Trying to find out what makes our man tick?'

'Trying.'

'If you don't have any joy, you might think of calling a profiler in. That guy from Heriot-Watt, for example. The Edinburgh boys speak highly of him.'

'I'll certainly consider it.'

She goes through into her office, kicks the door shut behind her, and starts going through the books.

Snakes. Snakes. Why snakes?

Trawl, note, think. *Why?*

Genesis, chapter three. 'Now the serpent was more subtle than any beast of the field which the Lord God had made . . . The serpent beguiled me, and I did eat. And the Lord God said unto the serpent, Because thou hast done this, thou art cursed above all cattle, and above every beast of the field; upon thy belly shaft thou go, and dust shalt thou eat all the days of thy life. And I will put enmity between thee and the woman, and between thy seed and her seed; it shall bruise thy head, and thou shalt bruise its heel.'

The Garden of Eden, where the serpent tempted Eve. The Garden of Eden, which

Matheson said couldn't have existed.

Does the snake somehow denote seduction? Blackadder as the snake, and Petra as Eve? Someone who'd showed Petra forbidden fruit? *Another* lover, one that neither Blaikie nor Scoular knew about? Another lover on the quiet. More deceit. Speaking with forked tongue?

No. Snakes use their tongues to smell, not to speak. Blackadder will know that.

Kate keeps looking.

'The tale of the snake in Eden can be seen as symbolising God's victory over Satan.'

Not in this case. The sex angle gives the lie to anything messianic.

'Perhaps paradoxically, snakes are often associated with healing—maybe because their constant skin shedding hints at immortality. A serpent is entwined around a staff on the badge of the Royal Army Medical Corps, after the Roman god of health Aesculapius. In some parts of the world, snakes are supposed to cure rheumatism, sore throats, headaches and backaches. Snake skins and gall bladders are used to ease childbirth. Snake flesh is used to help improve people's complexions, and snake fat is a popular antidote to premature baldness. The Chinese believe that eating snake flesh helps prevent tuberculosis, and use sea snakes to combat malaria and epilepsy.'

Health, immortality. On a dead body. Kate doesn't think so.

'Snakes have been objects of worship since ancient times. They were sacred to the Greeks, the Romans and the Minoans. The ancient Egyptians associated snakes with rain, and therefore fertility: the Egyptian goddess Ejo is usually depicted as a rearing cobra with an extended hood, and a similar symbol can be found on traditional pharaohs' headdresses. The Aztecs and Mayans also worshipped snakes. In contemporary times, the snake is venerated in many parts of Africa, Haiti (as part of voodoo rituals), south-west USA (especially among the Hopi Indians), and in India. In Rudyard Kipling's *Jungle Book,* the cobras killed by the mongoose Rikki-Tikki-Tavi were called Nag and Nagaina—the names given to the Hindu gods represented by that snake.'

Kate closes the last book with an angry thud. This is getting her nowhere. Give her a cut-and-dried domestic any day.

*   *   *

Frank isn't sure what's grating on him more: recurring flashes of the bodies on the sunken *Amphitrite*, or Lovelock's bullish stubbornness. Along with the heat, they're doing a pretty good job of unpicking his temper. He can feel himself fraying at the edges, and tries to relax himself back into full control. He knows that losing his cool will help no one. This is difficult enough without taking it down to a slanging match.

'Sir Nicholas,' he asks, being so reasonable it hurts, 'are you seriously telling me that the bomb theory story in the *Aberdeen Evening Telegraph* did not come from you?'

'I did not give them the story. They have good reporters.'

'Did you see it before publication?'

'Yes.'

'And you authorised its inclusion?'

199

'Yes. It's a legitimate line of inquiry.'

'But you didn't *give* them the story?'

'I told you. No.'

'OK. Then answer me this. The story was clearly written by someone who had seen the transcript of Christian Parker's statement. Some of the phrases he used are included verbatim, and the whole piece relies almost exclusively on his recollection of events.'

'Maybe the reporter spoke to him in person.'

'I rang the Infirmary before I came here. The only visitors Parker has seen are his family and myself. There is a policeman outside his door who confirmed this. No phone calls have been put through to his room. Therefore, the only people from whom that story could have come are those who've seen the transcript. And I know that no one in my office who's seen it has talked to your paper. *Your* paper.'

'I don't think I like your tone.'

'Every time I conduct one of these investigations, it seems that the MAIB is the only body interested in uncovering what actually happened. Everyone else has some sort of agenda to cover things up.'

'The fearless crusader for truth. Spare me.'

'And it's the same again here. Let me read this to you.' Frank picks up his copy of yesterday's *Aberdeen Evening Telegraph* and goes to a paragraph which he has ringed in red. He reads it aloud. ' "If the existence of a bomb on board the *Amphitrite* is conclusively proved, it will almost certainly prompt an extensive review of security procedures at ports throughout the EU. Ferry remains one of the easiest methods of travel:

check-in times are short, and in most cases tickets are valid for the first available vessel. Increased security measures would almost certainly make such procedures more cumbersome and time-consuming, and would provoke a vehement and concerted industry-wide response." '

Frank puts down the paper and looks at Lovelock.

'*Industry-wide.* That's the key, isn't it? If the *Amphitrite* was sunk by a bomb, every operator would be in the same boat. A bomb could happen to anybody. All carriers are vulnerable to external threats. So any security measures would have to be implemented across the board. Which in turn means that everyone would lose out, not just Seaspeed. If you have to suffer, you're going to make everyone else suffer with you. A bomb would suit you just fine, wouldn't it? It would mean that the *Amphitrite* didn't sink because of faulty design, materials or maintenance. Passengers put off by the bomb won't travel by ferry at all. But passengers put off by bad design or maintenance will switch custom to one of your competitors. If there was a bomb, it wasn't your fault. That's what it boils down to.'

'That's absolutely—'

'And now let me tell you this. There was no bomb on board that ship.'

Lovelock's reaction proves beyond doubt that Frank's diagnosis of Seaspeed's attitude was correct. The expression on Lovelock's face is more than disbelief: it is the anguished despair of having a main plank kicked away.

'That's impossible,' Lovelock says. 'Parker was quite definite on that point.'

'And quite wrong. The *Amphitrite* was not bombed, nor was it holed below the waterline in any other way. We checked that ship from stem to stern and back again.'

'No. No.'

'What we *did* find was that the outer bow door had been ripped off.'

'By a bomb.'

'No. A bomb would have blasted the door clean off. This had been *torn* away. There was no bomb on board. That is not a matter for debate. And believe me, I wouldn't say so unless I was sure. I received an anonymous letter in the post this morning, claiming responsibility for the bomb and threatening to send *me* a bomb—a letter bomb—unless I desisted from my investigation. I now know that the letter was a crank. But I only know that because I'm sure there was no bomb. And the quicker we disabuse the public of the notion that there was, the better. That's why I want my findings to be carried in your paper this afternoon, as fully and prominently as the original story yesterday.'

'Impossible.'

'Either that, or I shall get myself on every news programme from here to Plymouth and tell them not only that there was no bomb, but also how uncooperative Seaspeed are being. I will emphasise that Seaspeed are in financial trouble—yes, Sir Nicholas, I can read between the lines of the business pages too—and outline how and why the bomb theory suits you so well.'

Lovelock stares hard at him for long seconds before speaking.

'I can get the paper to print what you've found, but I can't guarantee where they'll put it or how much prominence they'll give it.'

'You own that paper. You can guarantee anything you like. Same place, same typeface, same size. Or I go elsewhere. Your choice.'

The muscles in Lovelock's cheeks stand proud under his skin.

'The editor's name is Cameron Shillinglaw.' He measures every bitter word. 'I'll let him know you're coming.'

*   *   *

A fruitless afternoon on the Petra Gallacher case. Everyone checking everything, and not a decent lead between them. One of those days when Kate feels as if she's walking in treacle.

She delays the afternoon meeting by fifteen minutes in order to deal with Petra's mother Eleanor, who has come to ask that Petra's body be officially released for her funeral on Friday. Kate checks with Hemmings that all the post-mortem work has been done, signs the necessary forms, and takes them down to the interview room where Eleanor is waiting.

The flesh round Eleanor's eyes is pink and puffy from crying. Kate squeezes Eleanor's trembling hands as she gives her the paperwork. She wants to tell Eleanor how she finds herself rooting for Petra even now, how she champions the dead girl's memory. She wants to say that she wishes she'd known Petra in life rather than just in death.

But Kate knows that Eleanor Gallacher doesn't want her sympathy. She wants her to catch the man who killed her daughter.

The coroner records a verdict of accident for Connie's death. He refuses to blame Ivan for what happened. He stresses that the family has suffered a tragedy, and that apportioning culpability—those are his exact words, the boy has to look them up in the dictionary at school—would be neither proper nor helpful. Ivan looks at Ailish when the coroner says this. She doesn't look back.

A few weeks later, Ivan gets a job deep-sea fishing. He is no longer trawling the shoreline on the short day runs, but going right out into the North Sea, in the wide-open ocean where the work is tougher and the pay better. He is away for long stretches now, two or three weeks at a time.

The moment Ivan's out of harbour, Ailish acts as if the boy doesn't exist. She talks to Kathryn and even to Hero, but never to him. His food is on the table and his plate is cleared when he finishes, but that's it.

The first time the trawler comes home, its deck slippery with blood and fish oil, the women run down to the harbour to welcome their men back. Ailish walks slowly behind them, trudging down the road with heavy steps. When she sees Ivan in his yellow oilskins step off the prow and on to dry land, her shoulders slump, and she turns round and goes back up to the house.

The boy hears her that night, while Ivan is in the pub toasting the catch with the rest of the crew. She is muttering to herself in a low intent monotone. 'He comes back. Folk lose husbands and sons. Lindsey MacQueen over the fields lost three in one trip. But not me. He comes back safe

204

and sound, and there's always some poor bugger who doesn't. Why can't that bugger be Ivan? I wouldn't grieve for him. I'd dance a reel on his grave and spit on the earth. Every minute he's on that boat, I pray for him to drown. Even when they're in harbour, I hope he slips on the deck and goes into the shallows, knocks his head or something, and by the time they fish him out it's too late. Fat chance. They say the sea gives and it takes away, like the Lord. Well, Lord, he's yours. Take him.'

*   *   *

The third time Ivan goes deep-sea fishing, Ailish begins her affair with Ivan's cousin Craig.

The betrayal is all the sweeter not only for being in the family, but for the long-held animosity between Ivan and Craig. Their fathers were brothers, and like many brothers, they fought and made up, fought and made up. Then they decided to go into business together, an ill-considered venture in the already overcrowded field of marine chandlering. The shop went bust in a spectacularly short period, each brother blaming the other first of poor management and then of fraud and embezzlement. This time, there was no reconciliation after the fight. The animosity lingered, festered, grew, filtered down through the generations.

Ailish and Craig aren't in the least bit subtle about it. Craig more or less moves in, eating with the family at breakfast and then again at dinner. Ailish says he's just staying while Ivan is away, because she feels safer with a man around the house. But the boy sees them when they don't think he's watching: Craig pressed up against her as she does the washing-up, the smug smile on his face as his footsteps echo round the house.

Kathryn and the boy don't speak much to Craig. They stay just the right side of polite, but they know that something is going on that shouldn't, even if they are too young to make proper sense of it. And at night they hear their ma with another man, Craig in Ivan's place and grunting like Ivan does, but now they can hear her too for the first time. She moans, and the boy wonders if she's in pain—then she laughs, and the boy is reassured that she's all right, and he rolls over, and as he falls asleep he wonders whether he heard just a smear of malice in that laugh, pleasure not just in satisfying herself but also in hurting Ivan.

Ailish and Craig talk in low voices around the house, afraid that the children will hear them. Terse, urgent dialogue, plans being made, modified. Maybe they're going to run away together. Maybe she's asking Craig to make himself scarce when Ivan comes home. Even on these long trips, Ivan's never away for more than three weeks, a month at the outside.

More conversation in these weeks than there has been in years with Ivan around. She takes the boy aside one day. Her voice is unusually tender.

'Not a word to your da when he comes back. He and I have got things to sort out.'

There is a terrible storm the day Ivan returns. His boat makes it back just in time, running for shore hours ahead of the maelstrom. They come into Aberdeen harbour with the exhilaration of burglars, those who have cheated the angry sea gods, taken their food—the boat is heaving with fish—and made it back. The ship docks just after dawn, and they spend all morning sorting the fish.

On his way back home, Ivan goes via the asylum in Stonehaven. His mother is there, but she is no longer the reason he goes. She hasn't even recognised him for the past few years. He goes because he's screwing one of the other patients: Cassie McKechnie, pale and lank and scrawny, cheeks hollowed and eyes which sparkle with the embers of perpetual challenge. Their sex is rough and loveless, the only way Ivan knows how. It is not even propelled by anything which could be dignified with the term 'lust'. He is there and she is there, and they come together with all the ease and passion of two people shaking hands.

Cassie is due for release. She lives in the next-door village to the family, and no one has come to collect her. Ivan says he'll take her home.

Why does he bring her back to the cottage first? Does he know about Ailish and Craig, and is determined to show that he too can go outside the marriage? Or does he just not think, because that's the kind of man he is?

Out in the bay, the storm has started. The rain falls in lancing swathes from clouds miles distant.

'Who's this?' Ailish's voice, harsh and peremptory. Her and Ivan have long since given up being civil.

'Cassie.'

'Where did you find her?'

They're talking about her as though she's not there. Cassie looks from one to the other. Her eyes are bloodshot.

'I went to see Ma. Cassie lives just over the hill.

207

They asked me to bring her back.'

'Been fucking her, have you?'

'And if I have?'

Ailish slides her gaze over Cassie. 'Fucking barnpot, are you?'

Cassie stares at her, says nothing.

'Well, there's nothing here for you. You can go now.' She nods towards the hills. 'Go on. Away with you.'

'Leave her be, Ailish. The least we can do is give her a cuppa.'

'Can we, fuck. Go on.' She flicks her hand, shooing Cassie as she would a seagull.

'For the love of heaven, Ailish. We'll give her a cuppa, and then I'll take her home.'

Ailish is opening her mouth to remonstrate when the scream comes, Cassie with her mouth wide open and her eyes tight shut, and the noise she is making is more feral than human.

They look at her in astonished stillness, Ailish and Ivan together, he half-turned and her with hands half-raised, frozen stiff by the noise.

Cassie's scream changes in pitch and volume and slides into words shrieked clear and staccato. 'How to tell the climax? Comes so quickly, see. Murder's strong right arm! She traps him, writhing. And now he buckles, look, the bath swirls red. Stealth in the cauldron.'

Her skinny chest heaves with the effort. Her eyes jerk open. Ailish runs over to Cassie and shakes her.

'Shut up! Shut up!'

Cassie looks straight through her. Ailish slaps her now, hard. 'What are you talking about? What, you loon?'

Cassie's head rolls with the blow, comes back to rest Her eyes slowly focus on Ailish. When she speaks, her voice is flat.

'This house breathes with murder.'

She breaks from Ailish's grip and runs back down the road.

*   *   *

Cassie comes back with the police an hour later. The family—ha! what a travesty, one child dead and both parents unfaithful—is sitting at the kitchen table. Ivan is still in his oilskin trousers, with his jacket hung on the peg behind the door. The rich, nauseating tang of fish has percolated off his clothes and through the house.

No one has said much since Cassie left. She has unnerved both Ivan and Ailish, no matter how much they try to dismiss her ranting as what it surely is, the tattle of a lunatic. But Cassie's fervour and intensity have made her words hard to ignore. Like many of those who live on Scotland's east coast, Ivan and Ailish are products of their environment. The harshness of the wind and the sea makes for suspicious and untrusting people. They say that on the west coast, where the weather is much gentler, the people are more open, milder. But here, they keep their front doors closed, and not only against the gales which swoop across the ragged expanses of sea. They trust only those they've known for ever, and often not even them. No one here is blind to the dark side of their natures. For them, good and evil are realities, not abstract religious concepts. That is why Cassie's outburst has affected them so. There's much in her that isn't so different from them, when you look closely.

And now she's back, with the police.

She stops dead before they reach the front door. 'Not going in there!' Her voice is shrill.

'Come on.' The heavy tones of one of the officers.

'No.'

'Come. Or we'll drag you in.'

'No!'

The terror in her cry is real. She may be mad, but she's not shamming.

'All right.' The same officer again, evidently the senior. 'Doddie'll stay here with you. I'll go and see what all the fuss is about.'

They hear him come over the threshold, rubber soles squeaking on the stone floor, and into the kitchen. He sizes them up in a quick, practised glance. A nuclear family the country would be proud of: the father as hunter-gatherer, the mother as homekeeper, the children polite and docile.

'Young fruitbat outside blathering on about murder.' His expression suggests that this isn't the first time Cassie has crossed paths with the law.

'No one been murdered here.' Ivan gestures around the table. 'Just the family, same as it ever was.'

'How did she come to be here?'

'Me ma's at the home up in Stonehaven. I went to see her this morning, and the staff asked me if I'd take Cassie home. She lives over the hill.'

Ailish says nothing. Her quarrels with Ivan remain within the house.

'In and out of places all her life, that one.' The officer looks fleetingly sorry for Cassie. 'Her "out"

210

has just changed back to an "in". Right. Sorry to have bothered you.'

His boots, leaving them, squeak on the floor and crunch on the gravel. The squad car's engine fades into silence. Ivan hauls himself to his feet.

'I'm going to take a bath.'

The storm reaches the shore at sundown, so unrelenting and primal that it seems more like divine vengeance than a meteorological phenomenon.

There are just three of them at dinner. 'Your da's gone out to sea,' Ailish tells the children. 'In the trawler, the little one he keeps down in the harbour. He's gone to look for the other boats out there, give them what help he can. He's nuts. I told him so. He's going to get himself killed.'

After dinner, Kathryn and the boy lie in bed and listen to the angry pounding of rain driven against windowpane. Ailish comes into their room, agitated. 'I'm going to look for your da. He shouldn't have been gone this long.'

The boy shudders when he hears this. No matter how bad the storm seems on land, it's always twice as bad out in the monochrome world of a night-time sea, the water black and white, the spray which streams from the broken surf, waves rearing up over the boat like striking cobras with backs arched before they slam down pulverising hard on deck.

Ivan, who hates his wife and fucks the lunatic, prepared to risk everything for the men he works with.

'You two, stay here,' says Ailish. 'For God's sake don't go out in this.'

She comes back in the small hours, soaked

211

through and breathless. Kathryn and the boy are still awake, unable to sleep for fear of their father out in the storm.

'No sign,' says Ailish. 'Couldn't see a thing.'

And so they wait.

The storm goes down, the sun comes up and the first searchers arrive at the harbour, Ivan's fellow fishermen in their bright yellow oilskins, climbing into their boats and heading out to sea, shaking their heads at his folly. The crowd on shore grows like Topsy. It tramps along the beach and pokes sticks in the shallows, a swarming pantomime of ineffectiveness.

The first trawler comes back in around lunchtime, and even before it's docked the boy knows they've found something. It's in the way the fishermen move on board. Usually they sway and roll with the sea's motion, but today they seem slightly out of kilter, half a beat off. Two of them on the foredeck, old Gordon Munro and young Murray McCulloch, arguing as they tie the boat up. Their yellow-clad forearms jab the air as they set off up the hill. McCulloch wants to hurry: he keeps making little jerky movements with his knees and shoulders, as if about to break into a run. But Munro walks slowly with his head bowed, determined to retain some dignity as a messenger of death, and he makes McCulloch travel at his pace.

They come into the house. There will be no preamble, no softening of the blow. Ailish would not expect it, and nor would she ask it.

'We found some timbers floating away in the next bay,' says Munro. 'One of them had *Orca* painted on. They're from Ivan's boat. I'm sorry.'

Ailish gets to her feet. Her expression is blank. 'I'll come and get them.'

*   *   *

A restaurant on the main shopping drag of Union Street, the same one they ate at the night before they set off for Norway. Same table, same places as before. Three empty chairs for where Davenport, Matt and Sylvie should have been.

No one is quite sure what this dinner is supposed to represent. A wake, tribute to the dead, gratitude still to be alive? Maybe all of them, or none.

Half a dozen young men are shouting and laughing at the next-door table. The waitress has to raise her voice to make herself heard over them.

'Oil workers?' asks Kate.

'You got it. Last night onshore before they go back to the rigs.' She pauses, looks round the table. 'You're not with the oil business, are you?'

'No.'

'I shouldn't say this, because I know they provide lots of money for the city and that, but—sometimes I just wish the oil would run out and they'd all piss off. All ten thousand of them or however many there are here.'

As if on cue, one of the men shouts across at the waitress. She spins around.

'I'm here to take your orders, not your shit,' she snaps. 'I'll be with you in a second.'

They whoop and holler sarcastically. Kate flashes her police badge at them, and they quieten fast.

The waitress goes round the table, writing carefully on her pad. She checks their orders back

213

at them and heads off towards the kitchen.

'Hey, Alex,' says Jason. 'Did you check out the arse on her?'

'For God's sake, Jason,' says Sinclair. 'Don't be such an oaf.'

Glowing with the warmth of their shared secret, Kate winks at Alex. He winks back.

The table lapses into silence, listening to the now subdued banter from nearby and lost in their own thoughts. Kate thinks about oil, and what it's meant for her adopted city. One of the lowest levels of unemployment in the country, and earnings way above the national average. A boom which has lasted since the seventies, when oil was first discovered in BP's Forties field, and which has been strong enough to survive two disastrous years in the mid-eighties when oil prices dropped by 800 per cent and 167 men were killed in the Piper Alpha explosion.

And what happens when the oil runs out?

The wine comes, sloshed into glasses and left untouched.

'Bugger this,' says Alex. 'Get your heads up, you bastards, and let's have a drink.' He takes a long, aggressive slurp from his glass. After a pause, Kate raises her glass, and then Jason, and in turn they all start to drink, and slowly the evening takes off.

Kate is sitting between Jason and Emmeline, and it is Jason who monopolises her to start with. A bandage is wound round his neck like a dirty white cravat, and Kate can see it flex when he swallows. With the weal on her cheek subsiding, Kate realises with a start that she is the only survivor without visible wounds. Alex has a large plaster on his left temple, Sinclair one on his cheek, Jean's right hand is in plaster, Emmeline is on crutches, and two of the fingers on Lennox's left hand are strapped together.

Kate's injuries are on the inside, buried beneath thick clothes and a desire to forget.

Jason is telling her about his divorce. She forces herself to listen and nod at the right places, though what she wants to do is drag Alex off to the ladies' and have him fuck her hard up against the wall.

'I feel as if someone has come along and torn my soul out. I still don't think it's really sunk in. It's such a cliché, but I half-expect to wake up and find that it was all a nightmare. And then the solicitor rings up for the fifth time in a morning, and I know it's not.'

As usual, he has placed himself slightly too near to her: Jason is the kind of man who could back someone into a corner in the Sahara. She can see the moisture on his lips all too well at such close range, and the sharp tang of his breath wafts around her face. Those apart, Kate thinks, he's not a bad-looking bloke. But he does himself no favours.

After what seems to Kate like hours detailing the minutiae of his married life, Jason gets up to go for a pee. The moment he's gone, Sinclair slides into Jason's chair and whispers in her ear.

'Something you want to tell me?'

She turns to him, smiling. 'Yes. The sooner science finds a cure for halitosis, the better.'

He laughs. 'His colleagues leave bottles of Listermint on his desk.'

'I'm not surprised.'

'And that's not what I meant about there being something you want to tell me. You and boy

215

wonder over there can hardly keep your eyes off each other. Which means that either you've just got it together, or you're just about to.'

'Well, when we get married, you can be best man.'

'Best man? I'll be the one giving you away, Kate.'

Frank outside the school, bending down to Leo, the letter in his shaking hands.

Kate, a daughter to the man who's not her father, and no daughter to the man who is.

Lovelock stands in the doorway of the restaurant, looking for them.

'Oh, look,' she says, glad of the distraction. 'There's Sir Nicholas.'

She waves at him. He raises a hand in reply and comes over.

'Sorry I'm so late. Got tied up with the inquiry. They've just recovered the visor.' He puts his head close to Kate's. 'Your father's a difficult bastard.'

She looks at him in surprise, unaware that he'd made the connection.

'Renfrew told me,' he explains.

'My father and I . . . we . . . I don't see much of him.'

She saw the paper this afternoon, saying there was no bomb. Guess it was a crank after all.

Lovelock hails the waitress. 'Could we have another chair, please?'

She indicates the three empty ones. 'You've got some there.'

'We'd like another one.'

The tone of his voice brooks no argument. The waitress shrugs, obviously marking him down as yet another difficult customer, and brings a chair over

216

from another table. Lovelock perches himself next to Sinclair, and they begin to chat.

Kate turns away, happy to let them get on with it. She gets up and walks outside, where she takes out her mobile and rings Bronagh.

'Auntie B, this may well be a late one. Is it OK if Leo stays with you tonight?'

'Of course. It'll be a pleasure.'

'How is he? Is everything OK?'

'Fine.'

Something in Bronagh's voice tickles at Kate. 'What?' Kate asks. 'What is it?'

'Leo's been asking who the man outside the school this morning was.'

'Did you tell him?'

'No. I thought you should be the one to do that.'

'I—I will. Thanks, Auntie B. I'll see you tomorrow.'

She ends the call and dials Ferguson.

'No joy on the snake men,' he says. 'Daniel Astbury's been on holiday since last Monday, Archie Forster's in a wheelchair, and Lawson Kinsella has never learnt to drive.'

'What about secondary follow-up? Internet, magazines, pet shops?'

'Most of the chat room stuff is pretty innocuous. Half of them were stupid e-mail names anyway— you know, Web Warrior, Knight Rider, that kind of stuff. *Snake Breeder* is sending its subscription list. I've got Lowe and Tennant trawling the pet shops. No joy as yet. Frozen rodents aren't doing that great a business, by the sound of it. Those they do sell tend to be small quantities. They're checking through the credit-card receipts. Of course, we're shafted if he used cash.'

217

'Anything else?'

'Lowe and Tennant are grousing about the job already. The others have taken to calling them . . .'

'The Pet Shop Boys?'

Ferguson laughs. 'Exactly. As you can imagine, they're chuffed.'

'OK. Let me know if anything else comes up.'

'Will do. How's your evening?'

'A laugh a minute.'

When Kate comes back to the table, she chats to Emmeline in sporadic bursts, and in between she watches the others: Jason now trying to flirt with Jean; Lovelock emphasising a point and Sinclair nodding; Lennox earnestly explaining sound and lighting techniques to Alex. 'The level 12 is all very well,' she hears Lennox say, 'but it only has two pre-sets. That makes it pretty limited. Once you get up to the Sirius range, the 24 and the 48, then you're talking memory and effects, and Bob's your uncle. You should see some of the things . . .'

Kate catches Alex's eye and winks at him again. He rolls his eyes theatrically. Lennox is in full flow, drawing diagrams on a napkin. He doesn't notice a thing.

It is past eleven when they leave. On the pavement, Jason hugs her goodnight and tries to kiss her mouth. She turns her head swiftly and feels his mouth smack damply against the corner of her jaw. If Kate didn't find the prospect so nauseating, she'd laugh.

Goodnights for all the others. A long lingering hug for Sinclair.

'You're going to be OK?' she asks.

'Fine.'

'I can always come and stay with you, if you

218

want.'

'That's kind. But I'm fine.'

She feels for him, home alone when everyone is hurting. But he's not the only one to live solo, and as he's often said to her, coming back to an empty bed is better than coming back to someone you no longer love or even like.

Kate and Alex work their separate ways round the group, little planets in their respective orbits. They come together when all the goodbyes are done and the group is dispersing.

Union Street stretches ahead of them, twinkling under the streetlamps as it shrinks to a grey-flanked vanishing point. They walk close together, not touching, talking easily.

'You're very close, you and Sinclair, aren't you?' he asks.

'He's been like a father to me. Whatever I've done, he's taken an interest in. He's advised me and supported me, but he's never judged me. You don't get that too often from people. And I can't tell you how many boyfriends he's been asked to pass judgement on.'

She feels his next question coming, and asks it back at him before he can get it out.

'What about your parents, Alex?'

'Dead. Both of them. Car crash, a few years ago.'

'I'm sorry.'

'You get used to it.' Pause. 'Well, you don't. But you live with it.'

*   *   *

In the bedroom later, wrapped warm in the duvet and around each other. Eyes shut, doze, eyes open,

219

world adjusting, eyelids heavy, eyes shut again. Kate sliding into sleep at last, random thoughts floating in her head. *Drew Blaikie, still in the cells. His forty-eight hours up at midday tomorrow. Charge him or let him go. Fire or fall back. The alarm clock. What time did I set it for? I can't afford to oversleep.*

She reaches out a hand. The clock is just beyond her reach—she can touch it, but not grip it. Her fingers push uselessly against its edge. It skitters off the bedside table and hits the wooden floor with a sharp 'crack'.

Alex starts, jackknifes, sits upright, rolling Kate away from him. He is breathing hard.

'It's OK,' says Kate. 'Alex, it's OK.'

He swallows.

'Jesus Christ. I'm sorry. I've been like that ever since—you know. Really jumpy. And yet really tired at the same time. Like my face is falling off, but I've got a massive speed buzz.'

She rolls back towards him and puts her head on his chest. His heart is racing.

'I'm a police officer, remember? I wouldn't know about speed buzzes.'

'Whatever you say.' She imagines him smiling. 'But the whole thing is weird. Everything's a paradox. I'm exhausted, but I'm alert. I try not to think about what happened, but I end up harking back to it the whole time. It's on the TV, it's in the papers, people talk about it in the street. As if *they* know the first thing about it. I just want to think about something else for once.'

'Blot it out. That's what I do.'

'Don't you think about it at all?'

'Not if I can help it.'

'Do you talk to anybody about it?'

220

'No.'

'Why not?'

'They weren't there. How can they understand?'

'I was there.' *I was there. I was there, and now I'm here.* 'I need to talk about it. And the person I'd most like to talk about it with is you.' She feels his hands move slightly over the swell of her buttocks. 'Come on. You can't resist it for ever.'

'Talk to you about it?'

'Yes.'

'Just you? Nobody else?'

'Just me.'

Moment after moment, spans marked on the second hand of her alarm clock.

'OK. But only to you. And vice versa.'

'But I . . .'

'If I trust you, you have to trust me back. It doesn't work otherwise.'

'Kate, you're . . .'

'You and me only. And only if I want to. Or nothing.'

'You're impossible.' He kisses the top of her head. 'Deal.'

She puts her hand between his legs. 'You know what they say?'

'What?'

'That there are only two types of men. Those who like blowjobs, and those who are dead.'

He laughs. 'Well, I'm very much alive.'

She gives him a playful squeeze. 'I can tell.'

*   *   *

Darkness and Alex is gone, the only trace a lingering smell on empty sheets. Kate flicks on the

221

light and squints at the alarm clock. Quarter to three.

He has left a note on the pillow. 'Couldn't sleep, didn't want to wake you. Sweet dreams.' Fluent and fast handwriting, sloping slightly right.

Kate knows that few things are more frustrating than lying wide awake next to someone sound asleep. So she can't really blame Alex for leaving. But still. It would have been nice to wake up with him. Another time, maybe. Hopefully.

She turns the light out and goes back to sleep.

THURSDAY

Bright camera flashes and the carcass of what a few hours ago was a woman. The cloud cover traps the heat as it hangs low and heavy over the city. When the sun shines on Aberdeen, the city sparkles like white marble: but when the day is dull and overcast, so the granite appears cold, hard, repellent and colourless.

Rather like Kate's mood as she looks at Blackadder's second victim, in fact.

Same pattern as last time. The hands and feet neatly cut off and arranged round the neck, and again the rippling black adder pinned to the chest, though this one watches the surrounding officers unblinkingly rather than lashing out. Kate and her colleagues keep their distance to avoid antagonising it.

Blackadder has again chosen woodland: this time, Tollohill Wood in Banchory-Devenick, south of the city centre and just off the Deeside Road. Between here and the coast, the oil company headquarters hulk and skulk through the haze: Total's elegant low brown block, the splayed glass and concrete of Shell.

Same pattern, and definitely the same killer. It can't be a copycat: the details about the snake and the severed extremities haven't been made public. But it is by no means a carbon copy of Petra Gallacher's death. Kate counts three, no, four, differences off the top of her head. For a start, this victim was old. Her hair is flecked with grey, and a lumpy tangle of varicose veins blotch the legs which lie twisted and visible where her dress has ridden up. Secondly, she has had her throat cut: a long grinning gash beneath her jaw, a second mouth. That apart, the attack looks to have been less ferocious than the one on Petra. There are fewer stab wounds, and those which there are look superficial. Four of Petra's wounds were fatal; here there is only one, and it is all too obvious.

It is the other two variations which catch Kate's eye the most, however.

A few yards away from the body is a knife, scuffed with dirt where it has been dropped. A typical kitchen knife, with a black handle and a smooth, sharp bottom edge. Single-edged, as Hemmings said it would be.

And on the victim's abdomen is a turd.

Ferguson points at it. 'Contempt?'

Kate shakes her head. 'At a guess, disturbed.'

'You don't say.'

'Not disturbed, as in state of mind. Disturbed, as in he was disturbed. Someone disturbed him. He's hyped up anyway. He gets a fright, shits himself and scarpers, dropping the knife as he does so. If he shat out of contempt, he'd have done it on Petra too.' She walks over to where Hemmings is standing. 'How long has she been here for?' she asks.

'I can't take a body temperature or check for rigor mortis until that damn snake has been removed. But I would say no more than a few hours.'

'Why?'

'There's no visible decomposition, and believe me, that wouldn't take long in this heat.'

'Not to mention that someone would surely have seen this in daylight hours. And Petra was killed at night.'

226

Kate turns to Ferguson. She can see herself reflected green in the anti-glare coating on his spectacles. 'You know what this *does* mean?' she says.

He nods. 'It can't be Blaikie.'

*   *   *

There are roadworks in town, forcing Ferguson to go the long way round via Justice Street.

'This was one of the main entrances to the city in the seventeenth and eighteenth centuries,' he says. 'Justice Port, it was called then. They used to decapitate notorious criminals and exhibit their heads on the gate.'

Kate looks at him. 'Now there's a tradition I wouldn't mind resurrecting.'

*   *   *

She bites the bullet and goes along personally to see Blaikie.

He is still asleep, sprawled across the cot with his blanket half kicked off. She turns on the light and watches without sympathy as he opens his eyes and instantly screws them shut again.

'Get up.'

He squints groggily at her. 'Huh?'

'You're not being charged with murder. You are being charged with ABH. The sheriff will see you this morning and arrange bail.'

'What time is it?'

'Ten past six.'

'I didn't get my full forty-eight hours. Shame.'

227

*   *   *

Kate can't face another stint in the autopsy room. She gets Hemmings to talk her through the salient points on the phone. He speaks in the cold language of his profession.

'Estimates from body temperature and degree of rigor mortis put the time of death at between three and four-thirty this morning. The fatal wound sustained is an incised wound of the neck. It measures 5 inches by 2, and is located at the level of the superior border of the larynx. The larynx and cervical vertebral column are exposed. The wound is diagonally oriented on the right side, and transversely oriented from the midline to the left side. Subcutaneous and intramuscular haemorrhaging—which shows up as very dark red, almost purple—is evident. The wound transects the left and right common carotid arteries, and incises the left and right internal jugular veins. All four have led to exsanguinating haemorrhage. The wound also transects the thyroid membrane, the epiglottis and the hypopharynx, and incises into the third cervical vertebra—though not into the spinal canal or cord.'

'In other words, he virtually cut her head off.'

'Exactly.'

James Buxton in Putney, the young army officer whom Silver Tongue had decapitated, a headless body on the floor, devastatingly out of place in a posh flat with hunting prints on the walls and the curtains tied back with tasselled straps.

'What else?'

'There are seven wounds to the left side of the neck and scalp. Five are superficial stabbing or

228

cutting wounds; the other two are largely indistinguishable from the main fatal wound. And there are multiple injuries to the hands: defence wounds, as before.'

'Those scalp and neck wounds seem terribly bunched.'

'Their angle and position would suggest that he inflicted them from behind. And the blood splatter and flow at the scene is consistent with the victim being face-down, her neck hyperextended, at the moment the fatal sharp force injury was delivered.'

'He held her down and pulled her head up.'

'Yes. Probably by her hair. The cut to the throat is clean, which indicates limited struggle. She'd probably have been immobilised by the constellation of neck and scalp wounds. And with that amount of haemorrhage, she'd have died in less than a minute.'

'Anything else markedly different from before?'

'Only that she'd eaten recently. Examination of the gastric contents reveals approximately 500 millilitres of chewed semisolid food in the stomach. Recognisable food particles are pieces of pasta appearing to be rigatoni, and fragments of apparent spinach leaves. The rest is partially digested non-recognisable food material. That apart, much the same.'

'Semen?'

'Yes.'

'Torture?'

'As before. Histamine and serotonin levels are virtually off the scale.'

Kate grits her teeth.

*   *   *

229

Faces turned towards her, expectant. The trail is fresh, and the hunters champ at the bit. Kate knows that the hard part often comes later, keeping morale up when days have gone by and still there is nothing. The irony that a new victim acts as a fillip to the investigation is not lost on her.

'The victim has been identified as Elizabeth Hart, aged fifty-two, a freelance editor and proofreader. Petra Gallacher wasn't just a one-off. He's in this for the long run. Let's use it. He's doubled the body count, but he's about quintupled what we know about him.'

She looks around the room.

'There are two things here: what, and why. Let's start with what. The presence of the faeces and the knife point to him being disturbed at some point in his three-part process: torture, killing, and arranging. Later rather than earlier, I would hazard. Hemmings said Elizabeth's histamine and serotonin levels were very high—"virtually off the scale" were his exact words—which indicates that he'd managed to get through most or all of the torture we saw with Petra. But Elizabeth's body wasn't as mutilated as Petra's, the snake wasn't pinned to the chest as securely, and the knot around her left hand was rather loosely tied. He finished off in a hurry, basically. So much of a hurry, in fact, that he dropped the knife and shat himself. Why? Because he could hear someone approaching, or because he was actually seen.'

Kate pauses, not only for effect but to let some of those scribbling notes catch up.

'It is absolutely crucial that we find the person who disturbed Blackadder. This person may not

230

even be aware that they did. It may have been someone in a car on the nearest road, the B9077, or lovers looking for some solitude. Anything near enough to frighten him. If whoever disturbed him *did* see what was going on, they may well have scarpered. Maybe they were doing something they shouldn't have been, and don't want us or anyone else to know why they were there. There are lots of maybes. But we simply have to find this person. Have to.'

She holds up the transparent evidence bag containing the knife.

'This is the murder weapon. A Jensen Laser. Single-edged, bog standard kitchen knife. Mass-produced, relatively cheap. Easy to buy, and he'd have used cash if he has any sense. He could have had it for years, and he could have bought it anywhere from here to Penzance. Even so, I want all sales records in the area checked. Just as importantly, I want all retailers warned that he may try and purchase a replacement—either this very model or one quite similar. Every time someone buys one, get the shop to call here. If the purchaser uses a credit card, the retailer can pretend there are verification problems. If it's a cash transaction in a large store, get store security to detain them. If it's a small store and we don't get there in time, we can at least lift the note or coins they used and fingerprint them.'

'That's going to be popular in the shops.' A voice from the back of the room. 'Armed police descending on innocent housewives.'

'Tell that to someone who gives a shit. Which—talking of shit—brings me neatly on to the next point. Now we know that the blood under Petra's fingernails came from Blaikie, and that Blaikie is not the killer, we're back to just the semen in terms of DNA matching. But we may also be able to get some DNA off the turd left on the body. A sample has been sent to the Forensic Science Service Unit in Birmingham. They have recently made some substantial breakthroughs in the field of mitochondrial DNA, which is found in faeces and other "dead" body tissue such as hair and bone. Mitochondrial DNA is located in a different part of the cell from conventional chromosomal DNA, and does not degrade. But it will take a week or two before any results come through, and even then we're dependent on there being a match with an existing suspect sample. So we can't rely on that.

'I want Elizabeth Hart's life picked apart. Did she and Petra Gallacher have any mutual acquaintances? It's doubtful, not only because they probably moved in very different circles— everything about them looks different—but also because Blackadder wouldn't be that stupid. So I particularly want to know where Elizabeth went and what she did. I want something which tallies her movements to those of Petra Gallacher. I want to know where he saw them. This is a *visual* crime, that's obvious in the ways the bodies are arranged. Visuals are very important to Blackadder.'

She pauses again.

'That's the what. Here's the why. Everything now points to Blackadder being a serial killer. As you know, killers of this kind usually fall into one of two categories: process-focused or act-focused, also known as disorganised or organised. The process/act terms are the ones used by the criminologists Holmes and de Burger, whose work some of you are familiar with. "Organised" and "disorganised" are used by the FBI, whose work I'm sure all of you are familiar with.'

There is a slight ripple of laughter.

'The divisions are by no means foolproof, but they're a useful guide. In this case, we are almost certainly looking at a process-focused, or disorganised, killer. Such a killer uses more excessive violence than his opposite number, and often engages in dismemberment or abuse of the dead victim. All three aspects are clearly prevalent in this case: the frenzied violence of the stabbing, the removal of the extremities, and the torture and sexual violation which the victims suffer. He's a sadistic sexual psychopath. He tortures his victims to obtain the maximal orgasm he can't get any other way. He doesn't want sexual partners, he wants casualties. His ultimate sexual turn-on is total domination and humiliation of a helpless prey. He murders for the thrill of it, not for the end goal of the dead victim. Such killers show little evidence of extensive pre-crime planning, and usually pick their victim at random or semi-random. Selection is often done visually—the killer sees someone and likes the look of them. Petra was an attractive girl. She would have been a sitting duck for someone like that.'

Sherwood it is who makes the obvious point. 'But Elizabeth was no beauty.'

'True. But who can tell what Blackadder's tastes run to?'

Sherwood makes a moue.

'I understand your scepticism,' says Kate. 'But if you want further evidence, look at the other side of the coin. Act-focused or organised killers murder

233

quickly and efficiently, and do not mutilate as often as the disorganised offender. They tend to plan out the crimes in great detail, perhaps stalking the victims for weeks on end, and they work out elaborate disposal schemes for the body. Blackadder made no attempt to hide either body. They were left there to be found by the first person who came past—as it happens, a morning runner and the night-watchman at one of the nearby reservoirs. They were *meant* to be found.'

*   *   *

Anger burning brightly at Kate's core, but still the cold won't melt.

'Hi. I'm Sally, the production assistant. Do you want me to take some of those clothes for you? It gets awfully hot under the TV lights.'

'I'm fine. Thank you.'

'It really does. That's why the newsreaders have to wear that special deo—'

'I said, I'm fine.'

'OK.' Sally checks her watch. 'You're on in three.' She hurries off, looking for someone else to infect with her busy nervousness.

The newsreader is reading through her notes. A flesh-coloured earpiece tails in tight curls around the back of her neck, and she talks back to the voice inside it. 'All right, John . . . No, that's fine. We can do the Pittodrie story at lunch.'

The studio buzz falters at the ramparts of Kate's mind. *What gives you the right, Mr Blackadder? How do you justify what you do? What is it? An absence of love, of empathy? Or maybe you think you're something special, that laws don't apply to you—or at*

234

least that you can pick and choose the ones you want to obey. We all do that, don't we? Break the speed limit, play our music too loud, have a joint now and then. But we don't go round slicing people's throats and cutting their hands and feet off. We don't mobilise just about the largest manhunt in Grampian Police history because of the way we get our kicks.

In the rational part of her brain, Kate recognises that she must remain as dispassionate as possible. Getting emotionally involved, wanting success too much, both will work against her. Kate tells herself that the best way is not to give a toss—the person who can walk away from conflict often has the advantage—but she can't bring herself not to care, not now she's seen the histamine readings, not when she has even the slightest concept of the pain Petra Gallacher and Elizabeth Hart went through in the hours before they died.

In the past, hunting killers or rapists, Kate has been surprised to find that she doesn't always dislike the unknown suspect. Not this time.

The monitor is running the story. Images of the scene in Tollohill Wood: striped police tapes flapping in the wind, forensics in their white suits. A shot of Elizabeth Hart's house, and a close-up on a grainy photograph of her. She looks like a sour-faced old bat. Probably just a bad picture. Back to the reporter in the woods, the microphone head mutated liquorice beneath his mouth, and then his name and location as he signs off. The newsreader turns to Kate.

'Detective Chief Inspector Kate Beauchamp is leading the investigation into the murders not only of Elizabeth Hart but of Petra Gallacher, the local reporter whose body was found two days ago. The

235

same killer is believed responsible for both murders. Detective, what kind of man are we dealing with here?'

Oh, he's a real sweetheart.

Kate remembers wryly what they taught her in media training: don't bother answering the question, just get your points across.

'Someone disturbed the killer this morning. We need to find this person, and urgently. If you were anywhere in the vicinity in the early hours of this morning, please come forward. Come to the Queen Street headquarters and ask for me, DCI Kate Beauchamp, or DI Peter Ferguson. You might have been driving on the B9077, you may have been at the reservoirs nearby. You may have seen something which only now makes sense to you, or you may be unaware that you came across a murder in progress. Maybe you were doing something illicit or illegal. I don't care, I'm not interested. I just need to talk to you.'

She has to make the witness come in, otherwise they'll have the world and his wife ringing in. Timewasters are less likely to present themselves in person. But equally she has to give that witness safeguards, an amnesty if need be.

'You heard our reporter talk about the climate of fear on Aberdeen's streets,' says the newsreader. 'We've got a record heatwave here, and yet women are too scared to go out alone. Just when they can go out and enjoy themselves, they have to stay at home. What advice would you give them?'

'Be careful. Public vigilance is one of the police's most effective weapons. If you see anything or anyone suspicious, let us know. If you know or live with someone whose behaviour has changed

236

recently, again, let us know. Don't worry that your suspicions may be unfounded. You are doing no one any favours by keeping quiet. We'd rather investigate a thousand duff leads than not know about the one which counts.'

'How close are you to catching this man?'

How close? What a moronic question. How long is a piece of string?

'We have a number of lines of inquiry which we're pursuing. I can't really . . .'

'Do you anticipate an imminent arrest?'

Stabbings of fury in Kate's throat.

She looks not at the interviewer but straight at the camera. Talk to them in their living-rooms, at their breakfast tables. Talk to them. Talk to *him.*

'If you are watching, I want to tell you this. You *are* going to be apprehended. We *are* going to catch you. It's not a matter of if, but of when.' Control slipping away from her like Sylvie sliding across the *Amphitrite*'s bar, but it's too late now, she's committed, she has to go through with it, she *wants* to go through with it. 'You think you have some kind of right to do what you do. Let me tell you something. I will not rest until you are found, do you hear? Every moment I have, I dedicate to tracking you down. I will go to the ends of the earth to find you, if I have to. I will pursue you over land and sea. Wherever you look, I'm going to be there, right behind you. I don't stop until you do.'

The newsreader is looking at her in astonishment.

Kate swallows once, hard. Her entire body is shaking with the force of her anger.

Her trembling fingers move to the microphone clipped to the neck of her jersey. She unfastens it, lays it carefully on the table in front of her, stands up and walks off the set without saying another word.

*   *   *

And how little do we learn? Redfern Metcalfe, letting the Silver Tongue case destroy his life because he made it personal. In the depths of that cold winter in London, when the killings kept coming and we could do nothing to stop them, I saw what my boss was inflicting on himself and vowed that I would never let it happen to me. I would win and I would lose, but I would never let it get under my skin. And how little do we learn?

*   *   *

In Elizabeth Hart's house now, trying to raise her from the dead and look inside what used to be her life. The white heat of Kate's rage at Blackadder has cooled to a manageable simmer, a pilot light which burns steady but can spark into leaping blue flame at any moment.

Elizabeth lived on Victoria Street, just beyond the western extremity of Union Street. It is a distinctively Aberdonian street, with two-storey terraced houses on the east side and one-storey cottages with large dormer windows on the other. Elizabeth's house is one of the terraced ones, doorways tucked back off the street and ringed with sharp granite surrounds.

Inquiries among Elizabeth's neighbours have revealed almost nothing about Blackadder, and plenty about her. It seems safe to say she won't be

238

much missed. The consensus is that she was a terminal busybody, a woman who'd dedicated her life to prying and gossiping, and who by all accounts had made a decent fist of it. She'd talk to anyone who'd listen, detailing lurid tales of infidelity, troubled marriages and uncontrollable children, often on the flimsiest of evidence or from isolated vignettes observed and then taken totally out of context.

Working from home gave Elizabeth endless opportunity for domestic espionage. Her desk was set up so she could look out and down on to Victoria Street, and her kitchen enjoys a panoramic view of the backs of the houses in the next street. Three separate rows of houses—hers, the one opposite and the one behind—and all human life laid out for her delectation.

Elizabeth lived here for some twenty years—*just about the same time as the cold war with Frank*—and always alone: no lodger, no housemate, certainly no husband. In the early years, her mischief-making caused trouble, precipitating at least two divorces after she saw men intimate with women who weren't their wives. More recently, she became something of a joke, everyone knowing to take what she said with a large dollop of salt.

Standing in this empty house, Kate's not sure what's worse: have the whole world hate you, or the whole world laugh at you. When she considers, she knows exactly. It is surely better to inspire revulsion rather than contempt.

Just about the only halfway positive comment has been from next door, who told Ferguson to prepare for an explosion in the local crime rate now Aberdeen's most effective Neighbourhood

Watch has gone.

How awful to have a life so empty that your only pleasure is in other people's.

This could be me in years to come—not the prying and the gossip and a life passed by, but that awful sense of loneliness when every night your house gapes mockingly barren, Leo grown up and gone and with girlfriends. I know that Sinclair manages OK on his own, but he's a man, it's easier for him.

Elizabeth's house is a curious mixture of lived-in and empty. It smells and looks like a place in which the occupant is almost always present: the smells of breath and skin and air freshener, the television pages of the newspaper laid out, programmes for viewing ringed in red pen. On the other hand, there is nothing which could be described as remotely personal; no trinkets or mementoes, no photographs or postcards, none of the clutter with which people stamp their personality on the places where they live. For a proofreader and editor, Elizabeth seems to have had surprisingly few books—half a shelf, no more. When Kate looks closer, she sees why. They are all from the library.

Elizabeth's atrociously pathetic lifestyle has at least made her movements yesterday easy to track. The newsagent at the end of the road remembers her coming in at around ten o'clock for her copy of *The Scotsman,* as she always did. The retired man across the road saw her returning home a few minutes later. That brief excursion apart, Elizabeth seems to have been at home all day. Four people remember seeing her at the window at various times during the day. Her constant surveillance seems to have engendered a Pavlovian response in her neighbours, rendering them incapable of

240

walking past her house without checking to see whether she was checking on them. Which, invariably, she was.

The contrast with Petra Gallacher is total. Petra was young and attractive, full of life and her interest in it, running two men at once. Elizabeth was menopausal and unattractive both to look at and to know, a spinster lonely beyond comprehension. Kate can't see why Blackadder would have killed both of them, let alone have had sex with them, though she also knows that there is often little resemblance between killers' victims. Maybe Blackadder was the first man Elizabeth had in years. Perhaps ever. The thought sounds facetious in Kate's head, but she doesn't mean it to be. She's simply trying to see the common threads between the victims, other than the single strand of them both being dead.

The only connection Kate can think of is curiosity. Petra was a reporter, Elizabeth a busybody. Curiosity. And everyone knows the old saying about curiosity and the cat. But nothing Petra wrote for the *Aberdeen Evening Telegraph* was controversial enough to have her killed, and surely nothing Elizabeth did was enough to have driven someone to murder. Those divorce cases were a long time ago, and none of the participants live here any more.

Blackadder saw them somewhere. That's the only thing which makes sense. Every other avenue eventually turns into a dead end.

What would he have seen in Elizabeth? Whatever it is, Kate can't determine it. She can't bring herself to identify with Elizabeth the same way she has with Petra. Sure, Elizabeth had a right to life the same as everyone else: and sure, her opinion of the victim doesn't in any way dim her anger at Blackadder. But Kate knows who she feels more sorry for, and that in itself makes her ashamed, for they're both equal when they're laid out on the slab and their judge is the unforgiving glare of the autopsy room.

*   *   *

The more Lovelock resists, the more Frank relishes their confrontations. He has never respected power for power's sake, and Lovelock's attempts to bully him reinforce rather than undermine this.

'As you know,' says Frank, 'we recovered the visor yesterday evening. My inspectors have been examining it continuously since then, and their conclusions are clear. The visor exhibits no trace of bomb damage. Nor does any other part of the ferry. There was therefore no explosion on the *Amphitrite.*'

Lovelock looks as if he is the one about to explode. 'That's impossible.'

Frank picks up a sheet of typewritten paper and begins to read.

' "Summary of the inspectors' report. There is substantial displacement of the visor in an upward and starboard direction. The visor exhibits sharp indentation and heavy scratch marks, especially on the starboard side. The bottom of the visor is heavily pounded and distorted, and has been compressed upwards. Both side locking lugs have been torn out of the visor bulkhead. The lugs for the opening cylinders have score marks on their starboard sides, and the bottom lock mating lug has

242

been stretched and pushed to starboard. From these observations, we can conclude the following:

'"The visor was ripped from the *Amphitrite*'s prow by the force of the storm. The direction of the prevailing winds correlates with the pattern and nature of visor damage.

'"Detachment of the visor could only have taken place with the visor open and/or suffering inadequate fittings to the hull. Maintenance records and stress load simulations indicate that a properly-attached visor should withstand twice the pressure of a Force 7 wind in open seas.

'"No explosive device was detonated in the vicinity of the visor."'

He puts the paper down again. Lovelock's face is wary.

'Parker said there was a bomb,' says Lovelock.

'That's not all. Point two of those conclusions points to an open visor and/or inadequate fittings. I checked the *Amphitrite*'s maintenance records again. Last November, when the ship was in dry dock, a fault in the closing mechanism was recorded. The visor was stopping a few feet short of its full travel.'

'I remember that. And I also remember that it was fixed.'

'It was *marked* as fixed.'

'It *was* fixed. The independent inspector demanded to see it at the time.'

'Three weeks ago, there was another entry in the maintenance log. Sporadic malfunctioning of the "visor closed" position sensor. The sensor was sticking on red when it should have been reading green. Complaint submitted by Captain Sutton. No record of it being acted upon.'

'So? It was a different problem. And a minor one, too. Who cares what the position sensor says, as long as the visor was closed?'

Frank shakes his head and plays his ace. 'What if the visor wasn't closed? What if it was the same problem as before?'

'Impossible.'

'Not at all. The fittings were fine, they were checked in dry dock. Therefore the visor must have been open. Therefore it . . .'

'The bridge crew would have seen it.'

'No. The bow doors couldn't be seen from the bridge.'

'But Parker said the doors were closed. The lights indicated so.'

'Parker was on the bridge. The only lights they had were for the visor side locks and ramp locking devices. Not the visor bottom lock. Not the position closed. It wasn't the position sensor which was malfunctioning, it was the visor travel. The position sensor was reading open because the visor *was* open.'

'You mean the *Amphitrite* sailed for three weeks with its visor ajar?'

'Not necessarily. Sutton described the malfunction as sporadic.'

'Your connection of these two maintenance records is pure conjecture.'

'On the contrary. It fits the facts perfectly. More to the point, it is the only possibility which does. Try this scenario. The *Amphitrite* leaves Bergen with ramp and visor shut: remember, Sutton's complaint was that the problem was sporadic. Even if the visor is ajar, there would be no problem for the first part of the journey, when the sea is calm

244

and the weather good. For twelve hours, the journey is uneventful. Then the bomb warning comes. Sutton acts swiftly and decisively, like the good captain he is. He ejects the suspect vehicle, at considerable personal risk. But when he closes the bow doors again, not all the lights go back to green. He still thinks it's a position sensor problem, and he's in a hurry. They've lost time already, and they don't want to lose any more. He probably gives it no more than a moment's thought.'

'This is . . .'

'But it's not a position sensor problem. It's a visor travel problem, which makes it very serious. The visor is now ajar, and the seas are getting up. Hundred-ton storm waves start to batter the *Amphitrite*'s bow. They're probing for the point of least resistance, and it's not long until they find it. A gap of a few feet, down near the waterline. It's not a small gap for long. The waves bash at it, start to prise it open, make it bigger and bigger. The visor can't take any more. It begins to shear away from the hull. Once it starts to go, that's it. The waves pull the visor off as easily as you'd rip a poster from a wall. The ramp is still closed, but the ramp isn't watertight. The ramp is pulled slightly away from its contact points, but by this time there's so much water on the car deck that it makes no difference.'

Frank taps at a piece of paper gridded with figures.

'All roll-on/roll-off ferries have a serious design flaw, and that's the car deck—an area bigger than a football field, without any watertight bulkheads. This means that even relatively shallow water sloshing around can seriously jeopardise stability.

245

Two thousand tons of water on the car deck—about two and a half feet—would have been enough to bring the first possible flooding point in other areas down to the mean water surface. In the *Amphitrite*'s case, this flooding point was the aft windows on deck four. Once the water started entering the accommodation decks, all residual stability would be impaired, and the ship effectively lost. You couldn't stop that flooding before the vessel sinks. You couldn't even stabilise it at any given level, because the water would just pour through the connections between the decks, the staircases and doors. Roll-on/roll-off ferries are basically death traps. They're designed for convenience, but this makes them extremely vulnerable to capsize. There's virtually no part of a roll-on/roll-off which can be effectively isolated. And when they go, they go fast. They have no transition period between survivable accidents and complete disaster. The *Titanic* took about two hours to go down. The *Amphitrite* took about fifteen minutes.'

Fifteen minutes.

'What about the explosions which Christian Parker mentioned? Lots of people heard *those*. I've talked to survivors, same as you.'

'Parker said he heard *bangs*. They were loud enough to be heard on the bridge, seven decks up from the car deck. If they were explosions, they'd have torn the ferry apart. But there was no bomb damage. Therefore the bangs were caused by something else.'

'Such as what?'

'Such as the water ripping the vehicle lashings away and flinging lorries against the side of the car

246

deck.'

Lovelock spreads his hands wide. 'Again, this is just conjecture.'

'No. It's a logical deduction.'

'You seem to think you have it all worked out.'

'Not all. There is one thing missing.'

'Which is?'

'The bow door was opened in the first place to eject a suspect vehicle.'

'And?'

'I want to know what was on that vehicle.'

'A bomb, of course.'

'No. Exactly the opposite.' Frank picks up a copy of Christian Parker's transcript and begins to read. '"I knocked the intercom out of his hand and yelled at him. 'You didn't get the right vehicle, did you?' That's what I said. I thought he was about to bite me. He looked like he'd lost his mind. He grabbed my shoulders and said: 'You could say that, Christian. You could say that.'"'

'That just confirms it,' says Lovelock. 'If there wasn't a bomb on board, as you contend'—the first time, Frank realises, that Lovelock has ever admitted that Frank might be right—'it must be because they tipped it out to start with. Sutton was wrong. He *did* get the right vehicle. The one he ejected had the bomb on it. The rest happened just the way you said.'

'There's only one way to find out.'

Lovelock sees instantly what he means. 'You're nuts.'

'Not at all.'

'That van had—*has*—a bomb on board. It was ejected an hour before the ferry sank. It had nothing to do with the sinking. And you've already

247

had a letter telling you to stop investigating. One way or another, you'll get yourself killed.'

Frank almost smiles. Lovelock, concerned for Frank's well-being. He never thought he'd see the day. 'I'm not your employee, and nor is my submersible pilot. What does it matter to you?'

'Of course it matters. There's a bloody bomb in that van.'

'I doubt it. Even if there is, it'll almost certainly have defused itself by now. Or gone off. Either way, the danger is minimal. And the investigation will be incomplete unless I find out for sure.'

'Just leave it. Please.'

Frank is so conditioned to Lovelock's bullying and intransigence that this—a plea, almost begging, did he imagine it?—comes totally out of the blue. If Lovelock asks for something, there must be a good reason for his doing so, and that reason must in turn be good enough to merit being denied.

'You have spent the past few days trying to convince the world that the *Amphitrite* was destroyed by a bomb. The moment I suggest finding the vehicle which is supposed to have contained this bomb, you try to stop me. It doesn't make sense. I'm going down there as soon as we locate the vehicle. Whatever I find, you'll be the first to know.'

*　　　*　　　*

Alex under his desk at lunchtime, his office deserted and a chance to grab back some of the sleep which eludes him at night. On his back, shirt undone and with his hands behind his head as if he's having a nap in the park. He twitches like a

248

sleeping dog, and his dreams are agitated.

He is on the *Amphitrite*, holding Kate's hand as they are about to jump. Then they're in the helicopter together, but the sun is shining and he is bone dry. He hasn't been in the water at all. He turns to Kate, but she is looking out of the window. When he follows her gaze, he sees a golden sheet of sea speckled with white points of light. The helicopter swoops hard and fast towards the ocean like a diving seagull, and they are underwater. He kicks hard upwards, and breaks surface in a swimming pool on the *Amphitrite*'s sundeck. Kate is sitting on the side of the pool, dangling her feet in the water. He swims over to her, and as he swims he is suddenly aware that he is in a dream.

The images fade into a dull orange. The inside of his eyelids. He tries to open them, but they are stuck. This always happens when he sleeps during the day. He relaxes and waits for his body to regain full consciousness. His eyes open once, twice more, still while he's asleep, and finally they open for real and he's awake. He rolls out from under his desk and stands up instantly, determined not to let himself be dragged back into sleep. His face is clammy.

Sinclair is walking past the door of Alex's office. He glances inside, sees Alex standing there looking dishevelled, and comes in. 'Are you all right, Alex?'

'Yeah. Just catching up on some sleep.'

'Too much nocturnal activity?'

Alex smiles. 'And what does *that* mean?'

'I think you know perfectly well. I saw who you left with last night.'

'I was helping her with her inquiries.'

Sinclair laughs, and puts his arm around Alex's

249

shoulders. 'And otherwise? How are you?'

'Pretty shitty. I'm not sure how much it helps, being back here.'

'Nor am I, sometimes. But I'd rather be here than in an empty house.'

'I know what you mean.'

Sinclair glances at Alex's desk. 'What are you working on?'

'A couple of appraisals for prospective sellers. Nothing too strenuous.' He looks at the clock on the wall. 'Jason's auction's just started. Fancy having a quick peek?'

'Thanks, but no. I should get back.'

They walk out into the corridor, and head their separate ways.

Alex, Sinclair and Jason have chosen to come back to work as soon as possible following the *Amphitrite*. Their colleagues have reacted fulsomely and predictably, drenching them in attention and solicitous concern. Alex can't remember even having to make a cup of coffee. Every time he stands up to do something, it seems that four or five people rush to help. He appreciates it and he's grateful they care, but at times it all gets a bit too much.

If anything, though, it's been most difficult for Jason. Alex and Sinclair are well-liked in the office, and the general anxiety for them reflects the affection in which they are held. Jason is less popular, something he is all too aware of. He once asked Sinclair why he wasn't more popular, a question which provides its own answer. The reaction to Jason has been tinged with guilt. If only two of the three could have come back, there is no doubt as to who the office would have chosen as

250

the odd one out.

Alex walks towards the auction room. Already he can hear Jason's voice, loud and hectoring as he directs the bidding.

'The bid is with the lady in the aisle, and against you, sir, at the back of the room—200 . . . And 20. And 40. And 60. And 80.'

The room is full. Alex stands at the back, the best place from which to view an auction, and watches Jason's head move back and forth as if he is watching a tennis match. That is the difference between Jason and Sinclair, thinks Alex: Jason appears to be a viewer, Sinclair the conductor. Jason's style of auctioneering is serviceable, functional, and eminently forgettable. Sinclair works the crowd, he *performs*. Lovelock once called Sinclair the Mick Jagger of Urquhart's, and he meant it as a compliment. Sinclair brings the same energy and vitality and flair to the auction room as he does to his directing, and the bidders love him for it. So does the auction house: Sinclair sells a higher proportion of lots above the reserve price than any other auctioneer on Urquhart's books.

'Now at 360 . . . 390 . . . 420 . . . 460 . . .' The increments rise with the price.

The lady in the aisle shakes her head. She doesn't want to bid any more.

'On £460, for lot number five, Etruscan terracotta sculpture.'

Jason looks round the room. Even from the other side of the room, Alex can see the sweat on his face.

'All through then?' The gavel comes down with a thump. 'Sold at £460 to you, sir, number'—Jason takes another look at the man's paddle—'32. Lot number six. A fine example of bronze . . .'

All these people here with their catalogues and their hopes, and for what? Items which won't make any difference to their lives, not really. These petty battles they play, trying to intimidate each other by jumping the bid or keeping their paddles raised throughout. And when it's over, someone's won and someone's lost. Someone goes home with the Etruscan terracotta sculpture, and someone doesn't.

Someone gets on the *Amphitrite*, and gets off again. Someone doesn't.

What do these people at the auction know about combat, real combat, when winning is a matter of life and death, when the people you beat are the ones you stamp down as you barge your way to freedom?

Alex turns abruptly and walks fast back down the corridor to his office. He fishes Kate's mobile number out of his Rolodex and begins to dial. He puts the phone down before he's finished punching out the number.

Why call her? What can she do for him?

Last night in bed, they made a pact not to speak to counsellors. Just the two of them, helping each other recover. What an idiotic thing to have committed himself to. Never take a decision when you've just made love.

Seaspeed offered him counselling, at his convenience. He's got the counsellor's name and number on a Post-It somewhere. One of the many dotted around the edge of his computer screen. There. Jane Bavin.

What does it matter, the stupid agreement? It's not like he's being unfaithful.

Alex picks up the phone again, and the number he dials is Jane Bavin's.

*　　*　　*

Nothing doing on the Elizabeth Hart inquiry. Drudge work, time-consuming and tedious, and always the possibility that a vital clue gets missed because the searchers are so enervated by the numbness of repetition and by the heat. The same routine as before. Vehicle checks and pedestrian checks, in the city centre and out towards Tollohill Wood. Receipts for the knife chased down. The snake connections gone over again. Same with the sex offenders. Everything which was cleared at first is back under suspicion. Chasing their tails.

Kate reads Elizabeth Hart's autopsy report. More of the same. Water in the lungs, presumably from one of the reservoirs. Petechial haemorrhaging under the eyelids. Oak grains on the back of the head, again from apparent impact with a tree. The snake the same as before, and again having eaten recently. Teethmarks on the abdomen. No sedatives. Rope marks above the severance lines. And absolutely no trace of fingerprints, saliva or hairs.

Kate can hardly think straight. She is just about to go out and grab a sandwich, as much for the fresh air as anything else, when her phone rings.

'Kate Beauchamp.'

'Kate, it's your father. Are you free for lunch?'

'You're joking.'

'Just a sandwich. Half an hour, tops. There's something I want to tell you.'

'Tell me now.'

253

'I'd rather do it face to face.'

'I . . .'

'Kate. Why do you have to turn everything into a trial of strength?'

Father and daughter, stubborn and pig-headed.

'I don't. You're the one who . . .'

'See what I mean?'

She clicks her tongue in annoyance, and is alarmed to find herself fighting back a smile.

'OK. I'll come.'

*　　　*　　　*

They get their sandwiches in a café round the corner from Queen Street.

'Do you want to know why the *Amphitrite* sank?' Frank asks as they sit down.

'Is this what you wanted to tell me?'

'No. Well, yes, but there's something else.'

'What's the something else?'

'I asked if you wanted to know why the ferry sank.' She shakes her head and hears her mouth saying yes.

Yelling at the woman on the ladder. 'You have to move. Come up or go down, but let these people through.' The woman doesn't even look at her.

Frank tells her about the visor not shutting properly, the indicator lights, the mystery vehicle at the bottom of the sea.

'You mean the *Amphitrite* had been sailing with open bow doors?' she says once he's finished. 'And this didn't really bother anyone?'

'Kate, almost every ferry sails out of harbour with its bow doors open. Timetables are so tight that they barely have time to get all the vehicles on and close the doors before the off. If every ferry which left harbour with its doors open sank, you could walk to France on the wrecks. No joke.'

She's interested, but in a detached kind of way. It's all shadow-boxing, she's waiting for him to tell her the big 'something' he promised. She doesn't push it. Whatever it is, she has gone all her life without knowing it: another few minutes aren't going to make any difference. And besides, she doesn't want to give him the satisfaction of her asking. Childish, she knows, but still. He's come back into her life at the worst moment possible. Having to run a murder investigation and get over the *Amphitrite* should leave her with little enough time to worry about anything else, but it has proved exactly the opposite. The less opportunity she has to deal with her father, the more vulnerable to him she feels.

Frank clears his throat.

'You know why I left your mother,' he says, midway between statement and question.

'This is what you've come to tell me?'

'Yes.'

'Right. You had an affair, and then you ran off.'

He shakes his head, more in sadness than contradiction. 'I wasn't the only one who was mucking around.'

Kate feels as if someone's just punched her in the solar plexus. She heaves the breath back into her lungs and presses her hands against the table. Nausea swirls in her stomach.

'That's bullshit.'

'It's not.'

'Mum was having an affair?'

'With Tony.'

255

'Tony? Tony, your best friend?'

Him nodding, her shaking her head.

'I don't believe this.'

'I found them in bed together.'

'Jesus.'

He shrugs. 'So I left.'

Kate at the top of the stairs while her parents raged on the ground floor: fifteen years old, on her bedroom wall posters of pop stars who sang of love and broken hearts and breaking up, and what they sang about was nothing like this, they never mentioned screaming matches and accusations going back and forth, back and forth, booming volleys of hate and backhands of rage. Kate can't hear the words, but she doesn't need to. As in opera, understanding the language isn't necessary. Listen to the rhythm, the passion, the emotion.

'But why did you tell me that it was just you who had the affair? You came to me—I remember this so well, both you and Mum came to me in turn and said exactly the same thing—and told me that you'd met another woman, and that you were going away to live with her.'

'We agreed the story between us before we spoke to you. You always adored your mother, Kate. More than you did me, at any rate.'

'I didn't dislike you. Not then.'

'Maybe. But she was your favourite. It used to hurt me, but I guess it happens often enough, that a child favours one parent over the other. That mother-daughter bond, you and Angie had it. So when this whole thing with her and Tony happened, we had a choice. Either we could shatter your illusions about her, or I could take the fall. We had the power to save your relationship with one of

256

us, but not both. That's why we pretended it was just me who had strayed.'

Kate looks down at her sandwich, seeing the marks of her own teeth. She has lost her appetite. When she looks back up, she sees that her father's eyes are wet.

'My affair was first, Kate. I wasn't a great father to you, just like I wasn't a great husband to Angie. Take what I did afterwards as my way of saying sorry.'

Kate grips the edge of the table, trying to anchor herself to reality. For twenty years she has adored her mother, first in flesh and then in memory, and during that time she has hated her father with an equal and opposite vehemence. And now that has been washed away. The faces they wore—one the guilty gloating lover, the other the humiliated cuckold—are now simply masks, lowered to reveal a truth behind.

The anger comes to her in quick bright flashes. *Why protect me for so long, and then undo the whole edifice that the lie was supposed to protect?* Kate knows it only too well from police work: if you're going to tell a lie, never go back on it.

Her new life, and nothing is as it seems.

She looks across at her father. She sees in his face how hard it has been for him to carry this around for so long, shouldering and perpetuating her hatred when he had the power to stop it at any time. He waited until he was back in her life, and he waited until they'd established a certain level of contact.

Her anger settles, simmers. The truth comes in many guises and at the most unexpected of times. She reaches out and touches his shoulder.

257

'Thanks,' she says. 'Thanks, Dad.'

*   *   *

Unlike many of the counsellors Seaspeed have brought in, Jane Bavin actually practises in Aberdeen. Her office looks like a living-room: framed pictures on the wall (she has hurriedly replaced the usual Roger Fisher seascape above the mantelpiece with a rather nondescript still life), two armchairs and a sofa, and a coffee table in the middle.

'Just start where you feel comfortable. Anything you want to say. We'll take it from there.'

Bavin tucks a stray strand of hair behind her right ear. She wears her hair down at work these days, ever since her sister told her that she looks too severe with it pulled back. And severe is not something she wants to look when dealing with traumatised patients.

Alex fidgets, looks around the room, and plunges in. 'This ferry thing, it just dominates my life. Everything I do seems to be related, one way or another, to what happened on board the *Amphitrite*. Flashbacks, insurance claims, getting my mobile replaced, people asking about it the whole time. I'm sick of it.'

'And you want to know why you're feeling what you're feeling.'

Alex nods.

'OK.'

Bavin spends half an hour explaining to him what post-traumatic stress disorder is and why he's affected by it, and then tells him how she can help him. 'The important thing for you to realise is that

258

PTSD is entirely normal. That's why counsellors such as myself always try and encourage people to talk about their experiences. By doing so, you'll come to realise that there is nothing unusual about your responses. You are not uniquely unworthy or guilty. And just because the problem is with your mind rather than your body doesn't mean that there's no way of treating it. There's no magic cure, but there are plenty of ways in which you can work through the trauma and therefore recover more quickly and more completely.'

She picks a booklet off the table next to her and hands it to him.

'What I'm going to ask you to try, if you're agreeable, is some cognitive-behaviour therapy. There's a technique known as systematic desensitisation, under which you're trained to recreate the traumatic event by physically relaxing and imagining scenes which more or less approximate what you remember. If done right, you will be exposed to an intermediate level of fear—not so great that you cannot process the trauma material, but equally not so little that you cannot engage with it. By exposing you to fear-producing stimuli and cognitions in a safe and supportive environment, we should be able to reduce the impact of these stimuli on your reactivity. Make a ten or fifteen-minute audio tape about the *Amphitrite*. Describe what happened and what you thought, what you felt, what you did. Once you've made this tape, play it once a day. You may well want to switch it off at times, if the memories it triggers are very painful, but try to resist the temptation. If you do switch it off before the end, only do it when you've gone through the

259

worst bit and come out the other side. Unless you accustom yourself to the trauma during the listening session itself, you won't find that your general condition improves day on day. What you *may* find, however, is that the particular aspects of the tape which cause you maximum distress vary as time goes by. Rather like a photographer, you'll take sightings of the trauma from new angles to try and make better sense of it. Is this all clear?'

'Yes.'

'You're happy with it?'

'Yes. It sounds good. I'll go away and make the tape.'

'Good.'

'Go with that for a week or so, and see what happens. If you feel you want to talk some more, let me know. I'm always here.'

Alex gets up, and impulsively leans down and kisses her on the cheek. 'Thank you. You've made me feel a whole lot better already.'

*   *   *

As before, Kate sits in an empty room with reference books and thinks one word. *Why?*

Sexual, sadistic, disorganised. Violence and rape. But no enucleation to prevent the victim from watching him, and no genital mutilation either. Neither the dismemberment nor the snake feature in any sexual fantasy she has ever heard of. The reference books through which she trawls detail obscure and unusual sex practices. She comes up blank. Knowing what amatripsis, biastophilia and chezolagnia are has not helped Kate discover Blackadder's motivation, and nor has it materially

260

improved her life in any other way.

She thinks of possibilities, writes them down, discards them. Nowhere Blackadder might have seen both of them. Elizabeth's range of movement was limited, Petra's wider, but their two spheres remain resolutely and frustratingly exclusive. Different parts of town, different circles of knowledge, different lives.

As before, Kate sits in an empty room with reference books and thinks. As before, she comes up with nothing. It's almost as if Blackadder has got one of them wrong. He could hardly have made it more difficult had he tried—which, Kate reflects ruefully, he probably did.

This kind of case offers up problems not found in normal crime, ordinary decent crime. There is no traceable motive. The motive is what he carries in his head. There are no informants, no stoolpigeons. With the DNA tests still nowhere near completion, there is very little Kate can do except plug away down the same old avenues and hope for the best.

No one would blame her if she cited the effects of the *Amphitrite* and handed the case over. No one bar herself, that is. She took this on, and she will finish it. She wants not only to find Blackadder, but also to look him in the eyes and tell him he's lost. To the victor the glory. But right now he is way ahead on points and showing no signs of flagging.

A thought comes to her with the penetrating directness of a laser beam. *I can't do this on my own.*

Almost before she's thought it she rejects it. Of course she can do it on her own. The battle is young, there is still everything to play for.

The thought comes again, and this time it forces her to doubt herself. More importantly, to question herself.

Why does she spurn what she thinks?

Because she wants to take the credit. No. It's more. She wants to *deserve* the credit. But if there is no credit to take, then what does it matter who deserves it? What matters is stopping Blackadder. Nothing else. Bizarrely, inappropriately, the words of Malcolm X come to her. 'Any means necessary.'

And in her head, another voice. Someone else's voice.

'There aren't an infinite number of hiding places. He's got to breathe and eat and drink and sleep. He's got to exist. But still he's in control. I look left, he goes right. I look right, he looks left. Someone once said that George Best was so tricky he gave his opponents twisted blood. Twisted blood, from chasing shadows.'

A possibility floats in her head. It wafts like a leaf on the breeze, there to be snatched.

What Kate is thinking of is a mindset unlike any other she's known. If she looks deep inside herself, she's known that she must do this from the moment she saw Petra's body. She's dealing with something beyond her ken, but not necessarily beyond that of this person.

No. It's impossible. It will reopen too many old wounds, for him and her alike.

Any means necessary.

She can keep the wounds closed long enough, she'll take that chance. When it's all over, she'll gladly surrender herself to them.

They—the powers that be—will never go for it. Too radical. Too many problems.

And if they don't? She's back where she started.

It's not as if she's got much to lose.

Kate leaves the quiet room and goes along to Renfrew's office.

'Any progress, Kate?'

'Not yet. That's why I've come to see you.'

He puts down his pen. She thinks that he shouldn't wear a blue shirt in this heat.

'You want off?'

'No. Anything but.'

'Good. Have you found a profiler yet?'

'That's what I want to talk to you about. Sort of.'

'What do you mean?'

'I want to bring Red Metcalfe in on this.'

Renfrew takes his time. He sits straighter in his chair and looks hard at Kate. He rubs his hand across his mouth and looks hard at her again.

'He's in Wormwood Scrubs, am I right?'

'Yes.'

'I can ask the Scottish Office to talk to the Home Secretary in London. But you know what they're like. That's a lot of bureaucracy just to go and see him.'

'I don't want to go and see him.'

'No?'

'I want him to come up here.'

Renfrew barks a curt laugh. 'Out of the question. Impossible.'

'Why?'

'He's a convicted criminal, Kate. You of all people must remember that.'

'Of course I do. And I also remember working with him. He didn't get his reputation overnight, sir. He was an inspiration in the Met. If anyone can help us here, he can.'

'Whatever I just said about bureaucracy, times

263

that by ten. The Home Secretary will never go for it.'

'Why not?'

'Why do you think? Politics. The law-and-order initiative London's just launched. There's an election to fight next year, in case you'd forgotten. Springing Red Metcalfe from jail is hardly going to be part of the Home Secretary's master plan. Imagine the publicity.'

'And imagine the publicity when Blackadder kills again. He's on a strike rate of one every other day at the moment, *sir*.'

'Kate, you've had a hard few days, and I think . . .'

'What happened on the ferry is nothing to do with this. I'm perfectly capable of doing my job. All I'm asking for is the tools with which to do it.'

Renfrew runs his hand through his hair. Kate can see he's considering it. She drives a wedge into the gap. 'All I'm asking is that you get Edinburgh to make the request to the Home Secretary, on my behalf. I'm prepared to make any guarantees he wants.'

Renfrew sighs. 'All right. Against my better judgement, perhaps.'

He makes the phone calls, asking, persuading, cajoling. Kate watches and listens as he is shunted from civil servant to civil servant. Long waits between calls while the wheels of government turn. Half an hour later, he has an answer. Sort of.

'That last one was the Home Secretary's private secretary, Tim Ayling. He says that the minister will consider the request and give us an answer by tomorrow morning.'

'He can't move any faster?'

'You heard me talking, Kate. It was all I could do to get that snotty little sod to take it to his boss in the first place.'

'I know. And thank you for your help. Tomorrow morning, yes?'

'They've got my numbers and yours. We'll know the moment they do.'

'I just hope it's not too late.'

*   *   *

Kate watches them together, her son and her lover. They are lying on the floor of Kate's living-room. Alex's long leg muscles snake from beneath the hem of his shorts, and a tuft of brown hair peeks cheekily out from the neck of his shirt. Leo has his toy multi-storey garage out, and is busy running all the cars up the ramp and down the spiral exit the other side. His little face is furrowed in concentration. Alex gives him the cars back when they're out of reach. Sometimes he makes two of them crash together, or he waves one around in the air so Leo can't get it. Leo laughs his high-pitched childish laugh and hits Alex playfully, and Alex rolls around the floor and begs for mercy as if he's just been smacked by Mike Tyson, and Leo laughs all the louder and jumps on Alex and shouts 'I am the winner!'

Leo has never liked any of Kate's boyfriends since David, his father, left. Not one, not really.

Alex glances up at her and winks. She has the feeling he knows exactly what she's thinking. *He's not your son, and maybe I wish he was.*

'How was work?' she asks.

'I spent all day multi-tasking.'

265

'Oh yes?'

'I read the paper and took a shit.'

She laughs. Leo grabs Alex's hand and tries to pull him upright.

'Come on, Alex. Let's go play football.'

Alex pulls Leo on to the floor, leaps to his feet, and pulls Leo back up again. They leave the room, Leo taking three steps for every one of Alex's. Kate tries not to let it choke her up too much. Death and destruction all day at work, and back home to find a man who's melting Leo's heart even quicker than he's melting hers.

She goes through into the kitchen, where Bronagh in full earth-mother mode today, tie-dye shirt and a skirt patterned with flowers—is drinking tea and reading a magazine.

'He's lovely,' says Bronagh.

'Not you too,' but laughing, pleased that the people Kate loves like him. 'Any tea left?'

'Should be some still in the pot.'

Kate pours herself a cup and sits down.

'You could do a lot worse, Katie.'

'It's hardly started. Give me a break.'

'I'm just saying.' The old woman's eyes twinkle. 'A lot worse.'

Happy screams from beneath the kitchen window. Kate looks out and down. Alex is flicking the football from one foot to another. He lets it drop and steps over it, first this way and then that. Leo scampers like a terrier as he tries to get it.

Kate wraps her hands around the mug and lets the warmth filter through the ceramic to her palms. The steam plays on her face.

Leo has the ball now. It comes up to his shins. He dribbles it unsteadily towards Alex, who

266

crouches like a goalkeeper, feet apart and arms out. As Leo approaches, Alex flings himself dramatically the wrong way. Leo runs past him and kicks the ball between the two flowerpots doubling as goalposts. Leo leaps in the air and shouts 'goal' at the top of his voice, his smile like a split galosh.

Kate turns back to Bronagh.

'You've got a lot stored up,' says Bronagh.

'A lot of what?'

'Love.'

'Haven't we all?'

'You in particular. All that love that you didn't feel for David. Or couldn't, or wouldn't, whatever. All the love you've poured into Leo. It'll do you good to spend some of it on someone else too.'

'You'll have me marrying him, if you're not careful.'

'Katie, I just want you to be happy. That's all.'

It's only on the way out to dinner, with Leo having reluctantly said goodbye to Alex and Bronagh beaming all over her face as she waves them off, that Kate remembers she didn't mention her father's lunchtime revelation to Bronagh. She smiles to herself. The old woman will have known all along.

*   *   *

It was supposed to be just the two of them, but Kate is so concerned about Sinclair, sitting in his house all alone, that she rings him up and invites him along too. He says he can't possibly impinge, she won't have made enough food. Only once she reassures him that they're going to a restaurant, and that he of all people should be there after the efforts he's made to get them together, does he agree to come along. If Alex minds, he doesn't say so.

Sinclair arrives a few minutes after them. He is still in his suit, and he has not even taken off his tie. He looks as immaculate at the end of a hot day as most people would at the start. As he walks in, Kate sees—not for the first time—what an aura he has. He is not the tallest of men, but energy crackles around him like a corona. People look at him, he draws their gaze.

Kate realises that she wants to show Alex off to Sinclair. Even though they all know each other, she still feels as if she's bringing a boyfriend home. Kate may be arguably more successful—certainly relative to her age, maybe in absolute terms—but the relationship she has with Sinclair is subtly tilted away from equality, and the imbalance shines through on occasions like these.

Just like a father would be—just like Bronagh is too, come to think of it—he is concerned that she is working too hard.

'You can simply give up this case,' he says.

'I can't.'

'Of course you can. There must be other people who could do it.'

'OK. I won't.'

'Why not?'

'Because he's *mine*. I want to see his face when I take him down.'

'But so soon after what happened on the ferry?'

'That's life. Things don't happen conveniently, sequentially, allowing you to package them neatly. They come tumbling on top of each other.'

'Only because you put yourself in their path.'

'Listen to me. When I became a police officer, when *anyone* becomes a police officer, a pact is signed. That pact is this. You accept there is evil in the world, and you agree to do your damnedest to stop it. You don't get to choose where and when you take up the struggle. It's with you the whole time, it never stops. The thing to do with evil is to fight it, not deny it. If you duck the struggle, you're denying or negating the reality of evil. The moment you're so used to it that you accept it is the moment you're lost.'

'You simply can't . . .'

'Let me finish. People always ask: "Why does evil exist?" They talk about God and Satan and Jesus' temptation and fallen angels, as if its roots are to be found somewhere in myth or religion. Or they try to explain evil away by accidents of birth. "Some people are born that way." Or they blame social conditioning, abused children, deprivation. Whatever their take, they're all doing the same thing: trying to give evil a context. By giving evil a context, you imply that if you remove the underlying causes of evil, you remove evil itself. But this is wrong. You cannot remove evil itself. It's the natural way of being.'

'That's bullshit.' Alex. 'How can you say this?' Sinclair.

'Because I see it, every day. The question people *should* ask is this: "Why is there *good* in the world?" It's generally assumed that this is a good world contaminated by evil. It's not. Quite the opposite. This is an evil world into which good has somehow got a foothold. Good may triumph over evil in religion and literature, but in science—in *reality*—the opposite is true. All things decay, all

269

things wither and die. The law of nature is based on survival of the fittest, and by fittest we mean the most ruthless and the most selfish. Mercy is an alien concept in the natural world.'

She lowers her voice.

'How do you think we all got out of the *Amphitrite*, for God's sake? By being good? No. By trampling over those who got in our way. On board that ferry, we were reduced to animals. Our existence was a straight fight for survival, without consideration of reason or enjoyment or all the things which sustain us every day, every normal day. And when we were reduced to animals, we showed no mercy, no love or consideration for our fellow humans. People are good because they're taught to be, because they're afraid not to be. If there were no consequences to be afraid of, then everyone would not only be evil, they would also act evil. The only difference between us and the man who killed those two women is that he is not sufficiently afraid of the consequences to stop himself doing what he does.' *And I hate him for that.*

'No,' says Sinclair. 'That's simply not true.'

'It *is* true. And by denying it, you're merely making my point for me. We know so little about the nature of evil that we lack the skill to heal it. The reason we know so little is that we have chosen not to look. It's there for all of us to see, and we choose to avert our gaze. The central defect of evil is not the sin itself, but the refusal to acknowledge it. Evil doesn't originate in the absence of guilt. It originates in the effort to escape it. You know what the most basic sin is? Pride. All sins are reparable bar the sin of believing that one is without sin.'

270

A couple of the other diners are looking across at them. Kate realises that she must have raised her voice again. She flushes, and slurps at her glass of water. 'OK. Sermon over. Let's talk about something else.'

So they do. They talk about life at the auction house, Jason trying to hit on the secretaries, upcoming auctions, how the other members of the Aberdeen Amateurs are coping, what films they want to go and see, which play the troupe should perform next. Kate tells them about her father and the revelation he sprung on her at lunch today. They ask her how it feels, and she answers as honestly as she can, aware that her answer is incomplete because her reaction is too. She can't assimilate its ramifications all at once: so much else is happening in her life that it comes to her piecemeal, as computer bytes fed down telephone lines will use any spare capacity they find, transmitting themselves in the moments when people talking on the phone system draw breath or pause for thought.

On one hand, tentative relief that she might be getting her father back. On the other, resentment that she has been fed a bright shining lie for so long, never been given the chance to make up her own mind. In the middle, the prospect that too much hurt and antagonism have passed for any rapprochement to be total.

Sinclair reaches in his pocket and pulls out a silver necklace with an oval of turquoise in the middle. He hands it to Kate.

'This was one of the unsold lots from an American sale we did the other day,' he says. 'It's Navajo. The vendor didn't want it back, so I bought it off him for the reserve price.'

'It's beautiful.' The turquoise is smooth under her fingertip. She twists the chain so it reflects the light. 'Absolutely beautiful.'

Sinclair clears his throat, a little diffidently. 'I'd like you to have it.'

She looks at him, startled. 'I couldn't possibly.'

'I bought it for you, Kate. And I don't think it would look so good on Alex.'

She glances at Alex, who nods, almost imperceptibly. Take it.

Kate fastens the necklace round her neck and leans across the table to hug Sinclair. 'Thank you. Thank you so much.'

As he hugs her, he cannot see the tears that prick her eyes.

*   *   *

Voices in the heavy-sexed darkness.

'I've got a hell of a day tomorrow.'

'Why?'

'It's Petra Gallacher's funeral.'

'The girl who was killed?'

'Yes.'

'Do you want me to come with you?'

'Why? You didn't know her.'

'I thought you might like the support.'

Pause. 'Yes. I'd like that very much.'

'What time is it?'

'Eleven.'

'Sure. I'll ring work in the morning and tell them I'll be in after lunch.'

'You're a sweetheart. Thanks. I really appreciate it.'

272

*   *   *

He is the guilty, one like this who hides his reeking hands; and up from the outraged dead they rise in flames, over his burning head to chant this frenzy striking frenzy, lightning crazing the mind.

Elizabeth comes to him like bait to the trap. She leaves the sanctuary of her watchtower for once, and this purely to continue her torment of him. She comes in doubles: two rings on his bell, his looking each way down the street after he lets her in to check no one's seen, double tap and she's down and out. Ropes hard round wrists and ankles. The gag wedged tight between her lips splits her twisted hideous mask of fury.

He slings her in the boot of the car, and chatters to himself while he drives. Heave in torment, black froth erupting from your lungs. Vomit the clots of all the murders you have drained. Go where heads are severed, eyes gouged out, where justice and bloody slaughter are the same. Castrations, wasted seed, young men's glories butchered, extremities maimed and huge staves at the chest, and the victims wail for pity. Spikes inching up the spine, torsos stuck on skewers. Your kind should infest a lion's cavern reeking blood.

The roadblocks are still up, officers in their shirtsleeves and the rims of their helmets slippery with sweat. In the boot Elizabeth Hart, trussed and bound, and in his head the knowledge of what happened to Petra and the anticipation of starting it all over again.

There is so little which conceals the truth from these policemen, and their prying eyes. A thin

273

sheet of steel between them and Elizabeth Hart, a thin curve of skin and bone between them and the knowledge in his brain. His voice is steady, laced with the proper amount of concern. No, officers, I didn't see her, but of course I read about her in the papers, what a crying shame it is, I hope you catch the monster.

He drives off without even the slightest motion of triumph. He knows that's how customs catch smugglers: they watch the ones who celebrate too early, relax or smile even before they're out into the arrivals hall, and then they haul them back and rip them apart.

Stupid, stupid police, chasing their own tails. They're rattled, that's plain to see. They didn't expect him to strike again so soon—they still had Petra's hapless boyfriend in custody, for heaven's sake—and it's thrown them off kilter. He's running the show here. Not them, and certainly not the detective chief inspector. He saw her on television this morning, yelling at the camera, at him. He had been led to believe she was better than that. Mind you, it's true what they say about television putting ten pounds on a person. She's much more attractive in real life than she was on screen.

He remembers what she said on the television, before she started that ridiculous invective. 'Someone disturbed the killer this morning. We need to find this person, and urgently.' Oh, lovely Miss Beauchamp. The shape of what you seek is there, but the detail eludes you.

He was disturbed this morning, yes, but not by a person.

It was a dog.

He's been terrified of dogs virtually since the

274

moment Ivan died. Craig moves in for good the day after Ivan's funeral, and with his arrival goes the last vestige of Ivan in that house, the last staples of protection for the boy. Craig hates the boy as much as Ailish does, and for the same reasons, because he reminds him of Ivan. Kathryn is caught in the middle. She's still a child, she can do nothing but watch the boy take the abuse, the slaps, the beatings, the neglect. At night in their room, they are silent and think their own thoughts.

Craig has been there a week when Ailish makes the boy eat from the dog bowl.

Dinner, four of them in the house and the table laid for three. Ailish serves Craig and Kathryn and then herself, all the time watching the boy, challenging him to ask where his place is. There is still food for him, but nowhere to eat it.

Ailish bends down and scoops his food into the dog bowl. It is sausages and mash. One of the sausages pivots on the edge of the bowl before dropping to the floor.

'That's where you're going to eat, you disgusting mongrel.'

In Craig's eyes, the cold contempt of a man beyond reach.

'Go on,' Ailish says. 'Eat your fucking food, you animal.'

He kneels on the floor, determined that they won't break him. He begins to eat, scooping the food from the bowl with his hands and shovelling it into his mouth.

A rap across his knuckles. He winces as the sharp pain pulses.

'Like a dog. No hands.'

He puts his hands on the floor and lowers his

275

head to the bowl. The mash is soft and warm against his nose.

Craig whistles, a simple sound shot through with sheer malevolence.

Running paws and an angry barking. Hero coming for his dinner, and they haven't fed him for two days. He's ravenous, and the boy in his way, at his bowl, on his territory.

He rolls away from the bowl, a flash in his vision of fleshy pink gums pulled back from snarling teeth. His hands rise in front of his face as the lurcher's jaws clamp hard on his forearm, shaking and ripping as it tries to tear him. In the distance, a keening screaming which he dimly recognises as his own voice. Kathryn crying and the dog growling deep in its throat. Warmth on the back of his legs and a sudden rankness in the air.

'Look, Ailish.' Craig's voice sounds mocking above the tumult. 'The little fucker's shat himself.'

And so again last night. Elizabeth already dead and mutilated and the arrangements all but complete. He hears running paws and a barking and it's happening all over again. He wonders whether he's imagining it, and knows even as he turns that he's not.

The dog is large and black, and comes out of the darkness as if unpeeled. He feels the pressure on his sphincter, and it's all he can do to rip his trousers open and down before the rush comes. The dog still coming, him with cloth piled round his knees and his vitals exposed: and suddenly the adder uncoils in its cage and hisses.

The dog stops dead.

The adder hisses again, and the dog turns and lopes back into the night.

The danger is past, but he is shaken now. He pulls his trousers up and over his soiled backside. His hands are trembling so violently that it's all he can do to finish attaching the extremities and secure the snake.

He carries the stench of his own ordure all the way to the farm. He is calmer by the time he arrives—calm enough to have remembered his lesson from the previous occasion, at any rate. This time, he opens the gate and leads the nearest pig through and down to the stream. He takes the spare knife from his car and kills it at his leisure, drenching himself in its blood and luxuriating in the brief remission of his madness.

*   *   *

The scars from Hero's attack are still lurid and raw the night Ailish calls him into her room.

She and Craig are going out to the village dance. Ailish is wearing a black dress which fastens up the back. A line of buttons runs from just above her coccyx to the nape of her neck.

'There you are,' she says. 'Help me with this, will you?'

She turns her back on the boy, indicating with her hand where she wants him to do her up. He walks across the room and takes the lowest button in his fingers. It is small and fiddly. He tries to fasten it, and it pops out. And again. Every time he takes hold of it, the fabric comes away from her skin, and he sees the swell of her buttocks. She is wearing no underwear.

The button slides through the hole. He moves on to the next one, and finds it even more difficult.

277

'What the hell are you doing?'

She twists her head round to have a look. The arc of her left breast is exposed.

The button comes away in his hand.

'For pity's sake. How hard can it be?'

She turns to face him. The dress slides from her shoulders and settles on her hips.

Her breasts almost in his face, he feels the hardening begin to distend the material of his trousers. His hands move to adjust it before she notices, but he is too late. She is already looking down, she has already seen it.

'You disgusting animal.' Her voice is low, measured. 'Beast. Vile beast.' She smacks him across the face, hand flicking from the wrist. 'Creature. That's what you are. Worse than the dog.'

Draped in shame, he can't find the words to protest.

'I can't have you sharing a room with your sister. Not if that'—she nods towards his groin—'is what's going to happen.'

She grabs him by the ear and marches him downstairs, to the living-room and beyond, right to the basement. The air is musty, and the sea echoes loud and distorted.

'This is where you'll live now, you little bastard.'

They bring his bed down there, and this is where he does live. He is allowed out for school and to eat, but he always sleeps here in the bowels of the house. The room is right next to the boiler and it can get hellishly hot, even in mid-winter. He lies on his bed with sweat springing like newborn plants from his skin, bare walls around him and the world above.

In the underworld, halfway between life and death, he prays that everyone on earth will die except him, and then he wonders what it would be like to be dead already.

His arrangements are meticulous. The basement is where everything is stored, and here he finds charcoal and a long mirror. On his trips up above ground, he collects the other ingredients: talcum powder from Ailish's bathroom, saffron and cochineal and a knife from the kitchen, blue chalk from school.

He is ready.

He places the mirror on its side next to his bed.

Face first. Talcum powder all over, to erase the living colour of the skin. Charcoal smeared under his eyes for a look of hollow darkness. Blue chalk on his lips. Heels of hands rubbed vigorously into his eyes until they are bloodshot.

Then the body. He mixes the saffron and cochineal to make fake blood. He takes an old T-shirt and stabs it four or five times, and then puts it on. Into the knife holes he soaks the fake blood.

He lies on the bed and looks at the mirror. He is perfectly still. His eyes do not blink or move, his body does not twitch. He is dead, and yet he is more alive than he has ever been. There are two of him now, him and the reflection which he desires, his only friend and true lover.

There is no magic on this earth, but life and death to balance birth.

He recreates this time and again, as the mood takes him. Sometimes he does it for many nights in succession, sometimes not for months. In these intermissions, he retreats in his head to his paradise, a place far from this inferno.

Prismed sunlight colours drifting cloud patterns above a drowned land, where sea lochs reach long wet fingers between splattered islands of grass and silt. Out here, he has all the solitude he could ever need. The sea is all around him, the same in every direction and yet always different. It is never static, never boring: at any given moment, it forms a pattern which has never happened before and will never happen again. It is not a homogenous entity, but an infinite myriad of separate water blocks and tidal systems, all shifting chaotic and disorientating. They come together and pull apart, pile up and slide down, roll over and duck under. He watches for hours. The soothing sea invades every part of him; right into the sanctuary of his eardrums, where it robs him even of his balance. And all the while his boat ploughs on, its prow reaching and splintering a new patch of water in every fraction of time one could choose to measure, and then on to the next and the next after that, an endless progression of birth and rebirth, creation and destruction entwined together.

At last he sees it. An island in the middle of the sea, with wide-open space all around. An alien form extravagant and defiant, rising from the ocean like the last peaks of a submerged land. Its outline dissembles and rearranges itself into a riot of stacks and skerries and promontories. Banners of cloud stretch away from the island's highest points, and the snowflake seabirds swirl all over the cliffs. As he comes closer, he sees that what he took to be uniform green is in fact a multitude of hues and textures: the bright green of the plantago maritima sward which swarms over the lower slopes, the red-brown of the deer grass higher up, rockface brown, wildflower violet, stone black and scree yellow. In the dull westerly light which bounces between the reflective expanses of sea and sky, the colours permeate the atmosphere with the rhythms of soft luminous energy.

He is at the top, where this place is almost lunar in its bareness. The wind and the water have ripped the grass and soil from everywhere bar the most sheltered hollows, where thick lush grass cowers in defiance of the elements. On the seaward side there are long striations in the granite, as if a giant has clawed his fingernails down the rocks. Scattered pieces of aircraft wreckage lie near the summit, whitened by the rain like gnarled bones.

A pair of peregrine falcons are performing intricate aerobatics above his head. Without warning they dive earthwards. They flatten their trajectories just in time to skim low over a rock wall and scorch straight through a group of oystercatchers, which make panicked high-pitched 'kleeping' noises as they scatter.

Now it is the turn of the fulmars, which glide on long loping helixes like miniature albatrosses. They fly close to him, landing on nearby ledges so that they can inspect the stranger who stands among them. Their short bodies and bull necks are at odds with the broad elegance of their wingspans. They appear to be two different creatures welded together.

When these fat and friendly birds tire of watching him, they set off down towards the sea. His eye follows them as they descend the cliff face until they are reduced to tiny white specks hovering and swirling at random far below. If he looks hard enough, he can pick out the gannets as well, circling lazily until they close their wings up and dive seawards. They send up little bomb-plumes as they hit the water. He has the impression not so much of looking down at the sea, but of looking up at a night sky filled with snowflakes. The cacophony of voices forms an unbroken barrier of sound, within which can be heard the distinctive cries of different birds—some of them wild and hideous, others more comfortingly human. In snatches too comes the singing of the grey Atlantic seals, faint and drifting, the music of sirens. But eeriest is the wind, which sighs and moans through the sea caves and throws up its complaints to the cliff tops strangely distorted, inviting him down.

FRIDAY

Tim Ayling, the Home Secretary's private secretary, rings Kate at seven-thirty.

'The Minister will see you at four o'clock this afternoon, in Queen Anne's Gate.'

'Has he made a decision yet?'

'He'd like to discuss a few of the issues with you first.'

'Issues? What issues?'

'I'm just relaying the Minister's instructions, Detective.'

'And that's the earliest he can do? Four o'clock?'

'The Minister is at a law-and-order conference in Brussels all morning.'

Kate bites her lip in frustration at all this bureaucracy. 'Tell the Minister I'll see him at four o'clock.'

Renfrew was right. Ayling *is* a snotty little sod.

She books herself on a lunchtime flight to Heathrow, and turns to kiss Alex.

'I wouldn't kiss me,' he says from beneath the sheets. 'My breath's atrocious. I should eat some dogshit. That'd make it smell better.'

*   *   *

A degree of progress in the Blackadder case, she thinks. Time to mirror that in the shower.

Yesterday—no, yesterday she was out in Tollohill Wood, so it must have been Wednesday— she managed to hold the spray to her head. The next logical step is to get in the shower fully: leave the shower head attached, and drench her whole being at once.

285

If I manage this, I'll find Blackadder. No. Too ambitious. *If I manage this, they'll let me have Red Metcalfe.*

Kate turns the shower on and lets it run, testing the temperature with the back of her hand every few seconds. The water bangs against the floor of the bath and bounces back up in fizzing spurts. It is just about as hot as she can stand when she steps in.

Head down so she can breathe. Water jetting on the back of her head—*where Petra and Elizabeth impacted against oak trees*—and down over her shoulders and breasts. It gurgles in the plughole between her feet. All of her soaked now as the water flows from the heavens, as if she is back in the rainstorm on the *Amphitrite*'s top deck.

Kate grips the top rung of the ladder, lowers her legs and kicks hard at the woman's hands. Two, three, four kicks.

She gasps as the water turns suddenly cold on her neck. But when she looks up, the shower head is still billowing steam.

* * *

Kate back in her car, Leo dropped safely off at school. The radio newsreader sounds cheery. 'There's still no break in the heatwave. Maximum temperatures in the Grampian region today will be 29 degrees Centigrade, 84 degrees Fahrenheit. And no change as we head into the weekend. Saturday bright and hot, Sunday more humid. Don't forget the sunscreen!'

Mid-80s, and still she feels constantly cold. She switches channels.

The front door of the Michaelhouse beckons her in.

A moment of indecision, and then she's out of the car and into reception.

Kate finds her father in his partitioned corner of the conference room, sorting out the day's agenda with Kirstie. He holds up a hand to let her know he's nearly finished.

'. . . and then maybe back to Seaspeed after that, if need be. OK? A quick typed copy would be very useful.'

Kirstie finishes scribbling notes, and begins to open the mail. Frank stands up and kisses his daughter.

'How's it going?' she asks.

'Fine. My boys are looking for the Transit van right now. With any luck, we should get a fix today. We know which course the *Amphitrite* took; all we have to do is work out where she was when she stopped, and search around there till we find it. You?'

'Petra's funeral at eleven. Off to London after that, to see the Home Secretary.'

'Moving in high circles?'

'Moving in bureaucratic treacle, more like.'

Out of the corner of her eye, Kate sees Kirstie opening a large brown padded envelope.

'Do you know what's in that parcel?' she asks sharply.

Kirstie glances up at her. 'One of the videos we ordered, by the look of it.' She looks for a brand name or corporate franking stamp on the envelope, can't find one. 'Funny. They normally come in company envelopes.' She reaches inside. 'Feels like a book, actually.'

Kate isn't sure what exactly first jags her sense of danger. Maybe it's the glimpse of an untucked wire, or the faint smell of marzipan which wafts up from the neck of the package. Perhaps she sees a grease mark on the envelope as Kirstie begins to pull the book out. Whatever it is, it kick-starts dormant memories from police training.

'Stop!'

Kirstie freezes. Her hand is still inside the parcel. 'What?'

'Kirstie—there's a bomb in there.' Kirstie looks blankly at her. 'Let go of the book, and take your hand out. Very slowly. Don't touch the sides on the way out.'

The sweat springs like storm rain on Kirstie's forehead. She does as Kate says, her arm stringed with tensed sinews as she withdraws her hand. One edge of the book peeps from the envelope's torn mouth.

'There's nothing under that parcel, is there?'

'No.'

'And it's on a flat surface?'

Kirstie nods, a quick jerky movement of her head. Kate turns so that she is facing back into the main body of the conference room and claps her hands loudly.

'Listen up, everybody.' She raises her arms above her head. 'I am a police officer, and we have just discovered an explosive device in this room. I want you to leave immediately. Leave this room, leave the hotel. Go now, in an orderly fashion. Pushing and shoving will just slow everybody down. And if you have a mobile phone, don't use it. Radio signals can set bombs off.'

There are about twenty people in the room. One

of them utters a short gasping cry, but the rest are silent. Their own shock and Kate's authority mean that they do as she asks. They get up from their desks and file out, some glancing back over their shoulders as if to convince themselves that this is really happening.

'You too, Dad.'

'Kate, I'm—'

'*Go.*'

He is the last of the MAIB staff to leave. Kate checks that the room is empty, and then walks quickly out and shuts the door behind her. The receptionist is coming round the corner. Her eyes are wide.

'They're saying that there's a—'

'Yes, there is. I want this hotel evacuated. *Now.*'

The receptionist stares dumbly at her. 'I'll have to call the manager.'

'Fuck the manager. You have an evacuation procedure for fire, don't you?'

'Yes.'

'Then use that. But not the alarm itself. Get every member of staff you can find. Tell them to go round every bedroom, all the restaurants and bars. Where's the fire assembly point?'

'On the bowling green at the end of the road.'

'Tell the guests to go there.'

The receptionist runs off. Kate dials 999 from one of the payphones off reception, and asks for the bomb squad. Then she goes out into the street. Some of the MAIB people are still hanging around near the front entrance. She shoos them away.

'Don't just stand there. Go to the end of the road. Dad, take them with you.'

Kate stops dead.

The children are still arriving at school. The usual bustling unruly mass jostles outside the main gates. But that is not what catches Kate's eye. She is looking a few yards further down the road, where a workman is pushing back red-and-white barriers. He is wearing large orange ear defenders, and he is about to start digging up the pavement with a pneumatic drill.

Time stands still, frozen on the edge of a precipice marked 'disaster'. No element of this teetering equilibrium—bomb, children, vibrations from the pneumatic drill—is safe or predictable.

Kate's father is still beside her. She turns to him. 'Is the window by your desk open or shut?'

'Shut. They all are, because of the aircon. Does it matter?'

'It does if the bomb blows the glass out into the street.'

He looks at her in horror.

The workman starts his pneumatic drill up, loud and pounding. Heads turn—mothers, children, guests spilling out of the Michaelhouse.

Kate and Frank start running at the same time: her towards the workman, him back inside the hotel. She sees where he has gone, but even as she turns to call him back it's too late. She glimpses his trailing leg as he disappears through the main entrance, back against the exodus.

She hasn't got time to go after him. She sprints across the road.

Frank throws open the conference-room door and runs over to the window.

Kate reaches the workman and grabs him by the shoulder, spinning him half towards her.

It is a sash window. Frank grabs the bottom edge

and pulls upwards. It doesn't move.

Surprise and anger crowd the workman's face as he turns to face Kate.

Frank sees that the window is locked. Trembling fingers unscrew the lock along its thread.

Kate gesticulates frantically at the drill, crossing and uncrossing her hands to indicate that the workman should turn it off.

Frank throws the window up as far as it will go. He can feel the drill's vibrations through the walls. The parcel squats malevolently on the desk, as if contemplating whether or not to self-destruct. He starts back across the room.

The workman turns the drill off.

Instinctively, Frank looks back towards the sudden silence. Still moving, no longer looking where he is going, he stumbles against the desk and starts to fall.

He is still falling when the bomb goes off.

*   *   *

Frank can't hear a thing, not even a ringing in his ears. Blood streams in rivulets over his skin and on to the floor. His right arm looks like someone's run a cheese grater over it. There's a large jagged tear across the left side of his chest, and a neat parallel of striations further down his stomach.

Warm liquid snakes across his face. He must have sustained head wounds.

The pain is surely on its way, though he can't feel it yet. Two thoughts chase each other through his head: that he's lucky to be alive, and that he shouldn't move an inch. He doesn't feel much like the latter anyway.

291

In the thin line of his vision, large swathes of brick wall muscle through unpeeled plaster, and floorboards curl up on themselves like restless sardines.

Feet appear, then Kate's face close to his. Her mouth moves, stops, moves again. It makes the same sequence of shapes three or four times before she realises he can't hear her. She disappears briefly, and comes back ripping one of the hotel's tablecloths to pieces. He feels the pressure as she applies the makeshift tourniquet to his arm.

The carpet patterns stretch away into the distance. He closes his eyes, and orange spots dance for him. He opens them again.

Now someone else's feet, and above them green trousers. The ambulance crew. They lift him gently on to a stretcher face-up, and the topsides of the world bump past him: the ceilings of the reception and the ambulance, drips swaying with the vehicle's motion, faces bending over him. The sirens wail silently for him.

He begins to fade in and out of consciousness. Maybe they've given him an anaesthetic, he's not sure. A hospital sign, the smooth motion of a trolley beneath him, gleaming walls and the smell of antiseptic. Kate's face again. Bright lights. The operating theatre.

Oblivion.

*　　　*　　　*

Kate shifts irritably in her chair, trying to find a comfortable spot on the hard plastic. Seats that make you want to get up and leave after twenty minutes may be fine in McDonald's, she thinks, but not in hospital waiting areas.

It's the not knowing which is the worst. Like many people who value control, Kate can stand almost anything, bad news included, ahead of ignorance. Every time she visualises Frank under the knife, she conjures up increasingly extreme images of his injuries: perforated eardrums, amputated limbs—*God no, not him too, not after Petra Gallacher and Elizabeth Hart*—internal haemorrhaging, drowning in his own blood, a long slow slide away from life.

Just when she gets her father back, she does her best to lose him again. Perhaps one day she'll see the funny side.

She was the one who told him the letter he got two days ago was a crank. What Frank found, or rather didn't find, beneath the sea simply confirmed this. Or so she thought.

And if she hadn't been there today, if she'd decided simply to go into work without popping in to see him first, Kirstie would have opened that parcel. She'd have lost an eye or a hand. Maybe both, maybe even more than that.

Some you win, some you lose. It gets evened out in the end, give or take.

Kate looks impatiently round the waiting area. Not so long ago—four days ago, in fact, almost to the hour—she was slumped here herself, with a sense of shivering coldness which even now won't leave her. She reads the posters which warn of meningitis and the dangers of drunk driving. On the wall to her left is a notice which tells her: 'Patients are seen in order of their illness/injury. Please be patient if other people are seen before you.'

293

Patients having to be patient. Patients and their patience.

She leans forward and flicks desultorily through the magazines laid out on a low table. *Marie Claire.* Safeways magazine. *Woman and Home. Petroleum Review.* She almost laughs. Only in Aberdeen, the last one.

A young doctor comes out into the waiting area. A stethoscope curls round his neck like a sleeping anaconda.

'Kate Beauchamp?'

She gets up fast and goes over to him. Now that the moment has come, she dreads knowing the extent of the damage.

Waiting for her exam results when he was still her father, in a time before this.

'What's happened?' Gabbled and breathless.

'He's going to be OK.'

She closes her eyes and, exhaling from her diaphragm, lets her shoulders drop. Only now, crumpled with relaxation, does she realise how tense she has been holding her body.

'What's the damage?'

'He has shards of metal in the right side of his head, though fortunately not in his brain or near his eyes. His right arm is badly lacerated. There are surface wounds to his abdomen and legs. No broken bones. His hearing is still impaired, but it's coming back. Nothing that time won't take care of. He won't even trouble airport detectors once we've finished.'

'Can I see him?'

'Not till this afternoon.'

'Doctor, I've got a funeral to go to now, and I'm leaving for London at lunchtime.'

'You simply can't. I'm sorry.'

Kate has seen enough accidents—and worse—to appreciate how difficult doctors' jobs are, even without the added hassle of demanding relatives and friends.

'Sure. I understand. And thank you, Doctor. Thank you very much.'

He nods courteously at her and disappears back through the swing doors.

*　　　*　　　*

Kate stands outside the church and thinks about sex. Funerals and memorial services always make her feel horny. Maybe it's because dirty thoughts are a big two fingers to the solemnity of the occasion. Or because sex is procreation, an affirmation of life in the face of death. Perhaps it's just because most people look good in black. Whatever it is, she can't help but look at Alex and remember that she had her face in his genitals a few hours before.

She cried on Alex's shoulder when she first saw Petra's coffin, and through her tears came a thought: the prime purpose of a coffin is not to hold the dead, but to hide them. Inside the thick varnished wood are things which bear no relation to what Petra Gallacher was like in life. A body slashed to bits, with its hands and feet neatly chopped. No open casket for Petra.

And now she's in the ground, under the same earth which three mornings ago soaked up her blood in the minute or so that she lay dying.

'Good morning, Detective.'

Kate recognises the voice without having to look.

She should have known *he'd* turn up.

'Mr Blaikie. I can't say this is a joy. I was rather hoping not to see you until your court case. Anyway, I thought you'd be too busy to make it. All that work you said you had.'

'I could say the same about you. Any luck in catching your man yet?'

She turns away without answering him and looks across the graveyard to Ferguson. In the crowd, Atkins and Ripley and Wilcox too. Blaikie has hit a raw nerve. That's why they're here, because they haven't got Blackadder yet. Kate would have come anyway, but a victim's funeral always attracts a strong police presence in case the killer turns up. Where better to relive the killing's joy and release than at its final confirmation? Where else can the suffering of those left behind be seen in such stark detail?

Before the service, Kate took Petra's parents aside and asked them as tactfully as possible if they wouldn't mind keeping an eye out for anyone they were unsure about. She located a couple of Petra's closest friends and asked them the same thing. And she organised for Sherwood to attend as the official photographer and take photos of everyone present.

And then the whole plan went to shit. The press turned up and with them a good hundred members of the public, people who never knew Petra but had been moved to come because it was simply awful that something like that could happen to such a pretty girl, especially in Aberdeen. In an instant, there was an entire crowd of potential suspects.

So now Kate and her five colleagues scan the clustered heads and hope against hope that they'll see a man whose face they don't know. As if that wasn't hard enough, the sun is bright, and many people are wearing sunglasses. They can't see whose eyes keep darting around, or whose stare is unnaturally level. They're having to do this blind.

Kate catches Ferguson's eye. He shakes his head.

Wilcox looks over and shrugs his shoulders. Ripley likewise. Atkins comes over to her.

'Nothing. He could be anyone. If he's here at all.'

'I've got to go to London. Let me know if Sherwood's photos show anything.'

*   *   *

Kate looks out of the window and waits for the Home Secretary to arrive.

She remembers the area well from her days at Scotland Yard, and the way in which it reeks of understated power: the massive grey squares of the Home Office, the armed soldiers at the barracks gates, and the colonial splendour of the Foreign Office across St James' Park, itself blooming with colour. Government departments, swallowing thousands of civil servants every morning and spewing them out again every evening. An army of grey suits toiling to provide the information on which the decisions of state are made. There is immeasurably more money in the Square Mile and immeasurably more innovation in even the smallest of business parks; but when it comes to sheer authority, nowhere else comes anywhere near this small fiefdom north-west of Westminster Bridge.

The Home Secretary comes bustling down the corridor. Kate stands.

'Detective Chief Inspector Beauchamp?' He shakes her hand. 'Please come through.'

He is smaller than Kate expected. She thinks of television's distorting power, the way in which it gives the viewer no clue as to the subject's real size.

They go through into his office. It is understatedly elegant, in the way that barristers' chambers often are: offices for men who like to think they are working in a house rather than a corporate building. The desk looks mahogany, and the fireplace on the far side of the room is real. Clearly New Labour's much-vaunted public austerity has encountered pockets of resistance.

'Good Lord. Aren't you hot in all those clothes?'

'I'm fine. Thank you.'

He guides her to a chair, and perches on the edge of the desk rather than going round to sit behind it. His movements are rapid and efficient. He is a man with more work than time, and determined not to waste a second of the latter. He comes straight to the point.

'Your request is unusual to say the least, Detective, and I cannot see any way in which I can honour it. Redfern Metcalfe is a violent man, and even a temporary release would cause major problems. Of course, he has not yet been consulted on the issue himself.'

'If it's publicity you're concerned about, sir, the answer's simple. There would be none.'

'It would set a precedent. An escorted absence from incarceration, which is basically what you are suggesting, can only be granted when all three of the following conditions are met: that the prisoner is detained in category C conditions, that the prisoner has four years or less to run on his tariff,

298

and that he is due to have his case reviewed by the parole board within twelve months. Even then, escorted absences are usually only to the nearest town, not halfway across the country. Redfern Metcalfe meets none of those conditions. He is a category B prisoner, he has the best part of eleven years left on his tariff, and he is nowhere near parole. If I agree to your request, I open myself up to every Tom, Dick and Harry trying a similar stunt. We're trying to tighten up the prison system, not liberalise it.'

'With all due respect, sir'—*how often that phrase translates as 'You're talking bollocks, sir'*—'the issue of precedent is largely immaterial. The amount of prisoner releases requested by a senior police officer is and will remain minute: certainly small enough to merit treating each case as a stand-alone. Redfern Metcalfe is a unique man and, I dare say, a unique prisoner.'

'You know why he's there, Detective. You were first to the scene, as I recall. *You saw what he did.*'

'And I saw how he was driven to it. I saw how he accepted—no, how he *insisted* on his own imprisonment. He is without doubt the most extraordinary man I've ever worked with.'

'The governor of Wormwood Scrubs is unsure what effect an excursion, particularly to crime scenes, would have on his psychiatric health.'

'Perhaps. But I would trust Red's own judgement on that. He has acute self-perception. He knows he should be inside. He knows what a thin line he walks. He knows what will hurt him and what won't. I don't. But what I do know is this. If there's anyone who can understand the mentality of the man committing these atrocities in

299

Aberdeen, it's Red Metcalfe.'

'In that case, show him your case notes. Take him the crime-scene photos. He could give you an opinion without leaving his cell, and whatever he saw would be at one remove. You'd get your help, he'd keep his sanity.'

'Sir—did you ever see Red work a crime scene?'

'No.'

'He's like a bloodhound. He doesn't just look: he smells, he listens, he touches, he tastes. He uses every single sense God gave him, and maybe a couple that he didn't. My showing him case notes and photos and autopsy reports simply won't be enough. It would be like giving him a travel brochure and trying to persuade him he'd been on holiday. If this is to have any chance of working, he has to get the scent back. He has to put himself in the killer's shoes. He has to follow the killer, sense him, feel him. *Be* him, almost. That's the way he works.'

'But even then, you couldn't guarantee success?'

'Of course not. You can't guarantee anything in this kind of case. But Red Metcalfe's my best shot. If I didn't sincerely believe that, I wouldn't be wasting my time or yours.'

The Home Secretary steeples his fingers under his chin, and Kate knows she has him.

'How long would you want him for?'

'As long as it takes.'

'No. Absolutely not. I'm not giving you an open-ended deal, I'm not having him out indefinitely. What's the minimum you need him for?'

'A night.'

'Why a night?'

'The killings have both taken place at night.

300

He'd have to visit the scenes under cover of darkness. There'd be no point doing it during the day. The whole ambience would be different.'

'Grampian Police are prepared to shoulder all protection and transport costs?'

'Yes.'

'It won't be cheap.'

'Nor is running a full-time incident room, sir.'

'You personally will take responsibility for all aspects of this—excursion?'

'Yes.'

His legs are crossed. He swings his right foot gently back and forth.

'If he agrees, you've got twenty-four hours.'

'That's—that may well not be enough.'

'It'll have to be, Detective. That's all I'm prepared to give you.'

'Thirty-six hours.'

'Twenty-four. Take it or leave it.'

This is how decisions of state are made, like haggling in the souk.

'Twenty-four hours, from when to when?'

'From the moment he leaves prison to the moment he's back there again.'

'That certainly wouldn't be enough, sir. It's a couple of hours' travelling each way, and that only if we cut it very fine. Can I not have him for twenty-four hours in Aberdeen itself?'

'Twenty-four hours, from the moment he leaves Wormwood Scrubs to the moment he leaves Aberdeen. Final offer.'

Kate knows when to stick and when to twist.

'That'll be fine. Thank you, sir.'

*   *   *

301

There are five main lifer centres in England: Brixton, Gartree, Long Lartin, Wakefield and Wormwood Scrubs. Red is in Wormwood Scrubs, and as so often it is running in excess of its official capacity.

Usual visiting hours on a Friday are 1.15 p.m. to 3.15 p.m. Kate has had to arrange special permission even to see Red. And since it's past normal visiting hours, she has to go all the way to his cell. They won't let her meet him in the visiting area, as they usually would. She can't be bothered to argue the toss.

No handbags, food or drink are allowed beyond the visitors' search area. Kate rummages in her bag for a pound coin, finds one, puts her bag in a locker, inserts the coin, shuts the door and takes the key. The warder who will escort her points to a sign on the wall asking visitors with bad news to tell staff before they see the inmate. Kate shakes her head.

Long corridors, footsteps and shouts echoing round the walls and in Kate's head. The warder walks ahead of her, keys jangling from his belt. She follows the back of his head. His hair is chopped slide-rule straight across.

In her navel a sense of fear which takes her a moment to decode.

Evasion.

Kate has only ever run from three things in her life, and they are all coming back to her at once. Her father, the *Amphitrite,* and now Red—not for who he is, but for what he reminds her of, the year they spent chasing Silver Tongue. Red is in here for the way in which he brought the case to an end—a

302

way which so traumatised Kate that she applied for a transfer from the Metropolitan Police that very week.

Her in with personnel, the staff giving her sidelong glances and none of them remotely capable of understanding her pain.

'Where do you want to go?'

'As far away as possible.'

'Yes, but where?'

Someone has a map of the UK in the back of their diary. They look at it. 'The furthest major town from London is Inverness.'

'Right. I'll go there.'

'But that was just a figure of speech, right? As far as possible?'

'I'll go to Inverness.'

They call Inverness. No suitable positions available.

'What's the next furthest?'

'Aberdeen.'

Aberdeen, where there is a suitable position, and where her Auntie B lives. All to get away from that case and everything which came with it. Jez, with whom she fell in love; Duncan, who sold them out; and Red, the man the Met called 'Golden Bollocks', finally up against a killer smarter than him.

The warder turns a corner and stops.

'Right at the end, on the left. When you want out, just come back this way and press there.' He points to a green button set at head height on the opposite wall.

Kate nods. Her throat is dry.

This is the far end of the prison. Under the Good Order and Discipline provisions, formerly the infamous Section 43, Red has been isolated

303

from the other prisoners. Most inmates who apply for GOAD are sex offenders, the nonces and beasts of prison slang. In Red's case, it's because he used to be a copper. Probably put a couple of his fellow inmates inside, at one stage or another.

Kate starts off down the corridor. White walls on either side afford her the haziest outline of her own reflection. There are no other cells on this corridor: just Redfern Metcalfe, former Detective Superintendent, the man who turned himself in and pleaded guilty to all charges, even when his entire defence team—and the prosecution too, truth be told—reckoned he would have walked in an instant had he pleaded self-defence.

More to this than professional memories. She looked up to Red Metcalfe. And when he went inside—when he put himself inside, in effect—that was it. She went to see him, and he wouldn't see her. She wrote to him, and he never replied. He wanted nothing to do with her. Not her, not his wife Susan, not anyone from his past. He cut her off as his own brother Eric had cut him off, after he'd turned Eric in for a murder buried deep in the past.

Thick belts of summer sun streak through the skylights and plunge to the floor. As Kate approaches, she sees the dense lattice of bars on Red's cell, horizontal and vertical like a fishing net of tempered steel. The smell of drains in her nostrils, there and quickly gone again.

Kate sees Red before he sees her. He is lying on his bunk, writing. Reference books are piled up to one side of him, their depths studded with yellow Post-Its. His face is paler and fleshier than she remembers, from lack of daylight and exercise respectively. Prison tan. His trademark red hair

304

rises like flames from his scalp, and he has a beard, red and slightly woolly. No TV cameras or aspiring detectives to look good for any more.

'Hello, Red.'

He looks up, startled. He must have assumed she was a warder.

'Kate.' His voice is curiously formal. 'My word. What a surprise.'

'What kind of surprise?'

'A pleasant one, of course.'

'Why "of course"?'

He sits up on his bunk. The squares between the bars are too small to frame his entire face: she sees an eye here, an ear there.

'I needed time to adjust, Kate. That's why I behaved as I did. To you, and to others. But I'm used to it now. My behaviour must have offended you, and I apologise. But you know it wasn't personal. I was like that with everyone, not just you.' He lays his pencil neatly across his pad, just below the place where his small neat writing ends. 'You should have told me you were coming.'

'It's rather short notice, I'm afraid.'

'How's life? You went to Scotland, yes? Edinburgh?'

'Aberdeen.' She's surprised he knows anything about her at all.

'The granite city. "One detests Aberdeen with the detestation of a thwarted lover. It is the one hauntingly and exasperatingly loveable city of Scotland." You know the quote?'

She shakes her head.

'Lewis Grassic Gibbon.' He smiles. 'Amazing how much knowledge there is to find, when you have time for it.'

305

Kate nods towards the pile of reference books. 'I can see.'

'They've put me in charge of recataloguing the prison library. It was a shambles. We had to begin right at the beginning—the Bible, Shakespeare, *Encyclopaedia Britannica*. There are about three thousand titles in there now.'

'What are the most popular?'

'That depends. Religion, probably the Koran. Non-fiction—*The Prince,* Machiavelli. And fiction'—he gives a little laugh—'Dostoevsky. *Crime and Punishment*, appropriately enough. But you haven't come here to discuss the reading habits of prison inmates, and you haven't come here for a social visit. What can I do for you?'

She plunges straight in.

'Two murders. Both female, one young, one old. No connection we can find, apart from the fact they're dead. Both stabbed. One had her throat cut, the other could have died from any one of four separate wounds. Both found in woodland. Hands and feet cut off and tied round their necks. An adder, live, secured to each victim's chest. Semen found inside each victim. No foreign object penetration.'

'And you want me to do what?'

'Help us.'

'Help you how?'

'Come to the scenes. Read the case notes. Do what you used to do. If you're willing, the Home Secretary says we can have you for twenty-four hours.'

'Twenty-four hours? Who do you think I am? Paul Daniels? Do you really think I can pick it up again in twenty-four hours?'

'I don't know. Do *you*?'

'Assuming I'm willing to do it at all.'

'You know what your reputation was. People still talk about you.'

'Do me a favour, Kate. Don't appeal to my vanity.'

'I'm not. I wouldn't. I'm appealing to—I don't know, your sense of duty. We found the first on Tuesday morning, the second yesterday morning. By the law of averages, the next one will be tomorrow morning. I've got to stop him.'

'I can't do it.'

'Why not?'

'Kate, this is my place. Here, in my cell, in the library. It's not exciting, but I'm here—I put myself here—for a very good reason. Doing what you ask would totally negate that reason. What I have, I have to suppress, you know that. I'm like an alcoholic. I can never ever have just one drink. I can never ever go back to just one case. It's only by ignoring what's in my head that I can conquer it.'

'We're talking about two dead women here, Red. Not one fucking drink.'

'No. We're talking about a very long shot.'

'I told my Chief Constable and the Home Secretary that you're my best shot.'

'In that case, I don't think much of your arsenal.'

She switches back, doing what he first showed her how to do: think like a boxer moves. Probe, look for the angle, cut back, start again. Keep the other person hopping.

'You remember what you had above your desk in Scotland Yard?'

'Yes, I do. And that's a cheap shot, because . . .'

'It was a quote. "Problem-solving is hunting. It is

307

savage pleasure, and we are born to it."'

'It's a cheap shot because that was a different time, and you know it.'

'And I know that there are two women dead. He tortured them. Their histamine levels were through the roof. You remember Bart Miller, the one who Silver Tongue flayed alive?' *Silver Tongue.* Even now, she can't bring herself to say his real name. 'Their levels were as high as his. That means they went through about as much pain as you can imagine. If we stop even one person going through that, isn't it worth it?'

'Of course it is. I'm not disputing that. But I'm not the right person to help you.'

'You are. You *are*. It's just that you won't.'

She can understand his reluctance, of course she can. But she's prepared to let this case do to her what it will as long as she gets Blackadder, and it sticks in her craw that he won't do the same. The anger is beginning to flood her, like the water on the *Amphitrite*'s car deck. And unless she uses it and channels it away from her, it will rise and rise until it tips her over and takes her down.

She won't beg him. Begging him's not going to work.

Kate inhales through flared nostrils and clenched teeth. She flicks her hand dismissively.

'You were my hero, Red. When you asked me to be on the team for the Silver Tongue case, it was the proudest moment of my professional life. I would have killed to work with you. You represented what I believed in, the reason why I joined the force: the struggle against evil. It sounds corny, but it's true, you know it is. And you taught me that, to combat evil, you first have to recognise

308

it. You can't fight it without knowing it. That's how you caught all the others, by letting yourself think like them. You surrendered to the dark side because you believed it was worthwhile. And it was. And it still is. It'll always be worthwhile. It's just that you're too gutless to put yourself through it any more.'

Red is silent. Kate wonders whether he's going to ask her to leave.

'You have a gift, Red. Empathy, projection, call it what you want. It's a very flawed gift, but it was given to you because you were man enough to use it. I don't have that gift.'

'You're a very good officer.'

'Sure. And I have what I've learnt, and what I've taught myself. But I'm not you. It's your bad luck to be the best.'

'I put myself in here because I surrendered once too often, Kate. I switched sides. I'm not with the angels any more. That's why I'm here.'

And switch again. Dance, jab, punch. 'Think of it this way. If I needed a kidney transplant, and you were the only possible donor in the whole world, would you do it? Give up a kidney for me?'

'Of course.'

'Of course. Even though it would cause you horrendous pain, and even though it had a pretty even chance of coming to nothing. But you'd still think it was worth it. You might wish it was someone else who had to make the choice, but you'd accept that you were the one who'd been singled out. You'd moan that it was unfair, but you'd live with it. That's what I'm asking for now. I know there's no guarantee of success, and I know what it might do to you. I don't underestimate that for a second. But it's worth the shot. End of story.'

Red covers his face with his hands and draws them slowly down over his eyes. The third and fourth fingers of each hand press against the side of his nose.

His eyes crinkle. He's smiling. He takes his hands away.

'Consultant role only. I'm not involved in operational issues at any stage.'

'They wouldn't allow that anyway.'

'And if you catch him when I'm there, I don't want to see him.'

'Done.'

'You must be a real pain to work for,' he says. 'I bet you always get your own way.'

'When it's for a good reason, yes.'

'When do my twenty-four hours start?'

* * *

A blizzard of calls from the prison governor's office and on Kate's mobile, often simultaneously.

Clothes for Red from prison stocks, inevitably ill-fitting: the legs are too long and bunch up round the ankles, the arms are too short and end an inch above his wrists.

Police protection to be arranged for the trip to Heathrow, in the air and throughout Red's stay in Aberdeen.

Escorted absence forms drawn up and signed. The Home Secretary's written permission biked over by special despatch.

The Scottish First Minister's office informed.

Grampian Police alerted and told to have the crime scenes ready.

310

Two quick personal calls: one to Frank in the hospital to check how he is and promise to visit him the moment she can get away, and the other to Alex, all geared up for a Friday night out with the lads.

Rooms booked at the Hugill, another of Aberdeen's business hotels, to include an external corner room on the third floor or above, and no immediate access to fire escape or balcony.

Six seats booked on the last outbound flight from Heathrow, with permission for four of the passengers to be armed. And hold the flight till they get there.

It takes off forty-five minutes behind schedule. An entire section of business class has been cordoned off for them. A couple of people make disapproving noises when they see that Kate, Red and the four men in suits which bulge in the wrong places are the reason for the delay. Kate gives the tutters a look that would have given Medusa a run for her money.

Red says nothing all the way to Aberdeen. He reads the case notes and looks at the photos, pencilling words in the margin when he feels it necessary. He doesn't look up or around him once, not even to wave away the stewardess when she comes round with drinks. Kate keeps a bottle of mineral water for him, and eventually drinks it herself. Like a young animal emerging into the world, Red looks slightly startled to be out in the open again; not that the back of a police car and an airline cabin can necessarily be classed as 'being out in the open'.

They are first off the plane at Aberdeen's Dyce Airport, which prompts more grumbling and another of Kate's death stares. The light is at last fading by the time they ease into a squad car and set off on the short journey to Woodend. Red sits next to Kate in the back seat and looks at the bright lights of a city gearing up for a Friday night out.

The crime scene is well secured. Arc lights are placed on the perimeter, and two squad cars block the bridge which leads to the hospital. Half the case detectives are here, together with those from the firearms division who have been deputed to watch over Red.

The car carrying Kate and Red stops on the perimeter. They get out. He points to the lights.

'I want them off. And no one in the area.'

'Because they'll distract you?'

'Yes.'

And because he's not sure how he's going to react. If he's going to freak out, he doesn't want to do it too publicly.

'I can put them on the perimeter of the crime scene. No further.'

He considers it, nods. 'All right. But everyone else back with them. Even you.'

Lights off. Him alone, in an area about fifty metres by fifty. If she didn't know him better, she'd say he was thinking about escape.

Know him better. She thought she knew him when they worked on the Silver Tongue case. Then she saw what he did to Silver Tongue. She hadn't known him at all.

'All right. But every part of that perimeter will be guarded.'

'I understand.'

Kate raises her voice. 'OK. I want everyone back, out of the area. Fan out along all sides of the

312

perimeter.' She does a quick head count. 'Seven or eight on each side, at about five-metre intervals. I want you quiet, too. Peter, kill the arc lights.'

'What?'

'Kill the lights.'

'Why?'

'Because they weren't here when Blackadder was. That's why.'

'Who the fuck does he think he is? We didn't fight Bannockburn for this.'

She marches up to Ferguson and shoves her face right in his. 'He's here because I asked for him, and while he is, you will treat him like fucking royalty. Got it?'

And so, in a cordoned square with an audience which watches his every move by moonlight, Red Metcalfe tries to get the scent back. It takes him a while. Twice he falters, twice he wants to walk to the edge of the cordoned area and tell Kate he can't do it.

He refuses to let this impotence fluster him. Slowly the control comes back, and with it the knack. It trickles through layers of resistance, something deeply buried but never extinct. Sometimes he digs for it, sometimes it rises to meet him.

He prowls round the area where Petra Gallacher was left, checks the lie of the land, looks at ingress and egress routes, picks up handfuls of earth or dirt, shines his torch on the photos or the witness interviews or the autopsy reports, checks details he's not sure about. He puts his face to the ground where she lay bleeding and sniffs it, feels it. Moves back and forth, stabbing in the air, quick motion and slow. He could be mistaken for a practitioner

313

of t'ai chi.

He is there for an hour before he comes over to Kate.

'Well?'

'Let's go to the second scene.'

There is a stirring of discontent. All that, and nothing to show for it?

'You heard him.' Kate claps her hands. 'We're going to number two.'

Ferguson comes up to her. ' "You heard him?" ' He mimics her words. 'Who's running this show, boss? You or him?'

'I am.'

'It doesn't look like it.'

She knows how this must appear to Ferguson. He will see it as Kate in some way abdicating her professional standing. She wonders whether he thinks she has designs on Red.

'I don't care what it looks like.'

They go through the same routine down in Tollohill Wood. Red is there for almost exactly the same length of time as at Woodend, though if he checks his watch, Kate doesn't see it.

'I'd like to go back to the hotel,' he says when he's through.

To Kate's left, an explosive 'For fuck's sake!'

She ignores it. 'That's it, everybody. Thank you all very much. In the incident room at nine o'clock tomorrow morning, as usual.'

She gets Red back into the squad car before anyone can have a go at him. He turns to her the moment the doors are shut.

'You've got it all wrong.'

'How?'

'He's not a sexual sadist. The stabbings and

314

mutilation do not disproportionately target the genitalia, breasts or face. And there is no penetration.'

'Not with a foreign object, no. But he raped them.'

'No. He masturbated first, and then pushed the semen in by hand. In both cases.'

'How do you know?'

'The semen was found relatively near the entrance to the vagina: six inches inside Petra Gallacher, five for Elizabeth Hart. Those were the maximum distances inside. Ejaculation would have propelled it substantially further.'

'What if he pulled out at the last minute?'

'You think he's concerned about birth control?'

'Why would he do what you're saying?'

'Confusion. To confuse us, because *he's* confused. Both, probably. He feels triumph when he kills them, and he expresses it through masturbation. But this is a symptom of the killings rather than the cause. He does not kill to get his kicks, but he gets his kicks when he kills. Does that make sense?'

'Just about. Though it is possible for killers driven by sadistic sexual fantasies to kill without attempting penetration of their victims or performing any overtly sexual acts. The "sexual" refers to fantasy, not activity.'

'Granted. But you must look at the context.'

'Which is?'

'These crimes are organised rather than disorganised, focused on the act not the process. You have it the other way round.'

'And for good reasons. They show all the signs of a disorganised killer: excessive violence,

315

dismemberment, abuse, no disposal scheme for the body . . .'

'Yes. But those organised/disorganised definitions aren't foolproof. Don't hold them as infallible. Once you accept that he's not a sexual sadist, what do you have?'

'A non-sexual sadist?'

'No. He's not a sadist.'

'He tortures them.'

'And then he cuts them up and arranges them. It's ritual. That's the key. The torture is part of the ritual. I would guess that Blackadder is one of the small proportion of serial killers who are genuinely insane.'

'You always said that no killer was insane. That every crime made sense according to its own logic, however twisted that may be.'

'And I stand by that. I mean insane in the medical sense of the word. Imperfectly grounded in reality. Blackadder is driven to murder by one or more of the following.' Red ticks them off on his fingers. 'Psychosis, or a break with reality; hallucinations, seeing or hearing things which aren't there; or delusions, immutable false ideas. In this context—and that's key, Kate, the context, I must emphasise that—his actions make perfect sense to him. The dismemberment, the adder, the rope of hands and feet around the neck: they all make perfect sense. To him.'

'And what is his particular psychosis?'

Red holds up his hands. 'That, I don't know. And that's going to be the hardest thing to find. If we're lucky, it's been triggered by an external event which we can work out. But many psychoses are internalised. Think of Richard Chase, for example.'

316

'Chase? He was the . . .'—Kate clicks her fingers rapidly while she summons the memory—'that vampire guy in California, wasn't he?'

'The vampire of Sacramento, yes. He believed his own blood was turning to powder, so he killed six people and drank *their* blood in order to replace his own. Or David Berkowitz, the Son of Sam, who said he was tormented by howling voices and mad fantasies. He said his neighbour was the devil and had commanded him to kill. His neighbour turned out to be an old guy who ran a telephone answering service. But that's my point. There are two genuinely delusional killers, and in neither case could you have uncovered their particular delusion simply from detective work. Or even from the murder scenes themselves, necessarily. Certainly not Berkowitz's. I don't know how much blood Chase could drink in one go.'

'Where do we start?'

'Childhood abuse. It's unlikely that a child who grew up in a stable and loving family will consistently prefer fantasy to real life. Yes, there are some killers who had blissful childhoods and who just happen to be born bad. But the law of averages takes us the other way.'

The protection team is waiting for them at the Hugill.

'I'll sleep on it,' he says. 'The answer's more likely to come if I don't force it.'

'I guess so.'

Kate fishes in her pocket and brings out a card. She hands it to him. 'You think of something, call me, I don't care what time of night it is.'

He opens the door and steps on to the pavement. The armed men cluster round him. As

317

they escort him inside, he looks back at her. His face is completely unreadable.

*   *   *

Bronagh is dozing in her armchair by the time Kate gets to her house. She opens her eyes, clears her throat, and squints at her watch.

'I'm sorry,' Kate says. 'It's been a hell of a day.'

'So what's new?'

'It'll get better soon.'

'That's what you always say.'

'I'll be fine. Where is the little terror?'

'Fast asleep, I should imagine.'

Kate goes into Bronagh's spare room. Leo is rolled up under a sheet. She bends over him. 'Petal, we're going home.'

He stirs, and wakes. Sleepy eyes, tousled hair.

'Mummy, I hurt myself in school today.'

'Where, sweetheart?'

'I fell over in the playground. Here.'

He unrolls himself from the sheet and pulls up his left pyjama leg. 'Look.'

There is a tiny graze on his knee. Kate has to look twice even to see it. 'Leo, that's nothing.'

'It hurts.'

'Not for a brave boy like you.'

'It *hurts*, Mummy.'

The anger comes without warning this time, ushered through her by pulsing fatigue. 'For God's sake, Leo. I've got corpses who've had their throats cut. My father's in hospital with pieces of metal embedded in his skull. Now pull yourself together.'

His eyes open wide and bewildered. There is a gasp at the door. Bronagh, who has heard Kate

318

snap and can't believe it either.

Leo starts to cry, and it is Bronagh who rushes to the bed to hug him, Bronagh whose face is smeared with reproach for what cannot be unsaid.

* * *

His eighteenth birthday. Alone in the house, no one there to help him celebrate his age of majority. Alone in the house, so he can emerge from the basement and pretend that it is his, all his.

There is a knock at the door. He opens it on to a thin woman with scraped-back hair. She looks vaguely familiar, though he can't place her.

'You're the boy.' Her voice is sharp and jerky. 'You're Ivan's boy.'

'My da's dead.'

'It's you I want. I've something to tell you, and you have to accept that it's true. *Have to.*'

It's her desperation to be believed that reminds him who she is. The mad woman whom Ivan brought home the day he was drowned. The one from the asylum he was screwing, the one who ran screaming to the police.

'Carrie? That's your name?'

'Cassie. Cassie. Now listen to me.'

He doesn't ask her to come in, and she doesn't ask if she can. Her eyes blaze with fervour.

'They told you he was drowned. Your da. He went out into the storm to look for people he could help, and he drowned. That's what they told you, right?'

'That's what *happened.*'

'He didn't drown.'

'They found pieces of his boat.'

319

'He didn't drown. I know how he died. Do you want to know too?'

Fishing nets distended with the timbers from Ivan's trawler. Slurping from the dog bowl as Craig mocks.

'Yes. I want to know.'

So she tells him.

*   *   *

The children go outside to play. Ivan hauls himself to his feet. 'I'm going to take a bath.'

He takes his time about it. Three weeks at sea have left him permeated with fish oil and grime and diesel fumes. The first time he fills the bath, the water turns black in seconds. He drains it and starts again. The water is cold by the time he's halfway clean, and he drains the bath on tidemarks of dirt and soap.

There are no towels.

'Ailish!' Loud and petulant. 'Ailish! Bring me a towel!'

She comes with one held open in front of her. As he reaches for it, it falls from her hands to the wet floor.

'For heaven's sake.' He bends to pick it up.

Head down, he doesn't see what she was holding hidden beneath the towel.

A fishing net. Thin mesh nylon, virtually indestructible.

She throws the net on to him. It spills from his crown and cascades down his body. The green gills entangle him. Struggle grapple now as he tries to free himself. The net's holes are prison bars, blotching a face contorted in fury. Ailish no longer simply holds the net: she has become part of it, she *is* the net, the snare, the bedmate, deathmate, murder's strong right arm.

'What the fuck are you doing, woman? What the fuck are you doing?'

Craig comes out from hiding and into the bathroom. He holds an axe in both hands, one at the foot of the shaft and the other below the head. Protests dying shocked in Ivan's throat and coming louder again as Craig swings the axe high above his head and down, top hand flying down the shaft for better leverage, two blows on to Ivan's chest, striped red gashes blooming on white skin freshly cleaned.

Ivan topples backwards into the bath. Craig hands Ailish the axe. Even in her thin arms, it feels light. A single clean blow through Ivan's neck, and off comes his head.

They work fast now. Ivan's body goes into an old trunk, and they clean every part of the bathroom, squeezing ragfuls of blood and gristle down the plugholes until the drains must surely cough them up again in protest. They scrub until their arms are numb. Molecule by molecule, they are erasing him from their lives.

They stop cleaning at nightfall. The bathroom is spotless, the axehead glistens as if it's new, and the clothes which they wore to kill him are in the trunk with his body and some of his clothes, his oilskins included. Not a single trace of him is left.

Ailish goes to eat with the children, and tells them that Ivan has gone off into the storm. When dinner is over, she puts them to bed.

The moon is a thin slice in the sky, and offers little light. No one sees them as they take the trunk,

Craig in the lead to shoulder most of the weight. They haul it down to the water's edge and load it on to Ivan's boat *Orca*. Craig fetches rocks from the beach to weight the trunk down further. They attach Craig's own launch to *Orca*'s stern, and set off into the storm.

Out beyond the bay they sail, the land's protection gone. The waves swell higher. Craig takes them head on, knowing that he cannot afford to have the boat turned and left broadside on. At the top of every wave they are suspended weightless for a moment before the boat plunges down towards the trough.

'This is madness,' cries Ailish, barely able to make herself heard above the storm.

On the deck, lashed down hard so it doesn't slide, the dead man's trunk squats impassive.

The water cascades down the gunwales as *Orca* shakes itself free from each dunking, and if Ailish thinks this is madness she's damn well right, but there's no turning back now. The spray whips across their faces in lacerating flat blades, and far behind them the waves explode against the cliff bases.

The most massive wave imaginable towers overhead, so large that they can't see the night sky around it. The water cracks into a leering smile as it hovers above them. Craig's hands on the wheel and Ailish's on the side-rail, holding on for dear life.

The wave crashes down, as hard and unyielding as falling concrete. The trawler pitches forward and round, stern chasing bow, and then another wave batters it back to its original course.

'Let the trunk go! Let it go now!'

Ailish takes the wheel, and Craig duck-walks down the deck. Brief moments of balance amidst the tossing, and he hacks hard at a section of railing: one blow and another quickly, grabbing a stanchion as they plough headlong through another wall of water. Three more blows and the side-rail tumbles into the sea.

Craig hacks at the trunk's lashings. The boat heels to leeward and the trunk begins to slide, Craig stepping deftly out of its path as it slips into the churning water. When he next looks, the trunk has gone, swallowed by the hungry sea.

Every sailor knows that when the sea has got its own it grows calmer. When they turn for home, it is into subsiding waves and an increasingly benevolent wind. They climb into the launch. Ailish bails the bilges, while Craig swings the axe at the *Orca*'s hull. He holes it twice below the waterline.

Once scuttled, the trawler sinks fast. Craig with quick hands slips the painter so they don't go down with it. They wait until *Orca* disappears for good. Then they start up the launch's engine and head back to shore, skipping lightly over the exhausted ripples of a spent ocean.

* * *

Cassie McKechnie, poor Cassie McKechnie. Given the gift of second sight, prophecy, ESP, call it what you will, and condemned to be labelled as insane and left scornfully unbelieved.

They sit in silence, outsiders together, waiting for Ailish and Craig to return. In the kitchen, as the family were when Cassie first came back with the police, all those years ago.

He is free in the house now. The terrible knowledge he has is liberating. Ivan did not give this house, his life, up to the interlopers. This is the boy's place—he is the son and heir, a king returning home from long exile.

Who can tear from the veins the bad seed, the curse?

Ailish and Craig come back at dusk.

Ailish knows instantly who Cassie is and why she has come. She has always known that this moment would arrive, that her secret is known outside the walls of the bathroom and above the waves of the sea. If she has borne that dreadful anticipation for every minute of every day, it is still a fraction of the price she owes.

She walks over to the sink. Craig stands by the door, uncertain.

A flash of steel in the air. The knife disappears inside Cassie's shirt, inside her chest. Surprise and anguish crowd her face, blood already circling on the fabric. Ailish grips the handle hard and pulls the knife back out. A sucking as the air rushes to fill the vacuum inside Cassie's dying body and Ailish striking again, but this time the boy is too quick. He grabs her wrist and bangs it against the table. The knife clatters to the floor.

Craig comes towards them. The boy down to the floor and up again with the knife, turning and thrusting under Craig's ribcage and into his heart. Craig keeps moving forward and down even as the boy yanks the blade free again. He is gone before he hits the floor.

Craig dead and Cassie dying. Son and mother now, just the two of them. Everything shines with

324

brightness unknown.

Ailish pulls her shirt off one shoulder. The cloth falls from the sagging frost of her breast.

'You have no respect for this?' She cups it in her hand. 'This suckled you. I am your mother. I gave you life.'

He hesitates. In the moment he sees that this is what he's always wanted to do, he cannot bring himself to do it.

The drips of her lover's blood hang on the end of the knife in his hand. Her face beseeches him not to go through with it.

His father begot him, his mother gave him birth. She is the furrow into which Ivan's seed was sown. Without the father, there is no birth. Ivan is the true agent of his being.

Behind Ailish's supplication, the deep belief that the boy won't bring himself to kill her.

She is wrong. The urge is too strong.

He slashes at her throat. She screams at him— 'Don't make your life an eternity of shame!'—and the cut comes, so long and deep that it all but takes her head off. The cry he hears as she goes down is his own. Her death-cry is his birth-cry. Mother and son, agonising out their evolution.

He throws her body against Craig's. Her head lolls back as if hinged.

Her voice, nagging and cursing and belittling. 'You disgusting animal. You little bastard. I gave you life. You are the snake I bore.'

He stoops to her fallen body. Colours in her neck. The pink of the vestibular folds, vocal cords pearly white, yellow the vocal ligaments. He rips out her larynx and stuffs it into the garbage disposal unit. He turns the switch, and the unit

325

spits it back up at him. Even when she's dead, he still can't silence her.

In this blood-strewn kitchen, he knows exactly what he must do. He goes through the house like a whirlwind, overturning tables, smashing pictures, breaking chairs, tipping clothes and possessions to the floor, staining some of them with his effluent. Ailish's life-force invigorates him. Her energy gives him the strength to obliterate the last traces of her existence, just as she did to Ivan. He charges through the rooms, up and down and up and down. The only place he leaves untouched is the basement.

When he has finished with the house, he carries Cassie's body up to the clifftops and throws it off. It twists slowly in the air as it falls. He watches as it bounces from rock to rock, and comes to rest spread-eagled and limp. The waves lick her, at first with the diffidence of a tentative lover, and then with increasing confidence. They slide her back and forth, land to sea and back again, until the soil relinquishes her and the waves suck her down.

The night sky vaults above him, and from its ceiling hangs a heavy moon. It is a couple of days off full, the time when the lunar pull drags the ocean's detritus on to the shore and the sea purifies itself. There is the sea, and who will drain it dry? Precious as silver, inexhaustible, ever-new, it breeds the more they reap it, tides of crimson dying their souls blood-red.

He walks down the path to the beach. The waves come in a whipping hosepipe across the bay, spray manes flying from their backs. They throw themselves at his feet and run back down again over the pebbles, bubbling in muted ripples of applause.

This is it. This eternal battle fought over millions of years, monotonous and repetitive. Its front line constantly shifts, but is always the same, the place where land and water collide. The sea can never be turned off, never quietened. The winds may be stilled and the sun may be blocked, but the sea refuses to be quelled. It is destined to beat this endless tattoo against the shoreline until the end of time. There is peace in the sea back down to man's origins. When the last man has taken his last breath, the sea will still remain.

Although he loves the sea, that does not make it his friend. The sea is a foe. It must be coaxed and flattered and cajoled, but never trusted. One must love the sea, but equally one must fear it. One must know its moods and caprices, must know when to risk taking liberties and when to obey without question. The sea gives freely, but it also takes.

Now he is close, he wants to immerse himself in the sea, give himself completely over to it. The water can hold him in salty suspension, embrace him, give him freedom and shelter. Wash him clean in its sympathy. He can drown, and the bubbles will stream from the sides of his smiling mouth and sound in his ears like the burr of ringing telephones.

Back to the womb.

The rest is logistics. He takes a car—everyone leaves them unlocked in the village—and drives into Aberdeen. He lets himself be seen in various places, and eventually goes to see Kathryn, who is working in the city. She is not there. He leaves her a note, carefully timed and dated. His alibi is secure. He rolls the freedom around his tongue,

327

and a more beautiful taste is beyond the parameters of his imagination.

He gets the last bus back home. Only then does he call the police and tell them that his mother and stepfather have been butchered and their house ransacked.

The case is a minor sensation. Ralph Whiteside, a local junkie with a record as long as several arms, is arrested. He was seen wandering round the village, so wasted he could hardly speak. He can barely remember his name, let alone what he was doing at the presumed time of the attack. For the police, under pressure to get their man, he is heaven sent.

Nine months later, Ralph Whiteside is tried, convicted and sentenced to life imprisonment.

SATURDAY

Kate sleeps fitfully. Her mind hovers by the telephone, waiting for it to ring and bring her one of two pieces of news—that Red has worked out the connection, or that another body has been found. The prospect of the latter hardens her skittering chills in the warm night.

At dawn, the phone still silent, she gets out of bed and runs a bath.

No matter how long Kate stands in the shower and how wet she gets, it does not count as full immersion. In a shower, only a small proportion of her body is in contact with water at any given moment. In a bath, every part of her can be.

As before, when she tried to have a bath after returning from the *Amphitrite*, she waits until the surface is perfectly still. As before, she breaks the surface tension with her big toe.

Not as before, the rest of her follows suit. Kate levers herself over the side of the bath and lowers herself to the water. It sloshes around her in lazy swells as she settles. Water up to her chest, and then to her shoulders as she lets herself slide downwards. Her knees make small islands. Lapping at her nipples, her chin. Warm water, steam rising and benevolent around her.

Every part of me.

She must put her head under. She has done it in the shower, she must do it here. Only when she puts her head under will she have finally conquered the fear. Eyes shut and quick duck, that's all it needs. She doesn't have to stay underwater, just in and out. She can finish it today, right here, right now.

331

Kate lies still. She listens for the phone, for Leo. For an excuse.

The water holds her life in suspension.

* * *

The hospital staff are still pushing the breakfast trolleys around the wards when Kate arrives. She has brought Leo with her. It is one thing palming him off on to Bronagh during the week—virtually all of Leo's friends have working mothers—but weekends are different. Other children see their mothers at weekends, and so Leo shall too.

Frank looks better than Kate thought he would. Bright white surgical dressings cover the wounds on his head, and his right arm is wrapped like a mummy from wrist to bicep. Kate reflects on the irony that the man in charge of investigating the *Amphitrite* has ended up looking like one of its survivors.

She knows it could have been much worse, but also that it need never have happened at all. She told him the letter was nothing to worry about. How wrong could she have been? And now she comes to his side as if to the scaffold. This is what it used to be like years ago, when Kate had done something wrong and suffered in impotent terror while her father decided how to punish her. She may be a grown woman now, but she sees herself as being at fault here, and childhood reflexes—no matter how dormant—are still hard to fight when they resurface. Guilt swamps her like a breaker.

It would be easier if Frank simply blew his top. But he never does. The only time Kate's ever seen him lose his temper was during his last fight with

332

Angie, just before he left for good. When he's angry, he seethes. Every movement is considered and deliberate.

As if reading her mind, he looks up at her and smiles.

'Don't blame yourself. It would have been a lot worse if you hadn't been there.'

The wave of dreadful anticipation subsides, and in its place swells sweet relief. She laces her fingers through his and strokes gently at his forehead with her other hand.

'And this must be Leo.'

'Say hello to your granddad, treasure.'

Leo smiles shyly. 'You're the man from the school.'

'Yes. Yes, I am.'

'Are those all for you?' says Leo, pointing to the crescent of get-well cards on the windowsill.

'Yes, they are.'

'Why don't you go and look at them, sweetheart?' says Kate.

Leo toddles across to the window. He is just tall enough to reach the cards, and he picks them down one at a time and studies the pictures on the fronts intensely.

'He's a nice kid,' says Frank.

'Thank you.'

'I'd like to see more of him sometime. Him, and my daughter.'

'What do my lot say?' Kate asks. 'As to who did it?'

'They don't know. Other than it was the same people who sent the letter.'

'Because the letter wasn't public knowledge, and therefore can't have been a copycat?'

He nods.

'Forensics must have got some clues,' she says.

'One of them came to see me last night. He said they'd found little bits here and there—pieces of envelope and detonator—and that they were still looking.'

'Plastic explosive?'

'Yup.'

'That makes sense. Nothing else would have done that much damage, not in such a small quantity.'

'How's the hotel?'

'Looks like a bomb's gone off.'

His face creases, first with laughter and then with a wince. 'Ow. Don't make me laugh. It hurts something rotten.'

'Sorry.' She pauses. 'Paperback in an envelope. Oldest trick in the book, pardon the pun. Wire up the explosive and detonator, put the contact points on facing pages of the book, insert a piece of cardboard between them, fold the cardboard back on itself outside the book and glue it to the inside of the envelope. When you pull the book out, the cardboard stays in. The points connect, the circuit's completed, and . . .' She gestures at his arm.

He smiles ruefully. 'My daughter, the letter-bomb expert.'

'I've seen my fair share, put it that way. When do they reckon you'll be out of here?'

'They want me in until Monday. For observation.'

'Do you want me to get you some books? There's a newsagent in the foyer. It'll take me five minutes.'

The phone by Frank's bed rings. He shifts

uncomfortably across and picks it up.

'Frank Beauchamp . . . You've what? Excellent, excellent. Good lads . . . I'll be there as soon as I can. Don't leave without me.'

He puts the phone down.

'You'll be where as soon as you can?' asks Kate.

'The heliport.'

'Dad, you're in hospital.'

'Not any more. I'm discharging myself.'

'What on earth for?'

'That was Charlie Fox. They've found the vehicle that Sutton pushed out. We're going down in the submersible to check it out.'

'Don't be absurd.'

'There's nothing wrong with me.'

'Apart from a head full of metal and one arm torn to bits. They want you here till Monday for a reason, Dad. Get someone else to go down to the wreck. There must be other people who can do it.'

'Says the woman who takes on a murder case the day after she was nearly drowned.'

'God, you're such a stubborn bastard.'

'Which I get from my daughter, no doubt. I have to go down because they've tried to stop me. They tell me to back off, and I don't, so they send me a bomb. Wouldn't *you* go down?'

'Yes, but . . .'

'But what?'

'I'm a police officer. It's implicit in my job that I put myself in that kind of danger when necessary. You're a marine investigator. Remember how freaked out you were when you got the letter in the first place?'

'Sure. And now they've done what they said they would, and I'm still here. What else can they do to

335

me? Every investigation I do, it's the same old story.'

'You get bomb threats on every case?'

'No, no. Nothing that extreme. But always, someone somewhere doesn't want something known. The shipping industry keeps itself closed tighter than a mouse's arsehole.' Frank counts them off on the fingers of his working arm. 'Designers create the vessels. Managers establish procedures and working conditions. Financiers hammer out takeover deals. Directors work out corporate strategy and direction. Politicians legislate and lobby. All to cover their own backs and each other's when things go wrong. This is just the same. The only difference is that it's come wrapped up in violence.'

'This is a terrorist act we're talking about, Dad. I think you're mad.'

He points to some clothes folded on a chair. 'I think you should help your old man get dressed.'

*   *   *

Kate drives from the Infirmary to Queen Street in silence. She called her father 'stubborn'. It's more than that. It's what she thought she learned from Red, but in fact now realises she had in her genes all along—an obsessive drive to find the truth, take what's hidden in darkness and drag it into the light. She knows she tried to dissuade her father from going down to the van because she recognises that he's just like her—she's just like him—and that scares her.

Kate parks in the underground car park beneath police headquarters and rides the lift up. She holds

336

Leo's hand. 'You've been here before, haven't you, sweetheart?'

Leo shakes his head.

'Never ever? I'm sure you have.'

They arrive at the fourth floor. Leo starts crying the moment they're out of the lift.

'What, darling? What is it?'

Kate down fast to his side after what happened last night, and now the screams come. She looks frantically round for what could be setting him off. A couple of uniformed officers are walking past, but that's about it. No Friday night drunks cursing and yelling as they're ejected after a night in the cells. Hospital waiting rooms aren't this quiet, this unthreatening. And yet Leo is reacting as if he's walked into the middle of a war zone.

'Leo, what's wrong?'

He points wildly around him. 'Don't like station. *Don't like station.*'

'Why not?'

'Want to stay with Mummy.' Loud keening sobs.

'You *can* stay with Mummy. That's why we're here.'

'Want to be home with Mummy. Not where Mummy works.'

'Mummy has to be here today.'

'Don't want to be where Mummy works.'

'Do you want me to take you back to Auntie B's?'

He nods, gulping. Kate hurries him back into the lift and jabs at the button for the basement. The silver doors slide shut on his anguish, and she cradles him close on the short journey below the earth.

337

This is Red's turf, the incident room. This is where he used to hold court, a conductor with his orchestra: fizzing ideas, adjusting manpower and tactics with the deftness of a chess grandmaster, galvanising his colleagues through sheer energy alone. He will have the floor for this meeting, and Kate's happy to hand it over to him.

Saturday morning traffic was light. Kate was at Bronagh's and back inside twenty minutes. She didn't even need to ring Ferguson and ask him to delay the meeting.

Kate and Red have a quick chat before the off.

'It's there,' he says, tapping his temple. 'Somewhere in there, I know why Blackadder's doing this. I know that I know, I should say. Something I've read, something I've seen. But it won't come to me.'

'Yet.'

'That's what I'm hoping.'

Kate has known frustration these past few days—at bureaucracy, at Blackadder, at the way in which her life sometimes seems to be running from her. She knows that Red's frustration is very different, because its relief is within his control. Hear a familiar tune out of context, and it can be difficult to place. You have to hum it through until the chorus, and even then it still might escape you, your brain might lead you off into other songs which sound similar.

'Ready?' she asks.

'Give me a second.'

He goes through the same accelerated routine he used to perform before any kind of public speaking: quick breaths in and out, wiggling his fingers and rolling his shoulders, to get the adrenaline up and the blood flowing faster. It's a physical thing, he would tell her. Your mind works quicker when your body does.

Kate clears her throat, and the room falls silent. She motions with her head to him. All yours.

In front of the entire Blackadder team, Red goes through the train of thought he outlined to Kate last night on the way back from Tollohill Wood: lack of primary sexual motivation, symptoms of organisation, delusional psychosis as opposed to sexual psychopathy. Kate listens to him, but it is her officers that she watches. She scans their faces, and what she sees more often than not is scepticism, distrust, dissent. She's disappointed, if not especially surprised. Even though she's invited him here, the odds are still very much against him. He made his name with the Met, which means he's instantly suspected of being a big-city cop without sensitivity to provincial conditions. Worse, he's a big-city *English* cop in Scotland. Even more pertinently, he's a convicted prisoner. He's crossed over, he's betrayed them. They'd rather be lectured by the Yorkshire Ripper. And he's telling them that they've been barking up the wrong tree. That never goes down well anywhere.

Red is barely finished when Ferguson jumps down his throat.

'You've offered a lot of theories, but no answers. What's to say that your reading of it is any more right or wrong than ours has been?'

'I was called in to give my thoughts, and that's all I'm doing. If you think I'm going to somehow teleconnect with him and suddenly go—oh, he's

339

five eight, wears combat trousers, has an earring in his left ear and likes his steaks rare, then I'm sorry, but that's not going to happen. All I'm doing is giving you an opinion on what's driving Blackadder, based on my expertise.'

'Which is a few years out of date.'

'I subscribe to police journals and psychiatric publications. I keep up to date with what's going on.'

'It's hardly the same as getting your dick wet on real cases, is it?'

'Human psychology doesn't change. It's just our understanding of it which does.'

Kate steps in before Ferguson can reply. 'Peter, you've made your point. Whether or not you agree with Mr Metcalfe, I hardly need remind you—all of you—that we have got precisely nowhere in discovering Blackadder's identity, let alone stopping him. Any new perspective on the case is therefore more than welcome, as far as I'm concerned. Anyone else want to say something?'

Atkins, the officer in charge of interviewing the sex offenders, raises his hand.

'All that stuff about immutable psychosis: could you repeat it?'

'Which bit?'

'The whole lot. It's all . . . Greek to me.'

The room laughs. Atkins has articulated what many of them were thinking, though he'd doubtless have used an earthier epithet than 'Greek' in private. Nor can Kate blame him. The way in which Red's mind works can be perplexing even for those who know him well, let alone a roomful of world-weary officers with a healthy disregard for bullshit and a strong faith in traditional policing methods.

340

Kate glances across—at Red, and catches her breath.

His mouth is slightly open and his eyes narrowed. Kate knows that expression. It is the one which signals an imminent connection.

She raises her hand for hush, but it makes no difference to Red. When his brain is working like this, he could think through a nuclear explosion. He is looking into the middle distance, but Kate doubts he is actually seeing anything. His gaze will be turned inwards, flashing through images stored in his head, watching as hundreds of separate thoughts flow, join together, race forward, tributaries spilling into a river which runs ever faster.

He shakes his head slightly as if jolting himself from reverie, and looks straight at her.

Kate can barely breathe. This is why she fought so hard to get him here.

'What sex were the adders?' he asks.

*   *   *

Silence as *Starsky* sinks towards the seabed, darkness creeping slowly up from below. Frank is champing at the bit, desperate to discover what's in the vehicle and scared of what it might be—if anything. It's the same mixture of anticipation and apprehension that he imagines Kate gets on police manhunts: a charge which is almost sexual in its twitching intensity.

Starsky's searchlights find the van, lose it, find it again. A white Ford Transit. Frank checks that audio and video channels are both recording.

Fox approaches the van cautiously, as if it might

explode at any moment. He circles it once from a good twenty metres away, all the way round. Then he comes in to half that distance and does it again.

The driver's window has been smashed. Tiny shards of glass cling to the doorframe's rubber seal.

'Must be how they got in to release the handbrake,' Fox says.

Frank nods, never taking his eyes off the van. A road atlas, now substantially more papier mâché than paper, floats above the dashboard.

Fox takes *Starsky* in close. They move round the front of the van, dipping the searchlight so the windscreen doesn't simply reflect the beam back at them.

There is a wood partition behind the seats. The loading bay is behind that partition, totally cut off from the driver's compartment.

Starsky moves slowly down the van's passenger side. The passenger window is intact. There are no other windows. Both exterior sides of the van from the partition backwards are solid metal, as are the rear doors. The name of a hire company is emblazoned on the side in large black letters. Fox holds *Starsky* a few feet from the van's rear and flicks the searchlight back on to full beam.

'Can we open those doors?' asks Frank.

'I was just thinking that myself.' He pauses. 'What about the mechanical grab arm on the front of this baby? That might do the trick.'

Fox pushes a couple of buttons and reaches for a joystick on the control console in front of him. Frank watches as the grab arm slowly uncoils itself and begins to stretch out towards the van's rear doors. The pincers at the end of the arm flex like primitive fingers.

Fox works the joystick with quick, efficient movements. He is totally absorbed.

The grab arm brushes the handle on the right-hand door, tries to gain some purchase, slides off. Fox clicks his tongue in annoyance and tries again. This time, he gets it to stick. He adjusts the pincers until they are gripping the handle tight, and pulls gently back on the joystick. The arm tenses, strains against the handle.

The doors don't move. Locked. Of course. Fox swears softly.

He pulls harder on the joystick. The handle suddenly comes clean away from the doors, a small strip of black plastic dangling uselessly from beneath the pincers.

Fox thinks for a moment. He straightens the pincers, so that they release their grip. The handle floats gently down to the seabed and lands in a small puff of sand.

Fox pushes the joystick away from him again and the arm snakes back towards the door, pincers locked straight. They smack against the metal, as near to where the handle was as Fox can manage. Frank feels the vibrations through *Starsky* as arm and door connect.

He's trying to punch a hole in the door. Smart man.

Fox backs the arm up a few feet and tries again. No joy. And again. The door is flimsy, made of thin aluminium. It can't hold out for ever, surely.

On the fifth attempt, the pincers break through the metal. Frank gives a little cheer, and Fox clenches his left fist.

He pushes the pincers through the holes they have made, right up to the hilt, and then curls them as far closed as he can, so that they are gripping on the door from the inside. He's going to rip it open that way.

'Ready?' he asks.

Frank nods. Ready as he'll ever be.

Fox pulls back on the joystick, and the grab arm takes the strain once more. The door buckles and begins to peel, first at the point where the pincers hold it, and then gradually above and below that. Finally, it gives altogether and swings open.

Starsky's searchlight sweeps into the van's interior, chasing the darkness from every last cranny, and the super-illuminated image it finds there seems to fly through the water and plaster itself on the submersible's glass. Frank ducks instinctively. He hears splattering beneath him as Fox empties his stomach.

Frank takes a deep breath and looks up, back towards the van.

Dante said there were nine circles of Hell. He was wrong. There are ten, and Frank is looking at the tenth.

*　　　*　　　*

It takes Kate a moment to register what Red's said, it sounds so nonsensical.

'What *sex* were they?' she asks.

'Yes. The adders left on the bodies—were they male or female?'

'I have no idea. Doesn't it say in the autopsy reports?'

'No. I would have remembered.'

'Well—I don't even know where they are.'

'They're downstairs,' says Ferguson. 'In a

344

storeroom.'

'I thought the university had them.'

'We took them back. They're evidence.'

'Who feeds and waters them?'

'The university said they'd send someone over next week.'

Kate remembers the problems Matheson had in getting the Malaysian temple viper to eat.

'Will someone go and get them? I'll call Matheson.'

Ripley and Sherwood are out and back in minutes, a glass cage each. Kate spends five minutes on the phone, cursing university departments for being skeleton-staffed on weekends. Cursing weekends full stop, in fact. She is shunted between three different people, each apparently more incompetent than the previous. They try to find Matheson in the building, fail to do so, try to locate his home phone number, again fail to do so, and eventually unearth a mobile number, seemingly more by accident than design. She dials the number and puts the speakerphone on. The low babble in the room subsides once more.

'Miles Matheson.'

'Miles, DCI Kate Beauchamp here. We met the other day.'

'I remember. How're y'doing, Inspector?'

'I've got a question for you.'

'Shoot.'

'Those adders we found at the crime scenes. You didn't check to see what sex they were?'

He pauses. 'Sorry, no.'

'You couldn't spare a couple of minutes right now, could you? I'm at police headquarters in Queen Street.'

'That would be a tad difficult.'

'Why's that?'

'I'm in Birmingham. At a conference. Is it important that you find out right away?'

Kate glances at Red. He gives her a sharp nod. 'Very.'

'Well, I can tell you how to do it yourself.'

'I—er—you mean examine them?'

She shouldn't have put him on loud. The whole room is listening. She can't back out now.

'How else are you going to find out?' he asks.

'Well—don't you have to be a trained snake handler, or something?'

'Hell no. All you need is a steady pair of hands. Piece of piss, Inspector. I'll talk you through it.'

Rows of faces turned towards her, expectant, enjoying her discomfort.

What did Matheson say to her, when she went to visit him? *You don't see the glorious array of colours on their skin. You don't see the beauty with which they move . . . You see only the scales and the venom and the danger.*

Too right, Mr Matheson. That's all I see because that's all there is. Venom and danger.

Kate hears her own voice bright and airy, and it is saying 'Sure'. Maybe she should give all this up and become an actress.

'Right. You got both of them there with you?'

'Yes.'

'Look at their tails. Are they about the same size?'

'One of the snakes is curled up. It's hard to tell. Why?'

'Males have got longer tails than females, and usually some kind of bulge at the base, where the

346

tail joins the body. You can easily see the difference.'

'How do I get it to stretch out?'

'Prod it.'

'With my hand?'

He laughs. 'No. Get a long ruler. Or a truncheon. You must have one of *those* there.'

A few officers laugh. One of the uniforms in the front row unclips his truncheon from his belt and passes it to her.

Kate's tongue is dry. She flicks it from side to side in her mouth to work up some saliva. She's not sure she wouldn't rather be back on the *Amphitrite*.

She reaches over the top of the cage and jabs uncertainly at the curled adder. It doesn't move. She jabs again, more firmly. Still no response.

'It's not moving.'

'Put the truncheon between its curls and straighten it that way.'

She reaches over again and does so. Her eyes dart from the truncheon to the snake's head, back and forth. Slowly, the tail begins to straighten, like a party paper whistle.

Kate takes the truncheon away. She looks from one adder to the other. If there is a difference, she can't see it.

'No. They both look the same.'

'What about bulges?'

'They look the same. I don't know what's normal and what's not. We might have different ideas of what a bulge means.'

The detectives laugh again. Kate doesn't feel like joining in. She glances at Red. He is not smiling either.

'Right. Have you got one of those pointers

347

there? The ones people use in lectures. To point at slides and that. A long rod, not one of those red laser jobbies.'

She looks round the room. There is one leaning against the wall, next to the whiteboard covered with Polaroids of the mutilated bodies of Petra Gallacher and Elizabeth Hart.'

'Yes. Peter?'

Ferguson walks over to it.

'Good. Have you got any water?'

'Yes.'

'Wet the end, to give it some lubrication.'

Ferguson goes to the water cooler and splashes the pointer under one of the taps.

Still Matheson's disembodied voice directing their every move. 'What you've got to do is probe under their tails. Now, this might well piss them off a bit, so make sure their heads are secured. You've got to hold that truncheon hard across the back of their necks, so they can't bite you.'

The officer who gave Kate his truncheon gets up and comes over. Kate hands him the truncheon. He reaches into the first cage and presses the truncheon down hard across the back of the adder's neck, just as Matheson said. The snake jerks under his grip. He moves one of his hands to the other end of the truncheon, so that it's held with equal firmness at both ends. Kate takes the pointer off Ferguson.

'Look at the tail, on the underside. There's a line where it joins the body.'

'I see it.'

'Put the probe in there. Just slide it under the first scale. Keep it at as shallow an angle as possible.'

'And then what?'

'Push gently until you can get no further. Then count how many scales in you've got.'

Kate reaches into the cage. The end of the pointer bumps against the adder's tail.

She forces herself to grip the tail with her free hand. The scales are cold and hard against her fingertips. She stifles the urge to wipe her hand on her trousers.

'It might help to twist the pointer slowly between thumb and forefinger,' says Matheson.

Kate has an absurd feeling that he's in the room, he can see what she's doing.

She does as he says. A soft, slight yielding as the first subcaudal scale opens under the pressure. She pushes the pointer gently in, and almost immediately feels the resistance.

'Two scales, maybe three,' she says.

'No more?'

'No.'

'Do the same on the other one.'

The officer helping her takes his truncheon away, fast as the adder lashes angrily upwards. They repeat the procedure on the second snake, truncheon held at both ends across the neck, Kate holding the tail still with one hand while she probes with the pointer in the other.

'Two scales again.'

She withdraws the pointer and her hand. The officer lets go with the truncheon. This adder hardly stirs.

'You're sure?'

'Yes. I'm sure.'

'Then they're female.'

Red is nodding, apparently satisfied.

349

'Definitely female,' continues Matheson. 'If they were male, you could have pushed it in about five scales' worth.'

'That's great. Thank you very much. Enjoy your conference.'

'Will do.'

Kate shuts the speakerphone off. She turns to Red.

'That's what you thought they'd be?'

'Yes.'

'Which means?'

'Which means that it all makes sense.'

*   *   *

'I knew that I knew. I knew something I'd read, something I'd seen, was like this. I just couldn't remember where or when, or in what context. And then you'—he nods at Atkins—'said "it's all Greek", and it came to me in a flash. What Blackadder does, the way he mutilates, is what the ancient Greeks did to the enemies they killed in battle. They cut off their hands and feet to stop the victim's ghost from pursuing the killer, and tied them round the corpse's neck. And then I thought about the other aspects of Blackadder's ritual, and of course the snakes come first to mind. You've been thinking of the snakes as adders, because that's what they're called here in Britain. But the technical term is *vipera berus*. Think of them as *vipers*, which is how the rest of the world knows them, and the connection is clear.'

He looks round the room. The faces which return his gaze are blank. Evidently the connection is not clear to them.

'What is ancient Greece's most lasting legacy?' he asks.

'Mythology,' says Ferguson.

'Exactly. And which mythological figures are most connected with vipers?'

'The Medusa. The Gorgons. The ones who turned you to stone when they looked at you.'

'Yes, but who else?'

The room is silent.

'The Furies,' says Red.

'What's this got to do with the sex of the adders?'

'All in good time.'

Ferguson virtually snarls at him. Red begins to quote. ' "Three hellish and inhuman Furies sprang to view, bloodstained and wild. Their limbs and gestures hinted they were women. Belts of greenest hydras wound and wound about their waists, and snakes and horned serpents grew from their heads like matted hair and bound their horrid brows." '

He looks round the room again. Their scepticism is beginning to vanish.

'Dante's *Inferno*. As I told DCI Beauchamp, I've had time to do an awful lot of reading over the past few years. The Furies lived in the underworld, from where they ascended to earth to pursue the wicked. They were just but merciless, and without regard for mitigating circumstances. They punished all offences against human society, and they did so by driving their victims insane. They're basically one's conscience, writ so large as to be inescapable.'

The savage triumph of working out a pattern. It never goes away.

'I told you Blackadder was delusional. That's exactly what he is. He believes himself to be

351

possessed by the Furies. He saw Petra Gallacher and Elizabeth Hart as Furies. That's why he killed them—to stop them possessing him, and to try and shake off the madness. And just as important, that's why he killed them the way he did. He cut off their hands and feet to stop their ghosts pursuing him after they were dead. He attached the snakes to symbolise their status as Furies. And he tortured them so badly because he wanted them to feel the kind of suffering they inflicted on him.'

'But why did he choose *them*?' asks Kate. 'And what did he do in the first place to inflict this on himself?'

'Why them in particular, I don't know. Something they did, something they represented. As for what his original crime was—that I do think I know. *That's* why I asked about the adders' sex. The Greeks believed the female viper was the dominant of the species. They believed that the female viper ate its mate, ate the male, and was in turn eaten by its offspring. And of all the offences the Furies could punish, they reserved particular zeal for one crime in particular.'

Red pauses. He is enjoying the moment.

'Matricide. Blackadder killed his mother.'

He has them now. They're hanging on his every word.

'Matricide is one of the hardest of all crimes to stomach. Look at the role mothers have in society. When you get people jumping up and down in front of TV cameras at football matches, what are they yelling? "Hi, Mum!" Who runs the majority of households, even nowadays? The mother. They're sacred, even among criminals. Look at the Mafia, look at the East End gangsters—men who won't

352

think twice about killing a rival, but equally won't have a single word said against their mothers. So it was in ancient Greece. Matricide was the one crime regarded as absolutely unforgivable, irrespective of the circumstances. The blood of the slain mother automatically called the Furies' wrath down on the perpetrator. Blackadder killed his mother. That's where you have to start. Whatever else you find out about him, I guarantee that that at least will be true.'

'If he killed his mother,' says Kate, 'then that must narrow down our field.'

'Yes, and no. If he was caught, imprisoned and has now been released, then he'll be easy to find. You can check prison and secure confinement records. But if he'd been caught and imprisoned, he would probably see himself as having done his punishment. The Furies couldn't get to him, because he'd served his time. So assume that he killed his mother and was never caught. If that's the case, you have to find all cases of women with children who've been murdered. Start with those that were never solved. If that yields nothing, go on to those where there was a conviction. Maybe it was mistaken identity, leaving the real culprit— Blackadder—still at large.'

'You said he's delusional. Couldn't it therefore be that the original victim was not his actual mother?'

'She may not be his biological mother, but she'll certainly have been a mother figure: a foster parent, guardian, stepmother, whatever. He's very literal in his delusions. It won't have been a stranger.'

'How long ago would this have taken place?'

Red spreads his hands wide. 'How long is a piece of string? Assume Blackadder's this side of fifty, fifty-five perhaps—he has the strength to carry out savage attacks. And assume too that the earliest he would have killed his mother was in his early twenties, late teens at a push. He could have killed her any time from thirty-five years ago to last week. Age is always just about the toughest thing to nail down when profiling a killer.'

'But surely he couldn't have harboured this secret, this grudge, for such a long time?'

'Of course he could. Psychoses can fester dormant for years, decades even. Then something triggers them and—bang! A trigger is usually, but not always, something damaging to the ego, such as getting divorced or sacked. Whatever it is, the fact that he's just got around to doing something about it doesn't mean he's just thought about it.'

'You said there were three Furies.'

'Yes.'

'That means he has one more to go.'

'It's more than that. Three Furies means that the moment he's killed the third, he's rid himself of his madness. Getting all three will free him from his torment. He won't need to kill again after that. He's one of the few serial killers who will be able to stop—who in fact will have no reason to keep going. And once he stops, he goes underground. He'll leave you no more evidence. If you don't catch him on what you've got, you never will.'

And I'll go to my grave never knowing who he was. No. No way.

'How are we going to find the third?' asks Kate. 'Before he does?'

'We don't know how he's picking them. Until we

354

do, we can't really hope to work out who his next victim's going to be.'

'Maybe it's chance. Maybe he just sees them, and something sets him off.'

'I don't think so. The Furies are usually portrayed as being utterly hideous. There's no way this could have been applied to Petra Gallacher. And she and Elizabeth Hart looked nothing alike. If he was doing it visually, they'd have looked more like each other. Whatever links them, it's not their looks. Which in turn means you can't eliminate any type of woman from consideration. Young, old, attractive, unattractive, single, married—they're all targets.'

'We've already got a city-wide alert telling all women to be careful, not to be alone.'

'Good. Keep it in effect.'

The third victim, walking round not knowing that she's Blackadder's next target.

The woman on the ferry, peeling off the ladder in stages, hands to chest to knees to feet.

A life to save, for the one Kate had to take on the Amphitrite.

The words of the Talmud: 'He who saves a life saves the world entire.'

'Let's get to it, everybody,' says Kate. 'Prison records, police records, mental hospitals.'

'So all in all,' says Ferguson, 'we've really got sweet FA to go on. No age, no firm parameters, no idea who his next victim will be.'

Red's stare oozes contempt. He doesn't even dignify Ferguson with an answer.

*   *   *

355

The helicopter's blades blat and the radio chatters, and all Frank can hear is the pounding in his head. Aberdeen laid out beneath him in the blazing summer sun, its people carefree and its trees lush—and behind his eyes the terrible image of what he's seen, an image which underlies everything he sees, as if in double exposure.

Movement oscillates through the heliport, men streaming to and from installations out to sea: Alpha North, Beatrice, Clyde, Forties, Harding, Magellan, Miller, Montrose, Stena Spey, Tartan Alpha. All these people on the move, thinks Frank, and for what? To suck up more oil from a reluctant ocean, and use that oil to run cars on endless pointless journeys and the silver streaks of airliners, and all simply fuelling lives lived in happy ignorance of what happens behind closed doors, in the back of vans at the bottom of the sea. Question things, you ingrates. Look up from your navels and around you.

Although the heliport is busy, most people seem to be arriving and leaving in private cars. The queue for taxis is mercifully short. Frank gets into the third one which arrives.

'You all right, mate? The taxi driver's eyes in the rear-view mirror. 'You look like you've gone the distance with Tyson.'

Half his head and most of his right arm swathed in bandages, and the video cassette juddering in his trembling hand. Frank knows he's looked better.

'You should have seen the other guy,' he says weakly, and pretends to dial a number on his mobile so the cabbie won't ask him any more questions.

The taxi drops him outside Queen Street police

headquarters. Frank gives the driver a £20 note for a fare the light side of £10, and sets haltingly off across the road without waiting for change. His co-ordination comes and goes in waves, as if he's drunk.

The foyer is cooler and less bright than outside. That may help.

'DCI Kate Beauchamp, please.'

The duty sergeant punches in a number and speaks. 'This is the front desk. There's a man here to see DCI . . .'

'Tell her it's her father. And that it's very urgent.'

Kate comes out of the lifts a minute and a half later. 'My God, Dad. You look *awful*. I'm taking you back to hospital right now.'

'It's nothing to do with the hospital.' He holds up the video cassette. 'Have you got somewhere we can play this?'

'Of course. What is it?'

'It's better if you see it for yourself.'

She turns to the duty sergeant. 'Derek, which of the meeting rooms are free?'

He consults an appointments book. 'One or four.'

'They've both got videos?'

'Yes.'

'One is nearer. We'll go there.'

She leads Frank along a corridor, left, left and then right. A door, 'MEETING ROOM ONE' spelled out in black letters on brown wood. The video and television set are in the corner, on a trolley.

Frank shuts the door. Kate takes the cassette off him, puts it in the video, and turns the television on. She takes a couple of steps backwards and waits

357

for it to begin.

'You'd better sit down,' he says.

She looks sharply at him. 'What *is* it?'

'Kate, just sit down, please. Sit down and watch.'

She takes the chair next to him.

'Here we go. It's starting.'

A blurring of grey static, and then the white Transit van abruptly in the searchlight.

'My God,' says Kate. 'That's the van we took to Norway. That's our van.'

*　　*　　*

She watches in silence, fighting the urge to hit the fast-forward button. Beside her, Frank looks gobsmacked. He had no idea who hired the van, of course.

Images on the screen. The smashed window, atlas floating above the dashboard. The puff of sand as the door handle drops to the seabed. The grab arm reaching out, piercing the metal, pulling the doors open.

Kate has an eerie feeling of being half-submerged. She takes a deep breath, and is relieved to find that what she inhales is warm close air.

Everything that should be in the van, is. Lennox's precious lighting system and sound-mixing deck, props from the set, parts of the artificial river bank—all in happy suspension, ignorant of their own waterlogged destruction.

And then the objects which shouldn't be there.

Kate gasps, recoils. She shuts her eyes tight. A trick of the light, surely. Shadows in the van from the searchlight. She shakes her head and opens her

358

eyes again. Still there.

Five bodies floating bloated against the van's roof, hands and ankles tied and their hair waving gently in the water.

Small bodies. Children's bodies.

* * *

The tape is still running, but neither Kate nor Frank are watching.

Her first reaction is to cling to him, such is the sheer horror of what she's seen. She buries her head against his chest and feels his arms around her, the right one held gingerly on the back of her jumper. His shirt smells of washing powder.

The implications tumble down on her like falling masonry. She forces herself not to think for a moment, knowing that she must let all the connotations fall before she starts to pick them up and stack them in a logical order.

Images and emotion first. *These children haven't even been buried, and there are few things more unutterably heartbreaking than the sight of a child's coffin. Coffins are supposed to be sturdy, built to withstand the rigours of the journey into the next world. They should make the pall-bearers stagger under the weight of a man's life and soul. But when the coffin is no larger than a window-box, and you feel that one man could flick it on to his shoulders without undue effort, then what can you do except shake with agony for all that might have been?*

Kate disentangles herself from her father, remembering not to knock his bad arm. She stands up. Her legs feel weak.

In her mind, she stands amidst piles of rubble.

The van they took to Norway and back has children in it.

The van wasn't supposed to have children in it. It was supposed to carry their equipment: what with the complex set and all Lennox's control decks, they needed a separate vehicle. The van for the equipment, and a minibus for them.

The children weren't there when they packed up the van after the last performance. The children must therefore have been loaded on the final morning, when everyone was doing their own thing before the *Amphitrite* set sail in the afternoon.

The children were loaded by one—at least one—of the Aberdeen Amateurs.

Ten people went to Norway. Minus the three who died leaves seven. It could have been one of those three, of course, but if it is then there's not much Kate can do about it now. Check out those who are still alive.

Seven minus her leaves six. Sinclair, Alex, Jason, Lennox, Jean and Emmeline.

Please God, not Sinclair or Alex. She couldn't bear it if it was one of them.

Who was driving the van that afternoon, when they got on board? She can't remember, and it's probably irrelevant anyway. The children would have been loaded by then, tied up and hidden, presumably drugged too.

Who drove the van usually? Most of them. She did a couple of times. So did Davenport. All the men still alive, they did too. In fact, the only people she can't ever remember seeing behind the wheel were Jean and Emmeline.

Scrap Jean and Emmeline, or at least give them lower priority for now. Not only did they not drive, but loading the children may have needed strength or coercion.

She thinks of something else.

'Dad, were there any unusual radio communications to or from the *Amphitrite* before the van was tipped out?'

'None that we found. Just standard radio traffic.'

No communication from outside means that whoever smuggled them on board got cold feet. Panicked, and wanted to get rid of the van before arrival in Aberdeen. So they cooked up a bomb warning, knowing that Sutton would have been left with no option but to do what he did. And Kate can't believe that any woman would knowingly send five children to their deaths. Jean and Emmeline are mothers themselves, like her.

Which leaves four. Sinclair, Alex, Jason and Lennox. Sinclair her mentor and Alex her lover, creepy Jason and nerdy Lennox. No prizes for guessing from which pair she'd like the guilty party to come.

Creepy Jason, who tried to kiss her outside the restaurant on Wednesday night. Jason, who tries too hard, invades her space, makes her feel uncomfortable. Easy—no, not easy, but not impossible either—to imagine him loading children into the back of a van.

Lennox, earnest and dorkish, boring Alex rigid at dinner about the technical specifications of sound decks. Quiet and innocuous, the kind of guy who wouldn't hurt a fly. The last person you'd ever have suspected. Isn't that what the neighbours always say, after the event?

It must be one of those two. They're the losers, the loners, the ones who life has passed by.

Because if it's not either of them, then it's Sinclair or Alex, and both of them are utterly unpalatable as possibilities.

It can't be Sinclair. He's too gentle and kind, too paternalistic. It would be like believing it of—well, of her own father.

But if it's not Sinclair, it's Alex.

Alex inside her, in her bed, her body, her *head*. Alex on the floor with Leo—with Leo, four years old, innocent and defenceless—making her precious child laugh. Alex, of whom even Bronagh approves. They can't all be wrong about him.

If it's Alex, she'll kill him herself, no question.

Kate rings Renfrew at home and explains briefly to him what Frank has found and what the implications are. When she has finished speaking, there is a good ten seconds' silence before Renfrew replies.

'I'll get on to the magistrate myself,' he says. 'Warrants to search their workplaces and homes.'

'I don't think we should do the homes just yet,' Kate says.

'Why not?'

'Wouldn't it be better to keep this as quiet as possible? Try to pin down the suspect's identity before alerting him that we're on to him?'

Another pause.

'OK. Just their offices, to start with. How many locations are we talking?'

'Two. The university physics department where Lennox Tait lectures, and Urquhart's auction house, where the other three work.'

'Good. I'm coming in right now. I'll handle this one myself. And tell your dad to stay put. I may need his help.'

It takes Renfrew an hour to get the warrants and organise search teams, and another hour for them to find the first piece of concrete evidence.

An e-mail on the central server at Urquhart's. It was sent three weeks ago and has since been deleted, but no file on a computer is ever truly erased. Even deleted files leave imprints, like those of a note on a pad where the pen has pressed through to the sheets below. A skilful operator can retrieve such files. And Holroyd, head of Grampian Police's IT section, is about the most skilful in north-east Scotland.

Although there is no longer sufficient information to determine if the sender used an individual account, and the message is unsigned, two aspects are unmistakable. The first is its content.

Phone contact impossible due to presence of others in office, hence use of e-mail. All arrangements now in place for trip to B. Cargo scheduled for delivery on a.m. of Sunday 9th. Five separate articles, as agreed. Transport vehicle and all necessary items for quiet and comfortable trip arranged.

The four is now three. The smuggler must be one of those who works at Urquhart's. But just as Lennox is now eliminated as a suspect, another person is introduced into the equation. For the second factor beyond doubt is the message's destination.

It was sent to Sir Nicholas Lovelock.

*   *   *

Lovelock is about to drive off at the ninth. Feet adjusted, club gripped securely, ball lined up. He is two strokes up and playing well.

He starts his backswing.

'Sir Nicholas.'

Lovelock drops his club and spins round, furious.

'What the bloody hell do . . . ?'

The words bounce off Renfrew's impassive gaze. Next to him, Lovelock's opponent shifts uncomfortably from foot to foot.

'I'd like a few words, please.'

'For God's sake.' Lovelock gestures towards the ball, perched on its tee and waiting forlornly for a shot that's not going to come. 'I'm in the middle of a round, can't you see that?'

'Perfectly well.'

'We'll be through in an hour or so. I'll meet you in the clubhouse.'

Renfrew steps closer, so that Lovelock's opponent can't hear.

'Do you really think I'd have come all the way out here myself if it could wait?'

*   *   *

'Told me it was something to do with the *Amphitrite*, and that was it. Not a fucking word after that. Like a bloody sphinx, all the way here. And now another hour in this sauna. There'd better be a damn good reason for this, that's all.'

Lovelock, still in pink polo shirt and checked plus-fours, looks ready to explode. At the table in

364

the stifling interview room, Piers Spitzer, Seaspeed's in-house lawyer, jots some more notes on a pad. He is young and slight, with ginger eyebrows arching over blue eyes. His pale skin looks almost translucent in the harsh artificial lighting, and he has a birthmark on the back of his left hand.

The door to the interview room opens. Renfrew enters.

'Not before time,' says Lovelock. 'Is this what—'

He breaks off in surprise as Frank comes in, a pace and a half behind Renfrew.

'Frank.' Shock, concern. 'I thought you were still in hospital.'

Frank and Renfrew sit down on one side of the table. Renfrew gestures Lovelock to the spare chair opposite, next to his lawyer.

'I discharged myself,' says Frank.

'Well, I'm glad you're feeling all right. Now, would someone mind telling me what the hell this is all about?'

'The reason Frank discharged himself,' says Renfrew, 'was to go and look at the vehicle which was pushed out of the *Amphitrite*. The MAIB found it this morning.'

Lovelock's tongue darts from his mouth and licks his lips.

'It was the van Kate's theatre group were using. Five dead children were found inside.'

'My God,' Lovelock says. 'My *God*.'

Renfrew takes a piece of paper from his pocket and slides it across the table to Lovelock. 'That's the hard copy of an e-mail retrieved from Urquhart's central server a short while ago. The e-mail was sent to you.'

'How did you find that?' says Spitzer.

'We have a search warrant for Urquhart's premises, and the security guard let us in.'

Lovelock is shaking his head. 'My God. Children. I can't believe it.'

He picks up the e-mail, reads it, puts it back down on the table and looks Renfrew squarely in the eye.

'I suppose you're going to tell me it's fake,' says Renfrew.

'I've never seen it before in my life.'

'It was sent to your e-mail account.'

'Then it must have been sent in error.'

'In which case, you'd still have received it.'

'I told you. I've never seen this before.'

'You don't know who it's from or what it's about?'

'No.'

'But you admit that someone in Urquhart's sent it?'

Spitzer opens his mouth to say something, but Lovelock stills him with an upraised hand.

'I admit nothing, because there's nothing for me to admit. If you tell me this e-mail was sent from Urquhart's, then I believe you. And if you think this is connected to what happened on board the *Amphitrite*, then of course I will co-operate with you as best I can.'

'Good. So you won't mind staying here while we clear this mess up, will you?'

*   *   *

Kate and Red travel to the airport the same way they came from it—in silence. She studies him

366

askance, wondering what he's thinking.

The public gardens are in full bloom, eruptions of colour so spectacular that they somehow look flat. A little bit of imperfection wouldn't go amiss, Kate thinks.

'The city's been banned from entering "Britain in Bloom" competitions, you know. It kept winning,' she says.

'You wouldn't play nicely with the other children?'

She laughs. 'You got it.'

They watch the parks slide by. Hordes of pasty white bodies lounge on the grass. There are so many of them, and so many with picnics, that the litter bins can't take all their rubbish at once. Bright wrappers and crushed drink cans overflow on to the paths.

A park attendant is picking up the debris and putting it in a black binliner. He is using a long forked stick with a trigger mechanism built into the handle, rather like a petrol pump: the jaws at the other end can be opened or closed by pressing or releasing the trigger.

Kate watches the attendant as he works the grabber in deft movements, scooping up the garbage and putting it in the binliner as adeptly as he would with his own hands.

Red is watching him too. Kate can feel his gaze blending with hers.

The thought comes to both of them at once.

This forked stick could pick up snakes.

Flashes in Kate's head of the adder on Petra's body.

The adder, secured to her chest by a metal hoop. Where else could such a hoop be found?

In a flowerbed, to wind fragile plants around and prevent the wind from ripping them out of the soil.

Kate yanks her mobile out and punches in Ferguson's number. 'Peter, it's Kate. I want you to get a list of everyone employed by the city park service. Also gardening shops, and any gardening organisations. He may well be using gardening equipment. One of those grab-hand stick things that parkies use to pick up leaves and rubbish, that's how he keeps hold of the snakes. And the hoops he secures them with, they're plant hoops. My aunt's a keen gardener. I've seen her use them before.'

Red taps her shoulder. 'Don't forget the ropes.'

'The ropes?'

'Which he secures the victims with. Ropes are ten a penny in gardening shops.'

Kate, back into the phone. 'Did you hear that?'

'Yes.'

'Good. I'll be back in half an hour. Thanks.'

She ends the call. 'We're closing in on him. I can feel it.'

'I hope so.'

He doesn't seem as excited as her.

'What's wrong?'

'I've missed something.'

'What?'

'I don't know. But I know I have.'

'I can't see what it might be. What you worked out was pretty comprehensive.'

'It always seems that way. Until you find out what's lacking. You write a report or something, and you think it's as good as it's ever going to get, and then someone else takes a look and says, "Change this, this and this", and you wonder how come you never noticed the mistakes before, when they were so obvious.'

'Well, be sure to let me know if you remember it.'

He smiles, and it fades.

'What did you think, Kate, at the scenes last night? When you saw me, what did you see?'

'Honestly?'

'Of course.'

'I thought you were loving it.'

He runs his hand across the bottom of his nose, takes his time before he answers.

'You're right. I was. But I was loving it in the way you love a doomed affair. Loving it even though it was no good for me—*because* it was no good for me, even. I stood at the places he'd killed, and I could feel him there, as sure as if he was standing next to me. You think of their lives, I think of their deaths. I've been away from it for years, and it comes back into my head like that'—he snaps his fingers—'like an oil slick, thick and pervasive, flooding me. And that's why I'll never do this again. Next time, I'd drown.'

'Do you wish you hadn't come?'

He shakes his head. 'No.'

'Even though it's brought it all back?'

'That's why I don't regret it. Kate, I told you I didn't want to stir it up, but deep down, I've always wondered what it would be like to try just one more time. I said it was a doomed affair. And you go back to doomed affairs, and back and back—and one day you go back that one more time, because you know that it will solve things one way or the other. And that only means one thing. That time is when you know for certain that it can't be. So it is

369

here. I've come back, and I know that I can't control it. I can't turn it on and off at will.'

The car passes under the entrance sign to Dyce Airport.

'I know that I'm not strong enough.'

*   *   *

Renfrew and Frank, together with six officers and Holroyd, go to Lovelock's house. The street sign says Golden Square, but it's not so much golden as grey, like everything else in this city. Nor is the house as grand as Frank expected. It is two storeys high, with a low parapet partially obscuring the slated roof. Maybe he has a castle somewhere in the hills west of the city.

Renfrew jabs at the bell. One of the uniforms hands him the search warrant, hot from the magistrate's signature.

The door is opened by the housekeeper, a woman in her mid-fifties who is wiping her hands on a tea towel. Her eyes widen when she sees the phalanx of officers on the doorstep. Renfrew shows her the warrant, and her eyes grow bigger still.

'What's going on?' The housekeeper's voice is plaintive.

'Just stay here, please.'

Renfrew pushes past the housekeeper into the hall. The others follow him.

Renfrew takes a quick look around. The dining-room and drawing-room are on his right, separated from each other by retractable partitions. To his left, the kitchen and the stairs. He turns back to the housekeeper.

'What's upstairs?'

370

'Sir Nicholas's study, the spare bedroom, and the master bedroom.'

'Are there any other rooms in the house?'

'There's an attic and some storage space on the top floor. Utility rooms down in the basement.'

'That's it?'

'Yes.'

'You don't live here yourself?'

'No.'

Renfrew divides the house up among the officers. One to the basement, two on the ground floor, two to the first floor, and one on the top floor. He impresses on them the need not to rush the search. Lovelock is still in Queen Street, and he's not going anywhere.

*   *   *

Holroyd goes to the computer in the study and sets to coaxing its secrets into the open.

Barely a mile away, at the Seaspeed offices down by the docks, another team of officers arrives. A skeleton staff is on duty, still dealing with fallout from the *Amphitrite.* The employees, bewildered and protesting, are shepherded from their desks and out into the street, where they are told not to bother coming back until Monday morning. The police allow Marita to change the company answerphone message and give her own mobile number for people calling with queries concerning the sinking.

Once the employees are gone, the police search the offices from top to bottom. Filing cabinets are opened and rifled through, folders ripped out and stacked in crates. Desk drawers receive the same treatment. They work with the merciless efficiency of a combine-harvester.

*   *   *

Renfrew and Frank sit in the kitchen. It is the least likely place for anything to be hidden, and therefore the best place for them to keep out of the searchers' way. The housekeeper sits with them, looking alarmed at the sounds of men turning the house upside-down. After half an hour, Renfrew turns to her.

'Where's the toilet?'

She points towards the door. 'Out of here, past the bookcase, first left.'

He leaves the room. A few seconds later, the officer who was searching the basement comes in. He is holding two objects, both in plastic evidence bags.

'The chief around?'

'Gone for a piss. What have you got?'

The man looks at the bandages on Frank's head and hesitates.

'I—er—I think he should see them first.'

'Why? What are they?'

The man still looking at Frank's bandages and Frank out of his seat, the connections fusing in his mind as he steps across the room and takes the objects.

The first item is a small brown square, maybe a couple of inches each side. It yields to the touch, and the smell of marzipan is strong even through the evidence bag.

Plastic explosive.

The second is a framed picture, black and white.

372

A group of young men lined up, healthy and proud and in immaculate uniforms. At the top a regimental crest, and in calligraphic writing the words: 'British Army on the Rhine. Explosives Ordnance Division.'

Lovelock is sitting front and centre, right next to the Sergeant-Major.

∗   ∗   ∗

Renfrew goes back to Queen Street alone. He doesn't want Frank confronting the man he now knows tried to kill him.

Lovelock rises in indignant protest once again as Renfrew enters the interview room. Renfrew ignores him. He places the explosive and the picture on the table and watches for Lovelock's reaction.

It is a split second, but it is enough. The tiniest slump of the shoulders and sagging of the jaw as Lovelock realises the import of what's in front of him. And then he comes up fighting.

'You searched my house?' says Lovelock. 'How dare you? How *dare* you?'

Renfrew gestures at the table. 'That's attempted murder, right there. If I were you, I'd start talking.'

'Planted. You planted them.'

'We planted a regimental photograph of you? In your own house? Come on.'

'That photograph proves nothing.'

'I've got a team of officers tearing your house to pieces, and another team doing the same to the Seaspeed offices. If you want, we'll hang you out to dry. If you come clean now, that might work in your favour. *Might.*'

373

'You have no idea who you're dealing with.'

'Attempted murder is attempted murder. I don't give a shit who you are.'

Lovelock shakes his head.

'You come clean now,' continues Renfrew, 'and I'll do what I can for you.'

'I haven't done anything.'

'You tried to kill Frank Beauchamp because you feared he'd find what was in the van. You knew what was in that van. You were involved in bringing those children over. *Children.* You know what cons do to prisoners who are there for child offences? Do you? It's not pretty, it really isn't. Come clean, and I'll make sure you're kept out of their way.'

Lovelock shakes his head again, but Renfrew's mention of prison has rattled him. A gap, and Renfrew drives a wedge into it.

'Where did they come from, the children? What were you going to do with them? Paedophilia, is that it?'

Renfrew has seen more often than he'd like—which is to say, at all—what paedophile rings do. He has seen the images they disseminate in glossy photos or high-resolution computer images. A child gagged and bound, being roasted on a spit above a fire. Children of no more than eight or nine performing oral sex on each other and on adults. A dark-skinned girl with neat razor slashes down her flank, staring at the camera with eyes so full of fear they looked as if they were about to burst.

'Don't be absurd. I'm not a paedophile, and I would never associate with them. I find the idea abhorrent.'

'What, then?'

374

'It was humanitarian. The children came from Russia. They were from the streets, orphanages, young offenders' institutions. We offered them proper accommodation, a better life. They took it up like a shot.'

'How did you get them out?'

'Through Scandinavia. They were taken across the Finnish border, near where the Finland Station used to be. From there, they were taken west—first by boat across the Gulf of Bothnia, and then through Sweden and Norway until they reached Bergen, which is where they were picked up.'

'By who? I need the name of the man on the ground.'

Lovelock continues with his narrative regardless. 'These kids had no life. We were going to give them one. If we could, we'd have exported them legally, but you know what Russia's like, there are no laws worth the name. So we had to do it underground. And it wasn't just the Russian end that was tricky. Once they were out of Russia, they were in the European Union, and you know what border checks are like. You start underground, you have to stay underground, because there's no documentation. It was like that Dutch cleric who used to smuggle Bibles behind the Iron Curtain during the Cold War. What was his name? Brother Andrew, that's it. "God's smuggler", he called himself. We were like him, except importing rather than exporting. We were going to bring the children back here and put them up for adoption. That's when the paperwork would have been sorted out, when they were safely here.'

'So what happened to change things? Why were they thrown out?'

375

'I have no idea. I told—my contact to be prepared, that's all. He panicked.'

'The decision to eject the van was nothing to do with you?'

'No.'

'No?'

'No.'

'Was Sutton in on it?'

'Yes. His job was to see that the van went on early. We wanted it near the front: customs rarely check the first vehicles off a ferry. Ask someone to take a playing card from a fanned-out pack. They'll almost always pick one from near the middle, won't they? If the van was pulled out unexpectedly, there'd be fewer cars in front. More chance of a quick getaway. And of course we needed him onside if things went horribly wrong.'

'As they did.'

'Yes.'

'So Sutton and—your contact cooked up a mythical bomb warning.'

'Yes. It was the only thing which could justify stopping the ship and tipping the van out. Justify to the other members of the bridge crew, that is. Not the passengers. They were told that one of the propellers had fouled. But the bridge crew would have known what was crap and what wasn't. A bomb warning was perfect. Impossible to disprove, imperative to take seriously.'

'Did Sutton know what was in the van when he tipped it out?'

'No. Not at the time. He'd been slipped £500 and told to ask no questions. He probably thought it was drugs or weapons. But he was told what was really inside after the van had gone, just to ensure his silence. He couldn't squeal without implicating himself too.'

Renfrew thinks back to Tuesday morning: he and Lovelock and Frank in Seaspeed's air-conditioned offices rather than a sweltering police interview room, and Frank saying how Sutton had panicked and turned the *Amphitrite* into the storm rather than away from it. Not because he'd got the wrong vehicle—he'd got the right vehicle—but because he'd just been told what was in the van he'd sent to the bottom of the North Sea.

Sutton in the chartroom as he calculates how much time they've lost and how much faster they'll have to travel if they are to arrive in Aberdeen on schedule. Then they hit the storm and have to cut their speed again. He needs to redo his calculations, but it's not difficult. The figures he writes are simple—distance remaining over average speed—but they make no sense, they shimmer and transmute into the bodies of dead children, children with no names and no future, trapped in terrible drowning panic in a metal prison . . .

'I'll ask you again. Who was the man on the ground in Bergen?'

Lovelock shakes his head. 'You won't get that out of me.'

'It must have been one of three,' says Renfrew. 'Sinclair Larsen, Alex Melville or Jason Duchesne. Tell me which one. Tell me, or I'll leave you to whatever slim mercies you find in prison.'

Lovelock shakes his head again.

*   *   *

The meeting room in which Kate and Frank

watched the video from *Starsky* is turned into a makeshift incident room. Five officers are tasked with obtaining access to Lovelock's bank statements, travel records, credit-card records, personal e-mail, mobile-phone records, and fax records. They keep in close contact with the three teams scattered throughout the city, at Urquhart's, Seaspeed and Lovelock's house.

A life in detail. Decades in the making, hours in the destroying.

*   *   *

Ferguson's mood has brightened since Red left. They have found three unsolved murders involving mothers: a woman stabbed in Banff in 1984, another killed in a suspected arson attack in Glamis in 1991, and one bludgeoned to death in Arbroath last year. They're checking each of them now.

They're cross-referencing all Park Service employees with criminal records, and of course any unsolved murders too. They're also checking out gardening centres, looking for anyone who might have bought such implements. Again, it will be useless if Blackadder paid cash, but maybe the sales staff will remember something.

The knife and snake searches continue, so far without success.

Kate walks into her office, and immediately hears a quiet electronic 'boing' from her computer, the one which signals an incoming message.

The screensaver is on: one she composed herself, three-dimensional text which swings and rotates across the screen as it slides through a succession of colours. One word, spinning and spinning.

'Blackadder'

Kate taps the 'return' key, and the screensaver disappears. She taps again, and the dialogue box disappears too.

The new message has no title and she has never seen the sender's address before—it's a Hotmail one—but she knows instantly who it's from.

Dear God. At last, he communicates.

Kate wonders briefly whether he'll have clipped a virus on to the message, but there is no attachment. She opens the message.

Two down, Miss Detective. And still you seem no nearer to catching me. I expected more from you, I must say. Your reputation preceded you. I guess it's true what they say: you're only as good as your next case.

Unsigned. Controlled. Taunting.

Kate thinks back to the last unsigned message she saw: the bomb warning sent to her father, blustering and crude. This one is neither.

Kate picks up the phone, checks an internal extension list, and punches out a number.

'Technical support.'

'This is DCI Beauchamp. I need a technician here, urgently.'

'We're rather tied up here now, Detective.'

'I could care less. I need one *now*.'

He comes through her office door ninety seconds later, red-faced and looking slightly frightened. Istvan Molnar, a Hungarian who's just started working here. His lank hair is smeared against the sides of his face like shower curtains, and his narrow chin and downturned mouth make him look permanently lugubrious. Kate points at the screen.

'I've just received this message. I need to know who's sending it and where he's sending it from.'

Molnar leans across her to peer at the screen. A half-moon of sweat nestles in the armpit of his shirt. She pushes her swivel chair back to give him more room. He nods an embarrassed thanks and presents her with an altogether charmless view of his backside. He taps at the keyboard, tuts to himself, taps again.

'Is impossible to tell,' he says, turning back to her.

'How do you mean?'

'You give any name you like for account.'

'But you must have to give details for Hotmail themselves.'

'No. Is free service, so no credit card needed. You give details when you log in, but they no check. You give name, birthday, postcode—all these you can fake.'

'There's no way you can find out who it is?'

'From one message, impossible. Over time, with much correspondence—maybe.'

'And how would *he* know *my* address?'

'Is easy. He find out server name—is on police website—and he know your name. Only certain amount of ways names is done on e-mail: initials, surname, and so on. He tries till he gets it right.' He shrugs.

'Right.' Kate twists her mouth in frustration.

'Thanks.'

Molnar nods and scuttles out like a monkey, torso bent slightly forward and legs splayed.

The message is still on screen. Kate reads it again.

Two down, Miss Detective. And still you seem no nearer to catching me. I expected more from you, I must say. Your reputation preceded you. I guess it's true what they say: you're only as good as your next case.

Above the text, the 'reply to author' icon stares impassively at her. She clicks on it and begins to type, not bothering with capitals.

we know all about you, viper man. you are nothing, you understand? whatever kind of hell you are in, you are there by your own choice. you made the decisions which put you there. and you could walk straight out of it, right now, if you so chose—except that your values are such as to make the path out of hell appear overwhelmingly dangerous, frighteningly painful, and impossibly difficult. so you remain in hell because it seems safe and easy to you. you prefer it that way.

Her finger hovers over the 'send' icon. With a sense of stepping into a void, she clicks on it. And waits.

What am I doing?

Trying to catch him, draw him out, make him say something which gives him away, gives her a clue as to who he is, where he is. By his words shall ye know him.

If he replies, it'll be worth it. She wants him to reply, the same way one wants a prospective lover to call.

What am I doing?

The 'boing', the dialogue box again. His reply.

Long is the way and hard, that out of hell leads up to light.

His own redemption. He does what he does so that he *can* walk out of hell. Red was right. When the last one is killed, the madness will go, and he'll disappear.

Kate looks back at the screen.

Where are you? Where do you sit? Where do you shroud yourself in the shields of technology? What do you look like? **Who are you?**

She stabs angrily at the power button, and the computer screen goes blank.

Holroyd is waiting at the front door for Renfrew when he arrives back at Lovelock's house.

They go up to Lovelock's study, where Holroyd points to the computer screen and stands back to let Renfrew have a look. Another e-mail, also sent from Urquhart's, also deleted.

I appreciate your desire to have the cargo auctioned as soon as possible, but enough people work late here to make a weekday evening unfeasible. The first available weekend would seem ideal. I have checked the building on three consecutive Sundays,

and found it empty. Sunday 16th would be suitable. A start time of c. 7 or 8 p.m. would ensure that we finish in darkness, with the consequent positive implications for security.

I received a call today from G. J., one of the prospective bidders. He was lax enough to use the Wilberforce word in open conversation. It must be worth re-emphasising to all clients the necessity of never using this word, even among ourselves.

Renfrew looks sharply up at Holroyd.

'This is exactly how it came up?'

Holroyd nods.

'And no way of telling who the sender was?'

'No. Urquhart's, that's all I know.'

'Have you shown this to Mr Beauchamp?'

'Not yet.'

Renfrew reads it again. It is all there, as before. No mistakes.

The children were going to be sold at Urquhart's. They were going to be *auctioned*. But Lovelock said they were destined for adoption. Why auction children for adoption?

Renfrew reads out loud, off the screen. ' "A start time of c. 7 or 8 p.m. would ensure that we finish in darkness, with the consequent positive implications for security." ' He turns to Holroyd. 'What do you think that means?'

'Presumably something about reducing the chances of being seen, if many people are leaving a place together.'

'Which means in turn they're doing something they don't want people to know about.'

383

But Lovelock just told Renfrew that all the paperwork would be sorted out in Scotland. He implied that, once the children were safe, the operation would be above board.

Renfrew reads the message for a third time, and this time one of the lines jumps at him.

He was lax enough to use the Wilberforce word in open conversation.

'What do you think "the Wilberforce word" means?' Renfrew asks.

'The only Wilberforce that springs to mind is William Wilberforce, the man who . . .'

Holroyd stops dead. Renfrew finishes his sentence for him.

'The man who abolished slavery.'

Slavery.

The evil seems to permeate through the screen.

An auction in human misery. After hours, by invitation, five lots only—all sold 'as is', imperfections and all. An exhibition before the start, so bidders can inspect the lots at their convenience. No reserve price, no registration, no credit cards, no catalogue, no sales code, no provenance. Lives under the hammer for a baying pack of sharks.

A child blinks uncertainly in the harsh light. The faces watch him intently, as if he is an exhibit in the zoo. Above him and to his right, a man is calling out numbers. If he could understand him, this is what the man is saying:

'Five thousand. And five. And six thousand. And five. And seven . . .'

Some of the people watching the child raise their

384

hands periodically. They hold paddles with numbers on them.

'Fair warning.'

The child flinches as the hammer comes down.

He is led away from all these people. In a back room, a man in a suit comes for him. The man says something which the child doesn't understand.

That man is the one who takes the child away.

Renfrew rubs his face with his hands. Years ago, Aberdeen exported stockings to Germany, followed by linen and granite to Gothenburg and Amsterdam. Then came the fishing trade, and after that the oil. And now they trade children.

*   *   *

They take twelve crates of documents from Lovelock's house to Queen Street. It is past six by the time they begin the laborious process of sorting through them.

The quiet calm of a white-hot day, brushed by the rustling of paper and the slide of forearms across sweaty brows. Frank, having been debriefed by Renfrew on the way back, mucks in with the search, and he is the one who finds what they're looking for.

A piece of Seaspeed notepaper. In Lovelock's writing, one below the other, five words.

Dover. Folkestone. Hull. Yarmouth. Poole.

All ferry ports.

And below them, a name in block capitals.

JASON D

Renfrew sends officers round to Jason's house. He is not there, and there is no sign as to where he's gone. Renfrew has a photograph of Jason circulated on a closed APB to all local police forces. He doesn't include details of why Jason is wanted for questioning, and he emphasises that this is not yet in the public domain.

Then he goes down to the cell where Lovelock is being held, on one charge of attempted murder and pending further charges pertaining to the illegal import of foreign nationals. Renfrew tells Lovelock that they know the truth now, they know the humanitarian story was a pack of lies, they know about the slave auctions, and they know who the man on the ground was. He also tells Lovelock to look forward to some special personal treatment in prison.

Lovelock says nothing.

*   *   *

Kate spends forty-five minutes with her father and Renfrew while they explain everything that's happened, and then she goes home. Her head feels as if it's full of water. She wants it all to be over— and when it is, she's going to spend a week at home and do nothing but be with her son.

Seaspeed is finished as a company, Kate knows that. It is in a precarious enough financial position anyway, and it will be dead the moment the truth about the *Amphitrite* comes out. Who's going to want to travel with a company which transports children from Russia to Scotland to be used as slaves? Who would put their reputation on the line

386

to try and resurrect it?

Both answers are the same. No one.

Kate thinks back to a story she was told last year. One of the toughest inmates in Shotts, she thinks it was, caught a robin. It was injured: one of its wings hardly worked. This man took it upon himself to nurse the bird back to health. He'd walk around with it in his top pocket. It was his pride and joy.

One day, one of the warders told this man he had to get rid of the bird. Prison rules: no pets allowed. The man protested. The warder was adamant. It was a hot day, like today, and the electric fans were all on. The prisoner walked up to the nearest fan, took out the robin and threw it in. It was killed instantly. Everyone was horrified, not least the warder. 'I thought you loved that bird,' he said. 'I did,' said the prisoner. 'But if I can't have it, nobody can.'

So it was with Lovelock and Seaspeed. That company was his baby. He'd rather it was destroyed than anyone else got hold of it. Lovelock and Seaspeed, the prisoner and the robin. A man of stature nursing an ailing beast, not only with love but with petulance and jealousy.

Kate rings Bronagh from the car. 'Hi, it's me. How's Leo?'

'He's OK, now.'

'Has he said anything about this morning?'

'Nothing at all.'

'Nothing as to why he freaked?'

'Nothing.'

'OK.' Pause. 'Auntie B, is it all right if you have him tonight?'

'Again? Are *you* OK?'

'Yeah. I'm just sick of the whole thing. I want . . .

387

you know.'

'Yes.'

'You're an angel. I'll ring you tomorrow.'

She ends the call, and rings Alex. 'Can you come round?' she asks.

'Sure. I'll be right there.'

He cooks dinner for her, and all the way through she talks at him, not caring to put a proper conversation or even a coherent monologue together, just letting it spill out in the same haphazard order it appears in her head. It doesn't even have to be him across the table from her: it could be anyone, anything, a lamp-post for all she cares, so long as it listens to her. When she grinds to a halt, as much through exhaustion as anything else, he comes round the table and holds her tight.

'How was your night out with the boys?' she asks.

'It was fun.'

'Did you tell them about me?'

'Of course.'

'All the gory details?'

'Don't be stupid.'

'Bet you did.'

'Did *not*.'

'But that's what all blokes want to know, isn't it? What's she like, what does she do, does she moan or scream, does she push back, all that stuff?'

'I told them you're great and you make me happy. That's all. Blokes don't ask that kind of stuff, not really. Women are much dirtier among themselves than men are. You'd tell your friends worse things than I do.'

'I don't have time for friends.'

'That's just as well, then.'

She laughs into his neck.

'I'll do the washing-up,' he says.

'That's a first. Every man I know runs a mile whenever Fairy Liquid's mentioned.'

'I quite enjoy it, actually. It's therapeutic.'

He goes over to the sink, squirts green detergent on to the plates piled there—piled like the bodies he trampled over on the *Amphitrite*—and turns the tap on, gently so that the water won't splash up off the crockery and soak him. Kate comes up behind him and puts her arms round his waist. He feels her breath against the side of his neck.

'Thank you for coming over,' she says. 'I'm glad you're here.'

Alex leans back against her and tips his head upwards, letting her nuzzle the underside of his chin.

'Someone hasn't shaved this morning,' she says.

'It's Saturday. Someone hasn't had to.'

He leans forward again, turns off the tap and begins to scrub one of the plates. She pushes her right hand up his shirt and feels for his belt with the left.

He turns to face her. His hands are bearded in soap bubbles.

In the bedroom now, moving seamlessly from one state to another: making love, dozing across each other, stroking hair and skin while the shadows lengthen outside and finally fade to night. They rock gently together, saliva smacking on parted lips as one or other gasps in delight. The sweat springs at the base of her throat and runs between her breasts and down her stomach. Alex lifts his head up and forward to kiss it away. She holds him inside her without moving, and then

389

suddenly clenches all the muscles from her abdomen downwards on to him until he thinks she'll never let go. For these drifting hours, their existence is entirely one another.

When Kate next opens her eyes, the alarm clock's luminous green hands are stretched as wide as they can go. Quarter to three. Exactly the same time as she woke up the other night, when Alex was gone.

He's still here this time, and he's out for the count. The sheet next to her rises and falls rhythmically.

Kate feels wide awake. She props herself up in bed, reaches across Alex and rootles around in the darkness, trying to find something—anything—which will tire her out and send her back to sleep. Her fingers roam the bedside table. They brush over the bandage box and the alarm clock, and settle on something cold and metallic. She picks it up and brings it into her chest, turning it over in her hands. Rubber buttons, a plastic cord. Alex's Walkman. Kate finds the headphones, puts them in her ears, and feels along the rubber buttons. 'Play' is always the largest.

Alex's voice sounds loud in her head. 'I will listen to this tape every day, and it will help me come to terms with what happened on board the *Amphitrite*. I have nothing to be afraid of. The horror will fade, given time.' Breath. 'I first realised that something was wrong at around—'

Kate jabs at the button until the tape stops. She rips the headphones from her ears, rolls over, shakes Alex roughly by the shoulder. He makes three or four snuffling noises, like a pig rooting for food, and then turns his head towards her.

'What's this?' she asks.

'What's what?'

She reaches behind her and turns on the light. He clamps his eyes shut.

'What are you *doing*?'

'What's this?' she asks, holding the Walkman up.

He opens his eyes a fraction. 'My Walkman,' he says groggily. 'What does it look like?'

'No. What's the tape in it?'

He's still half-asleep. He doesn't think before answering.

'The one the counsellor told me to make.'

'What counsellor?'

He snaps awake instantly, knowing that he has screwed up.

'What fucking counsellor, Alex?'

He sighs. 'I went to see one.'

'Why?'

'I wanted to get an impartial view on what I was feeling. I thought that talking to someone neutral who wasn't involved would help me get some perspective on it.'

'Perspective? Psychobabble, more like. What kind of bullshit did they spin you?'

'It wasn't bullshit. She told me I've got post-traumatic stress disorder, which is perfectly normal, and that I'll work my way through it.'

'Why didn't you tell me?'

'Because I knew you'd react like this.'

'We had an *agreement*. We agreed we'd only talk about it to each other.'

'I know.'

'I'm not enough for you now, is that it?'

'Kate, just cool down.'

'Don't tell me what to do. Fucking liar.'

391

Kate leaps out of bed and runs into the bathroom. Alex lies on his back, seething at her irrationality and his own stupidity in bringing the Walkman in the first place. After a few moments, he wearily swings his feet on to the floor and goes after her.

She is curled up in the corner by the bath, and she looks crushingly vulnerable. Her head is down, her knees are tucked under her chin, and she has her arms wrapped round her shins. Alex squats down beside her.

'Babe, I'm sorry,' he says. 'Come back to bed. We'll talk about it in the morning.'

She doesn't answer. He starts to stroke her hair. No reaction. He puts his hands on her shoulders, and she is cold to the touch.

She speaks without lifting her head.

'Go, Alex. Just go.'

*   *   *

This is the end of his time in the village. They try to sell the house, but there are no buyers, not with its history.

No longer a boy now, he moves to Aberdeen and gets a job working in the public library. The work is largely mundane, but the freedom is intoxicating. He relishes the start of every day as if he were a released prisoner seeing the sun for the first time. A flat of his own, a life of his own. This is all new to him, even if other people take it for granted. This is a rebirth.

He has opportunity galore to read. He takes a book home with him every night, and returns it when he arrives for work the next morning, already read. The less he gives of himself, the less likely his colleagues are to discover his previous life, the less he will show his greenness and naivety.

He comes out of his shell slowly. His colleagues know him as quiet and reserved, but the reality is slightly more complex. He keeps himself to himself until he learns how to do it—'it' being life itself. The conventions of social intercourse are new to him, and his silence is protection.

These people he works with, they are nothing special. The more he mixes with them, the less like them he realises he is. He is a blank canvas on which anything can be drawn. They are nothing, tangled in their petty lives and intrigues: inconsequential gossip, worries about promotion, the mundanities of life. Above all, they are stupid. Every day, his sneering contempt for them grows, and yet they have no idea.

At his first Christmas party there, one of the assistant librarians weaves drunkenly up to him and tells him how everyone thought he was such a cold fish when he first arrived, and they weren't sure whether it was shyness or superiority, but they now know it was the former, because he's started to come out of his shell.

What does he tell her? That it started out as shyness, but has metamorphosed from there to superiority? No. He smiles and mutters something non-committal, and she hugs him and tries to drag him under the mistletoe.

It's not hard, once he knows how. Shakespeare had it right, when he said that all the world's a stage. He acts his part perfectly. He observes human behaviour with the keen eye of an eagle, and he sees how easy much of it is to fake. He knows when to smile, when to place a hand on someone's shoulder, when a kind word can work wonders. He knows how to entertain, if not to be entertained. He knows how to express sorrow and sympathy and pity.

And here's the rub. He knows how to show warmth, but not how to feel it. The only emotions he feels are those edged with black: hatred, rage, and above all contempt. People are there to be used, and he uses them. That is what gives him satisfaction: seeing how they dance to his tune without even knowing that they are. Bewildered fools, the lot of them.

One night, just before the library closes, he goes searching for a book to take home that night. He is flicking through the spines in the drama section when he sees a book out of line. It has been put back on the shelf at an angle and too deeply, so it is half-hidden by another book. His hand moves towards it almost of its own accord. He pulls the book out and shakes it open.

Aeschylus. The *Oresteia*. A trilogy: *Agamemnon, The Libation Bearers, The Eumenides.*

He opens it and begins to read the introduction.

'Aeschylus was forty-five in 480 BC when the Persians sacked Athens and destroyed the shrines of the gods on the Acropolis. Soon afterwards, he fought in the forces which defeated the Persians at Salamis and Plataea. Aeschylus portrayed the Greeks' victory as a triumph over the barbarian latent in themselves, the hubris that united the invader and native tyrant as targets of the gods. The *Oresteia* perfects this vision of warning and reward. Its dominant symbol is that of light after darkness. It is a rite of passage from savagery to civilisation, from youth to maturity: a story of our recreation as we struggle from the past to meet the future.'

He is mesmerised. Standing between the metal shelves with the sparse early-evening crowd morphing around him, he pecks greedily at the words and steels himself against their resonance.

The introduction outlines the plot. Agamemnon, commander-in-chief of the Greek forces in the Trojan War, who had married Clytemnestra against her will. Orestes, Agamemnon's son, himself banished to exile. Clytemnestra, taking her husband's cousin Aegisthus as a lover while Agamemnon is away. Agamemnon, sacrificing his eldest daughter before he went away. Clytemnestra and Aegisthus conspiring to kill Agamemnon. Agamemnon returning home in a storm, with his mistress Cassandra in tow. Cassandra, caught in a prophetic trance, refusing to enter the house. Agamemnon murdered by Clytemnestra as he steps from his bath. Aegisthus adopting the trappings of Agamemnon's power. Orestes, in revenge, killing Clytemnestra and Aegisthus.

He slumps against the bookcase.

It is as if his life has been mapped out for him many centuries in advance, transposed from ancient Greece to a wind-lashed Scottish village. He is Orestes, struggling through his need for vengeance and his blood guilt. He is crime contagious, the dead pursuing the living for revenge. He is justice and injustice, equally justified in both.

He reads on, and what comes next freezes his blood.

After Orestes kills his mother and her lover, the

Furies come after him and drive him mad.

He flicks from the introduction to the text itself, looking for a reference to the Furies.

The man's clear trail tracks his guilt to light. He's wounded: go for the splash of blood, hunt him down. Over the wide rolling earth we've ranged in flock, hurdling the waves in wingless flight—and now we come, all hot pursuit, outracing ships astern. He's here somewhere, cowering like the hunted fox. The reek of human blood is laughter to my heart! Out of his living marrow will I drain my red libation, out of his veins will I suck my food, my raw, brutal cups.

They will come for him.

He sees now that he should have sought legal redress against his mother. He should have exercised self-control and respect for the law. Vicious as she was, the evil he has done by killing her has far surpassed her crime. They will come for him. Unlike Orestes, there can be no trial for him, no hope of salvation. They will come for him. He does not know when or in what guise, but come for him they will: and when they do, they will show no mercy.

SUNDAY

For the second time this week, the phone jerks Kate awake with the dawn. The chemical certainty of what it will be cuts through her sleep and the instant chill in her stomach.

The final body. Blackadder's there ahead of me, he's made his final sacrifice. His last victim, unspeakably violated because he's got this insane idea that he's being punished for killing his mother. That's it. He's going to disappear. I'll never find him.

She scrabbles for the phone. 'Kate Beauchamp.'

'It's Red.'

'Red, it's'—she squints at the alarm clock, her sleep-starved brain trying to associate their configuration with the time—'five in the morning.'

'I know. I'd have called you earlier, but it's taken hours to persuade these mulletheads to bring me a phone. I know what I missed.'

She sits bolt upright. Drowsiness flees from her as a gazelle flees a lion.

'I'd better spell the whole thing out, in case I'm wrong,' Red continues. 'Listen to me, and tell me if anything doesn't make sense. I don't want you just to take my word for anything. It's too important for that.'

Kate takes a deep breath. 'OK.'

'First of all, have there been any pig-killings reported since this thing began?'

'Pig-killings?'

'In ancient Greece, murderers—especially those who killed their own—would sometimes try to purify themselves by killing swine and pouring the pigs' blood over their heads. It was thought to absorb their blood-guilt as it flowed down their bodies.'

'Not that I've heard of. I'll check.'

'Right. Next. I told you there were three Furies, yes?'

'Yes.'

'Well, I've done a lot of reading since I got back. Three is the number usually cited, though not always. Greek drama, for example, used the Furies in a chorus of variable numbers. Both Aeschylus and Euripides had such a chorus when they wrote about Orestes, who the Furies drove mad after he killed his mother. But they're exceptions, and that I think mainly because of dramatic convention. So we can assume, as before, that three is the number we're looking for, yes?'

'Yes.' She wishes he'd hurry up.

'Those three are not interchangeable. They have names, separate identities. And they're almost always written in the same order. First is Tisiphone, the avenger of murder. Petra Gallacher was the first victim. Assume that Petra represents Tisiphone, in the strange vortex of Blackadder's mind. He sees her as having come to avenge his mother's death. She was a reporter. Maybe she'd cottoned on to the truth somehow.'

'Ferguson checked all the stories she'd done. There was nothing like that. He'd have found it.'

'Not if she was doing it off her own back.'

'Why would she do that?'

'She was about to lose her job, you said. Perhaps this was her last throw of the dice. Find a big story and wow the newsdesk into keeping her.'

'She'd have told them.'

'Not necessarily. Not if she was afraid they'd take the story off her, give it to someone more senior. You know what reporters are like, Kate. They're like detectives. They're secretive, they're territorial, they don't share. They're squirrels.'

'Who's next?'

'Megaera, the grudging. The unwilling.'

Kate grips her sheets. 'Elizabeth Hart. That mean old bat.'

'Exactly. The prying busybody. Trying to ruin lives with her gossip and her spying.'

'And the third?'

The line is silent. She wonders if they've been cut off.

'Can you hear me, Red?'

'The third is Alecto. Unceasing in anger.'

She opens her mouth to reply, but he is going on. His voice is curiously toneless, and what he plucks are not the words from her mouth but the thoughts from her head.

'Alecto, who has dedicated herself to tracking this man down. Alecto, who the case notes said went on TV and all but offered Blackadder a personal confrontation. Alecto, who lost her temper with me when I wavered about whether or not to help.'

She is begging for him not to say it, and she knows he must.

'Alecto is you, Kate. You're the last one.'

*　　　*　　　*

Queen Street turned into a fortress and Kate inside, the queen in her castle.

They are taking no chances. A cordon of wooden sawhorses and metal crowd barriers has been thrown up around the building, with a single

401

gap guarded by two armed policemen. There are twelve other armed men in and around police headquarters: two on each external corner, two in the lobby, and two outside the incident room. The anti-climb grease on the drainpipes which run up the side of the building is checked and re-applied where necessary, and the window-cleaning dolly which usually hangs from the roof has been dismantled and taken inside, just in case.

The detectives in the incident room—Kate's colleagues, for heaven's sake—treat her as they would a traffic-accident victim. They talk to her in low voices and risk quick furtive glances when they think she's not looking. She wants to tell them to act normally, but there is little normal about this situation.

She knows Blackadder won't go after any of her family, but even so she has Frank, Bronagh and Leo taken to a safe house and guarded. Alex, too. One less thing for her to worry about, at any rate.

She has Ferguson check through the records for any pigs reported killed over the past week. He looks as perplexed as she felt when Red first mentioned it.

Aberdeen awaking to a leisurely Sunday morning, long breakfasts over newspapers and walks on the beach after lunch, the heatwave now into its sixth day—enjoy it while you can, the weatherman says, it'll break sometime this evening—and for Kate the knowledge that Blackadder would do to her what he has done to Petra Gallacher and Elizabeth Hart.

It's not the dismemberment which scares her. He does that post mortem: she wouldn't be around to care by then. What makes her skin freeze under

402

three layers of clothes is the torture. The bastinado on the soles of her feet, and whatever else he does to them. She's seen their histamine levels, their petechial haemorrhaging. That says it all.

If it comes to it, she won't let him torture her. She'll make him kill her quickly. Petra Gallacher and Elizabeth Hart must have both fought for their lives, or at least talked for them. They must have begged and pleaded and implored. They thought they could still persuade him otherwise. And eventually they must have realised that nothing they could say or do would make any difference. That's when they would have looked into the abyss and begged for the end to come quickly.

She won't beg. Not just because it would be futile, but because she has come too far for that. She won't beg.

In Petra Gallacher, some of what Kate remembers being. In Elizabeth Hart, some of what she fears becoming.

Get a grip. This is all bollocks. I'm here, he can't get me.

Someone has brought in the Sunday papers. She takes them into her office, and is gratified to see that somehow the news of Lovelock's arrest hasn't yet made it to the headlines. Only a matter of time, she thinks ruefully.

All the papers have got large pieces on the ferry disaster, special investigations with lavish graphics. *Scotland on Sunday* has the most coverage, unsurprisingly: an eight-page pullout. Kate skims through it, sees there's little she didn't know already, and flicks desultorily through the rest of the news section.

On a left-hand page, tucked in the middle, a

headline tugs at her.

Scientists warn of Tollohill tree disease

Beneath the headline, a picture of someone with glasses and a hard hat standing by a tree. Kate reads the text.

Botanists yesterday warned that Tollohill Wood, south of Aberdeen, could suffer chronic Dutch elm disease unless steps were taken to prevent it at an early stage. Tollohill has one of the highest concentrations of wych elms in north-east Scotland. More than 90 per cent of the park is elm, with pines and cedars comprising the remainder. The warning comes in spite of wych elms' traditionally greater resistance to disease than other elms.

Kate snaps out of her mental cruise with the reflexive abruptness of a motorist swerving to avoid an accident. She grabs Elizabeth Hart's autopsy from her in-tray and rifles through it.

There, in clear black type. 'Traces of wood were found in a small area, approximately $1\frac{1}{2}$ inches by 1 inch, on the back of the victim's head, presumably from impact against a tree. The wood is identified as *quercus pedunculata*, the common oak indigenous to the UK.'

Kate takes Petra's autopsy. Her hands are trembling.

There it is again. The same, even down to the phrasing. Traces of wood, *quercus pedunculata*, common oak.

But there were no oaks where Elizabeth Hart was found. So how could she have impacted against an oak?

Simple answer. She couldn't.

Which means she must have been hit with something made of oak.

And if she was hit with something made of oak, so would Petra have been. Almost everything else has been the same.

Kate races through the autopsy reports again.

Neither victim suffered significant damage to the skull. No fracturing or displacement. So he didn't hit them too hard. Just hard enough to—what?

Knock them out. Subdue them. Make them groggy. Soften them up.

A string in the labyrinth of her mind, leading her to the answer.

Something made of oak. Hard enough to injure, but not to kill. Something easily handled, not too unwieldy. He'd want to be flexible.

Oak is a hard wood, one of the hardest in everyday use: way ahead of pine and sycamore and cedar. How does she know that? From David, Leo's father. He was big into carpentry. She remembers him telling her about density ratings one day, back when they were together. Density ratings. She's amazed she even listened. She's very glad she did.

Something easily handled, and a hard wood. Something small would be enough.

How small is small? Small enough to be carried in one hand. Small enough to be concealed.

An image begins to form in her head. It is blurred and blockish at first. The definition improves gradually. A picture being downloaded from her brain. It comes to her as things come in dreams—because one's been thinking about them recently, and they reappear in a different context.

405

Small. Oak. Handheld.

She checks the autopsies again.

'Traces of wood were found in a small area, approximately 1½ inches by 1 inch.'

Kate pushes her chair back and strides out of the room. The two armed men outside the door stiffen.

'I'm sorry, DCI Beauchamp,' says one, 'but we can't let you leave here unattended.'

'Well, come with me, then.'

They follow her down the stairs, three floors to the makeshift incident room dealing with the Lovelock case. Every side and corner is crammed with boxes and crates, and three officers are sorting through piles of items on tables pushed wonkily together in the middle.

'Where's the stuff from Urquhart's?' asks Kate.

One of the officers points to the far corner. 'There, mainly. Those yellow crates.'

Kate strides over and squats down by the crates. There are three, stacked uncertainly on top of each other. She puts the top two on the floor and begins to rummage through them.

'Er—they haven't been evidence labelled yet,' says the officer.

Kate ignores him.

The paraphernalia of an auction house. Prospectuses, insurance forms, appraisals, lot records, Rolodexes, a couple of telephones, a bidding paddle . . .

She finds what she's looking for, and almost falls on it.

A gavel.

She pushes herself standing and heads towards the door, holding the gavel up as she goes.

'I'll bring it back,' she says.

Back to her desk, and out with the ruler. The gavel has a circular head, and she measures across its diameter. Just over two inches.

Flipping through her Rolodex and punching out a number.

'Thomas Hemmings.'

'Dr Hemmings, it's DCI Beauchamp.'

'Good morning to you, offi—'

'Dr Hemmings, do you remember the traces of oak found on the back of the victims' heads? The ones killed by the snake man?'

'Of course.'

'Could they have been caused by a gavel? You know, what judges and auctioneers use.'

'Well, I . . . They were blunt force injuries. I think we all assumed that the victims had fallen or been pushed against the trees, but—yes, they could have been hit by a gavel, I'm sure.'

'The nature of those injuries is consistent with that?'

'Yes. But that doesn't mean they were definitely *caused* by that. We could rule that option in without ruling others out, if you get my drift.'

'I do. But you've already told me what I need to know. Thank you, Doctor.'

She puts the phone down and stares into space for a few seconds.

A gavel, as used in an auction house.

A gavel, as used by Jason Duchesne, who loaded up the children destined for auction.

A gavel, as used by Blackadder to subdue his victims.

Ever-decreasing circles.

Kate picks up the phone again and dials Ferguson.

407

'Peter, it's Kate. Any joy on the pig front?'

'I was just about to call you. Bankhead have one. Pig found knifed in a farm sty, early on Tuesday morning. The farmer said he must have missed the attacker by seconds. The pig was still dying when he got to it.'

'And Thursday morning?'

'Nothing reported.'

'What's this farmer's name?'

'Michael Gilchrist. Lives off the Inverurie Road.'

'Michael *Gilchrist*? That's . . .'

She knows exactly who it is. Jean's husband. Ferguson reads her the phone number. She jots it down, ends the call and dials the Gilchrists.

'Jean Gilchrist.'

'Jean, it's Kate Beauchamp here.'

'Kate, how are you?'

'Listen, can I ask you a strange question?'

'Sure.'

'Has Jason ever been round to your house?'

'Jason Duchesne?'

'Yes.'

'Yes. Quite a few times. You've been here with him, I'm sure.'

'When was the last time he was there?'

'Oh, a few months ago. He came for a weekend. When he was going through his divorce. Michael thought it would be nice to take him in hand and cheer him up. You know what Michael's like. Ended up working the bugger half to death on the farm.'

On the farm. Oh Lord.

'That's great, Jean. Thank you very much.'

'What's all this about?'

'I'll tell you later. Gotta go.'

Ever-decreasing circles.

Blackadder killed his mother. He must have had an unhappy childhood.

What if Jason wasn't merely smuggling those kids for money? What if he identified with them in some twisted way? Children, used and abused and no one to care for them? What if he wanted to get revenge for what had been done to him in the past? Or what if he wanted to save those children from what had happened to him? What if he thought he was doing them a *favour*?

Red talked about triggers, setting people off. The loss of a job, or a partner.

Divorce.

Divorce, and then the ferry. Enough to set anyone off.

Ever-decreasing circles.

Are the smuggler and the murderer the same person?

Blackadder has a name and a face. Are they those of Jason Duchesne?

*   *   *

He tries to escape the Furies. He twists, dodges, tries to stay a step ahead. He moves houses three times, and jobs twice: the second time to Urquhart's. He is cultured and knowledgeable, all the things they are looking for.

Leafing through the local paper one day, he sees an advertisement for an amateur dramatics group. They are touting for actors, directors, technicians. It seems like a logical extension of his life. The first time he goes, he sees that the word 'amateur' is all too well-applied. The members are enthusiastic but

409

incompetent, and—shamefully—they revel in the latter. They forget their lines or stand in the wrong place, and their idiocies cause them to shriek with laughter.

He sets about changing them. He suggests that they undertake a challenging project, one which reflects great issues of life and death and the human condition. It is time to wean them from their diet of frivolities and light comedy. They are unsure. What are you afraid of? he asks. Only the fact that you might fail. We're not good enough, they say. We're just doing this for fun. He asks what could be more fun, more rewarding, than mastering something difficult? He makes them an offer. He will find a play, and they decide whether they want to perform it. No strings attached. They agree.

He takes them the *Oresteia*. At first, they resist the idea of the trilogy entire. They want to do *Agamemnon* only. But he tells them it would make no sense that way. The *Oresteia* is thesis, antithesis, synthesis: disobedience, woe and restoration. The whole story must be played out. Through naked enthusiasm and sheer force of argument, he holds sway. When the *Oresteia* was performed in ancient Greece, some performances were so powerful that pregnant women miscarried. That is the effect he wants to have.

He is at the centre of it, the main character, the man they all look to. His own performance lifts them far beyond their own expectations. They play to packed houses for a week, and the reviews praise them for being better than the majority of professional productions. Every night, he relives his own life on stage, elevated to the pantheon. Memories of a life forgotten.

At Urquhart's, he gets to know Lovelock. They talk, briefly at first, as staff tend to with distant chairmen who are hardly ever in the office. But Lovelock is no hands-off figurehead. He may be a busy man juggling businesses galore, but he is also genuinely interested in the work that the auction house does, and he tries to attend auctions as often as possible.

They begin to have decent conversations, he and Lovelock. And gradually, they recognise a basic similarity between themselves.

Neither has a conscience.

He is not sure whether it is he or Lovelock who first suggests bringing the children over, and it hardly matters. The idea hangs in the air between them for a while before it is plucked down and brought to fruition. It is alluded to and examined from oblique angles before they are sure the other is keen, like two putative lovers who keep playing games until they cross a Rubicon and find that the only way they can go is forward. Plans are made, altered, discarded, modified, agreed on. A play in Norway as the cover: a significant challenge, but different enough to be exciting. One which requires a complex set and props, in order to justify the hiring of a separate vehicle.

The tension of the planning, so much going on and to look forward to: but still, all the time, he waits for the Furies.

The first one comes just before they sail for Norway, and she comes in disguise, to throw him off the scent. Not a hideous harpy, but a pretty young reporter. Petra Gallacher arrives in his office just before lunch one day. She apologises for the short notice, and asks him if he is free for lunch.

411

He has been working on a large auction for some time, and assumes she's come to preview that. They go to a pub round the corner.

'What do you want to know?' he asks.

She clears her throat and comes straight out with it. 'I saw Ralph Whiteside yesterday. He says he's innocent of killing your mother and her—your stepfather.'

He looks away and scratches at his ear, hoping to appear nonchalant and buying himself some precious seconds.

You are the master of manipulation, he tells himself. The man behind the mask, always saying one thing and feeling another. Don't let a teenager get inside you just because she's taken you by surprise.

'He wasn't my stepfather. They weren't married.'

'Oh. Right.'

'It's—I just haven't thought about it for a long time. It's been years, I don't know how many.'

This is a lie. He knows exactly how many years, and months, and weeks, and days. He always has done.

'I can imagine. I'm sorry. This must be painful for you.' Her eyebrows furrow in sympathy.

'What do you mean, Whiteside says he's innocent?' He hears his voice flutter at the edges. He can put it down to shock, if she picks up on it, rather than the unaccustomed sense of anxiety. 'That's absurd. He pleaded guilty. He signed a confession.'

'He says the police forced him to.'

'When did he say this?'

'Yesterday.'

'Yesterday?'

It sounds stupid, him repeating what she says. He must not appear stupid.

'His lawyer rang me. Well, he rang the paper's newsdesk. I was the one who picked it up. He—the lawyer—said that Whiteside's virtually on his deathbed, and he wants to talk to someone before he dies.'

'What's he dying of?'

'AIDS.'

'He's a junkie.'

'I didn't know who he was to start with. I found out soon enough from the clippings. I went along myself. He's in Glenochil, miles away. I don't think the lawyer was best pleased. He was wanting someone older, I reckon, more gravitas, more experience. I'm used to it, to be honest. In fact, I didn't even tell my news editor, because I knew he'd think the same thing. He'd have given the story to someone more senior.'

'So you're doing this on spec?'

'Yes. But it doesn't mean that . . .' She stops short, suddenly aware that she shouldn't have told him this. 'I mean, it's a valid story. Someone would do it.'

'What did he look like?'

'The lawyer?'

'No. Whiteside.'

She looks at him askance. Maybe it's an odd question to ask. 'Like he's dying. Thin. Painfully thin. His neck looks like piano wires, and he's got dreadful shakes. It took him about five goes to light each cigarette, and he must have gone through half a packet just while I was there.'

'And he said he was innocent?'

'Yes. Said he'd been framed by the police. They

413

said he was so bombed he couldn't remember where he was. He says that's bullsh— That's rubbish. He says he knew exactly where he was, and it wasn't anywhere near your ma's house'—his ma, she even knows what he used to call her—'and he told the police this, but they wouldn't listen, they said he was a junkie and had lots of previous, and he must have been looking for money for his drugs, and your ma and—and . . .' She clicks her tongue, trying to remember the name.

'Craig.' Deadpan. Not with the fucking contempt he deserves.

'That's it. Craig. The police said your ma and Craig must have come back while Whiteside was doing the place over.'

'That's what happened. They gave him a fair trial.'

'He says not.'

'And you believe him?'

'I don't know. That's why I came to talk to you. See what you thought.'

'This thing's been done and dusted, Miss . . .'

'Gallacher.'

'Ralph Whiteside was a habitual criminal. Why bring it all up again?'

'If he's innocent, then there's been a huge miscarriage of justice.'

'He's about to die. What difference does it make to him?'

'Maybe none. But if he's innocent, then that also means that whoever killed your ma and Craig is still free.'

He watches her closely as she says this. Her face is concerned, passionate even as she makes her point, but it covers no hidden depths. She doesn't

414

mean it in any way other than at face value. She doesn't suspect him. She's simply come to him as the person most closely involved: the person on record as finding two dead bodies in a lake of blood.

'Listen to me, Miss Gallacher. Ralph Whiteside was a bad man, he did lots of bad things. He was a junkie, a waster, a liar. He's lying now. He wants attention, someone to make a fuss of him before he dies. All you'll be doing is stirring up lies and a lot of hurt. Leave it be.'

'I'm really sorry to resurrect this. But all news stories are this way: someone somewhere doesn't want to talk about it. That's what makes it news.'

Petra Gallacher, barely out of school, talking in clichés and thinking she's Woodward and Bernstein all rolled into one.

She gets up to leave. The light is shining on her through the window, and as she turns from him her face passes into shadow. He sees her transformed. Her eyes, so full of wonder at the world, ooze a sickening discharge, and her flashing smile is twisted in hateful revenge. The knapsack protruding from her back sprouts stumpy wings of malevolence.

The dead take root beneath the soil. They grow with hate and plague the lives of men. Leprous boils ride the flesh, their wild teeth gnawing the mother tissue, and a white scurf spreads like cancer over these. He can see them—the eyes burning, grim brows working over him in the dark—the dark sword of the dead!—his murdered kinsmen pleading for revenge. And the madness haunts the midnight watch, the empty terror stakes him, harries, drives him on, a brazen whip which will

415

mutilate his back. There is no refuge, none to take him in. A pariah reviled, withered in the grip of all this dying.

And now the trip to Norway assumes the sordid aspects of flight. Far from home, he is sure she can't follow, but still he watches for her, always he catches his breath when he turns corners or opens doors for fear that she'll be there. And when the ferry sinks and he escapes with his life, she's right back in his face that very night.

It is a pleasant evening. They talk in the garden.

'I saw your name on the passenger list,' she says. 'What an awful coincidence.'

Coincidence. As if she thinks that will fool him for a second. He has seen the truth of her, and that is an end to it. There is only one way in which he can be rid of her.

Does she think he'll strike so soon? She is too wrapped up in the torment to be fearful of her safety. She torments him by not tormenting him, talking about the ferry rather than his ma or Ralph Whiteside, knowing as he knows that the anticipation can be as paralysing as the most dreadful of actualities.

If he sets her free, he redoubles his own torment. He has no alternative. He can see what they are, they drive him on.

He goes ahead into the house and calls for her. She thinks he is walking into her trap, but the truth is inverted. The moment she is out of sight indoors, he comes at her from behind and knocks her cold. After dark, he bundles her into the car and takes her out to the woods, where he does to her what she's done to him. Still she cries, professes ignorance, begs, pleads for mercy. Mercy for the merciless. She even tries to seduce him, offering her body for her life. He tortures her until she can stand no more, and then he does it all over again.

And then he kills her.

After Petra comes that meddling busybody Elizabeth Hart. Now the Furies know he's seen through Petra's disguise, they don't bother to dress the next one up. She comes as legend depicts, this hateful hideous old crone who knocks on his door.

'I saw her here,' she says. Her eyes drip loathing.

'Saw who?'

'That girl who was found in Woodend. She was round the night she was killed.'

Elizabeth Hart and her obsessive interest in other people's lives. He is silent, waiting for her to go on.

'Could hardly miss her, with that golden hair. You should be ashamed of yourself, associating with that harlot.'

'*Harlot?* You think I was having an affair with her?'

'You weren't the only one, by the sound of it. The papers said she used to put it about. Didn't give any names, of course. Otherwise yours would have been among them, I wouldn't doubt.' She pauses. 'Do the police know she was here?'

'I told them the moment I found out she'd been killed.'

'Did you? Did you now?'

'Yes.' *No.*

'What did you tell them?'

'That she was here.'

'That's all?'

'What else could I tell them?'

'What you were doing with her. Where she went

417

after she left you. To one of her other men, probably. Slut.'

It is all he can do not to laugh. At last, Elizabeth's nosiness benefits someone else. Elizabeth doesn't think he killed Petra. She's simply here to make mischief.

But will she ever drop it? Of course not. She'll persist, grudging and unwilling to let it go. She'll remind him at every turn of what he has and has not done. Unless he stops her.

As Petra died because of Ailish, Elizabeth dies because of them both. It is cumulative and linear, and the madness will rage until it is assuaged with the final sacrifice.

*   *   *

The gloves are off now. It is a straight manhunt.

Kate finds the APB Renfrew sent out yesterday afternoon and adds two urgent amendments: firstly, that Jason Duchesne is wanted for questioning in connection with the murders of Petra Gallacher and Elizabeth Hart, in addition to unspecified crimes connected with the sinking of the *Amphitrite*; secondly, that his details (photograph, physical description, car registration number) should be circulated to the public as soon as possible, together with all the usual riders about not approaching him.

They erect roadblocks in the city centre and on all major approach roads, and station watchers at any places he might try to visit: his house, Kate's house, Urquhart's. They put his bank on alert in case he uses his cashpoint card, and arrange to have the system slowed down the moment he attempts withdrawal—slowed enough to be plausibly an electronic glitch, but not enough to arouse his suspicions and make him scarper. Enough, perhaps, to get a spot on him, if they're lucky.

Kate wonders who'll handle the waiting better.

He has to break cover sometime. Make a phone call, use a credit card. Eat, drink. Make himself visible.

As for her . . . Physically, she can stay holed up here for as long as it takes. Mentally, she doesn't know how long she can prowl this cage before she goes spare.

Jason Duchesne, a man always slightly out of kilter with the world: inept at relationships and even friendships, always liable to misread the mood of an occasion. Kate had thought he was crass rather than actively malicious. And now she finds out not just that she was wrong, but how wrong she was.

The phone rings. She snatches it up. Ferguson's voice.

'We've got a sighting.'

*　　　*　　　*

Tomintoul is the best part of 60 miles west of Aberdeen. Even with moderate traffic, the journey can take an hour and a half. In a posse of squad cars with lights blazing and sirens blaring, it takes forty minutes.

Kate sits in the middle of a back seat, sandwiched by two armed men. She is wearing a Kevlar vest, on their insistence, to stop not bullets but knives. They didn't want her to come at all. She told them she'd trust them.

They race through Alford, once the terminus for the Great North Scotland Railway, and past deserted crofters' cottages, lonely witnesses to the effects of industrialisation on a once prosperous agricultural area. Ruined castles and hillforts stand carved against the horizon.

'That's Kildrummy Castle,' says Ferguson, pointing ahead. 'Robert the Bruce sent his wife and children there for their own protection when he was fighting the English. The castle blacksmith was bribed with as much gold as he could carry. He set fire to the castle, and it fell into English hands. Bruce's men captured the blacksmith, melted his gold, and poured the molten metal down his throat until he died.'

Sometimes Ferguson's propensity for the impromptu history lecture bugs Kate. Today, it gives her a welcome sense of normality.

They race up the hill to Tomintoul, the highest village in the Scottish highlands. It is long and thin, like a frontier town from the Old West. Around them rear the mountains which every winter host a modest skiing industry.

The newsagent is flame-haired and overweight, and he wears the look of proud disbelief which afflicts many people during their fifteen minutes of fame. Kate's protectors hustle her out of the car and into the shop, where they stand behind her and to the sides, watching her back and flanks.

'Bought a couple of Sunday papers and a can of Coke,' the newsagent says.

'Did he say anything?' asks Kate.

'No. I said I'd heard that the weather was going to break this evening, and he nodded. Queer-

420

looking fellow. Looked like he spent too much time doing this.' He licks his lips.

'Did you know who he was at the time?'

'No. It came on the telly about ten minutes after. Thought it was some kind of practical joke, or that he were famous or something. I had the sound turned down quiet, see. When I saw his face, I turned it back up, and that's when I heard. Lucky I didn't know at the time. Probably have shat me pants. Me hand was shaking so much when I went for that phone, I can't tell you. Nearly forgot the police number. I ask you! Three digits, all of them the same, and I nearly forgot it. Normally I can be quite sarky, but not with this chap. Luckily for me, else he might have filled me in. Maybe it was some sort of sixth—'

'You didn't see where he went?'

'No. Just out the door.'

'He didn't say what he was doing here?'

'He was dressed like a walker. Shorts, stick, hiking boots. You get a lot round here, on the Speyside trail. Most of them visit at least one of the whisky distilleries en route. Makes for an interesting journey back.'

Jason, alone in the hills, with no one's company but his own. All the solitude he wants.

'Where do walkers stay, when they come here?'

'Just go up and down this road. Hostels, B & Bs, hotels—you can't miss them.'

*   *   *

It takes them ten minutes to find out where he's staying. The fourth place they try is the Glennie House Hotel, and there he is among the registration cards—Jason Duchesne, room 26.

The manager gives them a key, so they don't have to break the door down or alert him by knocking first. Room 26 is on the second floor, and looks out on to the main street. Three armed men stand outside in case he tries anything stupid, like jumping. The sparse Sunday morning crowd watches open-mouthed.

Through the corridors softly, Kate and Ferguson at the back while the ones with the carbines take the lead. Key silently into the lock and the door bursting open, bouncing against the wall as they dive into the narrow space. Their barrels describe well-practised arcs which cover every corner of the room.

Jason is sitting on his bed, sections of the Sunday papers strewn around him. His legs are pale, skinny and hairless beneath his shorts.

'Down! Down! Face down on the bed, hands behind your back. Now!'

Kate, coming in behind the assault team, catches a glimpse of the shock on Jason's face as it disappears into the bedclothes.

Two of the armed policemen cuff his hands tight in the small of his back. They haul him upright while a third checks the bed for any concealed weapons, and then goes to the window and signals to the officers outside.

'This is absurd,' Jason says. 'Quite absurd. What's the meaning of this?'

Kate looks at him and tries to breathe deeply, but the Kevlar vest is tight on her.

'Kate, tell these gorillas to stop pointing those things at me.'

She makes herself turn away from him. Alecto,

unceasing in anger.

'Take him back to Queen Street,' she says.

*   *   *

Kate lets Ferguson handle it. She knows she can't trust herself to be rational.

She watches at one remove, through the mirrored one-way glass. What she'd like is Jason cuffed to a chair, alone with her in a room without observers and without consequences. Then he'd see what anger is.

Jason is remarkably cool about it, she has to give him that. He is co-operative and courteous. He answers every question they ask him with the air of a man who knows that right will out, as if this is all a terrible mistake which could be ironed out in a moment if only they'd all behave like adults.

Exactly the behaviour of a genuine psychopath, Kate thinks. A refusal to contemplate defeat, while enjoying playing other people for fools.

'You don't have any alibis for either of the nights in question,' Ferguson tells him.

'Why should I? I've done nothing wrong. I don't go round establishing my whereabouts on the off chance that the police will want to interview me.'

'What were you doing on those nights? Monday and Wednesday?'

'Monday night, I was at home, trying to sleep. It was just after the ferry disaster. I was still in shock. Wednesday night, those of us who'd survived that disaster—those of the amateur dramatics society, I should say—went out to dinner. Kate was there. She can confirm that.'

'DCI Beauchamp *does* confirm that, yes. She

423

also confirms that the meal ended at around eleven. Plenty of time after that for you to abduct and kill Elizabeth Hart.'

Jason shrugs.

'What were you doing yesterday?' says Ferguson.

'I was walking in the hills.'

'You take your laptop with you to go hill-walking?'

'I had some work to catch up on. I thought I'd do it after I'd had dinner.'

'The phone bill from the Glennie House indicates that you were on-line at the time when DCI Beauchamp received messages from the killer. And the Hotmail home page is listed on your favourites list.'

'I have an account with them.'

'In your own name?'

'Yes. You can check.'

'Any others?'

'No.'

'What you were doing on-line at that time?'

'I was checking the football scores. The TV in my room didn't have Ceefax.'

'You were on for almost an hour.'

'I surfed the net for a while.'

'What were you looking for?'

'Travel sites, mainly. I'm thinking of going away. America, maybe Australia.'

'I don't think you're going anywhere for a long time.' Ferguson gets up. He'll leave Jason to stew for a while. 'Could you ask DCI Beauchamp to come in, please?' Jason says. 'She's a friend of mine. She'll have this sorted out in no time.'

Ferguson laughs.

Ferguson confers with Kate and Renfrew in the observation room.

'Where do you want to start?' asks Ferguson. 'With the children or the killings?'

'The children,' says Renfrew. 'I want first go at him. The killings are done and dusted, but the smuggling may still be going on. The note in Lovelock's study suggests he was planning alternative shipments. If so, we've got to stop them. We need to know everything: his contacts, his clients, everything. He won't spill right away, of course. But I'll keep at him. He'll make a mistake. It'll take time, but he will.'

Kate looks through the glass at Jason again.

Civilisation. We call ourselves civilised because we have running water and electricity and we shop in supermarkets, but tear this away and see what monstrosities lurk beneath. How far have we come, when we can rip children from one hopeless life and dump them into another? How far from the Middle Ages? How far from the Stone Age, for that matter?

Jason Duchesne, suspected double killer and trafficker in human misery. A man she knew, travelled with, acted alongside. A man she never felt she could like. Maybe her taste in men isn't as bad as she sometimes fears.

'I'm going home,' she says. 'You want me, that's where I'll be.'

*   *   *

Kate does a quick TV interview before she goes, confirming that Jason Duchesne is helping police with their inquiries into the murders of Petra Gallacher and Elizabeth Hart. Between the lines, she implies that this is not another Drew Blaikie scenario. This time, they reckon they've got the right man.

Three people curled up in bed together and sleeping the sleep of the just. Kate and Leo and Alex, last night's argument forgotten as the nightmare at last begins to drain away.

Sunday pulses and scorches outside the windows.

*   *   *

Two hours in, and still Jason isn't breaking. He'd like to help, but they've got the wrong man. He knows nothing about any child smuggling. He spent the last morning in Bergen walking round town. Yes, on his own. His wife has left him. That's why he went round Bergen on his own, that's why he went to Speyside on his own, that's why he lives on his own.

Renfrew isn't worried. He's heard it all before. Not me. Not me. Someone else. Most suspects keep up this kind of act to start with. Lovelock did. Then they get tired and worn down. They can't remember what they did or didn't say. They make a mistake, which they try to bluff out. Then they make another one, and they know it's all over. That's the thing about mistakes: they breed from each other. After two mistakes, the whole thing comes tumbling out. The police spend hours, days sometimes, trying to get the fuckers to admit it, and when they do, it's all the police can do to keep up with the confession.

'How long is this going to go on for?' asks Jason.

426

'Until you come clean. It's entirely in your hands. We're in no hurry.'

'In that case, can I make a phone call?'

'To whom?'

'My mother. She's expecting me for dinner.'

Renfrew pauses for a second, as if he doesn't believe what he's just heard. Then he hurries out of the interview room and into the corridor.

'Ferguson!' he yells.

*   *   *

Kate gets out of bed, shrugs on her jersey and a pair of tracksuit bottoms, and pads to the kitchen. She leaves her boys sleeping.

Three in the bed and the little one said roll over, roll over.

The Amphitrite *rolled over.*

She splashes her face with water from the kitchen tap. Afternoon naps always leave her feeling groggy. She fills the kettle, puts it on to boil, and rummages around for mugs, tea-bags, milk and sugar. No tea-bags in the jar she normally keeps them in.

She's not going to think about anything. Tomorrow it can all start again, with the beginning of the working week like everyone else. Tomorrow, she promises herself, she'll lie in the bath and put her head underwater. She'll hold her whole body beneath the surface and know she's cured. Maybe if she puts herself under, she'll get rid of this dreadful cold sensation too.

Kate pours some milk into each of the mugs and scoops a teaspoonful of sugar for Alex.

The phone rings, loud in the quiet house. Kate

427

starts slightly and knocks the spoon against the side of Alex's mug. The sugar grains scatter across the Formica, white on white.

Her phone is cordless. She picks it up off the charger and continues preparing the tea.

'Kate Beauchamp.'

'It's Ferguson.' Breathless, urgent. Jason must have confessed.

'Tell me the good news.' She can barely keep the smile from her voice.

'He's just asked Renfrew if he can call his mother.'

'So . . .'

Blackadder killed his mother. That at least will be true.

'He's jerking you around. He's having his fun. Ignore him.'

'I don't know.'

'He's a psychopath. He wouldn't even *know* about the mother thing unless it was him.'

'He might just want to call his mother. He might not be our man.'

She opens a cupboard and runs her hand impatiently over cereal boxes and packets of pasta, looking for the unopened packet of tea-bags she knows is there. One day she's going to get some order in this kitchen. One day.

'OK. Why don't you let him call her? Then talk to her yourself and ask her to come in, with some ID. See if she really exists.'

'And if she does?'

'Then I'll come back in. But she won't.'

'OK.'

She ends the call.

Where the hell are the tea-bags?

Kate moves a packet of biscuits to one side. It slips off the shelf and down on to the sideboard. She picks the packet up, recognising it as a packet she brought back from Cornwall—when? Two years ago now, maybe three. They can have these with their tea, if the biscuits aren't inedible by now. She looks for the best before date.

It takes her a moment to work it out. The best before date is not printed straight, as it is on most products. Instead, there's a line of letters, followed by five consecutive two-digit figures. The letters represent the initials of each month, and the figures the year. One letter and one number are circled, to show when the biscuits should be eaten by.

The initial letters of each month. J F M A M J J A S O N D.

J A S O N D.

JASON D.

The words on Lovelock's pad, under the ferry ports. JASON D, all in block capitals.

July August September October November December.

It's June now. Lovelock was working out possible dates for the next shipment.

Not Jason Duchesne. Not the man who loaded up the children in Bergen.

And therefore not Blackadder either.

But she is convinced that Blackadder is the man who loaded up the children, and she knows that the man who loaded up the children works for Urquhart's. Which means that Blackadder is almost certainly one of Alex or Sinclair. Which in turn means that there's an even chance that Blackadder is, right now, curled up in Kate's bed.

429

With Kate's son.

*   *   *

Slow down. *Think.*

Kate feels the panic swirl around her, just as it did on the ferry and in the car wash. But this time there are no simple solutions, no straight choices.

The most important thing is that she doesn't alert Alex. He's no threat as long as he's asleep.

It can't be him. Please God let it not be him.

And if it's not him it's Sinclair, which is just as bad—but it's one of them, it has to be, and of the two, she'd rather it wasn't the man who's in her house right now, just for her sake and Leo's.

Kate forces herself to think back. Petra was killed on Monday night. Where was Alex then?

It was the night after the ferry sank. He could have been anywhere. As could Sinclair.

What was *she* doing? Sitting on her floor and trying to sweat the horror out. What did Jason say he was doing? Trying to sleep. They were all shellshocked.

All except one of them.

Elizabeth was killed on Wednesday night. The night they went to the restaurant. And Alex came back with her. They made the pact only to talk to each other about the ferry—*the pact which he broke*—and then they fell asleep.

And when she woke up, he was gone.

Kate pushes her face against her hands.

She rolled over to touch him, and all that was left was his smell and the note on the pillow. 'Couldn't sleep, didn't want to wake you. Sleep well.'

Couldn't sleep. He was sleeping perfectly well

430

when she found his Walkman last night.

It's not definitely him. Just because he left doesn't make it definitely him. But she has to know for sure.

She looks at the phone and wonders what to do.

Phone records.

Lovelock must have phoned his contact— Blackadder—at some time, either before or since the Norway trip. The team investigating the smuggling will have got Lovelock's phone records by now, but checking them won't be such a high priority, because they've got their man.

Correction. They *thought* they had their man.

Kate eases the kitchen door shut and dials the incident room.

'It's DCI Beauchamp. Get me Ferguson.'

'I think he and Renfrew are in with the suspect.'

'Then get him out of there. *Now.*'

'Do you want to hold, or shall I get him to call you back?'

'I'll hold.' She doesn't want this phone to ring again. Nothing which might alert Alex.

She waits and waits. The general chatter of the incident room sounds in her ear for long moments, and eventually she's put on actual hold and gets piped music instead.

Come on.

She watches the clock, the door. While she's waiting, she opens a drawer and pulls out the biggest knife she can find. If it's Alex and he comes at her, she'll kill him with that, and wouldn't that be a lovely irony? Maybe she'll chop off his hands and feet too. No adder to hand, more's the pity.

Ferguson comes on the line. 'He hasn't made the call yet.'

431

'Doesn't matter. Can you get me Lovelock's phone records?'

'Sure. Give me half an hour.'

'I need them *now*.'

'Are you all right?'

'Yes. But I need them right now.'

'Bear with me.'

If it's Alex, should she tell Ferguson, and have the police race to her house? No. She'd risk starting a siege, with Alex holding her and Leo hostage. Sieges can go wrong all too easily. She's seen it happen. She'd rather get out than be hemmed in.

More waiting. She runs her thumb across the knife blade.

'Here we go. Home, mobile, office. Take your pick.'

'Start with home.'

'It only goes up to last Sunday. Some computer problem at the phone company.'

Last Sunday. Exactly a week ago, when the *Amphitrite* was sailing serenely out of Bergen.

Last Sunday's no good. Blackadder was on the *Amphitrite*. Lovelock wouldn't have phoned him then.

Why not?

Blackadder and Lovelock were in it together. They could easily have talked just before the *Amphitrite* set sail. Maybe even during the journey, just to confirm that everything was going according to plan.

'Give me any calls made to mobile numbers from Sunday afternoon onwards,' she says.

She hears the printouts rustling as Ferguson flicks through them.

432

An 07961 number, dialled at 18.13, duration thirty seconds. Same number, dialled 18.14, duration five minutes twenty-three seconds. Obviously got cut off the first time.

07771 something, 20.29, three minutes twelve seconds. 07711, 21.54, fifty-five seconds.

An 07976 number, 23.45, one minute twenty-four seconds.

The digits clack in Kate's brain like lottery balls. She knows whose number that is.

23.45 British summer time. Quarter to midnight. About twenty minutes before Sutton had the *Amphitrite* stopped and tipped the Transit van out. A call *from* Lovelock rather than *to* him.

It wasn't Blackadder who made the decision to eject the van. It was Lovelock. It was Lovelock, and he rang Blackadder to give him the order.

Kate gets Ferguson to read the number out again, just to be sure. She wasn't mistaken.

It's Alex's.

*   *   *

It was Alex who Lovelock rang on board the *Amphitrite.* It was Alex who sent five children to their death, Alex who caused another 352 deaths. It was Alex who would have helped sell those children into slavery.

It was Alex who asked if he could come to Petra's funeral, when Kate and her colleagues were all watching for any signs of Blackadder.

It was Alex who made love to Kate on Wednesday night and then left, a few hours before Elizabeth Hart's lifeless body was found.

It was Alex's character in *Way Upstream* who

433

seemed an engaging Jack-the-lad, and turned out to be a raving psychopath.

It is Alex who's never invited Kate over to his house, who has always come to hers.

It is Alex who now lies in Kate's bed. With Leo.

The kitchen door flung open and Kate running through the house, bile rising behind clenched teeth, through the bathroom door and on her knees in a slide to the toilet.

When it's over, her face tingles with the effort of having thrown her guts up; and her mouth smarts warm and rancid. She lets go of the toilet bowl and slumps against the wall.

He must be waiting for nightfall, when he will suggest going somewhere to celebrate her solving the case. Just the two of them. Leo can go and stay with Bronagh: it's not going to hurt, not for one more night. And then, and then . . .

A tap on the head with the gavel, and it all begins again.

Ted Bundy had impeccable credentials too. He was intelligent, attractive, charming. He was a counsellor at a crisis clinic, an assistant director of Seattle's crime prevention advisory committee. He was a dream boyfriend. Just like Alex.

Kate pushes herself slowly upright and looks around the bathroom, at the *Far Side* anthologies piled on the cistern and the pictures on the wall. There is one of her receiving her new badge when she was made Detective Chief Inspector, and one of her on stage in *Amadeus* last year. She played Constanze and Alex played Mozart, and even then the others were already joking what a good couple they made.

Next to the picture, in the same frame, there is a

434

copy of the *Amadeus* programme.

Another connection fizzes in Kate's brain.

Red on the phone this morning. 'Both Aeschylus and Euripides wrote about Orestes, who the Furies drove mad after he killed his mother.'

She takes the picture off the wall and shuts the door. She doesn't want Alex to hear this either.

Kate brings the picture down hard against the side of the bath, glass first, as if she were breaking an egg on the edge of a saucepan. The glass shatters brightly. Jagged edges tinkle down the sides of the bath. Kate turns the picture back over, knocks a few more shards out, reaches in and extracts the *Amadeus* programme.

Through the pages. Adverts. Cast. Thanks.

About the actors.

Alex Melville, second after Matt Kellman, who had played Salieri. A black-and-white picture of him smiling at the camera. Fresh-faced and open, and evil to his core.

'Alex Melville (Mozart). Since joining the Amateurs four years ago, Alex has appeared in a variety of roles, most notably as Biff in Arthur Miller's *Death of a Salesman* and as Orestes in Aeschylus' *Oresteia* trilogy (*Agamemnon, The Libation Bearers* and *The Eumenides*). He works for Urquhart's auction house, and says he has obtained many of his acting tips from watching the auctioneers at work.'

He joined the Amateurs four years ago. Not long after his parents died in a car crash. Or so he said.

Alex as the lead character in a coruscating trilogy, the man who killed his mother and found that the Furies pursued him to the ends of the earth. But instead of Alex becoming Orestes,

435

Orestes became him. A role in a play which blossomed first into obsession and then murder.

Tisiphone. Petra Gallacher. Kate past.

Megaera. Elizabeth Hart. Kate future.

Alecto.

*   *   *

Kate walks back into the bedroom. Her knuckles are white where she grips the knife handle. She knows she must act calm, even if she feels anything but.

Leo is lying in the crook of Alex's arm. They are both still asleep. Very gently, Kate leans over and reaches out for her son.

The knife glints in a stray shaft of afternoon sunlight. She looks around and lays it gently down on the bedside table, as far from Alex as she can make it. It'll only be out of her grasp for a few seconds.

She works her hands underneath Leo's body, one on each side, slowly and with infinitesimal care so as not to wake either sleeper. She braces herself, and lifts Leo clear of Alex's arm and the bed. He snuffles and leans into Kate's body. His eyes half-open and close again. Alex sleeps on. Kate tucks one arm under Leo's backside, and with her free hand picks up the knife. She starts walking backwards towards the door.

Her life is once more reduced to a set of constant presents. The past has brought them to this point, the future is yet to come. All that matters is here and now, getting clear of the monster in her bed.

She glances over her shoulder to see how near to

the door she is.

Kate registers the sharp pain in her sole at exactly the moment she hears the loud scraping noise. One of Leo's toy cars, shooting across the floor from under her feet. Alex sits bolt upright in bed.

'What time is it?' His voice doesn't sound in the slightest bit sleepy.

Leo is awake too. He squirms in her arms.

'Kate, what on earth are you doing? Are you OK?'

'I'm fine.' Her voice wavers. High, much too high. 'Fine.'

He kicks the covers back and swings his legs on to the floor. 'I suppose you always carry a carving knife around.'

You would know, sunshine.

He's toying with her, just like he toyed with the others. Kate looks down at his crotch, to see if this is getting him hard.

'You come near me, motherfucker, I'll cut you, I swear I will.'

It doesn't sound like her voice, not at all.

'What's got into your head, Kate? Are you ill? Shall I call a doctor?'

She shakes her head so violently that her brain swims. He takes two steps towards her, reaching over.

'Here, let me hold Leo.'

Kate runs.

Through the open bedroom door, slamming it shut behind her, across the hall with Leo fidgeting in her arms and screaming, Alex's voice muffled and suddenly louder as he opens the bedroom door.

437

'What the fuck are you doing, Kate? Where are you going?'

Leo stops fidgeting and clings limpet tight to Kate's neck. Kate's knife hand shoots out and scoops up her keys from the hall table as she runs past. The blade scours a long scar in the lacquered surface. Keys dangling between her fingers, barely held, twisted into a firmer grip. Grabbing at the front door with the hand that holds Leo, quickly snatched open and her and Leo through the gap, pulling it shut as Alex looms.

Kate puts Leo quickly down, transfers the knife to her left hand, jabs the key in the lock and turns it savagely anti-clockwise. The handle turns even as she does so, Alex trying to yank the door open.

'Kate!' Bellowed.

The tumblers fall into place.

'Kate!'

The door shakes and rattles, holds firm. She bends down and secures the lower lock too, just for good measure.

'What the shit is going on? Kate! Open the fucking door!'

He is banging against the door now, big booming blows. She wonders whether the door will hold against his monumental rage.

Kate picks Leo up again and runs down the stairs. Out of the main door and into the street, warm air in her face.

'Kate! Kate! What are you doing?'

She looks up. Alex is leaning out of the window. The sinews of his neck ripple like wave crests. Leo is looking up too, bewildered desperation in his eyes. Kate opens the car door, bundles Leo inside and dives in after him. No time to get the child seat

438

ready. She plonks Leo on the passenger seat and pulls the seatbelt across him. Engine on, door shut, away from the kerb in jerky panic. Alex's shouts fade in her ears.

She gets to the junction at the end of her street, and realises with a start that she has no idea where she's going.

Just drive.

She turns left.

First things first. Kate leans across Leo, opens the glove compartment and takes out her mobile. She'd forgotten to bring it into the house when she returned from Queen Street. Something must be going right for her. She dials the incident room.

'This is DCI Beauchamp. Who's that?'

'It's DS Wilcox. Hello, boss.'

'Wilcox, listen to me. The man you're looking for, Blackadder, is called Alex Melville. He's in my house, right now, locked in. Take as many people as you can get and go round there.' She gives him her address, makes him repeat it. 'He may be armed, with whatever he's found in the house. So be careful. Ring me the moment you've got him.'

'Where are you?'

'I'm on the move, I'm OK.'

'Are you coming here?'

'I . . .'—*Leo crying, Leo screaming, 'Don't want to be where Mummy works'*—'just *go.*' She can hear him shouting to the other detectives as she ends the call.

The police station is the most obvious place to go, but she doesn't want to have Leo freaking out again. Nor does she want to be there when they bring Alex in.

They could go to Bronagh's. It's Sunday

439

afternoon, so she'll be out playing bridge, but Kate has a set of . . .

No, she doesn't. She doesn't even have a set of Bronagh's keys anymore. She gave them back because Bronagh needed them for the builders.

What about her father?

Kate dials Frank's mobile number, and is instantly put through to the voicemail. She curses, and tries the Michaelhouse switchboard instead.

'Just putting you through now.'

One ring, two, three, and she knows he's not in his room either. Story of her life, she thinks bitterly. Her father never around when she really needs him.

They don't even put her back to the switchboard, so she can ask for the conference room. The line rings and rings into an empty bedroom.

Who else?

Sinclair. She dials his number.

'Sinclair Larsen.'

'Sinclair, it's Kate. Are you at home right now?'

'Yes, of course. What's wrong? You sound like you're running a marathon.'

'I need to come round. I'll explain everything then.'

'OK. Sure. I'll see you here. Drive carefully now.'

'Will do.'

A safe haven at Sinclair's, half the Grampian Police on their way to arrest Blackadder, Leo beside her. Kate reckons the worst of it might be over.

*   *   *

440

Even though Sinclair's street is empty, she jabs impatiently at the doorbell, wanting to be out of sight as quickly as possible. Leo is trembling as she holds him.

Sinclair's feet hurry to the door. His face is suffused with concern.

'Good Lord, Kate. I hope you're going to tell me what this is all about.'

She nods. 'In a sec. Just let me get myself together.'

'Certainly.' He ruffles Leo's hair. 'How are you, little man?'

Leo presses himself even closer to Kate's chest.

'About as shocked as I am,' says Kate. 'About as shocked as you're going to be, when I tell you what's happened.'

'Let me get you a cup of tea first, eh?'

'Oh, God. That would be lovely.'

Sinclair steers them into the sitting-room. Kate slumps into the nearest armchair, and Sinclair disappears into the kitchen.

She wonders how much damage Alex is wreaking right now. For an awful moment, she imagines him finding her spare set of keys and letting himself out. Then she remembers that she keeps them at the police station. The only other person who has a set is Bronagh, but she's out. Even if Alex has thought of it, he couldn't get hold of her.

Kate can hear Sinclair pottering around in the kitchen. Normal, everyday sounds on a normal Sunday afternoon. Normality. That's something she hasn't enjoyed for a while.

She closes her eyes.

441

*   *   *

'Incident room.'

'Could I speak to DCI Beauchamp, please?'

'I'm afraid she's not here. Can I help?'

'Yes. This is Drew Blaikie. I was . . .'

'I know who you are, Mr Blaikie. What can I do for you?'

'I've just seen DCI Beauchamp on TV, saying you have a man in custody. I wanted to ask her what the hell she thinks she's doing wearing my girlfriend's necklace.'

'I'm sorry?'

'She was wearing a turquoise and silver necklace. That belonged to Petra Gallacher.'

'How do you know this, sir?'

'I gave that necklace to her myself. I gave it to her for her birthday, last month.'

*   *   *

Over tea, Kate explains everything to Sinclair. The smuggling, the connection between the two cases, the clues to Jason—and then how, pulverisingly, she discovered it was Alex. Sinclair listens with astonished horror on his face.

'I don't believe this,' he says. 'I simply don't believe this. And Alex, of all people.'

'Just goes to show how little you can know someone.'

Kate looks at her watch. Almost half an hour since she spoke to Wilcox. She's itching to call again and find out if they've got Alex. But she knows it will take them time to get to her house

442

and get in, subdue Alex if he's causing trouble, take him back to the station . . . She'll give it another quarter of an hour.

Leo is fidgeting. She wants to keep him occupied.

'Have you got anything for Leo to play with, or read?' she asks.

'There may be something upstairs. I'll go and check.'

Sinclair smiles at her, tender and benevolent, and walks out of the room. Kate bends down to Leo. 'Sinclair's going to find you something. He won't be long. You'll be all right, my precious.'

Kate gets up and starts to wander round the room.

Books. Hundreds of them, lined up neatly on the shelves. Good books, too. Penguin classics, contemporary literary fiction. In one corner, a shelf and a half of *Encyclopaedia Britannica*. Above them, a stereo system with a CD rack alongside. Classical, mainly. A bit of opera thrown in.

Cultured, definitely. But not very homely.

Through the ceiling come Sinclair's footsteps, moving around as he tries to find something for Leo. Kate walks through into the kitchen.

It is bare, functional at best. A bachelor's kitchen. She opens the nearest cupboard. Empty. And the next. Empty too. Nothing in the fridge apart from some milk and a packet of ham.

She hears Sinclair coming back down the stairs.

Kate goes to the window and looks out. Not much of a view. The backs of the houses in the next-door road.

A splash of colour in one of the windows. A blue and white striped 'X'.

Kate recognises it with a cold start. Police tape, marking a crime scene.

Police tape on a window looking out on to houses.

Elizabeth Hart's window.

Sinclair lives on Thistle Lane. One street down from Victoria Street, where Elizabeth Hart lived. Kate never made the connection. They came to the crime scene from the other direction, left that way too. Never went past Sinclair's street.

Elizabeth would have seen Sinclair, pried on him.

Kate steps back from the window. Something catches her eye. There, by the gas rings. An aberration in this orderly temple to emptiness.

A wooden knife block with six slots for knives.

Only five of them are filled.

The slat where the missing knife should be is about an inch and a half across. The width of the knife at the point where blade meets handle.

The width of the knife which was found by Elizabeth Hart's body.

The knives all have black handles. She takes one of them out of the block and looks for the name. There, stencilled on the blade.

Jensen Laser.

*   *   *

Facades and reality.

Behind the partition of a transit van, five children with hours to live.

Behind the good name of an auction house, an inhuman trade in human beings.

Behind the veneer of a man she loved and

444

trusted, the worst of them all.

She turns to meet Sinclair as he comes through the door, her hand already going up fast with the knife, but she's a fraction too late. He brings the gavel down and round on to her temple with an elegant flowing forehand, and Kate crumples to the floor with the thought that the puppetmaster has just cut her strings.

*   *   *

Sinclair watches in silence as his last adder slithers in her cage.

She moves with beauty. Her scales of perfect black overlap each other, and their trailing edges grip the ground where they find purchase. She progresses by using the sides of her body to push against irregularities in the environment he has provided for her. At any given moment, various points on her body are pushing simultaneously against a number of fixed points on the substrate. As she moves forward, new parts of her body come into contact with the same fixed points, allowing her to follow the same line. The steady fluid progression of the snake. Always the same and yet always different, just like the sea.

He has looked after them well. The cages are large and well-equipped with rocks, lichen, moss, water, branches and leaves. He keeps one end warm and light, the other cool and dark. And he has been meticulous in his feeding arrangements, thawing and cooking the frozen rodents with care and thoroughness. An hour's thaw for small mice, at least three for rats.

It is easy to cut corners. Some people zip the

frozen rodents in a plastic bag and place this bag in hot water, hoping to thaw and cook the animals simultaneously. They end up parboiling them, so that the skin comes off and the belly bursts. Nor does Sinclair microwave them. Microwaves cook inside out, and so it is hard to see how well the rodents are cooked.

Of course, he has been careful about concealing his hobby. He keeps the snakes in a locked room. He has never registered himself with the local authorities. The snakes he gets from the wild, the cages he made himself. He buys the rodents as far afield as possible, and always uses cash. He does not subscribe to any magazines, nor swap tips with fellow enthusiasts on the Internet.

Sinclair is as besotted with his snakes as any other amateur hobbyist, but he has always kept them for a specific and clandestine purpose—the arrival of the Furies.

The air is close around him. He knows that the Hopi Indians of Arizona and New Mexico use snakes in raindances, and he knows that no such ceremony will be needed here tonight. The heatwave is about to break.

When the adder looks at him, he sees that she has an opaque covering over her eye. This is the first sign that she is about to shed her skin. Soon, she will wriggle out of her old covering and be left with her new. Rebirth.

Were she in the wild, she would be breeding now. These warm months are when the adders mate. And the moment they give birth, they leave the young to fend for themselves. Parental care is very rare in snakes. The only snakes which show any consideration for their offspring are some

446

oviparous types, who lay eggs. But *vipera berus* gives birth to live young, and that is the extent of its interest. It abandons its children without hesitation or mercy.

This beautiful animal, and so like his own mother Ailish that it hurts.

*   *   *

Sinclair reaches for the wall and unplugs the cage's heat and light sources. It is time.

Wind on one cheek, something abrasive on the other, and a splitting headache in between. Kate keeps her eyes closed and tries to remember what happened.

A vague snatch of memory, her in Sinclair's kitchen. Police tape, a knife block.

A soft hissing rises and falls in her ears. She hears that the rise and fall are rhythmic, and understands what the sound is and what she's lying on.

Sinclair has brought her to the beach. Sinclair.

Leo.

Kate jerks upright, and immediately wishes she hadn't. A swell of nausea lifts in her throat—reaction to the bang on the head, no doubt—and her arms won't help her up. She tries to move them, and all she feels is a sharp cutting on her wrists. He has bound her hands behind her back. Even without looking, she knows that her feet will be secured as well. Kate flops back down on the sand in anguish.

She rolls over on to her back, tucks her legs up as far as she can, and uses her stomach muscles to pull herself into a sitting position.

Sinclair is stretched out on the sand, watching her. It is night and the streetlamps on the esplanade provide only a feeble light at this distance, but it is enough for her to see that he has a knife in his hands. The other instruments, props, call them what she likes, are arranged in a neat semi-circle around him.

A piece of rubber tubing. A biscuit tin, with a long strap and a Zippo lighter on top. A forked stick. A bucket. Something thick, like a branch. A ribbed cage with two mice running on a wheel inside. A plastic jerry-can. A toolbox. And a transparent glass box in which an adder, perfectly black, is coiled motionless.

The sea is a few yards behind her. In the distance, a low growling. Thunder.

Histamine levels and beaten soles and petechial haemorrhaging jump in Kate's mind.

'Where's my son? Where's Leo?'

'Leo's OK. I put him to bed.'

'Where?'

'In my house.'

'He wouldn't have gone to bed without saying goodnight to me.'

'Why not? He seems to have done so most nights this week.'

Ouch.

'Your house is empty, for God's sake.'

'I think your own welfare should be of greater concern to you.'

I won't beg. If nothing else, I won't ever let him say that I begged for my life.

'How?' she asks.

'How what?'

'How is it you, when it was Alex? It was his

448

mobile number that Lovelock dialled, it was he who played Orestes. It can't be you.'

'The mobile was pure chance. I tried to call Lovelock before I left Bergen, but my battery had gone dead. So I used Alex's. By the time I'd finished, we were boarding. I shoved it in my pocket and forgot all about it. He must have forgotten too: he never asked for it back. And then Lovelock called to say he'd got a tip-off from his mole in customs that they were on the lookout for a white Transit van. My number still wasn't working, of course. So he looked in his list of incoming calls for the number I'd dialled from, and rang that. I doubt that Alex even now remembers that he lent the phone to me. We've all lost a lot more since then.'

'He played Orestes. Blackadder's obsessed with the myth.'

'He played Orestes. So what? Remember what Hitchcock said. Actors are cattle. It doesn't matter who plays a part. It matters who *directs* it.'

'You directed the *Oresteia*?'

'That play was *mine*. Every inflection, every line Alex performed, I showed him how. A trained monkey could have got up on stage and played the part under my direction. Alex wasn't Orestes. *I* was.'

The faces the public see on stage, and the hands behind them. The hands that do what Blackadder does, and the face behind them.

The wind is getting up. It gusts in Kate's face, carrying tantalising to her the sound of traffic on the sea road which runs north to the Bridge of Don. The road is fifty yards away, seventy-five at most. On a dark night with a storm coming, it

449

might as well be on the moon.

The beach itself is deserted. Two miles of clean sand broken by groynes, an amusement park at one end and a golf links at the other. On sunny days, it is packed. Now it is empty. Even if she screams, no one will hear her above the wind and the sea.

Sinclair has to raise his voice when he next speaks.

'Oh Kate, I'm so glad it's you. You're special to me, you know that. Or you were. Until this week. I found out a few things about you, this week.'

'Like what?'

'Like you're an ungrateful bitch.'

'In what way?'

'I always said you were the daughter I never had. And you were. Any time you wanted, I was there for you. I gave you all the love and attention and comfort you'd expect from a father. But you didn't expect it from *your* father. You didn't *get* it from him, either.'

'It was my choice to shut my father out of . . .'

'And then he came back. Walked right back into your life, and what do you do? Take him back in. Just like that.' He snaps his fingers. 'No ifs, no buts. After all I'd done for you,'

Alecto, unceasing in anger. Kate, who won't beg.

'And why did he come back?' she snaps. 'Because the *Amphitrite* sank. Why did the *Amphitrite* sink? Because you were smuggling children. You brought him back, Sinclair. It was your fault he came back. You make your own fate.'

'Of course. And you've made yours. You vowed to pursue Blackadder to the ends of the earth, and you've done so. Everywhere we look, we see the same thing: people reaping what they sow.'

450

'What else?'

'What else what?'

'You said you'd found out a few things about me this week. What else, apart from being an ungrateful bitch?'

'That you're a bad mother.'

'No. That I am not.'

'Is that so? How many nights have you palmed Leo off on to your aunt this week, Kate? How much time have you given him? When you have a child, Kate, you make it your number one priority. I used to . . .'

'Don't tell me how to treat my son.'

'. . . think you were a great mother, Kate. I looked at you and Leo, and I was envious. I wanted to *be* him.' *First he wants to be my father, now he wants to be my son. This isn't happening.* 'I wanted to have a childhood like his, when everyone loves you and your mother dotes on you. Not one when your mother hates you and shoves you in a basement. Why do you think I brought those children over, Kate? Because they were me. Loveless, lost, no one caring if they lived or died. They were at one end of the spectrum, and Leo was at the other. But you're just like Ma was, Kate. Whatever you do is on your own terms.'

'Shut up.'

'Look inside yourself, Kate. Look and see what wrong you've done. Only then will you see how much you deserve to suffer.'

He gets to his feet, picks up the bucket, and comes over to her. She doesn't let herself flinch.

Sinclair grabs her by the hair and starts dragging her towards the sea. Intense darting pain in her scalp, made worse by the fact that she can't bring her hands up to her head. She scrabbles with her feet for propulsion as best she can, but they are bound tight.

At the water's edge, still with his hand clamped firmly in her hair, Sinclair kneels down beside her. The sea laps against her face. She tries to twist her head away from it, but he is holding her tight. Saltwater in her nose, her mouth.

Think of it as the shower splashing your face. You've done that.

He scoops the bucket through the water to fill it. Kate can see it sloshing over the top. Then her face down in the water so fast she doesn't even have time to breathe in, eyes and mouth squeezed tight shut and this raging cold stinging her skin, and on the back of her head a torrent as he empties the bucket over her. Kate helpless and bound, the torrent coming again and again as he fills the bucket and empties it on her, fills and empties, fills and empties, and this isn't like being in the shower, this is standing under a waterfall.

Kate jerks frantically in his grasp, and too late she realises that all she's doing is running down her air supply. He's not letting her go. Agony in the bottom of her lungs and massive pressure in her windpipe. She feels as if she's in a huge vice pressing her from front and back alike, grinding on her sternum and spinal column. Circling darkness closes in on her like a shrinking camera.

How bloody stupid, to fight so hard on the Amphitrite *and drown a week later.*

She can't hold it any more. She gasps a breath out. All she gets on the inhale is water, racing into her lungs and stomach even as she tries to cough it back up.

452

A sudden sharp pain between her shoulderblades, and night sky in her vision.

He has jerked her head up to let her breathe. She almost thanks him. The water dribbles down her chin as she splutters it out through swells of a heaving chest.

When she's got her breath back, he does it to her all over again.

It's not as bad the second time round. Sinclair knows what he's doing, he knows exactly how long he has to keep her under before it starts to get critical. This affords Kate a curious comfort. Whatever else he does, he's not going to let her drown. She has seen how it ends, and it's not this way. But she doesn't let herself think about what else he has in store.

A series of infinite presents. Survive one, and you can survive the next. And on.

Kate lets herself go away. She thinks of cyclists, and the way their torsos and heads remain perfectly still while their hearts beat furiously and their lungs heave and their legs spin round. This is what she does with her mind. She divorces it from what's happening to her body, and she thinks of anything but what's happening to her.

The Mercat Cross, the open circular arcade which marks the de facto centre of Aberdeen. A parapet above it divided into twelve panels, containing armorial bearings of crown and city, and portraits of every Stuart monarch from James the First through Seventh. A coloured and gilt marble unicorn above the parapet. Thank God for Ferguson, pointing these things out to her. The view down Marischal Street to the harbour, these enormous ships crowding into the too-small gap between the houses, outsize and slightly startled to be there, like the Guggenheim Museum at the end of a narrow Bilbao road.

Sand sticking to her cheeks. He must have stopped, though she can still feel water. When she looks, she can see the sand exploding next to her in small puffs. It has started to rain.

Sinclair presses his face close to hers, and it looks nothing like him. It's his features, but it's not him behind them. He looks right, but all wrong.

'You're going to beg. You're going to suffer as I have.'

She coughs a string of sea water and saliva on to the sand.

He picks up the rubber tubing. It is about eighteen inches long, and it sits straight in his hand. No flexing. Must be filled with something hard. Mercury, perhaps, or concrete.

She knows what he's going to do with it in the instant before it happens.

Reflexology works because every part of the body is linked to the base. The human body is mapped in its entirety on the soles of the feet. If you know where to look, you can find the points for every organ, every erogenous zone.

Every nerve ending.

The first blow knocks the wind out of her. Hard and fast and unyielding across the tender flesh below the ball of her foot, and the pain surges up her body, branching and multiplying at every turn. She tries to wriggle away, but all he has to do is sit across her shins to stop her moving. Her feet are bound and exposed. He can do what he likes to them, and he does.

All the way up her feet and down again. Across the toes and on their ends, squashing them hard as if she's stubbed her foot against a table leg in the night. On the soft part of the instep, where the veins crowd near the surface. Sometimes he stops hitting and instead rubs the tubing against her skin. The pressure on her raw flesh opens up whole new avenues of agony.

And I always thought my feet were a size and a half too big. If they were the right size, there'd be less of them to hit.

Kate never looks at him. It's the one thing she has control of. She doesn't have to watch him do this, she doesn't have to see the blows go in. If she does, she'll start anticipating the impact and the pain, and that will be even worse.

The rain comes in heavy drops and the lightning flashes in the distance, now forking between sky and earth in angry jags, now bursting wide and white in the clouds. Another fork. She starts to count the gap till the thunder.

1001, 1002, 1003 . . .

'Beg. You *will* beg me to stop.' Whack. Whack.

. . . 1012, 1013, 1014 . . .

Whack. 'The others begged. Petra offered to fuck me if I stopped.' Whack.

. . . 1020, 1021, 1022 . . .

'Elizabeth cried for her life.'

He grabs a handful of sand and scours her feet with it, smearing it on the places where he has drawn blood. She winces in the far corner of her mouth, so he can't see her.

. . . 1032, 1033, 1034.

The thunder cracks.

Sound moves at a mile every five seconds. The storm is about seven miles away.

'Why won't you fucking beg me?'

455

She doesn't answer.

He goes away. Lying on her back with her hands trussed beneath her, Kate looks wildly around, left and right, all the way down the beach. No one.

When Sinclair comes back, he is holding the knife.

The knife. He's going to kill me now.

He kneels on the sand next to her. Behind his eyes is endless night.

The knife rests tip first on her stomach, against her jumper. One of Petra's fatal wounds wasn't far from here. If he moves the knife a few inches to the left, he'll be right on her abdominal aorta.

Sinclair takes hold of her jumper at the hem and cuts it neatly up the middle, all the way to the neck. It flops back against her flanks like an open waistcoat.

He goes away again, and returns with the biscuit tin and the strap. He takes the lid off the tin and puts it on the sand. Then he turns the tin over fast and puts it on her stomach, mouth down. As he does so, Kate glimpses a flash of something white inside. She feels the tickling on her naked stomach, and she knows what it is.

The mice.

The mice enclosed by metal above and around, chasing each other over her skin below.

Sinclair takes the strap and loops it over the base of the upturned tin. He reaches under Kate's body and passes one of the strap's ends beneath her, bringing it out the other side. He threads that end through the buckle and fastens it tight. She can't reach the strap at any point, and the tin is secured tightly to her stomach.

For a third time, he goes away.

456

Flickering light at the bottom of her vision. In the wind and the rain, leaping flames. He comes back with hot orange licking from his hand.

What she thought was a branch is a flaming torch. He must have soaked it in petrol from the jerry-can and lit it with the Zippo. Nothing else would have caught light in this weather.

Sinclair has to shout now to make himself heard.

'This is the one that finishes them off. This is when they beg like they've never begged before. It's called the iron cauldron.' He lowers the torch to the tin. 'This end, the far end from the mice, becomes very hot very fast. The mice try and escape from the heat. But they're trapped. There's only one way they can get out.'

The flames settle and shape themselves on the metal.

'They try to gnaw through your stomach.'

Kate's mind goes blank. Literally blank. No words, no emotions, no basic concepts of fear or revulsion.

Tiny feet skittering against her skin, faster and faster as they panic.

She tries to drive her thoughts away again, but they won't go. They turn and come back to her, past her brain and down to her stomach. Every ounce of Kate's being is focused on the circle of her which is covered by the biscuit tin.

Please God no. Please no. Her breathing comes in quick shallow pants.

A nip at her skin, no more than a pinch. It is starting.

She watches the flames and feels the mice.

They are biting now. Short sharp bites, stabs of pain which flare and die.

457

Sinclair's voice comes from behind the flames.

'Only now can you see what I have suffered.'

The mice run backwards and forwards on her, gnawing and worrying and tugging, trying to find some way to escape the heat.

'Beg me. *Beg me.*'

Kate lets out an involuntary yelp as one of the mice tears deeply at her flesh. Longer pain now and more sustained, one to the right and one almost dead centre. They have found their spots. Agony pulses from her like radio waves.

Don't beg him. Don't beg.

The mice at her with teeth and paws, scrabbling and ripping as if they were digging a hole, and she wonders how far they can go, piling dripping chunks of her flesh as they burrow.

Pain in her and over her and all around her.

'Stop this. Please stop this.'

The flame stays steady.

'Stop this! Fucking stop it!'

And still the flame doesn't move.

It feels like the mice have gone all the way through her skin and are starting on her muscle.

'Sinclair, *please!*'

The entreaty is whipped away on the wind, and she's not even sure if he's heard her.

He takes the torch away and cuts the strap at her side. The tin falls away from her. One of the mice spills out on to the sand. Its mouth is red with her blood. Sinclair takes the other mouse, the one still in the tin, and drops it in the adder's cage.

Kate doesn't dare look down at her stomach.

He stands above her again.

'For you and I both, the pain is almost over. But before I can end it, there is one more thing I must do to purify my guilt. Orestes made an offering to the gods. An offering of himself. He took his finger, and bit it off.'

The little finger of his left hand disappearing inside his mouth, and his cheek muscles bulging like walnuts as he chomps down hard on himself. Kate hears the savage crunch of enamel on bone and sees the agony and concentration on his face as he forces himself through the pain. The screaming she hears is hers, a reflex to what she's seeing.

She tries to look away and can't. The sight holds her mesmerised. Kate cannot imagine, literally cannot begin to conceive, of what is living inside Sinclair at this moment. She sees it and believes it, but she cannot comprehend it.

Teeth are harder than bones. Of the three layers in a tooth, the two inner ones—dentine and cementum—are roughly the same composition as bone, and the outer covering of enamel is much harder and denser. Sinclair bites at the optimum point; right down at the knuckle where the fifth metacarpal meets the hamate. He misses three of the four muscles in his finger, though he has no way of avoiding the exterior carpiulnaris. He bites at the front of his mouth, using the sharp cutting edges of his canine and incisors.

His legs are buckling, as if something is hitting at the backs of his knees. He must pass out from the pain, surely.

And then his teeth snap shut and she sees the blood spurt from the severed joint.

Sinclair reaches into his pocket with his good hand and pulls out a length of white fabric, which he wraps round the stump and back on itself. It turns red in an instant. He winces as he presses it tight.

He spits his finger into his good hand and flings it into the sea.

Sinclair looks back towards her. On an adrenaline high now, and nothing more to play for.

He grabs the knife and rushes her. The blade glints in the moonlight's reflection on the waves.

With the clarity of white lightning, Kate sees what she has to do.

He is almost on her when she rolls away from him, front and back and mouthfuls of sand and the pain of the mouse bites. She feels rather than sees him tumble past her. She bangs herself down hard on the adder's glass cage. All her weight is on her trussed wrists, and the glass shatters beneath her. She grabs with her fingers at shards of stray glass and keeps rolling, fast off the cage as the adder rears up. Its throat is absurdly distended where it has swallowed the mouse.

What did Matheson say? *Catch snakes when they're eating, and all hell can break loose.*

Sinclair is picking himself up off the sand.

Kate's fingers are wet with her own blood, and something is pulsing in her right wrist. *Please God let it be a vein, not an artery.*

One of the shards in her left hand feels big enough to be useful. She flips it between her middle and index finger, and rubs frantically against the rope round her wrists.

The adder poised to attack, and Sinclair wheeling back towards her too.

He sees the snake rising from its cage, and hesitates.

Time spreads. Kate's own metabolism is racing so fast that, at the moment when the world should

460

be spinning for her faster than ever before, it seems to slow. She keeps sawing with the glass, not daring to think how much of herself she's slashing through.

Sinclair comes in measured strides, still watching the snake. The cage is between him and his forked stick, and the snake is angry.

Kate's right hand comes free with a jolt, her wrist trailing blood-soaked twine.

The snake's attention is on Sinclair. It is not looking at her.

She grabs the adder behind its head, as she saw Matheson holding *natrix natrix.* It jerks violently in her grasp, and she can feel the dead mouse through the stretched skin of its neck.

Sinclair is almost on her. She hurls the adder at him. Instinctively, he throws up his knife arm, and in doing so gives the snake a target it can't miss. It lands on his forearm and sinks its fangs deep into him. He screams, and drops the knife.

The adder hangs from Sinclair as it drains the venom into his bloodstream. It looks at him with eyes of unblinking coldness. The female of the species, utterly without mercy.

Kate throws herself forwards, grabs the knife from the sand, and cuts through the bindings on her feet.

A flash of lightning and she is up and running, a million darts of pain in her beaten soles. Kate runs with her legs high and her feet quickly on the ground and off again, as if the sand is burning hot to the touch rather than sodden wet.

The clap of thunder, no more than a few beats later. Less than five seconds, less than a mile away. Less than a mile is as good as on top of them.

461

Kate knows the basics of lightning survival.

Make yourself as small as possible. Crouch down, feet together, hands on knees. No metal. Drop the knife. Not so easy when your soles are in agony and Blackadder's after you.

Kate turns to see where Sinclair is.

He is standing where she left him. His arms are stretched skywards, and he holds the forked snake stick straight above his head. Its tip must be a good twelve feet above the sand. On a flat beach near a large body of water, he is the tallest target. Kate understands instantly.

He has lost. The last Fury has escaped. In his head, she will torment him for the rest of his days. Like the sea, the madness will never stop. Better to end it now. Better to die on his feet than live on his knees. He could step into the sea and put himself under, but then he gives her the chance to save him, fish him out when he's half-dead and too weak to resist.

Up to a billion volts surge through a lightning flash. It moves at a third of the speed of light, and the temperature at the heart of the bolt can exceed 40,000 degrees Fahrenheit.

Lightning travels upwards, from ground to sky. It comes not from above but from below: not from heaven, but from hell. From beneath the earth it comes for Sinclair now, brilliant and bright and thick as a telegraph pole. The image burns inverted on Kate's retina even as she falls, a black fork against a white night sky.

And in the middle Sinclair, the light raging aura beautiful around him.

EPILOGUE

They keep Kate in hospital for a week. Her feet are badly beaten, her wrists and arms heavily cut, and her stomach badly wounded. Nothing that time won't heal, they tell her.

The memories come back to her through the drugs.

The lightning striking Sinclair and her running to the beach road to flag down the nearest car, looking such a state that she has to stand right in the middle of the road to make the driver stop. Dripping blood all over his mobile as she calls first an ambulance and then the incident room. She gets Ferguson himself, and tells him to do three things: release Alex, get Leo from Sinclair's house, and send people down to the beach to clear up the mess. Sinclair on fire when she goes back to him, his clothes smoking and the wind whirling the smell of burnt flesh around her face.

As luck would have it, Kate ends up in exactly the same bed as her father did after the Michaelhouse bomb blast. It is from this bed that she receives a seemingly endless stream of visitors. Frank, Bronagh and Leo come the first morning. She waits until Leo isn't looking before she shows her father and aunt the extent of her injuries. Ferguson and the boys come round that afternoon, any bawdy police humour knocked out of them by the sight of her. After them come Emmeline, Jean and Lennox. 'I can't see us doing another performance, you know,' Jean says, and the others nod.

Jason sends her a note, stiff and formal, saying he understands why she has done to him what she did. She reads it twice and throws it away.

One of the nurses brings her a copy of the *Aberdeen Evening Telegraph*. 'Ferry chief charged with attempted murder, child smuggling,' shrieks the headline. Kate skims the text, and sees that Lovelock's own paper is already doing its best to distance itself from him. Like rats leaving a sinking ship, she thinks. Sinking ship, where the whole sorry mess began.

All the main players accounted for apart from two.

The first one comes the next morning, softly through the curtains around her bed as she dozes. She opens her eyes when he places his hand softly on hers.

'I didn't think you'd want to see me,' she says.

'I didn't.'

'What changed your mind?'

'A little birdie.'

'How little?'

He takes his hand from hers and holds it a couple of feet above the ground. 'About that little.'

'And what did this little birdie say?'

'He said that his mum was in hospital, and he thought she'd like it if I went to see her.'

'She does like it. Very much.'

They both know that there's plenty to say, about trust and betrayal and suspicion. But they also know that it can wait. They will broach it in their own time, when they're both up to it: and when they do broach it, they will do so fully and properly.

*   *   *

464

Kate has to wait until the third day before hearing from the second player. His greeting comes in the form of a parcel, because of course he can't simply come and see her as the others can. She recognises the writing on the envelope and the prison stamp before she opens it, and it is just as well: the parcel is a book, and Kate knows all too well how the previous occupant of this bed found himself in here.

She pulls the book from the envelope. It is a copy of *The Jungle Book,* and a Post-It pokes from the pages about a third of the way in. Kate turns to the yellow tab and sees what it is marking: the story about Rikki-Tikki-Tavi killing the two cobras, Nag and Nagaina.

*   *   *

The day she's discharged, Kate takes Alex and goes back to the beach where Sinclair tried to kill her. The heatwave has gone, and the sea breeze gusts at their backs. They walk along the long esplanade in silence, Kate's feet hurting through surgical socks. The leisure centre spurts chlorine and sweat as they pass it, and the dirty red hulk of Pittodrie football stadium squats away to their left.

'One thing I want to know,' she says.

'What?'

'Why you always come to my house. Never vice versa. I don't even know your address.'

Their footsteps on the pavement as he thinks.

'I've always been suspicious of falling in love,' he says. 'There's a part of me which thinks that, if you really fall in love, you lose your own identity to some degree. You peg your life to someone who might at any time leave you. If at the start you can live without them, and one day you find that you can't, hasn't that decreased rather than increased you?'

'Is that what worries you?'

'I wanted it for so long with you, Kate. Then it came to me, precious and cold, and it's exhilarating, I've never felt like this before, about *anyone*. And with that comes the fear that this is too good to last.' He stops and takes her arm. 'You've invaded every part of me. I feel more comfortable on your turf, in your life; when if it goes wrong I can just walk away and pretend that it never meant that much in the first place. That's why I've never invited you round. Where I live is the one thing I have left that's not you. Once you've been there, that's where you'll always be, whether you mean to or not.'

'And that's what scares you?'

'Yes.'

'I can live with that.'

Kate begins to shrug herself out of her coat. 'Is it me,' she asks, 'or is it hot today?'

It takes Alex a couple of seconds to realise what she has just said. By the time realisation spreads across his faces like the first rays of a new day, she has taken off her jumper as well.

And suddenly she is running across the road, slicing neatly between two cars and down the steep grass verge, bouncing off the end of an old bench painted duck-egg blue, down the concrete steps and jumping on to the sand. She kicks off her shoes as she goes and tears at her trousers, hopping awkwardly as they flail around her ankles. Her shirt is next, and then the surgical socks and her bra and finally her knickers. The sea water will soak her bandages and smart on the wounds beneath, and she couldn't care less.

Kate plunges into the sea, turning in mid-air so she is facing skywards.

The woman tumbles backwards, hits the water spread-eagled in an aura of foaming white, and disappears under the waves.

The water covers every part of Kate, and when she breaks surface again, she can hardly speak for laughing so much.